THE AURORA RESOLUTION

A conspiracy thriller

By Sam Nash

This is a work of fiction. Names, characters, organisations, places, events, and incidents are either products of the author's imagination or are used fictitiously.

Cover art supplied by Carantoc Publishing Ltd
First edition, 2018
ISBN 978-1-9999960-8-6
Carantoc Publishing Ltd.
www.carantocpublishing.com

Please note that this product was created by a British author. Except for slang and dialogue, spelling and grammar is corrected to **British English**. There are also scenes which may offend more sensitive readers. It is not deemed suitable for children

I dedicate this book to all the scientists who dare to teeter on the edge of conventional wisdom, to lead their research teams into unchartered realms. May you find the proof to turn fiction into fact.

Foreword

This is the third book in The Aurora Conspiracy series. It is advisable to read the books in order, but for those who wish to read them out of sequence or needing a little reminder of what happened to our luckless characters, provided below is a recap. **Be warned, it contains spoilers**.

Recap of Book One – The Aurora Mandate

Mary Arora witnesses the devastation of an earthquake in Japan via television footage and experiences a synergistic reaction to the pain of one of the victims. Other strange occurrences have her believing that there is something drastically wrong with her. Dr Parth Arora, Mary's husband, conducts tests on her in the Neurosciences department of the midlands university where they both work.

One of Parth's studies throws Dan Wildman, a local bookshop owner, into their path. Mary has an instant rapport with this chap, who has the remarkable ability to communicate with her telepathically. Later he discovers that he is in fact, Mary's brother, and that he has an additional memory wiping ability.

As the story progresses, Mary's full capabilities come to light. She has a unique electromagnetic sensitivity, allowing her to drift from her physical body to spy undetected on whoever she pleases. She can also produce an electromagnetic shock of varying force, to fry circuitry or to deliver a fatal blow to unsuspecting attackers. The third of her gifts, mindreading, allows her to combine all her powers and take control of people in far off destinations. This ability is extremely attractive to British Secret Services and to other unscrupulous factions across the globe.

In this first story, there are two main groups who seek to use Mary for their own gains. One is led by a Russian general. We know him by the name of Alexi, although for much of book one, he pretends to be subordinate to his co-conspirator, Lars Visser. Between them, they force Mary and their Russian Hive mind operatives, to initiate a series of man-made earthquakes using an Ionospheric Heater from an Alaskan research facility. Their primary aim, is to wipe out the Five-Eyes Data Centre in Utah, rendering British, US, Canadian, Australian and New Zealand surveillance systems redundant.

The second interested party is the British Secret Intelligence Service, MI6. They have been monitoring Mary and funding Parth's studies in secret for years. Their intention is to discover the trigger for these remarkable gifts and to create a formidable team of specialist agents, with a view to controlling heads of state in troublesome areas around the world. The head of operations for this division is Soviet born Yelena Plender, working in conjunction with her technical specialist, Agent Jasper Flynn.

At the end of the book, Mary is bewildered and shocked over the motives of both the Russian terror cell and by the actions of the British Defence Minister. With her brother's help, they devise a way to escape the suppression of MI6, but they know that it will not protect them for long.

Recap of Book Two – The Aurora Manifesto

Book two in the series, sees Mary beginning her PhD studies at the University where her ex-husband works. He discovers methods to modulate her powers, utilising them for a whole new purpose; to supply free drugs to poor nations in the hope of earning himself a Nobel Prize.

Mary is under close scrutiny from British Secret Services. Her latest activities prompt an immediate invitation to a government run estate in Oxfordshire, where the Prime Minister awaits an explanation. With this revelation, comes a new raft of problems, ones which cabinet ministers are not keen to address. With all the tell-tale signs, Mary confirms that she is carrying her ex-husband's child.

The Secretary of State for Defence issues a kill order, sending Mary and Parth running for their lives. They hide with an old friend in London, whose internal conflicts with science and religion render Mary a target for holy censure across the entire nation via the internet. The Prime Minister uses this twist in circumstance to announce Mary's mental health concerns, suggesting that she seeks medical intervention.

After evading gunfire, and surviving an intentional car crash, Mary and Parth limp to a quiet hotel. Their assassin follows, lacing Parth's food with a variant of a shellfish toxin. He is paralysed, and close to death, when Mary assists the medical staff in a procedure to draw out the toxins from his body, thus saving his life.

Fearful of further powerful individuals emerging, the ministers arrange for a suppression additive to be dispersed into the national water supply. Without trialling the effects of this chemical, many vulnerable people become sick, flooding hospitals with emergency cases.

Mary and Parth are trapped at the hospital, surrounded by religious protesters and flanked by MI6 agents. She is warned by her old adversary, Alexi, not to drink the water, but it is too late. The suppressant causes Mary to miscarry the baby.

Concerned for her welfare, her brother and grandfather arrive at the maternity ward, and witness the colossal scale of harm from the water treatment. Pip pushes his granddaughter in a wheelchair to check on Parth's progress, only to find the assassin making another attempt on his life. There is a struggle, and Pip is shot dead. Distraught and angry, Mary fries the killer's head with a massive burst of electromagnetism.

Mary and her brother, Dan, escape the hospital and catch the train to Brighton. Here, at their grandfather's house, they discover the contents of his floor safe. It contains a passport under a new name for Mary, Pip's journal, and an heirloom brooch bearing the Greek letter Lambda.

Once again, government agents descend to ransack the house. Mary makes a run for it, hiding in her home town among friends, one of whom is a jeweller. He informs Mary, that the brooch contains a gemstone unlike anything he has ever seen, offering to have it analysed on her behalf. She declines, taking the jewel to back to the Indian Consulate in London, with her rescuer, the Indian nobleman, Karan Shinde.

At Karan's request, Mary meets chief executive officer of a global pharmaceutical company, who offers her a job. Mary also discovers that it is her company supplying the suppressant, and that they are involved in shady depopulation schemes under the guise of philanthropy.

Running again, she takes shelter at a friend's house, with the aim of using the fake passport to leave the country. As she hops on the London Underground to go to the airport, she is accosted by young, disgruntled Christians, on their way to a protest march. Under duress, Mary is delivered to Parliament Square, and forced to address a crowd of fifty-thousand religious protesters. With anxiety bubbling to the surface, Mary loses control on stage, blasting all electronics in her path. The commotion is recorded on camera, and broadcast live.

As MI6 arrange uniformed officers to extract her from the crowds, emergency crews arrive at the Houses of Parliament in response to hundreds of workers and politicians falling sick. At first, it is handled as a pathogenic outbreak, sealing the buildings under quarantine.

Mary deduces that the symptoms are the same as those falling ill from the water suppressant. The Prime Minister is one of those stricken. With hospital supplies of medication scarce, Mary is asked to use her gift to generate more.

With the Prime Minister's health failing, she makes promises to Mary that legislation will be altered to protect the British population from any further attempts to medicate them without their knowledge or permission.

Before Mary can create more of the necessary drug, the Secretary of State for Defence, accuses Mary of being in league with terrorists, while hoping that the PM will die, leaving him a strong candidate for leadership.

The PM is surreptitiously given the treatment, foiling the Defence Minister's plot. He retaliates by having Mary arrested and bundled into a prison transportation vehicle. With all hope lost, Mary is resigned to her fate. When the van stops, she is confronted by her old foe, Alexi. He had orchestrated the parliamentary poisoning using a concentrated dose of the suppression chemical, to prove his loyalty to Mary.

With no other options open to her, Mary leaves with Alexi for Heathrow Airport.

Manhattan, NYC

The connection between the siblings, a telepathic tether crossing the choppy waters of the Atlantic Ocean through western airwaves thick with greed and mistrust, was tenuous.

"It seems our grandfather kept his own special talents a secret from us all. He was an avid and prolific journal writer."

"Uhuh..."

"Hey, Mary. Listen to this entry. Pip writes: This vision had me quaking in my shoes all through the morning. The scenes played over and over in my mind. So many gruesome deaths, carnage; complete pandemonium. The dark skies lit up with an arcing pulsation, electric blue and deadly. The shock waves spread in concentric circles, decimating all circuits, communication and power lines. Substations exploded, collapsing nearby buildings. Hospitals plunged into chaos, without backup generators or torchlight. Streams of highway traffic coasted and collided into fatal accidents.

"And there was screaming. Loud, terrified screams of the afflicted. Burns so deep, the whites of the bone shone through the bloodied flesh. Children impaled by shards of steel and glass, lay lifeless in the streets. Looters stepped over bodies to claim bales of toilet rolls and porridge oats. There were shopping carts piled high

with bottled water and dog food. I saw Times Square cast into darkness. The Eiffel Tower was a mass of lethal sparks and the London Eye crashed into the Thames.

"I cannot recall a moment within the premonition which could indicate a potential date for this catastrophic event, but from the technology I saw, it will be soon. More importantly, we must be prepared..."

Their transmission dipped; a moment of silence before the connection could be re-established. Mary groaned. Pain radiated throughout her lower torso. Excruciating spikes of intense distress numbed all other bodily sensations. She pressed the cotton wadding closer to her abdomen, flinching from the pressure. The medic jabbed her arm with a cannula needle and attached a bag of fluids to the end of a tube. Mary drew breath across her teeth. The rocking motion of the emergency vehicle mounting a ramp, reverberated in her belly. Perspiration formed on her top lip and forehead. The throbbing, incessant agony proved impossible to contain. Mary's concentration dimmed; her grasp on the present diminishing with the blood loss.

"Mary? Did you hear that? What's happening, are you okay?" Dan caught his sister's distress, which in turn spawned panic in his neural pathways. Three and a half thousand miles away, Dan was powerless to lend assistance. "*Mary, what's happening? Tell me what is going on...*"

"Now is not really a good time, Dan. I've been shot."

Chapter One

The fasten seat belt sign illuminated above the door to the cockpit. "We are making our final descent into JFK now. If you would like to adjust your watches, the time is ten pm, eastern standard time. Forecasts are good, although there is potential for rain later tonight. Please allow cabin crew to dispose of any remaining items of food or drink. Have a pleasant stay." The pilot's echoing voice halted with a static click.

Mary sat upright in the leather chair and re-attached the lap belt. She ground a knuckle into her tear duct and yawned. The mesh fabric from the blond wig, itched her scalp. She leaned across to her travel companion and whispered into his ear. "You had better know a man this side of the Atlantic too, or we are in serious trouble."

Alexi took a final sip of his champagne and smiled, before the obliging steward cleared away the debris from their first-class meal. He watched Mary pack the complementary travel mask and slipper socks into the airline goody bag, and shook his head. "You don't need those. You will have everything you need." His English had improved significantly since their first fateful meeting, but the Russian inflection was hard to shake.

Mary ignored him, coveting the mini toothbrush and paste, the wireless earbuds and bottle of facial spritz. Clutching the freebies tight, she felt her stomach drop inside as the small jet lunged into its descent. As the wheels skidded to the tarmac below them, Mary released the pressure from her ears, swallowing hard while holding her nose.

They taxied for what seemed like miles. The aircraft turning in sharp bends until they reached the terminal building. First-class accommodation emptied first. Mary stood up against her aisle seat, stretching up to the overhead compartments. She was at least a foot too short to reach. A kind man in a crumpled suit, suppressed a smile and opened the locker, retrieving the only feminine looking bag inside. She thanked him and a mild embarrassed flush warmed her cheeks.

With her goodies stowed inside her satchel, Mary dug out her passport and flipped it open to the photocard at the back. She looked at her younger self; the bleached student hair and wrinkle free features. Those were happier days. Days of youthful petulance and insignificant worries. A time when she could call her father for help, and her mother still nagged her to make her bed. An era when her grandfather would bring her doughnuts from Brighton Pier. A spiral of loss twisted her innards.

I still have Dan. She thought to herself. *I am never alone while I have my brother.* Another glance at her documents, before smoothing the wig against her neck. *Remember my new name. I am Mary Sedgewell.*

"Come, Mary." Alexi chirped. "We go now." He waved her towards the exit. Kneading her fingers into fists, Mary followed. They trudged through the hollow, clanking passageway from the aircraft door, and into the customs foyer. Mary held her breath, imagining a large party of uniformed and armed men awaiting their arrival.

There were none. Just the streams of passengers and staff, shuffling through to the document checking queues. Mary heaved a massive sigh, breathing in the stale aromas of old alcohol and breath mints. She indicated towards the shortest queue and began walking. Alexi grabbed her sleeve. "No. We go this way." He said, steering her towards a cordon bearing the sign: VIP.

The lounge was plush. A glass internal wall looked out on to the thoroughfare which split between the green lane signposted *nothing to declare* and the red walkway for honest travellers. Lines of grim faced customs officers flanked the passageway, compelling each visitor to look up and make eye contact. Seasoned travellers shuffled at speed, eyes cast down to the wheeled cases of those before them.

Mary launched herself into a beige linen seat, content to wait for the two Saudi gentlemen to conclude their documents check with the only member of staff on duty. Alexi thumbed his phone. It made a whooshing noise, carrying a text into the airwaves. Within moments, a man of indeterminate age, scurried into the VIP lounge. He wrestled with his uniform, buttoning his jacket and fastening his ID badge to a lapel. His hair was ruffled and one eyelid drooped.

"Ah, sir. Madam. May I take your passports and visa cards." He said, smirking at Alexi. Mary waved hers aloft. Alexi took it from her, adding his own plus the visas which Mary had filled out on the plane, and gave them to the customs clerk. "If you would like to help yourself to refreshments, I will arrange for your luggage to be sent along shortly." The man winked at them, and then turned to his colleague to bestow a solemn nod in his direction, before disappearing the way he came.

Alexi sat by Mary's side. "You look tired." He said. "Can I get you anything?"

Mary shook her head. "It's hardly surprising, given that it is three am in London right now." Her mind raced back to all the events that had culminated in fleeing her homeland. The confrontation with the Secretary of State for Defence; his continued insistence that she was a threat to national security. Mary was wanted in Britain and all allied countries with extradition treaties. Her hopes lay in the recovery of the Prime Minister, and whether she would keep her promises. It was a fragile hope at best. One which assumed that an unrecorded, undocumented deal, made in haste with a dying woman, would retain validity when the crisis was over.

If you cannot take the word of a British Prime Minister, whose can you take? Mary recalled the exact words she had used. No mention of a promise, or a deal well struck, just the deflection of another question. This was the woman who had set loose the Defence Secretary and his band of military mad dogs. Together they had conspired and killed hundreds, maybe thousands when the count was finally done. They had been the cause of her grandfather's brutal death. Mary's optimism faded. There would be no return to her former life and home.

Mary gawped around and then straightened her wig. In the steamy lounge room, she ached to be rid of the clinging artificial hair, and get away from the uniformed officers. She pondered on her dilemma. What would it take for Alexi's customs chum to turn traitor and hand her in to the authorities? The allure of promotion perhaps, or a hefty bonus on his pay slip at the end of the month? Had he seen her on worldwide news bulletins, with Dr Hugo Blom, standing on a stage addressing fifty-thousand disgruntled Christians?

Reams of memories choked rational thought processes. The mire of events exhausting the neurons in her hippocampus. When had she last slept? Her eyelids fell. Just a moment or two of rest. *Nope... can't sleep now. Can't give in.* Forcing her eyes open she pushed back at the giddiness and blinked away the blurring of her vision. Staring through the side windows into the customs passageway, she saw a man she knew well.

He strode passed the armed officers and customs officials and through the green channel. Despite her exhaustion, Mary dragged herself to her feet and walked closer to the window. Craning her neck, she watched him stand aside from the pedestrian flow to greet a woman in her mid- twenties. Mary could see her face on. Something about her wide smile, her freckled nose and the mechanical tilt of the head, prickled her senses. She seemed familiar. The man dug into his coat pocket and then held out a small plastic device in his palm. A memory stick perched beneath four stubby digits; the little finger conspicuous by its absence. *Flynn. What's that slimy bugger doing here? Was he on our flight? Has Yelena sent him to fetch me?* Mary observed Flynn beaming at something on his smart phone, before nodding to the woman, and dissolving into the crowds once more.

A little spike of adrenalin, refuelled her common sense. This was no time for complacency. She helped herself to a bottle of spring water and sat back down next to Alexi, who was firing off texts at speed. Alexi's friend returned with their documents and cases twenty minutes later. He led them through a secondary doorway, into the main concourse near the front entrance. A conspiratorial handshake later, and they were free to leave.

Mary stacked her satchel on the top of her case, and dragged it towards the taxi ranks.

Alexi called after her. "Where are you going? We have car waiting. Driver is here to take us."

"Thanks, but no thanks. I can make my own way now." She yelled over her shoulder, not stopping to look back. Alexi stood still as his driver approached him. They watched Mary through the automatic doors as she dragged her luggage to the rear of the queue. It took a few moments for Mary to notice the police car, parked in the pick-up bays; another minute to spot the officers making their way through the crowds. One of them was talking on his radio, his eyes darted along the lines of tourists in the floodlit taxi queue.

Could be coincidence. No one knows that I am here. No one is looking for Mary Sedgewell. Nausea wafted in waves, heating her face. *Stay calm. Mary Arora is under suspicion in the UK. They are not looking for me.* As soon as the thoughts manifested, Mary lost her courage. She turned back towards the entrance, and returned to Alexi's side. "A lift to Manhattan would be appreciated. Thank you."

Alexi peered at her little frame. "You think it easy to find cheap hotel in middle of night?"

Her sagging shoulders and slow blink aged her. Mary shrugged.

"I have place you can stay. We go there first. It is a little further, but better." He reached forward to take control of her suitcase. Mary looked perturbed. The memories of her incarceration still fresh and sensitive. Alexi softened his voice. "You don't like it when we get there, you leave. I have driver take wherever you want, but at least come and rest."

Still Mary resisted. Her mouth puckered around her gritted teeth, while she grappled with suitable expletives.

Alexi persevered. "If I lie, you can zap me." He mimed an explosion to his head with his hands. "Boom. I dead."

"Fine." She conceded, "but I am warning you. Any funny business and I will fry you."

Mary relinquished control of her wheeled case to the driver, but kept hold of her trusted satchel. Parked near to the empty police car was a large black four by four vehicle. Alexi took the front passenger seat, giving Mary space to stretch in the back.

There was not much to see from the freeways and overpasses on their way out of JFK Airport. Mary tried to keep a mental note of the signposts as they zoomed past, but the monotony of asphalt and the late hour weighted her eyelids. By the fifth junction on the spaghetti-like roads, Mary was asleep.

***

Alexi roused her to consciousness as they drove through a small town. The scant streetlights gave the place an antiquated feel. It was as though time had not touched it for a hundred years. Paint peeled from lacquered signs. There were no parking bays or white lines marked on the roads. Buildings were scattered as though town planning was an unnecessary and foreign concept. There were a few shops, a red brick town hall and a prominent, well-lit diner, but little else.

Mary sat up straight and squinted through the windows. "Is *this* where we are staying? I at least thought we'd be in the city. Is there a nice hotel?"

"This is the nearest town to where we are staying. We have not arrived at place yet." Alexi smiled. Her reaction to the vast distances and luxury of space amused him. "A few more miles only."

The main street petered out to nothing but straight tarmac, bordered either side by woodland. Trees, trees and more trees, as far as the eye could see. Their eerie fingers protruded over the roadside as they shed their summer foliage. The moon was high and fat, spreading its cold light between tall silhouettes across their path. Every now and then, their headlights would pick out a mailbox, posted at the end of a track leading into the dense forest.

"People actually live around here?" Mary said, suddenly alert and frightened. This was not what she had envisioned when they left the airport.

"Private place. Keep to themselves. Very good for us." Alexi looked to the driver for confirmation. The thick set man nodded, and then returned his gaze to the road ahead.

"Where exactly, are you taking me?" Her tone forceful and accusatory. "I warned you Alexi…"

"Will you trust me, for once. We almost there. You like it, I promise."

They rounded a long bend in the road. Ahead of them, the trees thinned and tall brick pillars either side of a set of steel gates, came into view. They pulled off the road. The driver reached to the dashboard for an electronic device and pressed a remote button. The gates juddered open on their hinges, and closed automatically as soon as the car drove through. The plaque on the gate read:

Summerfield Retreat – Private Property

"A retreat?" Mary enquired.

"Very nice. You will like. See it better in morning."

Mary looked at the gates through the rear window. She felt pretty sure that she could scale them, if the need arose. The vehicle came to a halt outside a large building. Some of the lights were still on inside. A network of pavements snaked around the edge of the building towards several smaller ones either side.

"So, this is what? A spa resort?"

"No. Communal centre. Many uses. We not staying there. Come." Alexi followed the driver to the car boot and lifted out their luggage. He thanked the man and dragged their cases along a path up an incline. "Come…"

Mary looked about her. Beneath the street lights, she could see that the entire place was deserted. It was difficult to estimate the size in the dark, but it looked to be a considerable acreage. With few options open to her, and exhaustion eroding her belligerence, she followed.

Each dragging footstep took her closer to a row of exclusive lodge houses, tucked away on the hillside. Alexi stopped at the foot of the steps leading up to the first house. "This one yours. I next door if you need anything." Alexi pointed to the house a few hundred metres to the left.

"Seriously? The entire lodge… just for me?"

"It is not locked. Food in fridge, and many tea." Alexi giggled, depositing her case before dragging his own towards his assigned lodge house. "Goodnight Mary."

She stood dumbfounded, watching Alexi ascend the wooden steps in the distance. His case bumped against each tread, slowing his progress. Beneath the porch light he turned and waved, and then disappeared inside. She was all alone.

Chapter Two

Could be a trap. I could wander inside only to find three armed men with a syringe full of sedative. Mary looked back towards the communal building. *How do I know that occupants there would be any friendlier?* With her senses on high alert, Mary bumped her case up the steps to the porch. The lights were on inside the lodge. Through the windows, she could see a comfortable seating area and an open plan kitchen beyond. A vase of wild flowers topped the mantelpiece, skimming the frame of a watercolour painting above.

Leaving the luggage to fend for itself, Mary burst in through the door, holding her hands high to counter any potential attacks. She stood in the empty hallway, panting and snapping her head in all directions, but saw no one. She did a lightning search of the ground floor, and then the upper floor. Eventually, the heightened state of anxiety reduced. She was indeed, the only resident.

With her heart still rattling inside her chest, Mary retrieved her bags and locked herself inside. Under calmer scrutiny, the cabin was warm and welcoming. Her brain informed her of a need to explore, but the aching muscles in her neck and shoulders told her to sleep. Leaving all the lights on, Mary climbed the stairs to the nearest bedroom, and flopped onto the bed. And there she stayed, fully clothed, asleep on the eiderdown.

***

Mary's tongue lolled at the side of her mouth. As she stirred herself fully conscious, she remembered her new surroundings and jolted upright. Stock still and listening intently, she took in the absence of sound and that the bedside clock read two minutes past midday. She had slept the morning away, and yet no one had disturbed her. No pestering Alexi, no armed men. No one to badger her into fulfilling their whims and needs. She took a swig of water from the airport bottle, and sauntered into the bathroom.

Her shower was brief. It goaded her into water efficiency with a countdown timer actuated the moment it was switched on. Mary scrubbed and rinsed at speed, fearful that it would turn itself off while her mass of dark curls was still soapy. The time ran out with a long beep, shutting off the water supply, just as she had suspected.

Mary stepped out on to a woven bamboo mat and searched for a toothbrush. The cabinet above the sink, yielded more bamboo items, including a toothbrush with natural bristles. *They certainly like to be environmentally friendly around here.* With no wrapper, Mary thought it might belong to the former occupant, and so instead, used the travel brush from her flight bag freebies.

Opening the suitcase that Alexi had packed for her, proved most disconcerting. For one, it reminded her of how they first met, and his talent for duplicity. How easily he slipped into the role of genial host, while secretly planning terror attacks of catastrophic proportions. His choice of clothing for her, was also alarming. She found the same style of grey jersey sweat pants and tops he had provided for her during her enforced captivity in an abandoned cottage hospital in Britain. Mary shuddered at the thought. From the bottom of the case, she found light cotton underwear and a t-shirt. *These trousers will just have to do me for another day.*

Dressed, but with her hair still dripping wet, she made her way down the stairs to the kitchen. She examined the solid wood cabinets and polished beech worktops, tiled flooring and a neat little breakfast table. *This is nice.* She scanned around the ceiling, searched in between the decorative plates on the dresser and peered under wall cabinets. She could find no cameras, nor listening devices anywhere. *Okay, what's the catch?*

Mary opened the massive fridge and lifted out a large glass container of milk. There was no fancy seal, just a lid to keep out the dust. She stuck her nose inside the container and sniffed. *Smells just fine. Could be drugged, can't risk it.* She returned it to the shelf inside the door.

There was something weird about all the produce stacked inside the fridge. Lush carrots, the green tops still attached, eggs of all different shades and sizes, irregularly shaped butter stored in a glass dish. She opened the salad drawer. More fresh produce nestled inside; whole heads of lettuce, a mixture of tomato varieties, and paper cartons of mushrooms. *Not a single supermarket label, plastic bag or tie anywhere.*

She opened the cupboards. Inside, glass containers, displaying the dried products within; rice, lentils, flour and much more besides. Her stomach growled. A bread crock harboured some English muffins and a loaf of granary. Fortified with toasted buttered muffins, and a pot of black tea, Mary explored the rest of the lodge.

The ground floor of the building was largely open plan, with a downstairs cloak room and utility area to the rear of the kitchen. The lounge and dining area, terminated with bi-fold French doors and a balcony suspended above the hillside. Mary drank the last of the black tea and stood out on the wooden platform, taking in the view.

From the vantage point, she could see the extent of the compound, right to the tree-lined boundaries in the distance. Chalets, villas and more permanent structures dotted the clearing on one side of the communal building. On the opposite side, large tracts of land devoted to arable and dairy farming, polytunnels and reed beds that seemed to stretch for miles.

Men worked teams with shire horses ploughing fields, alongside more modern machinery. Groups of workers harvested crops inside the polythene tunnels, while others dipped sheep outside the farm buildings. Every acre of land had a purpose. Beyond the vast area of arable land were rows of wind turbines, and solar arrays, biomass shredders and methane digesters. Despite the mild breeze, the turbines were still.

Outside the communal building, a group of people wearing sports gear trained in unarmed combat, throwing each other down on crash mats and throttling their opponents into submission. Other's sat at tables in the sunshine, labelling pickle jars. *What the hell is this place?*

Mary watched, transfixed as a tiny electric vehicle appeared from nowhere, the slope of the ramp hidden behind shrubs and trees. Two more vehicles surfaced from what Mary assumed was some sort of underground garage. This time, they were large haulage trucks. The car stopped a few hundred metres from the entrance, and a slight figure got out. He walked to the driver's window of the first stationary truck, spoke to the men inside, and then returned to the little car.

The trucks veered off towards the gated entrance, while the electric car headed in Mary's direction. As it drew closer, she could see Alexi waving to her through the windscreen. He parked close to her lodge stairs, and then stepped out of the driver's seat. Yelling up to her, Alexi said, "you sleep okay? Everything good, yes?"

Mary nodded, but could not quell the deep-seated suspicion festering in the back of her mind.

"You want to come down and look around? I give you tour." He waited for some indication of acceptance. Mary paused. Her curiosity was piqued. She did not feel threatened, particularly since Alexi knew of her capabilities. One false move and she could send a jolt of electromagnetic energy right through his skull, cooking his brain inside.

"A quick look, and then I must leave. I'll be down in a minute." She yelled. *I'll take my stuff with me.* She mused, returning to the bedroom to stash a few essentials into her bag.

They began on foot, walking the short distance to the communal centre. Alexi donned a baseball cap and tinted glasses, shielding himself from the early autumn sun.

"You like cabin? It has all you need?" Alexi held open the heavy door, ushering her inside.

"Yes, thank you. It is very nice." Mary noticed that even out of the sun, Alexi did not remove his sunglasses. The communal centre was packed with people. Most wore the same sweat pants and t-shirts that Mary found packed into her suitcase. It unsettled her. They shuffled their way past the crowds queueing at the canteen for lunch. "Are you hungry? They have nice goulash here. Or maybe you like pizza? All fresh made."

Mary declined, but found herself lingering to view the cheerful faces of people sharing their meals together in what looked to be family units. Other tables supported groups of friends, discussing their work, scribbling on napkins, in animated discourse. The entire dining hall had an uplifting aura about it that made her smile.

"Come, I show you rest of place." Alexi tapped Mary's arm, urging her towards the west side of the building. "Here is medical wing…" They peeked in through the doorway. A medic was stitching a fresh wound in a man's shin. "He very clumsy. Seen him here before." Alexi added, striding off towards the rear of the building. "Here is food storage and over there, food waste um… recycled. Correct word, yes?"

Nodding, she followed the excited chap to the east side of the building. Pointing through an external window towards an adjacent structure, Alexi said, "over there, school rooms, centre for to look after babies…" He clicked his thumb and fingers together, tapping them against his forehead.

"Creche." Mary offered.

"Yes, that is it. Creche." He smiled at her, and then returned his attention to the large empty rooms in the east wing. "This for group activities, but is sunny today. They all outside instead." He wandered off through a side exit, loitering in the doorway for Mary to catch up. "Ah, I must show you orchard, and my bees. Come, come…"

She trailed after him. It was difficult for her to maintain her suspicion in the face of such enterprise. Everywhere she looked, people laughed and smiled in their endeavours. It was almost idyllic. A short walk took them closer to the great open spaces reserved for crops. They passed a few cages protecting soft fruit canes and vines from wildlife, before nearing a large mature orchard. Long grass interspersed with wild flowers, cherry and apple trees, pears and plums, providing a home for Alexi's beehives. The view was stunning.

"This is where the flowers in my lodge came from." Mary said, launching herself through the grasses to lean against a low cherry tree. "It's beautiful."

Encouraged by her response, Alexi drew closer to her. "Modern world very bad for my bees."

"You mean all the chemicals? Pesticides and herbicides sprayed onto the land?"

"Yes, but not only. Modern frequencies disturb bees. Cannot find their way home. Mobile phones and cell towers, broadband, wireless Internet, all mess with wildlife, birds, bees. Colonies fly away, queens die, crops fail, we all die." Alexi's perky mood ebbed. "I have proof. Will show you later. Science studies."

Mary patted his shoulder. "But not here though, surely? Come to think of it, your little car is the only electric thing, other than a fridge, that I have seen since I arrived." Her own words, puzzled her. All those people at lunch, and none were using mobile phones. There were no monitors, televisions or computers. "Why is that, Alexi? How do people around here keep in touch with what is going on in the world?"

"There are some electric things. Most are stored underground, packed away or um…disabled." Alexi saw the look of suspicion reappear across her features. He bent low and picked a pink meadow flower and handed it to Mary. It did not deflect her attention.

"Why are they stored underground, Alexi? What are you up to?"

"I not up to things, Mary. We build a nice place here, eh? You know, you should make use of facility. You learn self-defence. We have teacher. Come, we find him."

Mary persisted with her interrogation all the way back to the open grassland in front of the communal centre, but Alexi would not divulge any more. They watched the groups of people engrossed in Tai chi, some made natural soap on portable gas hobs, while others learned martial arts in the shade of a large American beech tree. Each of the areas were connected by small service roads and cycle paths.

"You meet nice teacher. He help you defend yourself, yes?"

"No. I really must leave now, Alexi. Please can you ask your driver to take me to that town? I can make my own way from there."

Alexi made a hang-dog face at her, pouting his lips in a down turned smile. "You want to go already? You don't like this place?"

"It's lovely, really, but I need to leave now."

"If you want, but you must eat before you go. Will tell driver to take you." Alexi ambled towards the communal centre entrance. Mary trailed after him. She thought about refusing his offer of food, but her stomach, like the rest of her, was still working on Greenwich Mean Time. It would be about time for an evening meal back in England.

The canteen had thinned of crowds on their return; people drifted off to their duties or studies for the afternoon. Only a few of the animated groups of friends remained.

"Does this canteen stay open all the time?" The delicious aromas stimulated her salivary glands. It had been some time since Mary had eaten a proper meal. The choices listed on the chalk board were varied and enticing.

"All day yes. Close at ten pm." Alexi collected a tray from a neat stack and balanced it on a metal shelf next to the hotplates. "What would you like? Italian, Indian, French, or maybe from my homeland? Some very tasty pirozhki? They do an okay lapsha…"

"All these different cuisines in one canteen?"

"Da, people from all over world here. Food make everyone happy. Come." He gestured for Mary to take a tray and join him at the counter. She observed as Alexi ordered something called Koulibiaca. The man serving took a huge knife to a giant, sized free-standing pie, and sawed a couple of inches from its end. As it toppled onto the plate, Mary could see the colourful layers of sticky wild rice, dark spinach, hard boiled eggs, black mushrooms, sun-blushed tomatoes and slab of rare beef inside.

"They do a veggie kind too… you like?"

Mary thought for a moment. Everything looked appetising.

Alexi saw her indecision. "I think you would like pirozhki, soft and tasty, with mushroom sauerkraut and potatoes. The man serving handed Alexi a small bread-like roll with a pair of tongs. Alexi ripped it apart revealing a steamy mushroom and egg filling. "See, very tasty."

Warm dill and pepper tingled her nasal linings. Alexi handed half to her and munched on the other. Mary took a bite. The herbs, piquant flavours and soft textures danced on her tongue. "Wow, that is amazing."

The server gave her a wide grin, stacking a plate high with the filled rolls and adding portions of the accompanying dishes. She thanked the man and shuffled along to where Alexi was helping himself to fresh juice.

"Can have tea instead, if you want?" Alexi said, pointing back at the man serving another resident. "I can ask them to make you some."

Mary shook her head. "Thanks, but I will just eat this, and head off to that town." She took a glass of orange juice and followed Alexi to a long table. They sat next to a group of people, whose vibrant discussions had caught her attention earlier in the tour. As she sat down, their conversation halted, and their postures changed to a more formal and upright stiffness.

"Gentlemen, ladies…" Alexi said, his voice dipping low and gravelly.

"General." The group replied, with varying intonation and timing.

Mary felt a painful memory stab her brain. Alexi was not her friend. He was former Soviet military, and a ruthless extremist. No amount of delicious food would alter that fact. She looked at the expressions on the young people's faces. They were watching her. There was a growing expectation for her to say something to them, but what?

She cleared her throat. "Um, hello everyone. I am Mary."

"We know who you are Mrs Arora." The voice came from a large man sitting closest to her. The accent distinctly Scottish. His t-shirt stretched taught over his biceps. "We are all very glad that you have joined us."

"Oh no, I haven't joined anything. I am just having a quick bite to eat before I leave." She picked up a fork and stabbed a buttery potato, directing it to her mouth.

The group looked first at each other, and then at Alexi, who shrugged his response. Mary peered up at them, their attention trained on her. In that instance, all their hopes and fears transmitted across the space and lodged in her mind.

"That is distressing news, Mrs Arora." The voice was low and husky, but fainter than before.

Wait... Mary stopped eating. Her thoughts expanding into a multi-directional wave. *I heard that inside my mind. No one actually spoke. These people are like me.* She twisted in her seat to face the large man at her side. *"Are you able to hear my thoughts?"*

"Indeed, Mrs Arora. We all can." The man replied. Mary looked at all the other faces around her. Each of them smiling and nodding in her direction.

"Are you Alexi's new Hive Operatives?" She asked, keeping the conversation internal and shielded from their general's ears.

Again, the group exchanged glances. This time the look was of puzzlement. *"What is a Hive Operative, Mrs Arora?"*

Mary was stunned. How could they not know of Alexi's former missions? How could they be unaware of the hundreds of military personnel, trained in extra-sensory perception and kept in a constant state of collective consciousness, via coma inducing and hallucinatory drugs? How had Alexi gathered up these English speaking people who exhibited extraordinary mental abilities without the use of medication? And for what purpose? Was this entire complex devoted to gifted people? All at once, it hit her. This was no spa retreat. This was a military command centre.

Chapter Three

They were waiting for her answer. Seven young, earnest and innocent victims of Alexi's latest plot. Could they hear her inner turmoil as she wrestled with her conscience? How much should she tell them? How much did they already know?

"Do you know why Alexi has brought you here?" Mary launched the question into the airwaves, trying to keep her features in a neutral expression, so as not to alert her host. She watched the group struggle with their internal lines of communication. Hand gestures overtook their telepathic discourse. The larger man nodded towards a woman on the opposite side of the table.

She replied in a weak transmission. *"The general is training us to use our gifts. In return, he is taking care of my mother's medical fees."*

Mary squinted at the blond, who scratched her dry forearms and then picked at her nails. She appeared timid, but Mary detected something defiant about her. An obstinacy of sorts, apparent in the way she sat slightly apart from the rest of the group. The provided sweat pants were cut off way above the knee to reveal her long, tanned legs. Trouble simmered beneath the veneer of compliance. Mary turned her attention to the rest of the group.

"Is this the case for all of you?" Mary enquired of them. Their responses were instantaneous and

deafening. Mary received all their answers at once, in a neural cacophony.

"Nah, I just needed a job... my sister volunteered us, stupid cow... the money was too good an offer..." And so on, drowning out Mary's cry to stop. These were not the experienced military Hive minds that she was expecting. They were barely able to control their own abilities, let alone infiltrate anyone else.

Alexi sat at the end of the table, eating his Koulibiaca and watching their faces.

"So, this is your little game, is it? Show me some Arcadian orchard and a luxury cabin and you think I will fall in line with your cadets? What were you expecting… that I would become queen bee of this new hive, and train them for you?" Mary snapped at him.

Alexi placed his cutlery down on his plate. "You not happy I find more like you? I found you new friends, people who understand. They part of our family now."

"I don't need a new family." The sentiment caught in her throat. She drew breath and composed herself. "Whatever you are planning, Alexi, forget it. I'm outta here." Mary untangled her limbs from the bench seating and grabbed her bag from the floor.

Alexi scuttled after her. "You don't have to be friend to them, only stay. I get you whatever you want." He stopped at the front entrance to the communal building and watched her storm off towards her cabin.

At full stride, Mary hurried to Alexi's electric car and jumped in. Whatever his latest devious plan was, someone else could stop him. It was not her problem. There was no ignition key, just a starter button on the dash. With a foot on the accelerator pedal, she zoomed past a sulking Soviet general, and out of the open compound gates.

Mary turned right onto the tree-lined road, and followed the signs to little township. The sense of freedom was exhilarating. With the windows fully lowered, she breathed in the refreshing forest air. About five miles into her journey, she realised that the blond wig was still in the lodge house bedroom. She would need to buy another, or some hair dye if she was to use her fake passport again. *Which, easily reached country, has no extradition treaty with Britain? Somewhere in South America perhaps.* Before she could settle on a destination, a red warning light flashed on the console.

Mary peeped at the power gauge next to the LED. *Shit. Just my luck.* Taking another right turn, Mary cruised towards the main street of the little town. There seemed to be more churches than houses; mostly of wooden construction from the colonial era. The Stars and Stripes hung motionless in the humid air from every porch and veranda. These were proud Americans.

A loud beeping noise accompanied the flashing light, as she reached a small cluster of shops. There was just enough juice to coast into a space directly ahead, before Mary applied the brake. With the car abandoned, Mary walked past the knife and gun shop and into the diner. She sat against the counter. A woman in a pink uniform plonked a mug in front of her and hovered with a glass jug of coffee.

"What can I getcher, sweetie?" She said. Mary could see the mass of grey gum stuck to her upper teeth when she spoke.

"Could I have a cup of tea, please?"

"Ah just love that accent. Where yer from?"

"Oh, um, Brighton." Mary said, rummaging in her satchel for her purse.

"Where's that now?"

"It's in the UK."

The waitress chewed again, shaking her head.

"England?" Mary blew out her cheeks. Still the waitress looked confused. "London?"

"Ah London…how niiiice. Tea yer say?"

"Please."

The waitress took the mug away and filled it with hot water and a splash of milk. It was returned to Mary with a teabag resting on a saucer next to a spoon. Mary looked at the anaemic broth and thanked her.

"Oh, no." Mary clutched her purse to her chest.

"What is it, honey?"

"I haven't any US dollars. Is there a currency exchange? Somewhere I can swap sterling?"

"Tell you what," the woman in pink said. "This one is on the house." She smiled and wandered off to wipe the counter top.

Mary touched the money roll her friend Connie had given her in London. What use was it, if she couldn't exchange it for dollars? Use of the debit and credit cards in her purse would pinpoint her location, even if there was a delay between British and US Intelligence Agencies. She drank the insipid tea, and thanked the waitress again before leaving.

Hurrying down the vast open spaces of the main street, Mary found a bank. It sat all alone with a drive through facility encircling the building like a moat. *That's novel. Very convenient for robbers- they wouldn't need to leave their get-away vehicles.* Before entering, she peeled off a couple of fifty-pound notes and stashed them in a pocket inside her bag. With her passport in hand, Mary held her head high and walked into the building. Two bank tellers sat behind their glass screens chatting to one another. There were no other customers. Mary stood at the front of the queue, waiting to be called to the counter.

The tellers looked at Mary, and decided that she had not waited long enough to warrant service, and so returned to their conversation. She peered about the foyer. The ATM machine looked tempting, but Mary knew this was a bad option as far as tracking her whereabouts was concerned. A man in a suit sat behind a desk in the small business section, playing patience on his computer.

Mary tried to look suitably humble, in the hope that this would prompt the legendary customer service that US politicians boast about. Eventually it worked. Mary was called to the nearest counter.

"I'd like to exchange all this sterling into dollars, please." She said, preparing herself for an explanation regarding her passport and change of appearance.

"Can't do currency exchange at this booth. That would be the counter over there." The woman pointed to a shuttered window at the end of the row.

"Is it possible to open that booth, please?" Mary implored, giving the woman a piteous and desperate look.

"Delores does exchange."

"And where is Delores?"

"She's on a break."

"Then may I wait for her break to end over there?" Mary pointed to the seats next to the small businesses' manager.

"You'll be waiting a while... she's on maternity leave." The tellers sniggered together, and indulged in a slow high-five palm touch.

Mary persevered. "Is there anyone here prepared to help me? This is all the money I have, and I cannot spend it in your lovely town as it is." One of the tellers turned away and shuffled administrative forms and papers. The other, folded her arms across her chest.

A man's voice boomed out from behind her. "Stop being so God-damn awkward, Shandy. Open the counter and serve the lady." It was Mr Patience, rising from his seat to assert his authority. Grumbling, and at the slowest speed humanly possible, Shandy wandered to the exchange booth and raised the shutters.

Mary clasped her passport beneath her satchel, framing reasonable sentences in her mind and preparing for a battle, but it never materialised. Shandy was too focused on the glacial rate at which she counted out the notes. Armed with US dollars, Mary left the bank without having to show any form of identification.

"I hope y'all have a nice day." Mary muttered as she passed through the exit. "And then choke on your apple pie."

I just need to get to a city. There must be public transport of some description. Mary looked around her. There was just one short row of shops with a large area of grassland opposite. Scattered between massive road junctions were an odd assortment of buildings, from the fire station to the Town Hall. Everywhere had drive-through facilities.

Retracing her steps, Mary returned to the diner and sat on the same stool as before. She took a ten dollar note from her purse as the waitress approached.

"Hello again." Mary said, waving the cash at the woman. "Please may I have another cup of tea? I can pay for both cups now."

The waitress simpered and turned her back to retrieve a mug.

"Could you tell me where the nearest train station is please?"

"Oh honey, there ain't no train station. There's one over in the next town, if you can hitch a ride, but it only goes to Hoboken. Where yer headed?"

"Ideally, Manhattan." Mary said, dunking the teabag into the warm milk mixture.

"There's a bus...but that's in the next town too. Really, you need to get there first." The waitress looked down at Mary.

"I don't suppose that the petrol station behind the bank is able to recharge an electric car either?"

"Oh, you British people with your sense of humour." She shrieked with laughter, and then grabbed the TV remote. "Let's find a channel to make you feel more at home." Within moments, the wall mounted monitor showed re-runs of Downtown Abbey above their heads.

Mary gave the waitress a thin-lipped smile. Looking out of the window, she tried to gauge the likelihood of hitching a ride. She stared for a full five minutes. Not a single vehicle passed by. *Great. I'm stuck here.*

"How far is it to the next town? Could I walk the distance?" Mary enquired.

"Sweetie, you can't walk there, it's a full fifteen miles."

Hmm. She looked at the wall clock. *I could probably make it there before dark, if I took plenty of water.* "Could you give me directions please? I'll walk it all if I have to, but I might catch a lift if I am lucky."

"Aww, honey, forecast gave storm warnings. I wouldn't risk it. How bout, I ask around during the evening rush, see if anyone's headed out that ways that can give yer a lift?"

"Thank you. That's very kind." Mary looked about the deserted diner and figured that obtaining assistance could take some time. The frustration tired her. Despite the morning spent asleep at Alexi's compound, her body was still running on British hours. She drained the last of her tepid drink. "Is there at least a hotel, somewhere I could get a room?"

The waitress thought for a moment. "Well, you could try your luck at the Kent's place. Closest thing we got to a guest house round these parts. But she's a bit on the strict side."

"Great, thanks. Where will I find the Kent's place?"

"It's over by the library. Walk up to the corner there and hang a left. It ain't far. But don't say I didn't warn yer." The waitress wagged an amused finger towards Mary and laughed.

Mary smiled hollow pleasantries and left. She passed an odd assortment of shops; a manicurist salon, the gun shop, a Chinese takeaway and a steakhouse. Every corner construction and yard bore a flagpole. The wide spaces between buildings were laid with immaculate lawns and punctuated with maple and fir trees. If the early settlers were attempting to replicate England, they missed their target by a country mile.

Most of the houses were timber, clad in planks decorated in tasteful muted colours and well-tended. A few brick buildings peppered the landscape, but those were signposted with more municipal functions – the firehouse, town hall, library and community school.

The Kent's guest house was exactly where the waitress had directed. Two pristine stretches of lawn away from the library. The structure was of the same colonial style as the majority of properties, but at more than twice the size. The woodwork was fresh painted grey, with white windowsills and door frames. Bedding plants dripped in long festoons from hanging baskets either side of the porch entrance.

An elderly lady rocked in a chair on the veranda. She did not look up from her crochet work in her lap as Mary approached.

"Hello there. May I …"

The old woman raised her arm, silencing Mary. She extended a bony finger towards a sign pinned to the door frame. It read: *Ring bell for service*. Threading the wool around her fingers once again, she continued her labours.

"Right… I see. Thank you." She turned around and pulled the cord attached to the brass bell. It rang out clear and loud. From inside the house, Mary could hear scraping and sloshing, and heavy footsteps.

"Confound those blasted children, if I catch you this time it'll be… Oh." The large woman appeared behind the screen door, and considered Mary. She wiped her hands dry on her apron and moved closer. "Can I help you?"

"I hope so. Is there any possibility of me booking a room for the night, please?" What was it about being abroad, that prompted a forced clarity of English? Mary heard her own perfect speech and suppressed a giggle.

She stepped aside as the screen door opened towards her. Mrs Kent was quite as formidable as the waitressed had warned. Her muscular forearms tensed as she leaned against the door jam.

"One night, you say?"

"Yes, please."

"Travelling alone?"

"I am, yes."

"With no luggage?"

"I was not anticipating an overnight stay, but um, my car broke down on my way to the next town."

She peered at Mary from her messy dark curls to the mucky leather sandals on her feet. "Oh, I will take my shoes off in the house, I promise. I need to buy some new ones, but I have not yet had the chance."

Mrs Kent's eyes narrowed further still. It was a carefully conveyed warning. She turned and stomped back into the house, expecting Mary to follow.

"It'll be a hundred dollars per night, fifty up front. Breakfast is at eight am sharp and will be an extra fifteen dollars." She glanced back to see that Mary was still standing out on the veranda. "Well, come in girl." She screeched.

Mary balanced on one foot, wrestling the sandal from the other. In rapid succession, the second shoe was dislodged and tucked beneath her arm.

"Mind the floor, it's still wet."

It was splendid inside. The sitting room lay to her left; stripped wooden flooring, woollen rugs, antique dark stained furniture and porcelain ornaments over the fireplace. Mary dawdled after the disciplinarian along the hallway to the foot of the stairs. A small shelf supported a stack of three tattered bibles, beneath a carved wooden crucifix and china figurine of their lord and saviour. Mrs Kent noticed Mary staring at Jesus.

"You are welcome to join us in prayer at seven thirty this evening." She waited for Mary to respond. When no answer came, she continued, "my son will give you the Wi-Fi password, if needs be."

"Thank you, most kind." Mary jogged up the stairs after her landlady.

"This room is made up, I'll bring clean towels along presently. I don't provide evening meals, but there's the steakhouse, a Chinese and the diner stays open till nine. Bathroom is along there to the right, and there's a small room safe with instructions in the wardrobe." She swung open the door to a room at the top of the first flight of stairs. The windows were all open and the net curtains were billowing outside. Mrs Kent gathered them in and slammed the windows shut. "That'll be the storm on its way."

She turned and stared at Mary with her palm outstretched. Mary came to her senses and grappled with the money envelope Shandy had provided at the bank. She fanned out the currency and selected two twenties and a ten, placing them into the woman's calloused and muscular hand.

Mrs Kent scrunched the notes tight to her bosom. "I don't allow additional visitors at any time. I'll be back with the towels."

It was spotlessly clean - hospital corners, sparkling water carafe, ironed pillow cases on which you could cut yourself. She scanned the room. A disturbing lithograph of Christ, stared back. She caught sight of her dishevelled appearance in the mirror above the vanity unit, and felt an urge to find her hairbrush and tame her locks into something which might earn the landlady's approval.

Her thunderous steps announced Mrs Kent's return, carrying a stack of white towels and the residents' book. "You'll need to sign in and provide some form of ID."

Chapter Four

Mary was expecting the landlady's demands for identification, and had her passport ready and waiting. The woman scowled at the photograph.

"Oh, I dyed my hair back to brunette. That was taken during my blond days." Mary produced her most disarming smile. It bounced off Mrs Kent without leaving a mark.

"Sign here, Mrs Sedgewell, and I'll leave you to settle in." Mrs Kent delivered another non-verbal warning. One that said, *I don't trust you lady. Cross me at your peril.*

Mary did as she was told, finding the new name awkward to reproduce on paper. No matter what instructions her brain relayed to her muscles, her hand slipped into an automated response beginning her signature for Mary Arora. The result looked like a squashed insect.

Mrs Kent slammed the register closed, and stomped from the room, leaving Mary to contemplate her surroundings. No television, no phone, no books. Just a copy of the bible on the nightstand next to the water carafe. A quick inventory of her bag did little to cheer her spirits. She had just two pairs of cotton knickers, taken from the luggage provided by Alexi, and the travel toothbrush and paste from the flight freebies.

There has to be a supermarket or other shops somewhere around here. Mary mused, searching around the bale of towels for the room key. She went out on to the landing, leaning over the banisters.

"Mrs Kent?" She hollered. "Hello there?" Mary descended a few steps and tried again. "Mrs Kent?"

An alternately high and low pitched voice answered her. It broke in the middle with a discordant squeal. "Mom's out back, taking in the washing."

Mary followed the voice back up the stairs and along the landing. The boy's bedroom door was ajar. Mary double tapped it and peered through the gap. "Excuse me?" She could see the teenager sitting close to his computer monitor, smashing the cursor keys on his keyboard to direct a cartoon figure on his quest. "Where will I find the room key?"

He didn't take his eyes from the game. "Ain't no keys. Put yer valuables in the safe. Mom locks the front door at eleven every night."

"Thank you." She waited for his reply. When none was forthcoming, she returned to her room. The money envelope bulged with low denomination bank notes, a gift from her dear friend Connie. It was all she had with which to start a new life. *Perhaps it would be wise to lock it away. I'll only take a few notes with me for food and such.*

Mary opened the wardrobe door. The electronic safe was bolted to the inside wall. A small card gave instructions on how to programme the digital code to a new pin number. She decided to use her grandfather's birthday digits. As she typed in the numbers, she remembered the golden lambda brooch, taken from the floor safe in her grandfather's study. It was nestling at the bottom of her satchel. Mary fished it out and traced her finger over the symbol. *What were you up to*

Grampy? I so wish you were here with me. I miss you. Fighting back the emotion, Mary placed the brooch, her passport and the money in the safe and clicked the door firmly in place.

She went to the window and looked out along the street. The wind had picked up and the Stars and Stripes now whipped against their restraints. A single pickup truck passed by, turning left at the end of the road. The solitude gave her a longing to connect with the outside world. *How does anyone find out the news in this place? Wait, didn't the battle-axe mention a Wi-Fi password? Yes, I'm sure she did.*

Mary ventured back out into the hallway and edged closer to the boy's room. Knocking gently, she heard him tut at the disturbance.

"Hello there. I'm sorry to bother you again, but please may I borrow your computer for a few minutes? I need to check my emails and look something up online, that sort of thing."

The boy pressed a couple of keys, pausing his game, and then swivelled in his chair to face her. "Ten dollars for five minutes." A crooked smirk formed across his face.

"Five dollars for ten minutes, final offer or I'll tell your mother." Mary surprised herself at her quick thinking. She almost sounded authoritative.

"Fine..." He whined, strolling from the room to claim his money.

Mary flicked the door closed and minimised the boy's online quest. With a new browser window open, Mary typed in the Reuters news web address and trawled through the headlines for any updates on the failing health of the British Prime Minister. Instead, she found reams of articles, placing the British Defence Secretary at the heart of a scandal which involved trading defence technology and intelligence with Iran. Her friend Constance Cadot, was credited for breaking the story worldwide. *Well at least with the Ministry of Defence in turmoil, they won't be looking for me.*

Another browser window, another trawl. This time, she picked through her Facebook feed. Hugo Blom was capitalising on his new-found fame. Legions of Christian worshippers flocked to his side in support of the struggles he faced daily over his *unnatural desires*. His impassioned speech at Parliament Square, recorded in video snippets, littered Mary's Facebook news feed. Her name was tagged on every post and tirade. Someone had created an animated gif of Mary's explosive appearance on stage, her electromagnetic discharge played over and over in a loop. This was not going to fade quietly into the background.

Mary held her head in her hands. The likelihood of the Prime Minister keeping her promise grew ever more doubtful. The door creaked. Mary whipped her head around to find the boy watching her through a sliver of a gap. Busted, he bound into the room.

"Time's up lady." He stood next to her, reading the visible comments on the screen. Mary quickly closed the browser windows, glaring at his intrusion. She had seen enough. Her notoriety continued building in Britain but, as yet, they were unable to pinpoint her location. Time was on her side.

Wandering back to her room, a bumble bee ricocheted from the window, reminding her of Alexi's issues. His insistence that technology was killing worldwide bee populations, followed by a memory of large trucks leaving an underground facility. *What was Alexi up to? Not my problem anymore. He can go on playing with his bees and erecting more wind turbines to his heart's content. But, why would he need a team of telepaths unless he had another grand plan in the pipeline?*

Mary pushed him from her mind. Her new life was all that mattered, not his potential to destroy others. She grabbed her satchel and crept down the stairs. Mrs Kent was still in the yard. Mary could see her through the rear windows, wrestling with billowing bedsheets from the washing line. *An eleven-pm curfew, eh? I'll be back long before then.* She skipped down the porch steps and out onto the street.

The wind cut through her flimsy clothes, chilling her skin to ice. She had just enough time to register the first few spots of rain, before the deluge arrived. Mary ran the five hundred metres to the end of the street and sought shelter beneath the shop awnings. Soaked through, she looked about her for a potential haven. Her choices were slim. Most shops had closed for the evening, leaving her with the steakhouse, a Chinese takeaway, or further down the road, the diner.

I can't imagine Mrs Kent allowing me to eat a Chinese takeaway in my room; all those foreign smells and messy noodles. A vegetarian in a steakhouse would not fare particularly well. The diner it is then. Clutching her satchel tight to her chest, Mary ran the length of the block, back to the diner.

Bowling in through the doors, she almost ran into the waitress.

"Back again, honey? Did you find the Kent's place okay?"

"I did, thank you. It is wild out there."

"Sure is. Wilder still across the border in Philly." The waitress nodded towards the television above the counter. "The storm has wrecked no end of buildings. Let's hope it blows northwards, eh? What can I getcha?"

Mary sat at the counter, along with a number of workmen, fresh from their shift. Most ate in silence, watching the news play out on the screen. Behind her in the booths, sat families with young children dressed in a variety of after school apparel, from cheerleading outfits to martial arts garb.

"I am rather peckish. Do you have any vegetarian dishes?"

"We can do you an omelette, or grilled cheese, or an omelette?" The waitress scratched her head with the end of her biro, in quiet thought.

"Thank you, an omelette sounds lovely."

"You want fries with that?"

"Yes, please. May as well go the whole hog."

"Pardon me?"

"Fries would be lovely, thanks."

A man sitting near to Mary bellowed a garbled instruction to the waitress. She seemed to comprehend him fully, dashing to the remote control and raising the volume on the TV.

The reporter stood beneath a glass overhang, speaking to camera. Behind her, blue flashing lights and medics wheeling a trolley into the rear of an ambulance. "As far as we can tell, the senator is alive and fully conscious. At present. All we know for sure is that at six thirty this evening, Senator Luca Bonovich was struck by lightning at the opening ceremony of the new Bonovich Community Baseball field." The reporter paused, while the storm rampaged around her and her crew, knocking them sideways in the force of the wind. A hand appeared in the shot, wiping the rain from the lens.

"Witnesses say that shortly after the ribbon was cut, the senator was invited to pitch from the mound. It was at this point, that the senator was struck. Medical teams rallied and re-started his heart at the scene. We will follow his progress and update viewers as events occur. Back to the studio."

A few people murmured their concern for the politician. One woman looked to be uttering a prayer, before kissing the crucifix hanging around her neck. Most returned their attention to the food on their plates without comment.

The news broadcast ended with a weather forecast for the region. Once again, the diner grew silent, listening out for the predicted trajectory of the storm. Confident that the epicentre was shifting in a north easterly direction, the broadcaster gave warnings to towns and cities that lay in its path. Their township was not among them. Tension in the diner visibly eased. The babble of community life returned to full volume, and the waitress adopted a relieved smile. "Poor man. Let's hope he recovers soon. Would anyone like more coffee?"

Within ten minutes, Mary was presented with a steaming plate of omelette and fries, and a tasteless cup of tea to wash it down. She tucked into the meal with relish, complimenting the waitress for the perfect eggs. This tiny iota of praise, prompted the waitress to grab the remote and switch channels on the television. Her customers wailed and moaned, but it made little impact.

"Would you like a channel from your neck of the woods, honey? We got cable."

"Really? Thank you. Do you have access to the BBC news?" Mary asked, without putting much thought into the outcome of such a request.

"Sure do…" The waitress pressed a menu, scrolled down to the BBC and selected the option.

World news events, bored the clientele. One or two sitting at the counter squinted up from their meals every now and then, but most ignored the broadcast. The Italians were celebrating a papal visit with another dignitary, the French bemoaned fishing quotas and the Swedes were congratulating themselves on a new method for treating Alzheimer's patients.

Mary recognised two customers arriving at the diner, each holding a raincoat over their heads. It was Shandy and her friend from the bank. She clocked Mary at the counter. Her response was to choose a booth to Mary's left, allowing her ample opportunities to be seen sneering and glowering.

Time rolled on. Eventually, the world news swung back to Britain. Mary peered up at the screen to see the familiar red curved settee in the BBC news studio. She almost choked when the next guest was introduced. Dr Hugo Blom perched on the sofa, soberly dressed in V-neck sweater and cotton slacks. Twisting around, Mary was relieved to see that no one in the diner paid Hugo any attention. Video footage of the pilgrims' march through the streets of London, stopping at Trafalgar Square before marching along to Parliament Square, were of little interest to the inhabitants of a New Jersey township.

The RSS feed of headlines scrolled along the bottom of the screen. *Prime Minister stricken by legionnaires outbreak at the Houses of Parliament. Pharmaceutical giant fined for dumping illegal waste into river channels and water courses.* Mary scoffed at the deception, tucking into her omelette and skinny fries.

The waitress had the remote control again. She squinted at the television, and then down at Mary, and back to the screen. "Hey, ain't that you up there on that stage, honey?" She squeezed the volume button, and gestured across the diner. "Hey everyone, we have a star in our midst. Quiet now…" The township residents all hushed at the command, obliging the waitress with their attention.

Mary shrank down as low as her posture would allow, shutting her eyes tight to the revelation. She had no need to watch. She knew the replay would show her standing centre stage in front of the Arch Bishop of Canterbury, addressing a crowd of fifty-thousand irate Christian worshippers. The dissent which ensued after viewing a YouTube video of Mary performing actual transubstantiation in a laboratory at Imperial College, London. Some were in awe of the possibility that she might actually be the new messiah, others threw their jaunts and jeers in verbal combat.

"So, what?" Shandy sneered. "So, she is a bit famous in the back end of Europe. Who cares?" She slammed her burger down on her plate, sending the cutlery crashing to the table. "Switch over to the game. No one wants to see this snooty Brit on TV." The waitress shushed her, delivering a scornful glare. She increased the volume a few more notches.

The video clip paused, the cameras cut back to the studio, where Hugo Blom preened.

"That was quite a feat you pulled off there, Dr Blom, how did you achieve those numbers in such a short span of time?" The lady presenter asked.

"Well, it was simple really. The video I posted online, girded such overwhelming support, I felt it was my Christian duty to act." Hugo picked at a fragment of lint from his knee, doing his best to look chaste and innocent.

"And this is the video claiming to show the unusual abilities of Mary Arora?"

"Yes, it was taken as evidence for an experiment suggested by her husband Dr Parth Arora."

"Can we see the clip now?" The presenter touched the small device in her ear. "Yes, we can go to that now."

The picture altered to one of Parth and Hugo, celebrating their discovery with mugs of wine.

The diner was silent but for the sound of clattering pans from the kitchen. Mary braced herself as her ex-husband uttered those fateful words. The phrase that had sent a ripple of revulsion through the faithful around the virtual globe. The statement that gave rise to the British Prime Minister denouncing Mary as mentally ill.

"Mary," Parth shouted from the monitor. "Turn this water into wine for us."

It was as though the whole world simply stopped. Every mouth hung open in the diner as they watched the colourless liquid transform into a dark syrupy burgundy with just a touch. Scrabbling with her purse, Mary knew it was time to go. Thrusting a few dollars beneath the edge of her plate, Mary gathered herself up, and turned to leave.

Shandy led the charge. "I just knew there was something off about her…didn't I say…?" The family of cheerleaders and karate kids flinched as Mary approached. "Move away from that woman, Chet, before she turns you into a frog or something." Workmen sat at the counter watching in awe. The video feed had returned to images of Mary on stage. Chanting from the masses grew in a crescendo, all baying for Mary to show them her capabilities.

The small woman alone on the stage looked harassed and agitated. Mary looked up at the playback of herself losing control of her electromagnetic discharge, frying the cabling, circuitry, sound systems and giant screen in a spectacular array of electrical sparks and secondary flames. The workmen gasped, waiting for a slow-motion replay. The waitress dropped the remote on the counter and stepped backwards, her gum resting on her trembling lips. Even Shandy was muted.

Mary hurried towards the door. "I never intended for any of this to happen." She yelled over her shoulder. "I didn't mean to offend anyone." She ran. The rain pelted down, flattening the curls to her face and chilling her bones. She could hear them coming after her, scraping the counter stools across the hard flooring and yelling swearwords through the closing door.

The diners spilled out onto the pavement beneath the shop awnings. Mary sprinted around the corner and across the wide road. Street lamps flickered on in the stormy evening light, distracting her from the commotion up ahead. As she passed the edge of the library building, Mary saw vehicles screeching to a halt outside the guest house. Some of the vans had aerials and satellite dishes mounted on the rooves.

Emblazoned across the side of the vans and people carriers were the letters CNN. The United States media circus had arrived.

Chapter Five

Mary dashed behind the trunk of a Maple tree. *This is crazy. How the hell did they get here so fast?* She sneaked a look towards the guest house. Mrs Kent's son stood sneering on the veranda. The old woman packed up her crochet, strained to rise from the rocking chair, and shuffled past her grandson and into the house. This was his carnival, and nothing was going to stop him.

A slew of reporters, camera and sound engineers bundled from the vans and rushed to the porch steps. Mary could hear several people speaking at once, but nothing distinct. She scurried from the tree to the front stoop of the library. The overhang gave little shelter in the swirling storm and it faced the main drag of the street. The reporters only had to turn around and they would spot her in an instant.

Slipping around the side of the building, Mary found a covered area, enclosing the library rubbish bins. Hunkered down, between the dumpsters, she tried to rationalise her options. *I doubt anyone from the diner would give me a lift to the next town now. I will have to walk the distance in the morning. How the hell am I going to get the money and Grandma Phebe's brooch from that bloody safe?*

Van doors slammed, metal poles clanged together and engineers muttered brief instructions from the roadside. The camera crews were setting up their encampment. A siege, just for her. *I wonder if the boy knows that I am not in my room? Little sod must have back-tracked through my browser history and spotted the YouTube links. I wonder how much CNN agreed to pay him for my whereabouts?*

Mary hugged herself. The last grey fingers of daylight slipped away. Wasps gathered around a patch of sticky liquid, oozing from the base of the trash cans. The stench of rotting coffee grounds and spilled soda invaded her senses. *If I could just…* An idea popped into her thoughts. She squeezed between the dustbins and found a squashed cardboard box. Ripping it open, she lay the flat sections of dry board on the floor, in the most sheltered section of the covered area, and sat down.

With her satchel beneath her knees and her back against the library wall, Mary closed her eyes and hummed a tune to herself in the darkness. The same tune that harmonised her brain waves to match that of the Earth's resonant frequencies. The Beatles number that her grandfather would sing to her in infancy. With her alpha rhythms in sync, Mary disassociated her mind from her body, and flew.

In a roiling mass of energy, Mary's consciousness slipped around the corner of the library building and soared high above the Kent's guest house. The camera crew were still unrolling cables and connecting their microphones up to record an interview. The boy had a massive grin plastered across his pimply face. There was no way that Mary could feasibly take control of him, without drawing attention to his actions.

The grandmother was a wholly different entity. That was who she needed to find. Commanding her nebulous mass, Mary pushed her consciousness through the roof of the guest house and descended the central staircase to the hallway. She could see the boy through the open front door, his stance as confident as his mother's. With no time to lose, Mary shifted towards the rear of the building, passing the dining room and into the kitchen.

Mrs Kent stood by the oven, slipping her hands into heatproof mitts. The grandmother was shuffling towards a high-backed chair next to the range, clutching her crochet bag to her body. *Rather her than Mrs Kent...*Mary mused. Steering herself to face the old woman, Mary blended with her sight, and took control of her central nervous system.

The pain was instant; an ache in almost every joint. Spasms in her left hip caused Mary's energy to fluctuate, forcing her to concentrate hard on the task. She batted the grandmother's psyche into a sleep state, and dropped the crochet bag on the chair. Turning around, she shuffled the old woman's body back through the kitchen and into the hallway.

This is taking forever. No wonder the poor old dear just sits on the porch all day with her wool. Grabbing the banister for support, Mary dragged the body up the stairs, one agonising step at a time. By the tenth tread, Mary was aware of a dull ache in the lower abdomen. A sinister mass of cancerous cells divided and multiplied at a lethal rate. The invasion was impossible to ignore.

Mary swallowed, and refocused. There was nothing she could do to help, except leave the woman's body alone. Guilt swept through her consciousness. *I'm using a dying woman to collect my belongings. I'll be as quick as I can grandma. Bear with me.* At the top of the stairs, Mary had to stop to allow the body to draw breath. Lactic acid built in the muscles to displace the pain from worn joints.

A few more steps, and she was inside her room. She moved to the wardrobe and opened the doors. The safe was just as it had been left. For a brief moment, Mary wondered if the boy had tampered with the lockbox; perhaps overridden Mary's programming with an admin code and helped himself to the money. *What if he has taken Phebe's brooch?*

In cold alarm, Mary jabbed at the keypad with a bony knuckle and fumbled with the latch. The brooch lay on top of the money wallet and passport. All was well, until Mary heard the bedlam from the media crew growing louder; the rumble of multiple footsteps on the stairs, drawing nearer. The boy had invited the reporters inside.

Mary scooped up the safe contents, tucking the flat items into the waistband of the old woman's skirt, and tightening the brooch into her fist. She slammed the wardrobe closed and shambled as fast as the old body could muster.

There was a light tap on the door. Mary was trapped. She rehearsed sentences inside her mind. Coaxing them into an excuse for his grandma's presence, but what could she say? Did the old woman have an accent? How would she sound to them?

The boy sprang into the room, followed by a rush of eager people. They did a three hundred and sixty degree sweep of the room, ignoring the old woman entirely. "Oh, she's not here." The boy uttered. "She'll be in the bathroom."

The crew followed the boy back out of the room and down the corridor. Mary used the diversion to scoot granny out of the guest room and begin the climb back down the stairs. *Old folk really are invisible. They didn't even say hello to her. That's so awful.*

Relaxing into the anonymity, Mary shuffled into the kitchen. Mrs Kent stood at the range stirring a skillet of foul smelling onions and beef mince, her back to the old woman. Mary swiped a bag from the counter top. It contained just two slices of cut bread and the crust.

Keeping the momentum going in the frail limbs, she toddled through the back door, tipping the bread out onto the wooden boards of the veranda.

It took a minute or two for Mary to coordinate the stiff fingers, but she managed to stow the money envelope, passport and brooch in the bag. *I'm sorry to do this to you, grandma, but I need your help for a bit longer. I'm sure you won't melt in the rain.* Clutching the bread bag to her chest, Mary edged down the steps to the back garden, and compelled the legs to carry her to the front of the house.

The technical crews sat inside the vans. Mary could see them wearing headphones and concentrating on their computer screens. Only one man looked at her through the windscreen as she crossed the service road to the library, before returning his attention elsewhere. *I think I could rob a bank in this body and no one would notice.*

Rain soaked the old woman right through to her undergarments. Mary detected shivering. *This is so wrong. This poor woman has suffered enough, but I need that brooch back.* One unsteady step at a time, bowed back and ambling, the old woman finally reached the covered refuse area at the rear of the library building.

Mary looked at her own body, slumped behind a dumpster, unconscious and vulnerable. Her recent ordeals had paid a toll on her. Fine lines around her eyes were more pronounced now, as was the emergence of white hairs intermingling with the dark brown of her curls. A swell of regret and pain infused her senses. Where did it all go wrong? Just a couple of months ago, she was content and in love with her husband. How had her life descended into this empty and directionless state?

The old woman's body shook with the cold. There was no time to linger. Mary compelled the woman's arm to extend. She dropped the bread bag into the lap of her own sleeping body, and began the shuffle to the guest house. Stiff and exhausted, Mary delivered grandma back to the kitchen. She stayed just long enough to hear Mrs Kent's shrieks of dismay at the state of her mother, before prising her consciousness from the old woman and floating back to her own body.

Fully dark now, the temperature fell rapidly. Mary tucked her knees up to her chin and rocked herself for comfort. *I can't stay here or I will get hypothermia. Can't go back to the Kent's with that wretched boy's camera crew waiting for me. Can't go to the diner without them calling a priest to have me exorcised. I have a real talent for screwing things up.*

Perhaps I could sit in the steakhouse until it closes? That must be what passes for a bar around here. I could buy a drink and sit in the warm until I get dry. She got to her feet and plucked at her wet clothes where they clung to her skin. The storm was beginning to shift. Rain clouds delivered sporadic downpours, and then stopped for a minute or two before resuming the same intensity. It was the brisk wind that froze her to the core.

Retracing her steps, Mary made her way back towards the row of shops, pleading with an absent deity to clear her path of diner customers. Keeping in the shadows, Mary sneaked past the gun shop and takeaway, and scuttled into the bar entrance of the Steakhouse. The smell rivalled that of the dumpster. Half raw slabs of meat, swimming in tiny rivulets of blood, mixed with smells of steaming wet dog. Clearly this was the place for the *real* men. Wall to wall checked shirts and dirty denim; lank unwashed hair and steel toecaps.

The door slammed closed behind Mary, drawing attention to her presence. She could not have looked more out of place if she had tried. With every eye trained on her soaked t-shirt, Mary made a dash for the bar at the farthest end of the room.

The barman leaned his fists on the steel counter, dipping low to Mary's level. "You lost or something, ma'am?"

"More than you could ever imagine. Is it okay if I buy a drink and shelter from the storm for a little while?"

"As long as you're buying, you can stay as long as you like. What'll it be?"

"Could I have a glass of lemonade, please?" Mary clambered up on to a high stool, cradling her satchel while ferreting inside for her purse.

"You a Brit?" He said, watching her struggle, his amusement ill-concealed.

"That obvious, is it?"

The man snickered, grabbed a glass and pressed a button on the syphon, squirting the soda up to the fill line. Gradually, the clientele returned their attenti on to the sports channel, roaring and crowing in unison over the propulsion of a ball.

One or two men approached her with caution, attempting pleasantries, but were shooed away by the patriarchal nature of the bar keep. Mary nursed her drink. The atmosphere was warm and she could feel the chill in her bones receding. She glanced across the bar to the mirrored shelving supporting the more expensive liquor. Her hair had almost doubled in size, and now resembled something out of a nineteen-seventies sit-com. She groaned, patting the sides down, but it sprang back to its original position. At least the t-shirt was drying off, even if her trousers still felt damp.

For all its menacing potential, sitting among these bar flies and sports fanatics calmed Mary's nerves. It was the first time since London where she did not feel ill at ease. No one made demands of her. They allowed her a safe haven from the storm. For a long time, Mary observed their rituals; the camaraderie between old friends. Great bearded men laughing and teasing each other over pool losses and team scores. Their sweet manners towards the waitresses leaving their shift for the evening and closing the kitchen. How long had it been since Mary saw any of her friends? Those old bonds of childhood and of college house mates, once steadfast and loyal, now unfettered and blown to the four winds.

Parth had filled the void. He was her everything; friend, lover, confidant and protector. Had it all been faked from the start? Was his interest in her purely academic and financial? She had allowed the ties of friendship to wear thin during their year-long world trip. On their return, her marriage to Parth consumed her time and energies so fully, there was little room left for her friends. They too, found fresh life paths and drifted to new promises and expectations. In all the marital fervour, Mary had not replaced the circle of friends she had lost.

How careless that decision turned out to be. Her trust in Parth so absolute, so unshakable, so mistaken. Did he engineer her isolation to retain better control over her life? To steer her towards the goals imposed on him by those funding his neuroscience studies? Had the Ministry of Defence overseen her entire life? Mary stifled the erupting hysteria. This was not the time to lose her cool.

I still have Dan. She chanted to herself to steady her tattered nerves. Cleared of brain fog, Mary attempted a telepathic connection with her brother in England. *"Hey Dan, can you hear me?"* She waited, listening for his soothing low voice. *"Hello?"* Nothing. Not a single murmur. She looked up at the clock, registering the time

– 11.45pm. *Ah, they would be five hours ahead in the UK. He'll be fast asleep.* Her glass was empty, the ice melted in her grasp.

"Please could I have another one?" She asked of the kindly barman.

"I'd like to serve you ma'am, but it's almost closing time. You got a place to go to?" He took a step backwards, distancing himself from the responsibility of helping her, should her answer be in the negative.

Mary took the cue. "Oh yes, thank you. I will be fine." She affected a light and breezy air, even though it was a lie. *I cannot go back to the Kent's and I cannot walk through the storm for fifteen miles along a deserted road to the next town.*

Some of the men bid her goodnight as they grabbed their coats from the hooks by the door. The bar emptied rapidly. The barman fixed his stare on Mary. She could feel it pushing her out of the building. Avoiding eye contact, she drained the last drops from her glass and set it down. He swooped, grabbing the glass and stacking it in the dishwasher. Another man spilled out of the lavatories and hurried after his companions at the exit.

"I'm sorry, ma'am, but I have to close up now." He said, trying to mask the pity in his voice.

"Oh, I fully understand. Thank you for your hospitality." She left some dollar bills on the bar and slid down from the stool. The bar man followed her to the door, bolting it shut the moment she passed the threshold.

The storm was winding down in intensity, but the rain persisted. The shop awnings provided little protection. Her choices were limited. *Well, even if the news crew have given up and gone away, I don't trust that little shit. He could come creeping in while I sleep to film me.*

Neither do I fancy a night with drowsy wasps between the dumpsters.

Mary leaned against the wall of the gun shop. A four by four vehicle cruised by, the blue lights mounted on the roof bar startled her. *Christ, I don't want to get picked up by the police for soliciting.* She dipped her head low and started walking. At the end of the row of shops, she peered around the corner and strained to see towards the library. She couldn't be sure, but the illuminated grey blobs at the roadside were more than likely the CNN vans.

Too risky. Mary turned and walked back the way she came. Passing the steakhouse, she scanned around for the police car. The streets were empty. *I know, I can sleep in the electric car. It won't be comfortable, but it will be dry and free from wasps.* At a smarter pace, Mary rounded the corner and hurried towards the spot where the electric car cruised to a halt.

In the darkness, she could make out a figure leaning against the bonnet, holding an umbrella.

"Are you ready to come home now, Mary?" Alexi smirked, holding open the passenger door to the car with his free hand.

Chapter Six

Mary stopped short in her tracks. "How did you know where I was?"

"Easy. You never go anywhere without your bag. Friend at airport place tracker. You want to drive?" Alexi let go of the passenger door handle and gestured towards the driver's side.

She waited, contemplating her options. It surprised her that she no longer felt Alexi threatening. Despite his twisted ideas and missions, he had done nothing towards her that could jeopardise her safety. Match that to the fact that if he did try anything, she was certain that she could bring him in line with a painful jolt of electromagnetic discharge. Still Mary wavered.

"I never hurt you, Mary. You know this."

"Hmm, that may be so, but whatever you are planning, I want no part of it. Whatever sick, warped and inhumane deal you have going on back at your ranch, it has nothing to do with me."

"Fine. As you wish. Do you want to spend night out in cold rain, or in nice warm cabin?"

Mary looked down at herself. The muddy splashes seeping through the gaps in her sandals soaked her feet. The dark t-shirt drenched through all over again. A warm, timed shower surrounded by bamboo would be better than the alternative.

"One more night. I'll be off first thing in the morning."

The grin on Alexi's face provoked her own smile. "But that car is useless," she said. "The battery is dead."

"No, battery replaced. Driver brought me here with new one."

She dashed around to the driver's side and hopped in the car. As she pressed the starter button, and strapped herself in, she looked up at Alexi. For all his heinous antics, he was all she had to rely on for over three thousand miles. Steering the car into a tight U-turn, they headed for the compound at Summerfield.

"I tell you Mary, you surprised me when you took car. I did not know you could drive. I thought you only had your bicycle for travel."

"I passed my test before I went to college. Driving rather lost its appeal after my parents' death in that car crash." *Why am I telling him this? He is not my friend. Pull yourself together.*

There was a lull in conversation as they reached a cross roads among the trees. Mary stopped the car and read the signs, inwardly noting the direction to the next town and filing a rudimentary map in the hippocampus of her brain. A short distance into their journey, the rain ceased altogether and the howling wind stilled to a mild breeze. As they neared the gates, Alexi sent a text message to someone inside the compound. They waited for a minute or two in the floodlit driveway until the gate juddered open, before driving inside.

Mary rather expected to find the place utterly deserted as they had the night before. Everyone squirrelled away in their cabins and bunks, ready for another productive day come daylight. Instead, they were greeted by a series of revellers outside the communal centre, singing and laughing in boisterous cheer.

"What is all this?" Mary smiled, slowing the car to view the commotion.

"Celebrations. Someone give birth. Nice lady, healthy baby, but big...very big baby. Must have hurt." Alexi shuddered at the thought.

Mixed emotions resurfaced in Mary's mind. Joy for the new parents and pity for herself. With events in London so tumultuous, she had not had time to process her own grief. They passed the group of young men spilling out onto the sodden grassed area, their drinks splashing as they tumbled about. They parked outside Mary's lodge. Stepping out of the car, she paused, looking back at the fun the men were having.

Alexi watched her. "You want to go join them? Have a vodka to wet baby's head?"

"It's late. I ought to go to bed." She said, looking wistful as the men toppled over one another, re-enacting the childhood game of leapfrog. "They are little more than children themselves." She did not mean to say it out loud, but her general demeanour conveyed her feelings to the astute Soviet general.

"Come, let us have one drink. It is time you had fun for change." He threaded his arm through hers, led her into the communal hall and found them seats near to a table filled with bottles of alcohol. Mary did not object. Everywhere she looked, people laughed and chatted, drank and smiled. The happiness was infectious. By the time Alexi had poured her a shot of vodka from one of the many bottles, Mary found herself smiling too. The pinched lines in her forehead relaxed and the tension in her abdomen dissipated.

"I'd introduce you to new father, but that is he, over there." Alexi said, pointing to a young man passed out in the corner of the hall, stacked uncomfortably between plastic chairs.

Mary tittered. "Children." She muttered beneath her breath.

"We toast?" Alexi held his glass high.

"To the new born. May he always be happy and healthy." Mary sank the colourless liquid down. It burned every inch of her gullet making her gasp and her eyes water.

"Za lyoo-bóf!" Alexi supped the contents of his glass and refilled both his and Mary's.

"What does that mean?"

"To love."

Mary's grin faded. Suddenly she didn't feel like drinking anymore.

"More, yes?" Alexi swung his glass around, getting into the spirit. Mary pushed her shot glass away, shuffling more upright in her seat. He put the vodka back on the table, comprehending her thoughts. "You know, Parth very bad man for you. Do not upset. You beautiful lady, will find better man in no time." He patted her arm. "If I liked ladies, I would love you." His countenance so sincere, his gesture kind. Mary sniffed and patted the back of his hand in return.

He raised his glass again. "To Mary. Be happy." She reciprocated, a forced smile and half-closed lids hemming in the sadness. The second chugged vodka burned a little less. By the third toast a large man, whom she had met once before, joined them at their table.

He greeted them and his Scottish accent jogged her memory of their meeting. He was one of the new telepaths.

"You're back then?" He said, launching himself into the seat next to Mary.

"Just for the night." She giggled at his attempts to focus on her face.

He squinted and tried to raise his drooping eyelids with his brow muscles. "Aye, glad to have ye here. Did ya get caught in the storm, Mrs Arora?"

"I did, and it's Mary."

He nodded. "Lachie, well Lachlan, but you know."

"Nice to meet you Lachie." She watched his attention drift as a petite woman with long ginger hair increased the volume on the music system and dragged two beautiful black twins onto the dance space. Their initial resistance dissipated as the track changed to an upbeat and iconic millennial number.

The red head dancing between the Amazonian black girls, struck a coy pose and pointed at Lachie. She curled her index finger, beckoning him onto the dancefloor. Even in the dim lighting, Mary could see him glowing red. Lachie shook his head, inanely, and then returned his focus to Mary.

"What's her name?" Mary asked.

"Which one?"

"The one you can't stop drooling over."

Lachie's pink blush renewed, a shiny film of perspiration added to his embarrassment. "It's Oona. She's a bit of a flirt, but you know, a nice flirt."

"Uhuh, she likes you too."

"You think so?"

"You should dance with her."

"Ocht, no. I cannae dance. All arms and legs. Uncoordinated mess me."

Mary sighed. *Children.* She thought once again. "You can sway, can't you? Take her into your arms and sway."

Emboldened, Lachie struggled to his feet and headed towards the girls. As he reached the centre, he was abducted by the twins, who gyrated and undulated about his person as though he were a pole in a nightclub.

Lachie wobbled about on the spot, enjoying the attention. Affronted, Oona flounced off towards the exit. Lachlan did not notice.

Mary watched the spectacle with great amusement. She turned to Alexi. "This is like high school all over again, but with greater quantities of vodka."

Alexi smiled to himself, and pushed the full glass towards her hand. Mary drank it, fully immersed in the clumsy attempts at seduction playing out in the hall.

***

The morning brought a coated tongue and an ice pick headache. Every movement sent her brain reverberating from the inner walls of her skull. Sitting upright in bed, it took a full minute to recall the events from the night before, although how she made it to the cabin and undressed were little more than a hazy blur.

Staggering to the bathroom, she held her head beneath the tap and slurped at the cool water, but it did nothing to slake her thirst. She stripped off her t-shirt and knickers and stepped into the shower. Closing her eyes, she stood beneath the gushing stream and tried to fill in the blanks of her memory. *Lachie and Oona, then a fourth vodka and then…something to do with…um…*

The shower alarm sounded. "Arrghh, stupid thing, I have barely had time to wash, let alone do my hair." She jabbed at the buttons on the control panel, trying to reset the functions but to no avail. Dripping wet and uttering curses, she grubbed around the room looking for a bath towel. There was a loud knock on the door downstairs. "Now what?" Wrapped in a soft white bath sheet, Mary descended the stairs, noting that her calf muscles were stiff and gave her pain with each step.

Standing on tiptoe, Mary peered through the abstract glass panel in the door. It was Lachlan. Twisting the lock, she unlatched the door and let it swing open. The daylight blinded her. "Come in, shut the door." She muttered, turning and wandering towards the kitchen.

"Ah didnae mean to disturb ya, I just wondered if we could chat?"

"Hmm…what about?" Mary picked up the kettle and shook it from side to side, judging the mass of water inside. Plonking it down on the power base, she flicked the switch on.

"About Oona. I tried to speak to her last night, but she threw an empty beer bottle at ma hee'd." He sat down at the kitchen table. Mary held a mug aloft, offering Lachie a tea. He declined with a shake of the head.

"I don't blame her. I'd have done the same thing in her position."

"Really, why? What did a'do?"

"Men really are dense. She put herself out there, invited you to dance with her, not with those stunning twins."

"Ah."

"And then when she stormed off, she expected you to follow and make it up to her…"

"Is that so?"

"Instead, you got down and dirty on the dancefloor with two other women."

Lachie pulled a contorted face. One of embarrassment and regret. "Okay, I can see her point. Now, what do a'do about it?"

Mary closed her eyes and sighed. "Children. Go pick her some wild flowers and say you're sorry. Tell her how you feel. And none of that ambiguous crap that most of you blokes spout either."

"Flowers? Ah don't know flowers from weeds. Would yer come with me, Mary? Please?"

"Dear god, give me strength. Make me some tea and stick some bread in the toaster. I'll have another attempt at a shower."

Grumbling her annoyance, Mary returned to the bathroom and completed her ablutions. She dressed in the same grey sweatpants and t-shirt as everyone else on the base, and found a pair of sturdy black trainers in the wardrobe. Ditching her sandals in favour of the new footwear, she left the bedroom, grabbing her bag on her way out.

Despite the hangover, she rather enjoyed playing mother hen to Lachie; a big strong chap in need of her advice. She ate her breakfast and together they walked to the orchard in search of late summer flowers.

The rising sun evaporated the remnants of the storm's moisture, which steamed in a haze at shoulder height between the trees. Bees danced their chatter across the roofs of their hives, preparing for the last few rounds of nectar collection. Many of the flowers hung limp from their broken stems, battered by the rain. Only the most hardy and fresh burgeoning blooms remained for the bees and for Lachlan to pick.

Freed from burden and restraint, Mary allowed herself an hour or two to decompress and recover from the effects of the vodka. More of Lachie's group arrived at the orchard, in dribs and drabs. Some smoked peculiar smelling cigarettes, others shook the branches for the early ripening apples.

There was the tall blond woman, who introduced herself as Judith, but who everyone shortened to Jude. Her jaw clenched every time they misspoke her name. She seemed also to have a particular affection for

Lachie, who was wholly unaware of the power he held over the female members of the group.

Ronica and Raeni, the twins of the dance fiasco, bickered constantly. Mary observed one to be bookish, while the other was quite the attention seeker. Which one was which, remained a mystery. Two other young men joined them, but stood farther away, content to observe from the outer battlements of the gathering. Oona was conspicuous by her absence.

Mary observed each of them with the same detachment she adopted during her long years as a lab technician at a British University. The students arrived, fresh faced and eager in the first days of the autumn term, wrote their assignments and attended tutorials with assiduous attention. By the third week of term, their good habits had fallen by the wayside. Social activities and lust drove their waking hours. Mary gauged this to be the group's third week at the facility.

Mary had no need to read the minds of these novices. There were no ulterior motives beyond their own selfish desires. This was easy money in a comfortable environment. It made no difference to them if Mary joined the team or not.

The gathered flowers lay in a flattened area of grass, awaiting Lachie's collection. With Judith and the twins watching his every move, he looked decidedly edgy. Mary saw his eyes dart to the simple bouquet, shortly followed by an imploring glance in her direction. Mary took the hint.

She scooped up the stems from the ground and tightened them into her palm. "Come and walk with me Lachie. There are some things I would like to discuss with you."

"Right, yes. Catch you all later." He said, dusting the debris from his trousers as he rose from the damp orchard grass. Together, Mary and Lachie walked in silence until they were no longer in earshot of the others.

"Where is Oona likely to be?" Mary said, thrusting the blooms at his hands.

"Ocht, you'll need to come with me Mary, or I'm likely to bottle it." He pushed the flowers back at her.

"You know, for a big bloke, you are such a baby."

He guffawed and snorted at the same time. "Sometimes she sneaks down into the underground storage bunker. They have a few computers hardwired down there. She gets tech withdrawal worse than the rest of us."

"Lead the way, big man."

Mary was anticipating a long walk to the ramp entrance where she had witnessed Alexi driving in the electric car. Instead, Lachie took Mary to a large building which had not featured in the compound tour. Constructed of brick and steel, the few windows were of reinforced safety glass and did not open. They entered via a metal door, and walked through a dark corridor illuminated by a single light at the terminal end. There, Mary could just make out a standard safety sign on a door – stairs.

"Cosy." Mary remarked. Her attempts to lighten the mood futile. She felt her mouth dry as Lachie opened the door, and gestured for her to make the descent into the storage bunker. "What's down here." She said, pausing at the top of the steps and peering over the banister at the abyssal drop in the stairwell.

"Oh, all sorts of things. Food, clothing, vehicles, equipment, the computers of course, you name it. It has its own electricity supply, I guess from some of the alternative energy sources that are hooked up around here."

"Why haven't they connected all the power sources?" She asked, and then chided herself for being drawn in. This was not her problem.

"No idea."

The deeper they descended, the less they had to say. Mary was acutely aware of her leg muscles cramping in pain with each step. She stopped beneath one of the wall lights and rubbed her shins.

"You feeling the effects from all that dancing last night, Mary?" Lachie stopped and waited for her to catch up.

"What dancing?"

He cackled with laughter, slapping her shoulder, and then continued down the steps. *Oh jeez. Note to self – no more vodka – ever.* Eventually, they reached the bottom. Another ill-lit doorway, and out into a cavernous space, filled with massive trucks, farm machinery, forklifts, a helicopter and side partitions, stacked with metal storage cabinets.

"The computer room is down this way," Lachie tipped his head towards a series of rooms on the opposite side of the cavern. They wove their way through the vehicles. Mary could see the computers in neat rows through an internal window. Oona was busy at one of the stations.

"Here." Mary said, handing Lachie the wilting blooms. "You have to do this bit on your own."

"But what do a'say?"

"Just say you are sorry for being an oaf, and give her the flowers." Mary pushed him forwards, and then took a diagonal route through the tall trucks to the far wall. Standing in the doorway of a room filled with freezers and chillers, she watched Lachie make his approach. An enormous smile appeared on Oona's freckled face the moment Lachie entered the room. Mary turned away, two minutes later when they started kissing.

It was curiosity that forced Mary inside the freezer room; alarm, that drove her to open the door marked with a biohazard symbol, and fear that sent her reeling from her discovery.

The frosted sheen coated the man's body inside. It had one finger missing from his hand.

Chapter Seven

Mary shrieked, clapping her hand over her mouth and stumbling backwards. That crystallised stare, the unnatural twist of the neck and the gaping mouth, sent a cascade of memories from her brain. Scenes of shared duplicity at the hands of the Minister for British Defence; a recollection of drone strikes and the loss of many lives. This was the MI6 agent she had seen at JFK airport on their arrival.

The squeal brought Lachie and Oona dashing to Mary's aid. They peered into the freezer and gasped, recoiling at the sight of their first dead body. Lachie cradled Oona in his arms.

"That's it. That treacherous bloody Russian has gone too far." Mary said, slamming the lid of the freezer down and storming from the room.

"What'll you do?" Lachie said, trailing after her and leading Oona by the hand.

"Leave, and so should you, before you get embroiled in whatever scheme that degenerate has planned." Mary scrambled towards the electric vehicles, testing each door for ease of entry. None were unlocked. In desperation, Mary tried the trucks, hopping up onto the footplates and yanking each handle. Alexi, it seems, had anticipated her moves, securing every vehicle in the compound.

"We can't leave, Mary." Oona said in a weakened, trembling voice. "The penalty clauses in our contracts are…."

Mary jumped down from a US Military truck cab. "Are what? What clauses? Nothing can be as bad as sticking around here under Alexi's control."

"The general will release evidence against each of us if we break contract." Lachie said, his tone grave.

"Evidence of what? I can't imagine any of you have done things to warrant aiding and abetting a terrorist?"

"None of us are clean. That's why he picked us. Oona was awaiting trial for serious hacking offences when the general's men intervened…" Lachie paused, squeezing Oona's hand tight.

"And you?" Mary barked, her head still on a swivel looking for potential transportation.

"Misadventure. I thought I was helping an animal liberation group, I used ma'gift to find the access codes to the lab. I didnae know they'd bomb the lab after releasing the wee beasties. People died. The activists got caught. They gave me up straight the way."

"Even still, you can't stay. Look around you…" Mary flung her arms wide at the stacks of resources and supplies. "Whatever Alexi has planned is big, and you can bet your bottom dollar that you lot will be at the heart of it all."

Oona swallowed, her breathing laboured and shallow, on the verge of tears. "There are a lot more freezers in this bunker, I've seen them. What's to stop the general putting us in them? All the people here look happy and compliant, but they are all military personnel except for our little team. He has them stationed everywhere. We would not make it five miles without them tracking us down."

For all her internal pep talks, Mary could not help but feel moved by their plight. They were in the same limbo as she; caught between the conflicting powers of the government and a wealthy terror faction.

"I don't know how, but I will find a way to get you out. Just try and lay low. Do as little as you can get away with." Mary was not sure what prompted her declaration. She was barely able to secure her own freedom, let alone seven gifted individuals with government targets on their backs.

They followed her into another side store where Mary found a series of bicycle racks. "Perfect. Pedal power." She said, grabbing a baseball cap from a locker and tucking her hair up inside as she slipped it on her head. "Do I look like all the other female personnel?" They nodded. Lachie helped to yanked a bike with a front basket from the racks and wheeled it out into the main cavern. Mary secured her satchel in the basket, and wound the strap around the handlebars.

"Trust no one but each other, got it?" Mary said, scooting along on one pedal before swinging her leg over the crossbar to the other. Mary did not look back. She pedalled along until she saw a spiral ramp twisting up towards the surface. "Not the best time to have aching shins…" Mary mumbled, dropping the gears and pedalling hard up the continuous incline. She stopped just twice to catch her breath, before the dizzying ascent brought her to another large space. This level was buzzing with Alexi's military personnel.

Enormous army trucks with canvas rooves were lined up in a convoy ready to leave. Their engines idled, generating a smog of diesel fumes. Mary dismounted, crouching low and wheeling her bike along the edges of the bunker walls. She watched as the uniformed men climbed up the sides of the trucks, to secure the load.

Great rubber bungee straps were stretched across black metal crates, stacked high on each truck bed.

Mary crept closer, keeping low behind the stationary farm equipment on the opposite side. She was almost level with the trucks when she saw the first symbol. The yellow triangle supporting three black arc shapes, equidistant around a black circle. Mary's heart fluttered in dismay. Hazard warnings had been part of her job for many years. This one struck fear in the hardiest of lab technicians. Alexi was transporting nuclear material.

Holy shit. How the hell did he get hold of that? And for what purpose? I need to tell someone in authority, but who? She crept on, pushing the bicycle slowly to mitigate the ticking noise as the wheels turned. As she neared the foot of the main entrance ramp, the trucks leapt into action. Mary ducked down, holding her breath until the dense fumes had dissipated. They powered up the ramp in a noisy cavalcade and disappeared from view.

A few personnel remained, stowing unused bungee straps and wheeling fuel tanks back into storage compartments. Mary waited. Her feet cramped with holding the same crouched position for too long. Just when she thought she might lose her balance, the men drifted into the stairwell and vanished.

A quick glance about her, and Mary was off. Pedalling furiously, she gathered momentum and hit the ramp at speed. The last few metres required all her strength, forcing her to pedal standing up. She crested the bunker, and out into the bright sunlight, several hundred metres from the communal centre. Aiming the bike towards the main gates, Mary pounded through the gears.

To her left, on the grassland, three men were busy inflating enormous metallic weather balloons. They rose in elegant wafts, as the gases pumped into their innards. The men peered at her as she zoomed by, but made no attempt to stop her. *Must be something to do with Alexi's bee obsession. Perhaps he tracks weather data alongside the changes in the electromagnetic spectrum.*

The steel gates were just ahead of Mary, and wide open. She squinted at either side of the posts. No one manned them. They were electrically controlled, but she knew not who maintained them. She crossed her fingers and charged at the opening, sweeping through the aperture without resistance.

That was a little too easy. How did Alexi find me before? Shit. He arranged for a tracker in my satchel. Mary kicked down the gears and pedalled away from the compound at speed. When she was fully passed the long bend in the road, she pulled onto the grassy verge and tipped the contents of her bag into the handlebar basket. Sifting through her belongings, nothing looked out of place.

It was when she felt in each of the internal pockets, that she found a tiny device, no larger than the end of a cocktail stick. Mary snapped it in half and threw it into the ditch. Scooping everything back into her bag, she set off once more towards town. This time, she followed the signs at the junction to Washington, New Jersey.

Despite the maelstrom of questions whirling inside her mind, the ride was pleasant. It felt good to be back in the saddle after such a long abstinence. *Fifteen miles eh? I can do that. Might get bum ache, but I can recover on the train. There must be a connection to Manhattan, or a bus maybe. Anyway, I am free. I can hide in a big city. Start again. Maybe get a little job for myself. Connie's money won't last me long in New York City.*

A few miles further and her mind slipped back to Alexi. *How the hell is he funding that entire set up? It must have cost millions, perhaps billions. And for what purpose? He cannot possibly mean to spread nuclear material around the United States. That would irradiate his precious bees.*

Maybe he sells the nuclear material to countries like Iran or Iraq. They seem to always be threatening nuclear weapon capabilities. But where did he get it from? How am I going to warn the authorities without getting detained myself? If I telephone them, it would be dismissed as a crank call. One step at a time. Get to Washington, find a train link to NYC, and then worry about it.

Mary slowed to avoid a pothole in the roadside. The deviation allowed something to invade her peripheral vision. Glancing skyward, in what she estimated to be the general direction of the Summerfield Retreat, she saw a bright glint. Rising ever higher were two large weather balloons, lashed together in support of a black box beneath. She grasped the handbrakes and set her foot to the ground. The balloons were mesmeric, reflecting the sunbeams in a circular array. She watched as they became faint specs on the outer edges of the atmosphere, before resuming her journey.

How freeing it is to fly. She remembered the feeling well. Her last disembodied flight being when she returned the old lady's body to the Kent's guesthouse in the storm. *Why would Alexi be collecting his own weather data? Surely, he could just look online at national weather centre information.*

The last few miles of her bicycle ride, saw the woodland thin once again. Open farmland and wide spaces between properties, marked the outskirts of her destination. Soon, she was in the thick of regimented housing and industrial estates. Taking the routes that signposted the town's centre, Mary eased the gears into second and coasted between queuing vehicles. Finally, she rode along the main shopping precinct of the large township.

She cycled the entire length of the shops and outlying centres, but saw no signs to a train station. Sweating profusely and in desperation, she drew level at a set of traffic lights with an elderly couple in a pickup truck. Tapping lightly on the passenger's window, the old lady lowered the glass.

"Excuse me, but could you tell me where I can find a train station around these parts, please?"

The woman looked taken aback, and then she gave Mary a beaming smile. "Are you lost, honey? Where you headed?"

"I'm trying to get to Manhattan, but it is proving more difficult than I anticipated." Mary, was red in the face from her exertions, and panting. The traffic lights changed.

"Merl, pull over there, so I can talk to this young woman." She screeched at her husband. Merl did as he was told, turning at the junction and allowing Mary to scoot her bicycle around the corner to meet them.

The nice old couple explained the difficulties in reaching Manhattan by train, persuading her to take a coach from the bus stop along the main street through the centre of town. Mary thanked them, and pedalled off to seek out the bus shelter, between the liquor store and a memorial home.

A single metal sign with the number forty-seven embossed into its surface, was her only indication of finding the correct stop. With great reluctance, Mary wheeled the bicycle to the rear of the shelter, and leaned it against the back wall. *Wish I could take it with me. Doubt they would permit bikes on coaches like they do the train.*

Mary waited at the roadside for no more than twenty minutes, before a coach arrived. She checked with the driver that her destination was possible on his route. He snatched the ten dollars from her hand, nodded, and said 'Exact fare only, no change." Moving in jolts and bumps, Mary navigated to the rear of the bus. The air was thick with cheap deodorant and hairspray; the air conditioning feeble at best.

Finding an empty double seat on the shaded side, Mary settled down with her satchel next to her and the strap wound around her wrist. She pulled the cap down over her eyes and relaxed into the jumble of emotions. *I wonder what Dan is doing back in England, right now? What time is it there?* Projecting her neural frequency out into the ether, she reached out for a connection to her brother.

"Dan? Can you hear me?" She waited, blocking out the noisome sounds from the other passengers and concentrating on the silence inside her head. *"Dan?"* Another wait, more silence. *"Hello?"* She opened her eyes, lifted the cap, and stared at the bus interior. There was nothing about it that was unusual. No additional metallic structures, nothing which could block her telepathic signals. Closing her eyes once more, she tried contact again. *"Hello?"*

A faint sound came back to her. A distant voice dipped and grew louder in turn. An odd cadence that was both familiar and strange at the same time. *That is not my brother. Who on earth have I tuned into?* She listened again, straining with all her might to hone in on the sounds. The more she concentrated, the louder the blend of voices became. A mixture of guttural and harsh sounds, interspersed with an inflected accent. She reached out to the source. *"Hello there, who are you?"*

A part of her grew suspicious of the interaction, another part, excited at the prospect of stemming the loneliness.

"Mary..." The voice tapered off, struggling to maintain the frequency.

Shit. They know my name. Who are they? The realisation that this was no accidental broadcast frightened her. *Is this the result of Alexi training the new recruits back at the compound? It didn't sound like Lachie and the others. It sounded foreign, one of the Baltic states, Russian perhaps.* She swallowed hard, recollecting her last and final encounter with the Soviet telepaths. *That did not end well for them. It cannot be the captain and his men. They were all killed in the drone strike.*

Mary sat fully upright, removing her cap and mentally shaking herself from the borders of sadness. She took a swig of stale water from the airport bottle, chiding herself for not buying more before boarding the coach. Stuck in the confines of a stifling hot and stinking bus, she hunkered down for the remainder of the trip.

The many delaying stops and the dense traffic slowed their progress, but after almost two hours of jolting travel, they crossed the Hudson at Fort Lee, on the New Jersey Turnpike. The route took them along the western riverbank, past miles of grey jigsaw tower blocks, with barely a pin's breadth between them. The vista changed to a seemingly endless stretch of parkland, flanked by the river on one side, and apartment blocks on the other. At a small marina, the coach took a ninety-degree turn on a roundabout, and ventured into the heart of the city.

Boutiques, salons and the tree-lined Hayden Planetarium, announced their arrival. Here, at the west side of Central Park, Mary disembarked into another world. She stretched, taking a moment to find her land legs and her bearings. The bustle and the buzz from the streets were exactly as she remembered. It had been a long time, since she and her ex had visited New York. It was their final destination in a year long trip, before returning home to England.

Those days are long gone. I need to find a new place to take root. Start afresh, but after I have had a cuppa and a wee. Mary hurried past the planetarium to a café on seventy-seventh street and achieved her objective, grabbing a tea and a bagel to go after using their facilities.

Crossing the road, Mary followed the pathways towards the lake and settled on the rocky outcrop of Hernshead. A Japanese tourist party took turns to pose at the famous spot, passing their cameras around to snap the shots for one another. She watched them, as they linked arms and smiled. No silly poses or finger wagging bunny ears above the next person's head. Each and every visitor, so dignified in their adventure. The bagel was dry and chewy, but it sated her hunger. The tea, weak and tasteless. *This will never do. If I am to make a new life here, I have to find a better source of tea.*

Her mind made up, Mary was determined to locate the little specialist deli, close to the United Nations building, which Parth had found some eight years ago. Heading back to the roadside, she hailed a cab and directed the driver to the corner of East Fortieth and Second. The cab driver took the scenic route, clocking up a handsome fare. Mary checked her cash situation, vowing to make this a one-time indulgence.

Despite the cost, their drive through the park and down Fifth Avenue took her past some of the most iconic buildings of all time. Tiffany's, The Rockefeller Building, Saks and the magnificent library. They turned left into a one-way system, long before reaching East

Fortieth Street, but The Empire State and Chrysler Buildings remained in view from almost everywhere.

Hopping out of the cab, she handed the driver his fare, who then glared up at her. “Oh God, of course. A tip. I completely forgot that about America. I meant no disrespect.” Mary gave him another note, hoping that it would suffice. He took it without a word, pulling away into the traffic without a backward glance.

Mary ambled around the corner. Outside the international delicatessen was a large black limousine, sporting a tiny Indian flag on the bonnet. As she drew nearer, a striking man, dressed in a cream silk Kurta, exited the shop. His secretary carried a paper grocery bag and fussed about him. Mary’s heart pulsated in her chest. She recognised him at once. It was the Indian nobleman, Shrimant Karan Shinde.

Chapter Eight

"Mary? But how...? Forgive me." Karan placed his palms together and bowed his head. "Namaste."

Mary repeated the greeting. Seized with confusion, she stammered and fidgeted, before forming a coherent sentence. "Shrimant Shinde. It is good to see you again."

"Mary... what's with the sudden formalities? I am sorry for how things were left between us." Karan was acutely aware of his secretary and driver, listening to their conversation. He flicked his hand at the wrist, dismissing them both to the limousine.

"I suppose I reacted badly too. You were only trying to help me, and I repaid your kindness by running out on you." She smoothed her hair as she spoke, wincing at her reflection in the shop windows. Karan smiled. The warmth spread to her cheeks.

"We were both a little hot headed, if I recall. Can we start afresh? I would dearly love the opportunity to catch up. Heal the rift, as it were."

"I'd like that too. Perhaps we should steer clear of politics."

"An excellent idea. Where were you going? Could we give you a lift?" His hand reached out to her arm, but stopped a few centimetres distant, turning his palm outwards towards the car.

"Oh thanks, but no it's not necessary. I was just going to stock up on decent tea and check into the hotel on the next street. I've stayed there before."

Karan nodded. "I remember you telling me about this deli when we were at Ditchley together."

"That's right, I did. The UN building is just a couple of blocks from here, isn't it?" The recollection of their first meeting flooded her mind. The intensity of their discourse, the jealousy displayed by Parth, the petrifying escape from the Defence Minister's agents. She remembered too, her brief stay at the Indian Consulate, and how his manipulations gave her grave concerns.

One hundred different emotions crashed into her prefrontal cortex, warning her to keep her distance, each one completely overridden by a forceful desire. She felt dizzy. Was she hyperventilating?

"I would very much like to see you again. May I take you out to dinner this evening?"

Those soulful dark eyes unravelled her. She blustered, pulling at her t-shirt and sticking her leg out to emphasise her apparel. "I'm afraid this is all I have to wear. Another one of my ill-timed mad dashes in borrowed clothing. It's a lovely offer, thank you, but I really need to check in to that hotel and then buy some clothes."

"Will you permit me to come to your aid once more?" Did she see a faint glow beneath those perfectly groomed cheeks? Was he embarrassed by his offer?

"Really, Karan. You have already done so much for me, I couldn't possibly accept."

"It would be my honour." He could not make eye contact with her. His gaze drifted to her feet. This was a man wholly unused to refusals. "There are guest rooms in the consulate, just off Central Park"

"Oh no, I couldn't. Thank you. That did not turn out so well last time. The hotel here will do me just fine."

"Then allow me to be your Richard Gere, as it were… not that I think you are a prostitute… oh dear, I mean only that I can assist you with the clothing issue, so that we may dine together this evening. I do apologise." The glow intensified into a rich magenta.

Mary erupted with laughter. "You want to re-enact the film *Pretty Woman* with me as Julia Roberts? That is hysterical. I could not be further from her tall, svelte, red-haired appearance if I tried." Karan giggled too. It suited him. His serious face broke into a devastating smile, fringed with the most adorable dimples above the line of his neat beard. Mary weakened. "If it is not too much trouble, that would be lovely, thank you."

Buoyed by her response, Karan regained control and summoned Gupta, his secretary.

"I know a wonderful place nearby, which does the most perfect afternoon tea."

Gupta hopped out of the front passenger seat, and opened the rear door for Mary. Karan slipped into the opposite side. Relaxing into the leather seating, Mary breathed in Karan's sandalwood cologne. *Yesterday, I am sheltering between smelly dumpsters, today I am luxuriating with nobility. My life never ceases to amaze.*

***

Just as Karan had promised, the afternoon tea was divine. Despite the uneasiness of sitting in sweatpants and trainers in the lounge of the exclusive Palm Court of the Plaza Hotel, her initial fears of being evicted from the opulent stone pillared tea lounge were unfounded. Karan, being one of their coveted and regular customers, could do no wrong, and that extended to his guests. To stave off her protestations, Karan and the Maître d' agreed to a table on the concourse level, where the families with young children dined. Mary indulged in a sensory overload of finest Assam, cucumber sandwiches and tiny eclairs.

From there, Gupta arranged a private shopping experience at Saks. With the financial implications squared away, Mary was encouraged to browse at her leisure. Mary felt awkward. She grabbed at the first black dress she could find, and balked at the price tag. Everything seemed way beyond her simple tastes.

Karan looked impatient, his brows cinching together as he peered at his watch.

"I am sorry. You must have so many other things to do. I'll just get a pair of jeans, then we can meet up sometime for a veggie burrito."

"A veggie burrito?" He chuckled. "Sounds horrific."

Gupta stepped forwards and handed Karan a mobile phone, whispering the caller's name to his employer.

"I'm sorry, Mary. I have to take this." Karan gestured for Gupta to assist Mary, and then stepped away to a quiet corner for his telephone conversation.

Mary pawed at the clothes racks, all the while watching Karan pace along the polished department store floor space. His initial look of calm, soon morphed into one of deep concern. His free hand massaged his left temple. His lips barely moved, as he listened intently to the disturbing news from the other end of the line.

One of the personal shoppers returned to Mary with a selection of casual wear for her approval. A short time later, another woman appeared with expensive garment bags draped over her arms. A young trainee tottered behind her, balancing stacked shoe boxes on a small trolley. She paid them little attention. Her interest lay within Karan's fretful demeanour as he ended the call and hurried back to her side.

"Is everything okay?"

"Not really," he said, "there is an important matter I must attend to. I am sorry to leave you, Mary, but you are in capable hands with Gupta. Buy whatever your heart desires. I look forward to dining together this evening." Karan bowed. "Namaste." Before Mary could return the gesture, he turned and rushed away. Gupta made a poor Richard Gere. He stood a respectful distance from the fussing personal shoppers and tapped away on a tablet PC, in sporadic bouts of activity. Mary felt trapped. The shopping assistants had clearly been offered a bonus for every high value item purchased, but Mary would not be swayed. Taking a biro from her satchel, she wrote a list of basic and essential clothing items and their sizes on the lid of a cardboard shoe box.

Jeans x two – British size twelve,

cotton underwear x seven in white, x seven black

t-shirts…

And so on. She gave her completed list to the most senior personal shopper, whose puckered features conveyed her annoyance at the loss of commission.

From the garment bags, Mary selected a simple black cocktail dress, with lace panelled sleeves. She held it up in front of Gupta.

"Is this suitable for wherever Shrimant Shinde is taking me tonight?" Gupta peered up from his tablet PC, gave a single nod and returned his gaze to the screen.

"Good," Mary thrust the dress back at assistant number two. Please can you wrap this up, along with those strappy sandals over there?"

"But madam, what about lingerie? Surely you will require a selection of…"

"Fine. Throw in a couple of lingerie sets and some tights."

"Tights?" The assistants looked puzzled.

"Stockings, nylons… hosiery"

The personal shoppers looked at her as though she were speaking a foreign language, and then began locating her requested items.

"I thought this would be fun." Mary murmured, flouncing down into a soft chair near to Karan's secretary. She looked up at Gupta, who opened his mouth to speak, thought better of it, and closed it again.

"Say what you have to say, Gupta. Your boss is not around to hear it."

"Shrimant Shinde is a very wealthy man, madam. You should do as he suggests, and buy whatever you like. It won't make a dent in his finances." It was the first full sentence she had heard him speak since her time at the government run estate at Ditchley. He seemed greatly emboldened when Karan was not present. Did his comment stem from a dislike of his employer, or a liking for her? Mary could not tell.

"Nevertheless, Gupta. I am tired and spending another person's money does not sit right with me. At any rate, I never was one for shopping."

"In that case, madam, may I recommend a similar selection to that which was provided in London, be sent to your hotel?" Gupta stood, poised once again with his tablet computer, ready to set the wheels in motion. How often did he perform this ritual for Karan? It seemed altogether habitual, as though Karan doted on a new ragamuffin to elevate into the lofty halls of the diplomatic corps, every month. She estimated how long her exchanged dollars would last her in Manhattan. Not long. And she would require suitable work clothes, and something to wear to a job interview. That would seriously eat into her funds. As much as she loathed the notion of relying on Karan's generosity, Mary found herself accepting Gupta's kind offer of assistance.

She watched the diminutive Indian gentleman take control. His serene authority and grasp of logistics, soothed her anxieties. Within minutes, the store assistants were beaming with renewed hope of bonuses, and scurrying around the departments. Gupta returned to Mary's side and bowed. "Shall I escort you back to your hotel, madam?"

"I can get a cab, thank you Gupta. You have done more than enough to help me."

"Shrimant Shinde would expect it of me, madam. Please."

Mary weighed Gupta's response. Was it simple good manners, or a fear of displeasing Karan? It was difficult to judge. Was Karan harsh with his staff? Either way, Mary was unable to refuse. She allowed Gupta to issues commands to the assistants, who trailed after them carrying the evening wear and accessories, down to the front entrance, where a black city car awaited them.

Mary slid into the back seat, allowing the whirlwind of activity to continue around her. Finally, when all was loaded into the boot, Gupta sat in the front passenger seat and directed the driver. Within moments, they were heading back towards Central Park. Mary shuffled forwards in her seat.

"Gupta, this is the wrong way. Even with my terrible sense of direction, I know that thirty-ninth street is the other way."

"That is correct, madam, but we are going to your hotel."

"I don't understand…"

"Shrimant Shinde requested a suite for you at the Plaza Fairmont. It is walking distance to the Indian

Consulate." Gupta spun around in his seat. He tried to administer a reassuring smile, but it came off as creepy. Mary got the distinct impression that smiling was not part of his job description.

"Where we had tea earlier? That's insane. I cannot afford a posh hotel, Gupta. Thirty-ninth street will do me just fine."

"Shrimant Shinde insists on retaining the suite for you. It will cost you nothing, madam."

Mary knew she sounded like a whining and ungrateful child. She also knew that to resist, would result in further insulting Karan. Something she was keen to avoid this time around.

Rocking her head back into the seat rests, Mary thought about her previous time with Karan. Seated among the most important politicians, world diplomats and a sprinkling of nobility, Mary wondered if she was in for a repeat performance. One where she was the main attraction, invited to display her peculiar talents to the highest bidder. Was this another opportunity for Karan to introduce her to VIPs with shady ethics and broken moral compasses?

Mary had learned a great many lessons in the last couple of months. It saddened her that those bitter experiences corroded her trusting nature, leaving her to question the motives of even her closest friends and allies. It was more isolating than she imagined. *I still have my brother. He is the only one I can trust. If there is anything fishy about Karan this evening, I can simply walk away.*

The short drive along Fifth Avenue, deviated on a circuitous route to comply with the irritating one-way systems. They approached the prestigious entrance via Central Park South, their black town car pulling up to the chequered pavement and wrought iron awning. Mary cowered behind the tinted windows. The doorman was heading for the car. Gupta peered around the shoulder of the front seat.

"Is everything alright, madam?"

"I should have changed into something more appropriate at Saks. Now I look like a tramp trying to gain access to Claridges."

"People will think you have been for a run in the park. Do not worry yourself, madam. Leave everything to me." Gupta left the car and darted around to her side. The Plaza doorman, back tracked his steps up the red carpeted stairs, and held open one of the two main doors. Gupta slipped him a bank note and ushered Mary through to reception.

Gilded light ensconces, marble flooring and chandeliers as large as a family car, crowded her senses. Every inch of the wide reception area was decorated or patterned in a lavish display of wealth. A bank of four elevators lined one wall, their gilt cages missing only a winged creature to complete the illusion. In the centre, a perfectly arranged seating area, decorated with fresh flower arrangements. It looked as though no one had ever sat there in a hundred years. On the opposite wall, a long marble reception desk, supporting two uniformed men on duty.

"You will need to sign in, madam." Gupta gestured towards the front desk. Mary hesitated. She fumbled inside her satchel for her passport. How could she show her fake ID in front of him? He knew her only as Mary Arora, a name which would surely flag up some international alert via The Plaza's computer systems.

Gupta frowned. "Is there a problem, madam?"

"I'm not sure this is a good idea, Gupta. It is very kind of Shrimant Shinde, but perhaps I would be more at home in the hotel on Thirty-Ninth Street. Please could you hail a taxi?"

"Madam, please. Your apparel is of no consequence, and will soon be rectified. Shrimant Shinde would be most upset if you are unhappy with the arrangements." He looked imploringly at her. Would Karan really take the refusal out on Gupta? Mary glanced across to the receptionists. They were listening to every word, in the echoing and empty foyer. She swallowed hard and nodded, tucking the passport back inside her bag.

With his hand inches from the small of her back, Gupta guided her to the desk.

"Good afternoon madam, sir. How may we be of assistance."

Gupta stepped up. "We have a Carnegie Suite reserved, courtesy of Shrimant Karan Shinde, in the name of Lady Mary Sedgewell."

Chapter Nine

Mary's eyes bulged from their sockets. Her jaw slackened, allowing her tongue to loll at the edges of her lips. A prudent interruption from Gupta prevented her from spilling her shock out verbally into this public arena.

"Madam, if you will sign in, please."

Mary staggered to the open register and scribbled her new name into the section reserved for her signature. In what felt like slow motion, she produced the fake passport and slid it across the counter. With barely a glance, the receptionist scanned the document on a machine to his left and returned it to Mary with polite thanks. Half expecting the ruse to disintegrate around her, Mary froze to the spot.

"Shall I accompany you to your suite, madam? Make sure that everything is to your satisfaction." Gupta gently touched her back, propelling her forwards. Another man in a uniform arrived to chaperone her to the suite. He introduced himself as the chief concierge but Mary, lost in confusion, failed to hear the given name.

She held her tongue as the lift carried them to the nineteenth floor. She stayed silent while the concierge opened the door to her suite and handed her the key card, and again when he explained the electronic control of the suite and services. Gupta tipped the man for his efforts and closed the door behind him. It was only when Mary and Gupta were finally alone, did she burst with a flurry of dread.

"What the hell, Gupta? How did you know about my fake passport? Who are you really working for? What do you want from me?" She blurted, much to the shock of the small Asian man.

"Madam… I know not of what you speak. That was the name under which Shrimant Shinde requested your suite. I was simply following instructions." He backed away from her and towards the door.

"Don't give me that. Was it Alexi? Tell me… who is pulling the strings? And what's with all this lady malarkey?" She was close enough to feel his breath on her skin.

"Madam, please. I am just a lowly secretary. If you have questions, I suggest your pose them to Shrimant Shinde this evening." He grappled with the door handle behind his back and levered it open. "I shall convey your displeasure to him. He will be most upset." The gap in the doorway widened, and Gupta slipped through.

"Not half as upset as I am."

He was gone. It took a full minute of pacing for her heart rate to lessen from erratic. During that time, her thoughts veered from grabbing her bag and running once again, to waiting until she could form a coherent debate with Karan to ascertain his allegiances. Her mouth felt dry. For the life of her, she could not recall the information from the concierge regarding services. Opening doors and cupboards she found a small sink unit, an expensive looking coffee machine and a tea kettle. The minifridge beneath the sink unit was stocked with a few groceries. *This must be what that man was muttering about – a butler's pantry.*

Mary made herself a cup of tea, and unwrapped a pack of Scottish shortbread biscuits. She munched and supped, and tried to figure a possible connection between the former soviet general and a member of the Indian royal family; a UN Ambassador. Both declared an interest in her unusual neural capabilities, but the longer she dwelled on the issue, the less likely the linkage became. Even still, it gnawed at her well-being.

By her second cup of tea, a knock at the door saw the concierge reappear with the clothes and shoes from her shopping expedition. The parcels and bags contained far more than she had chosen; evidence of Gupta's thoughtful additions. Mary felt miserable. It was not Gupta's fault that her new name was public knowledge. Karan could have discovered it via an internet search of posts following the stormy debacle at the Kent's guesthouse. Mary felt sure that Mrs Kent's son would have willingly sold a photocopy of Mary's signature from the resident's book.

Her new name may well be common knowledge on the internet, but from where did the title of lady originate? This was not the first mention of such a title. Mary trawled her memories. Who was it who had first referred to her as such?

With her explosive mood tempered, Mary resolved to broach the subject at dinner. She also thought that a heartfelt apology was in order, the moment she next saw Gupta. There had to be a simple explanation, and Karan was the only source of answers.

The garment bag containing the black lace dress hung in the bedroom. She wandered in, skirting around the king-sized divan, and unzipped the plastic sheath. *God, I hope it fits. I should have tried it on at Saks.* The telephone rang. Picking up the handset from the power cradle, Mary listened to the man at the other end of the line. It was the receptionist, informing her of a salon appointment at six pm on the ground floor of the hotel complex. *I guess Gupta thought of everything*. Mary scanned the bedside clock. She had an hour to soak in the bath and find something casual from her new wardrobe to wear.

As she turned the gold-plated taps on, allowing the water to spill into the carved Earth Stone bath, she heard a knock at the door. "Jeez, it's like Piccadilly Circus around here." She found yet another man in a uniform, wearing crisp white cotton gloves.

"My lady, allow me to introduce myself. My name is Harvey, and I shall provide the butler service for the duration of your stay. My services are listed on the complementary iPad, along with a remote bell service. One press is sufficient to call for me, from 7.30am to 11.30pm." His accent was a flat British one, and genuine.

"Thank you, Harvey, but I can manage just fine. I found your pantry and have already made myself tea." She began to close the door on him.

"Erm, my lady, will you permit me to replenish the stock used with fresh supplies?"

Mary let the door swing open fully. "Just as you like, and it's not *lady* anything. That must be a mistake at registration. It is just Mary Sedgewell."

"As you wish, Ms Sedgewell." Harvey took a couple of large strides past the cloakroom to his pantry, and checked the contents. He turned around, listening to the running water. "Did you want me to draw your bath, madam? I can set it at a preferred temperature?"

"That's a joke, right?" Mary said, tittering and wandering towards the bathroom.

"No, madam. I am most sincere."

Mary looked up at the tall gentleman. Something about him was comforting. He had a parental aura, as though he looked upon her as one of his charges in need of protection.

"Harvey, thank you for the offer, but I can take care of myself." She rifled through her satchel in search of a bank note.

The butler pre-empted her actions. "Madam, your friend took care of tipping, and was particularly generous. Please use the iPad to ring for me, should you require anything." He closed his pantry and retreated from the room. Locking herself in the bathroom, Mary stripped off the loathsome sweatpants and t-shirt and stepped into the carved stone bath. With little time to spare, she scrubbed her skin and tried to frame the questions that she would pose to her dining companion. A few rehearsed phrases might prevent her from losing her temper, thus maintaining an open dialogue.

***

Mary gathered a stocking into a ruche, slipped it over a toe and gently pulled it towards her thigh. Sitting on the edge of the bed, the CNN report caught her attention on the television. She increased the volume.

"Following yesterday's debilitating lightning strike, we have learned from his campaign director, that Senator Luca Bonovich has in fact, discharged himself from this hospital. In the released statement, the senator thanks everyone for their kind thoughts and good wishes and for keeping him in their prayers. Senator Bonovich intends to continue with his gruelling schedule of public appearances and benefits, but warns that he may have to wear unconventional attire to cover burned tissue until it has fully healed." The report was punctuated with video clips of a black vehicle, speeding away from the press pack. Luca Bonovich sat in the front passenger seat, smiling and waving to the crowds. Taped to his neck, was a large cotton bandage.

Mary slipped on the silk chemise and the lace dress, taking care not to smudge her makeup.

Harvey tapped lightly on the door and entered. "Your guest has arrived, madam. Shall I say that you are ready to receive him, or direct him to the bar lounge?"

Mary stood in front of the tall mirror, stunned at the transformation. The salon had performed miracles with her hair, taming the knots into a tumbling cascade of soft curls, pinned loosely with discreet pearl tipped clips. The lace dress fitted in all the right places, flattering and balancing her top-heavy form. She looked at Harvey's reflection. He could not contain the slow smile or the lazy eyed blink of pride.

"Will I do, Harvey?"

"You look lovely, madam."

For once, Mary chose to accept the praise offered. She supposed that it was something he said often to residents; all part of the job. "Thank you. I'm ready, I think. I can go down to meet the car."

"Madam, forgive me, but you should insist that your date comes to escort you. If you will wait here, I shall inform reception to send him up." Harvey's self-proclaimed guardian mantle resurfaced, his smile converting into a frown. With a few taps on his iPad, he transmitted instructions to the receptionists.

Her first date since Parth. An actual date. Mary had not paired the event to the word in her mind. Afternoon tea, followed by an invitation to dine with a regal and important rich gentleman. This was a formal date. Her confidence crumpled. She sat heavily on the settee.

"Is everything alright, madam?" Harvey drew closer.

Mary's complexion paled. "I'm going on a date." Her inhalations increased noticeably. "I haven't been on a date since before I was married. This is huge. I'm not sure that I am ready."

"Should I send him away when he reaches this floor, madam?" Harvey was earnest. His guests' comfort was his priority, even if it meant facing down a powerful man.

"No, thank you. That would be too mean, too ungrateful." As she said it, she realised that the room, her clothes, even Harvey, were all baited hooks. Karan was reeling her in. How easy it was to fall for the allure of wealth and luxury. She reminded herself of this temporary arrangement; in that her primary aim was to find a job and attain independence.

Harvey answered the door when, at last, the knock came. Mary took a few steadying breaths, and left the security of the bedroom to meet Karan in the sitting room. His expression said it all. For a few moments, he was unable to form words, such was the metamorphosis.

"You don't like the dress?" Mary faltered, her forehead wrinkling above her nose.

"Quite the opposite. I am speechless." He could not stop staring as she fidgeted before him. "Are you ready to leave? Gupta has arranged something special for us."

"Yes, in just a sec." She bolted back into the bedroom and with a backward glance at her trusted satchel, picked up the tiny clutch bag that matched her shoes. "Talking of Gupta, I owe him an apology. I was rather cross with him, when really I should have been annoyed with you." They left her suite for Harvey to tidy, and stood by the elevator doors.

"He said that you were riled about the name Sedgewell."

"That, and bestowing the title of *lady* on me, yes. How could you have possibly known about my fake passport? Please tell me that you are not in league with Alexi?" They entered the lift, stood next to the attendant and waited for nineteen agonising floors until they were able to continue speaking unheard.

"Who is Alexi?" Karan said, striding out across the polished marble foyer. "In my position, Mary, security teams complete background checks on everyone I come into contact with. The closer the alliance, the more thorough the search." They left the building and crossed the chequered paving to the limousine. Mary shuffled along the back seat, allowing Karan to slip in beside her. "Please don't be angry with me, but your search began the moment we met at the Ditchley Estate."

Mary did not know how to process this information. It left her more perplexed than ever. How could a background check have uncovered the use of a fake name? "Are you telling me, that your security team discovered the name of Sedgewell before I left Ditchley?"

"I'm saying that there are some puzzling lines of enquiry surrounding your poor grandfather's death. Again, I am sorry for your loss, Mary." He bowed his head in respect.

Mary did not want sentiment to undo her at such a critical juncture. The mention of her grandfather caught her unawares. It invaded her senses so completely, to acknowledge the feelings would wreck her entire evening in hysteria. She swallowed down the anguish and ploughed on. "So, it had nothing to do with that repellent woman, Bernie Feinstein, and her cabal of pharmaceutical philanthropists?"

"Nothing at all. I do wish you would forgive me over that regrettable incident."

"Do you still have dealings with her?" Mary analysed his face for any indication of lies.

"My ties to Bernie and her conglomerates were tenuous at best. I thought she could help you."

"You said, *were*. Does that mean that you have changed your mind over her outrageous assumptions regarding de-population schemes?" Mary bit her tongue. This was not the time to debate global politics. She was steering him off course.

"Let's just say that her methods have caused me considerable problems. I am… reconsidering my business and personal alliances."

As pleasing as it was to hear him declare a shift away from the US elite group, she had to refocus the discussion back to that of her family. "Is that why you ordered a deep background check on me? Do you plan on us forming a personal alliance?" She reached over and lay her hand on his. He did not flinch at the touch as she had anticipated. Instead, she could see him smiling in the dim evening light. They remained still, basking in the possibilities, until a sharp turn pulled them from their reverie.

Karan snapped to first. "You must understand that checks are standard procedure. My job leaves me vulnerable to those who would try and leverage my position as ambassador. Our security teams are allied to the United Nations. They are able to pull on worldwide resources; collate current chatter from the most secure sources. In truth, they are still trying to piece your data together."

"But my life is as simple as it gets. I am no one at all." She removed her hand, returning it to her own lap. The moment of intimacy shattered.

"How can you say that, Mary? You are far from simple. Look at all the incredible gifts you have; the ability to read minds, the electromagnetic sensitivity, the whole spying without your body thing… You are truly unique."

Mary frowned. Her mind wandered to Alexi's compound and the team of trainees he had at his mercy. She also felt a brief moment of pity for the perished soviet operatives who had formed a Hive Mind together. She was not unique at all. Fearful of Karan's motives, she kept the insight to herself. "So, this background search discovered that I had used a fake passport in that New Jersey guesthouse?"

"That was taken from a reporter's notebook, yes. In truth, they were not sure as to the validity of that claim."

"And what of the title, lady? Where did that come from?"

Karan shifted uneasily in the seat. He was playing for time, unable to frame his answer. His mouth pursed, as though he was debating internally over how much to divulge. "That little nugget was sifted from a top level file. Gupta should not have let that slip until it can be verified."

Mary was on the verge of refuting the claim entirely, until a memory flitted into her thoughts. A vision of a thin man in pinstripes handing her a condolence card on Parliament Square. The former friend of her grandfather, conveying his respects to the family. He had addressed her as, *my lady*. He had been the source of Connie's news story, which condemned the Defence Minister for illegal technology trades. Could there possibly be some truth to this wisp of intelligence?

And then there was the discovery of her grandfather's journal, the inner inscription denoting that he was the Eighth Earl of Sedgewell. Dan and she had taken that as a joke. What if it had been the literal truth? She shook it from her thoughts. It was too incredible a notion to entertain.

The limousine stopped at sixty, East Sixty-Five Street, and Karan climbed out. Holding out his hand to Mary, she took it and did not let go. Only when they reached the revolving door into the restaurant, did she release him. Karan gave his name to the hostess, who then swept them away to a quiet corner reserved for dignitaries. Mary felt the keen eyes of the other diners straying towards them. Far from affording them privacy, their sheltered spot highlighted them as different.

"Mary is a vegetarian," Karan explained to their personal waiter. "Please can you give us a selection of your finest dishes?"

She could not prevent the swell of elation welling up inside. He had remembered her dietary preferences. He really was trying to put the animosity behind them. The waiter hurried away to place their order.

"Dare I ask how your ex-husband is faring. Is he still recovering in that London hospital?"

"In truth, I have no idea. The last I heard, he was making a slow recovery, but that was before g

Grampy..." She couldn't say it. The words stuck in her throat. Her eyes glazed with a slick of saline. Karan anticipated the rest and recognising her distress, reached out for her. The touch that he now craved. Their hands locked across the white linen of the table.

She gaped up at him. Those rich dark eyes looked back. During their last meal together, Mary found herself unable to read his mind. He had forged an unconscious barrier from years of studied meditation and mental discipline. She was interested in seeing if her abilities had strengthened. Could the block still resist her intense foray into his thoughts?

The connection took just a few seconds to achieve. Her penetrative stare latched like a deadbolt onto his optic nerve, securing her access to his neural transmissions.

In that moment, she heard his foremost thought. *"My family would never accept her."*

Chapter Ten

Karan's thoughts bewildered her. It was their first proper date, and already he was contemplating long term ramifications. She hardly knew anything about him, and all his information about her originated from a secret file. The waiter returned with the wine list, breaking her concentration.

The food was beyond divine. Tiny masterpieces, mounted and framed in bespoke china, exploding the taste buds with inexhaustible flavour. Each dish, came and went in a flurry of excitement, until Mary could consume no more.

Loathed to break the convivial atmosphere, Mary broached the subject which had preyed on her mind since first she saw him outside the international delicatessen. "Karan. Is there a way of reporting an incident to the US authorities without incriminating myself in the process?"

"Why, what have you done?" His face sank. Gone was the perpetual smile and hazy blink. The concentrated frown unsettled her.

"Nothing… much. It's just with all the problems I had with the Defence Minister targeting me, well you recall my terrifying run from Ditchley that night… I had to use fake documents to get into JFK airport. There is still an outstanding warrant for my arrest in connection to all those dreadful things that went on at the Houses of Parliament. Not that any of it was my fault."

"So, what do you need to report?" Those dark accusatory eyes were unbearable.

"The chap who helped me to escape, Alexi, is a known terrorist. When I got to his compound, I saw trucks transporting nuclear material."

"You know that there are private companies that specialise in transporting nuclear waste, don't you?"

"It's not that. I am convinced that he is plotting something dreadful. Didn't you hear me, Alexi is a terrorist."

"Then why were you with him?"

"Because I had no other choice, look you are missing the point. Alexi is a bad man. He has nuclear material in a large compound in New Jersey. Shouldn't it at least be reported so that the authorities can mount an investigation?"

Karan stroked his short beard in thought. He gazed into her fright-filled eyes and smiled. "Leave it with me. I will look into it for you." Clearly, this was not going to spoil his evening. Piloting their conversation away from further turbulence, Karan navigated them back into the romance of childhood dreams. He banished the diplomat and negotiator; letting slip his guard to reveal the man beneath. They spoke of adolescent memories, of family holidays, boarding school dramas and nursery foibles; each fascinated by one another's tales.

"How is it that you are not already married?" She blurted, regretting her inquisition the moment it left her lips.

Karan picked up his glass and took a long sip. The light-hearted banter evaporated. She could see his eyes narrowing, contemplating his answer. The wait seemed interminable. Was he resurrecting those barriers, banishing her from his intimate thoughts? She watched his indecision and unease.

"I'm sorry," she whispered. "It is none of my business. Please forget I ever asked." She looked so contrite, he softened.

"I was supposed to be married a long time ago. An arrangement of my father's." There was a break in his voice. He coughed to mask his distress.

Mary was fascinated. He had left a tiny crack in his defences for her to crawl through. Perhaps it was the wine, or a little of her growing confidence, but she was determined to discover more.

"You did not like his choice of bride?"

"She was a nice enough girl, and it would have been a fortunate match for my family." He was talking in hushed tones, drawing Mary in closer.

"Why didn't the marriage take place?" She matched his timbre, the intimacy blossoming once more.

"My father was very angry when I voiced my opinions. He said that he regretted sending me to England for my education. Thought that I had picked up too many western notions and had forgotten my roots, my duty." He drained his glass. Mary stayed silent, hoping that he would complete his emotional outpouring. He did. "I relented. The wedding plans took weeks. It was tedious in the extreme." He had difficulty swallowing, his mouth dry with anxiety. Karan gestured to the waiter to bring another bottle.

"What happened?"

"My father died. I became head of the family."

"Oh God, I am sorry."

He waved the pity away. "We were not close. The funeral arrangements took precedence over the wedding. When things had settled down, I visited the bride's father and convinced him that his daughter favoured another. Out of respect, I would not allow my mother to arrange a second match." He looked down at his plate, embarrassed by his vulnerability. Mary reached across the table and offered her hand. He took it and gave it a light squeeze. The waiter returned with his wine. Karan snatched his hand away.

Gupta appeared a respectable distance from their table and tapped his wristwatch with an index finger.

"Ah, that is our signal that we must hurry or we shall miss our ride." Karan stood up and held the back of Mary's chair. "Gupta has arranged for a carriage through Central Park."

They walked towards the exit, allowing Gupta to take care of the payments and tips. Once through the revolving doors, Mary felt the night breeze, and shivered. Bundling into the rear of the limousine, they knocked their heads together. Mary found their graceless collision hilarious, her lyrical laughter infecting her dinner companion. Giggling and fumbling with her seatbelt, Karan was enchanted. He swept his finger along her jawline and kissed her. Just a glancing touch of the lips, exploring how far he could extend the liberty.

"Do we have to drive through the park in a cold carriage?" She murmured, all inhibitions dissolved in Chardonnay.

He kissed her again, this time with enough passion to inflame all her senses. "We can do whatever you desire."

"Then let's go back to the Plaza."

He stopped kissing her and pulled away. Mary sat upright, dumbfounded. "What's the matter? What did I do wrong?"

"Mary, are you not concerned for your reputation? I do not want people to think that you are my… mistress, put up in a nearby hotel for my convenience."

"What does that matter? No one knows me in New York. We can do as we please." She could not believe that she was arguing in favour of spending the night with a man whom she had met only once before. She grappled the lapels on his jacket, pulling him closer.

"Mary, please. I have respect for you, even if you do not. Let us allow things to develop naturally. Take our time." He pushed her arms away and pressed a button on a control panel, lowering the glass partition between the rear and front seats. "Gupta, we are taking Mary home."

"Yes, Shrimant Shinde."

The driver heard the instruction and altered their course. Mary sat on the back seat, wishing she could sink into the leather creases and disappear. With her arms folded across her middle, Mary hugged herself. She recalled her previous bungled attempt at passion with Karan at the consulate in London, and flushed hot. How many times must she be rebuffed by this man and his vacillating affections? When they arrived at the entrance to the Plaza, Karan got out of the vehicle with her, and pecked her on the cheek.

"Don't be angry with me, Mary. I just don't want us to rush this."

"Thank you for a lovely meal, Karan. Goodnight." As she scurried up the steps towards the entrance, she heard him calling her name, but she did not look back. She stood in the lift with tears streaking her mascara. On the nineteenth level, she dashed across the hallway and searched for the key card inside the clutch bag. In her haste the card slipped from her hands onto the floor. Harvey witnessed the pitiful scene from the doorway of his supply cupboard. Mary tried several times to pick up the key, its flat surface sitting flush against the marble tiles.

"May I be of service, madam?" Harvey crouched down and used a thumb nail to gain purchase beneath the card. He touched it against the sensor, opening the door. Mary cuffed the back of hand across her wet cheek, and walked into the living room. Unbidden, Harvey followed. There, her tears gained momentum. Harvey moved a ceramic container of tissues to her side on the settee and made her a cup of decaffeinated tea from his butler's pantry. As he delivered the cup and saucer, her upset dried as her insobriety decreased.

"I'm sorry, Harvey. I should not wallow in self-pity."

"I take it the date did not go well, madam?"

"No, that's just it, it was perfect, until the end." She sniffed and wiped her smeared eyes with a damp tissue.

"Did he hurt you?"

"Only my pride. I really thought… never mind. You men have no idea how humiliating it is to have your advances rejected."

"I think I can safely say, on behalf of all men, that we have a fairly good idea of that feeling, madam." It raised her smile. He tidied the pantry, walked into the bedroom and turned down the sheets. On his return he said, "perhaps you will feel better after a good night's sleep."

Mary took the cue, rose from her seat, and walked towards the bed.

"Mary…"

She turned around to face the butler. "Yes, Harvey?"

"Pardon me, madam?"

"You called my name."

"I did not, madam." They both looked puzzled. "Is there anything else you require before my shift ends?"

"No, thank you, good night."

Mary lay awake for a full hour, watching the ceiling spin and listening to the incessant traffic noises from Central Park South and Fifth. What was she doing playing princess with an Indian nobleman? How had her life become such a mess? An ex-husband, plus half the staff at the Houses of Parliament recovering from near fatal poisoning, a warrant for her arrest issued by a man under suspicion of trading defence technology, and Alexi up to his old tricks again. All this, and yet Karan was her primary concern.

In the early hours of the morning, Mary made the decision to prioritise her independence; find a job and her own place to stay. *I must talk to Dan about Alexi's latest venture. He always gives me clear advice.* The pillows were so soft, her mind so tired, she slipped into slumber mid thought.

***

Mary awoke to the smell of toasted bread and freshly pressed orange juice. Dragging herself from the comfort of the divan, she wrapped herself in the complementary cotton robe, used the facilities and went through into the sitting room.

"Good morning, madam."

"What's all this?" She lowered herself onto the settee, each movement exaggerating the dull ache inside her skull. The daylight offended her eyes, piercing the pupils with flint like pain.

"I took the liberty of ordering for you madam. I did not think you would feel well enough to breakfast downstairs." He poured her a cup of tea from a Wedgewood pot and set it down on the coffee table.

"You thought right, Harvey, thank you." Grabbing the teacup, she drained the warm liquid and held it up for more. "What's the time?"

"A little after ten, madam." With the faintest of smiles, Harvey poured her a second cup, and then reached to the butler's trolley for a tiny serving plate. On it, two oblong tablets lay on a miniature paper doily. He set it down in front of her.

"Paracetamol?" She protected her eyes with the flat of her hand.

"Yes, madam."

"You really do pre-empt all our needs, Harvey, but I wish you would stop calling me madam. It makes me feel like a maiden aunt. Can't you call me Mary?"

"It would not be appropriate, madam - hotel policy."

"Marvellous." She gobbled up the pain killers and sipped more tea.

"A number of packages and deliveries have arrived for you. I told the concierge to wait until you had risen. Shall I inform him to bring them up now?" He acknowledged her nod with rapid taps and swipes on his iPad. Within five minutes, a stream of porters carried garment bags, shoe boxes and several arrangements of flowers into her sitting room. Mary stood bewildered, surrounded by an abundance of gifts. The young men and women deposited the items and filed out of the door.

"Oh God, tips. I haven't given them tips." Mary tried to find her purse, and then remembered that it was still inside the clutch bag.

"It is all taken care of, madam. Do not trouble yourself."

"Really? How?"

"I believe Shrimant Shinde insisted on leaving a cash donation, to be equally split among the wait staff, with a separate and very generous annuity for me." He placed a paperknife and an envelope down next to her teacup. It was made from heavy weight cream paper, edged with gold leaf.

Inside, she found a gilded invitation to a charity auction and a handwritten note from Karan. It said:

Dear Mary,

We seem to always be out of sync with each other. I apologise if I caused you distress last night. Please allow me to escort you to the charity function tonight, and I will endeavour to make it up to you.

With warmest regards,

Karan.

Harvey unzipped the closest garment bag, draped across an occasional chair. The silk of the cocktail dress slid through the aperture. "Shall I hang this in the bedroom, madam?"

"Yes, please." She swung her legs up onto the settee and lay back on the cushions. *I'm a kept woman. I have gone from having Parth make all my decisions for me, to having Karan make them. I have got to get out from their control and start steering my own future. How on earth am I to get a job without a green card? How am I to get a green card with fake documents? If only I could go home. I'm sure the professor would let me continue my PhD studies.* She sat up and reached for the suite's iPad. Tapping in the memorised web address, Mary sifted through the links on the BBC News page, for any signs of an announcement from the Prime Minister. Other than a brief paragraph of lies, stating her recovery from a minor case of Legionnaire's Disease, there was nothing to give Mary hope.

Abandoning the iPad, Mary directed her attention to the massive television screen on the wall. The menu of channels was immense. "Harvey... how do I get cable channels on this?"

He abandoned the new clothes and floral arrangements to attend her. "Was there something specific you would like me to find?"

"I want to see what is going on back home."

Harvey scanned through the options on screen and landed on the BBC. He returned the remote to Mary, and continued his work.

"Thank you." She murmured, lost in the tickertape ribbon of headlines scrolling beneath the newscaster. It read: *Defence Minister detained over allegations of treason... Prime Minister recovering well and scheduled to return to Downing Street later today... Deputy PM stands in at the MoD and warns cabinet reshuffle imminent.*

"Nothing about water contamination or the Mental Health Bill?"

"Pardon me, madam?"

"Oh nothing."

Harvey finished stowing away the latest gifts from her admirer and cleared away the breakfast items. Mary locked herself in the bathroom and took a leisurely soak in the tub. With the Prime Minster out of action, there seemed little chance of her lifting the warrant for Mary's arrest.

As she lay in the warm soapy bubbles, Mary contemplated her next move. The anonymity of a big city would not last forever. If a teenage boy in a small, New Jersey town could out her as the famed Miracle Mary, it wouldn't be long before news crews tracked her location. She really ought to decline Karan's offer to escort her to the charity auction. It could be surrounded by media teams.

Mary pulled the plug and dried herself off. Wrapping the soft towel around her body, she walked into the bedroom and touched the midnight blue silk of the new dress. It moved like a living creature, undulating through her fingers.

I shouldn't, but I really do want to see Karan tonight, if only to ask him what he has discovered about Alexi. Maybe those ladies, downstairs in the salon, can spruce me up so that no one would ever recognise me. I could ask Karan to drop me off at a service entrance so that no one would see me arrive. Harvey had placed the matching shoes under the hanging gown. Their allure was too great to resist. Mary slid them onto her bare feet and sighed. *What is wrong with me? Am I so shallow as to be seduced by all this materialism?*

Dressing in jeans, a red cotton blouse and jacket, Mary grabbed her key card and satchel, and descended in the lift to the foyer. Taking big confident strides, Mary left the hotel and crossed the road to the park. Without the distractions of wealth, she had a better chance of thinking clearly. She strolled along the busy foot paths and cycle routes before settling on a bench to watch the wildlife upending in the lake.

"Dan?" She reached out into the ether for her brother's telepathic frequency. *"Are you able to talk?"* She waited a few moments, and then tried again. *"Dan?"*

"Yep, am here... two secs..." Another short wait, and he returned with his crisp intonation. *"Sorry, I was driving. I have pulled over with my hazards on. Good to hear your voice. How are you doing?"*

"I'm okay, thanks. How's your mum?"

"Much better. I'm heading to the hospital now. She thinks they will discharge her today. Still on medication, but the specialist said that she should make a full recovery."

"Oh, that is good news. I hope to God that the Prime Minister has recovered too. She needs to get back to the day job and fulfil her promises."

"Don't hold your breath on that score, little sister. Where exactly are you now?"

"Central Park, watching the ducks."

"How the other half live. And no dramas, so far?"

"Well, I wouldn't say that, exactly." Mary refrained from blurting out the whole of her worries; her fear that Alexi was preparing for yet another grand scheme of the terror variety. On reflection, there was nothing to be gained by burdening him with her concerns. He could not do anything to help.

"Mary...? You are alright, aren't you?"

She changed the subject. *"Hey, Dan, I'm sorry that I lumbered you with sorting everything out over..."*

He felt her sadness. The surge of emotion that stung his own eyes. The mutual grief over a beloved grandfather. *"They haven't released his body yet. I have been battling with Yelena over his personal effects. She says they are part of the investigation, but that is such bullshit. As if MI6 need to investigate what happened. Anyway, I'm seeing her later. Apparently, Pip was carrying a journal when... it happened."*

"Grampy carried a diary around with him? That's an odd thing to do. It must have contained something important. I can't believe I didn't know that about him."

"It seems there were quite a few things we didn't know. I received a condolence card in the post, this morning. There was a metallic business card inside, embossed with a whole bunch of contact details."

The disclosure crystalized a thought from her memory. Mary reached into her satchel, pulling out the sympathy card the Thin Man had handed to her on Parliament Square. She unfolded it and read the message once again. *"It wasn't from a man called Jenkins, was it?"*

Chapter Eleven

"You got one too? Who is he?"

"No idea. He didn't give me a business card though. He just handed me the envelope and called me, My Lady."

"How peculiar. I really need to look into this, especially after finding that Earl of Sedgewell statement. Maybe Pip's journal will shed some light on it. Right, got to go or I'll be late for my mum. Take care, Mary."

The moment she felt her brother's mental halter release her, the solitude invaded. Surrounded by dog walkers, joggers, tourists and an ensemble of native New Yorkers, Mary had never felt so alone. For a full half hour, Mary just sat and watched the world go by, pondering her circumstances. It was only when a man sidled up to her bench, sat down and shuffled closer to her, did she move.

Wandering aimlessly, she gravitated to the area where she had first arrived in Manhattan, close to the Hayden Planetarium and American Museum of Natural History. The signage directed her around the corner from Central Park West to the entrance at Eighty-First Street. The massive grey sphere encapsulated in the glass box was magnificent; its attraction was irresistible.

Mary paid her fee at the ticket desk and followed the crowds into the main theatre. Distracted by the Big Bang feature, she allowed herself time to forget her problems.

From there, the exit led her from inside the sphere down a long and gradual spiral of time. The entire history of the cosmos laid out in images, explanations and interactive screens. The atmosphere felt rarefied, concentrated by the hundreds of astonished children, gasping at the displays and running through the exhibitions.

It was when she reached a darkened area to view the Earth Event Wall, that Mary shuddered. The real-time data streaming from thousands of seismographic and meteorological centres across the world, showed a minor tremor occurring in New Zealand. Her heart raced, sending a flush of heat through her chest. She did not want to be reminded of past ordeals; the events that culminated in the deaths of ten innocent people by her own powers. The disquiet made the memory real. Her abilities were a menace, not an asset. Turning on her heels, Mary hurried from the exhibit.

She took time with the rocks and meteorites to banish the thought from her mind. Here, she touched the five-foot mass of red rock, cut along its length and polished to a shine. Its cool surface reflected the artificial lighting above, which flickered as people, moved forming shadows.

"I don't know why you are even considering it, frankly. Give a man a PhD and he thinks he has the right to pontificate on all subjects equally."

Mary turned to watch them from a discreet distance. The man who spoke was familiar. She recognised him from the television; it was the widow's peak hairline on his perfect black forehead, the cheeky grin and engaging way he explained complex concepts to children and adults alike. The second man Mary saw, looked fraught.

"Even still. You can guarantee that they will contact you about this, so you ought to have an answer prepared."

"It is not worth my time. He's a goddamn neuroscientist. His theories about the ionosphere are irrelevant." The charming black man dismissed his colleague with a waft of the hand.

"Can you just have a brief statement prepared for when the media come calling? It would make my job a whole lot easier." The fraught man scratched idly at his eyebrow, closing his eyes to his surroundings.

"Why would they contact an astro-physicist about atmospheric layers and consciousness? It doesn't make sense."

The men walked further from Mary, their voices became harder to hear. She wandered closer, her inquisitiveness piqued.

"If what this Arora guy says is credible, it will initiate a massive round of televised debates. You are the obvious choice."

Mary reeled. It couldn't be Parth, could it? Why would he be releasing statements about this ionosphere? In a flat spin, she fidgeted, looking for any access to the world wide web. There were interactive screens, but all were locked into the child friendly interface displaying the cosmos. In desperation, Mary dashed to the nearest exit. She had to get back to the hotel to search for any recent activity tagged to her ex-husband. If only she still had her smart phone. The thought crossed her mind that she ought to buy a SIM card and register it with her new name.

Racing across the park, Mary ran in a straight trajectory, dodging the many obstacles until she arrived at the front entrance of The Plaza. The doorman tipped his cap to her as she bolted past and ran into the silent foyer. When she reached the elevator doors, the operator pressed the button for the nineteenth floor without her asking. Mary spent the vertical journey, doubled over panting. As the lift doors opened, she signed the thumbs up to the young man, and rummaged in her bag for her key card.

Upon entry, Mary discovered Harvey hanging the dress, from her dinner with Karan, up in the wardrobe. Its nylon sheath evidence of the dry-cleaning process, Harvey had arranged. He scuttled to the sitting room. "Can I be of assistance, madam?"

"Nope. Just needed the iPad, thanks Harvey."

He loitered, tidying his pantry and switching on the small kettle, anticipating her need for a drink. Mary flipped the cover open and the device sprang to life. With a new browser window on screen, Mary typed Dr Parth Arora into the search bar. Within a millisecond, over a hundred thousand entries scrolled before her eyes. Each post began with a sensational headline.

Online tabloid services led with variations of, MIRACLE MARY'S HUSBAND CLAIMS HEAVEN IS A MYTH. Broadsheets focused on his neuroscience qualifications to lend them credibility. Theirs read; IONOSPHERE IS HUMAN MEMORY REPOSITORY. *Oh god, what has he done now? I thought he would still be in hospital, or at least recuperating at home with his sisters taking care of him.* She clicked on a link to an illegal upload of a debate aired on British terrestrial TV channels. The studio was decked one side with a live audience; the stage area supported four chairs lined up in a semi-circle. Parth sat at the end of the row, almost facing the TV host. Next to him, a man in a black suit and clerical collar. The final seat was occupied by Danish quantum physicist and Christian, Dr Hugo Blom.

Mary lowered the volume control on the iPad and touched the play arrow. The audience applause died down and the host introduced each of the guests. Parth looked especially gaunt. His freshly shaved cheeks caved in either side of his chin, the whites of his eyes yellowed from the toxins leaving his system. Mary swallowed back a twinge of pity. Even a near fatal poisoning could not dampen his fervour. If Parth could not collect a Nobel Prize, he would have to be content with media infamy. Mary observed the passive-aggressive exchange of looks between the former college house mates and sighed. This is what comes of having a competitive nature.

The host gave a precis of the events, which had culminated in a march of fifty-thousand disgruntled Christians through central London. It was punctuated by video clips illustrating Mary's abilities in all their uncontrolled glory. The discussion began with an explanation from the guest cleric, The Archbishop of Canterbury. Mary recalled his compassion for her on that fateful day. How he had rescued her from the clamouring masses with his undeniable charisma. A kind, highly articulate and dignified man, who diffused the mob mentality with a simple prayer. A reminder that forgiveness, not judgement was part of the tenets of faith. His introductory statement left him sitting squarely on the fence. A tactical move which neither condemned Mary for her abilities, nor made claims of her Messianic potential.

Hugo charged in with both guns blazing. His animosity prepared in advance, to appease his following among the online trolls and religious zealots. While the Archbishop attempted to temper Hugo's belligerence, Parth sat in silence, absorbing the petty bickering and semantics. The host gave Hugo free rein.

"I still think that Mary should be held to account for her blasphemy. No other faith would permit such mockery of their prophets." Hugo was almost pouting, his nose held high in the studio air.

The Archbishop countered. "I don't believe that she did mock our faith. It seems to me that Mary is as unsure of her abilities as we are. She should not be judged for being blessed with unique gifts."

"Blessed?" Hugo lunged forwards in his chair. "You think God has blessed her with the ability to turn water into wine, to heal the sick and blow up electrical equipment?"

"Of course. Just as you have been gifted with abilities in theoretical physics. We each excel at something in life." The Archbishop interlinked his fingers and balanced them on crossed knees. Mary thought he looked most sincere in his opinions.

Hugo would not be swayed. "Well, I know a collective of fifty thousand people who would disagree with you there."

"That is my point, Hugo. Parliament Square was filled with impressionable people. You influenced their collective conscience into bitterness and antagonism; dare I go as far as hatred. You should be using your drive and celebrity to steer people for the betterment of society."

Parth snorted, and then excused himself, masking his retort as a sneeze. "It is interesting that you use the term, *collective conscience*. It is making quite the revival in scientific circles. This ability to influence others has nothing to do with charisma. There are a couple of notable scientists investigating this hypothesis. One refers to this collective as Morphic Resonance; the ideas of one can become the ideas of many, even without direct contact. Sheldrake's work centred on learnt mammalian behaviour, while Persinger favours aspects of the electromagnetic spectrum aligning, allowing transmission of thoughts. Being a Neuroscience myself, I naturally lean towards Persinger."

The host looked utterly perplexed. "Can you boil that down to essentials for us layman here, Dr Arora? What exactly are you saying?"

"I am saying that there is growing evidence to suggest that when our brain waves quieten to approximately seven to eight Hertz, we can align with the Earth's natural electromagnetic frequencies, and communicate our thoughts along the ionosphere, much like radio signals."

"But then, to where do our thoughts go?" The host was intrigued, allowing this tangent to blossom.

"It is but a theory, at present, but initial suggestions are that the ionosphere itself is a repository of all our memories and ideas; a true collective consciousness. If you think about it, those atmospheric charged particles are no different from the magnetic tape still used in some computer networks to backup data. It is certainly large enough to contain seven billion peoples' thoughts. And it would account for why there are so many copyright and patent infringement lawsuits in the world, if we are all tapping into the same information streams."

"That is preposterous." Hugo blustered. "What have you been smoking? What evidence are you citing?"

"I did say it was a theory, Hugo. There is no need to be defensive." Parth shot him a glare; a warning to allow him time in the spotlight. For the first time since she began watching, Mary was aware of Harvey listening in on the debate. She increased the volume to make it easier for him to hear. It seemed pointless to try and hide the video from him. It had already accrued millions of views worldwide. She angled the iPad towards him and gestured for him to sit beside her. He blushed, but then accepted her offer and sat down.

"All I am saying," Parth continued. "Is that each thought and idea, takes approximately twenty minutes to form linkages in the brain. The tiny branches at the ends of the nerves are electrically labile - that is liable to change, can be easily altered. What if during those twenty minutes, the frequencies of our brain waves allow thoughts to be directed outwards too; sent as a transmission into the atmosphere?" Parth looked at Hugo. The antsy frown morphed into a glazed eyed introspection. Parth elucidated further. "It is proven that neural activity emits photons, even if they are too few to actually see. And we all know that where we have photons, the nuances of quantum physics come into play. What was it that Einstein said? Spooky action at a distance."

Hugo was lost in the complex ramifications of Parth's account.

The Archbishop drew in breath. "You are suggesting that we all access the same pool of information?"

"Only when we are immersed in sympathetic electromagnetic frequencies. If, for example, there was a particularly strong geomagnetic storm, the turbulence would undoubtedly prevent a connection. But, while our brains are at rest, particularly in the dream states of alpha rhythms, we would be at our most congruent. That's probably why we tell people who need to make decisions or have problems, to 'sleep on it.' The solution is found by tapping into the font of all knowledge - aka, the ionosphere."

The Archbishop smoothed his beard and re-crossed his legs. "Can anyone do this, do you suppose, or would you have to be trained in yogic practises or meditation?"

"Anyone who can calm their mind down to match the Earth's Schumann Resonance of 7.83Hertz. Isn't that what you do when you pray? You try and sync your mind with a deity who will listen and give advice?"

Mary winced at Parth's pronouncement. He was deliberately provoking them.

Hugo bit first. "That is an outrageous suggestion. How dare you?"

"With all due respect, Hugo, Has God ever replied to any of your prayers? Could it be that you were simply transmitting your problems and wishes into the great backup in the sky? That there is no God to hear you, only a collective consciousness of seven billion people, or by logical progression, hundreds of billions of people since Homo-erectus died out in the Pleistocene era."

"You are dismissing two thousand years of worship for the sake of a shaky argument over an unproven hypothesis." Hugo snarled.

"I am merely proposing an alternative approach to a current trend in consciousness experiments. It just seems curious that the more we bathe ourselves in artificial electromagnetic fields of telecommunications, the less able we are to empathise with one another. If we switched off all the interference in our lives, we might all have a telepathic ability with each other and with our ancestors. Might we achieve genuine harmony? No one sector of society could sequester information at the expense of all others. No one group could retain control. No rich, no poor, no corrupt governments. True equality could be achieved."

"Hold, for one moment, Dr Arora." The Archbishop interjected. "Let us circle back to what you just said. A connection with all our ancestors?"

"Precisely, isn't it logical that the ionosphere retains all our memories and thoughts even after we die."

"Are you suggesting that the ionosphere is Heaven?" The host chimed in.

"I'm saying that there is no heaven."

Chapter Twelve

Mary hit the pause button. The video froze with Hugo's mouth wide open. It was not a flattering look. She could guess his reaction to Parth's assertions. She knew that Parth was hellbent on antagonising his old college friend in retaliation for his part in ruining his chances of a Nobel Prize. This latest outpouring would reignite the science versus religion debate, sending it into a stratospheric level of global conflict. Did Parth's motive also include raising the potential backlash for Mary too?

Resting the tablet PC on the arm of the sofa, she closed her eyes and rubbed them. Did Parth really believe that anyone could tap into a collective consciousness? A tethering much like her own abilities, but with the wider implications of connecting all mankind. If his theories were correct, there could be many more people with gifts like her own. People who had managed to stay off Alexi and the British government's radars. More importantly, if the essence of a person's character, memories and thoughts are preserved after death in the ionosphere, could she still make contact with her grandfather? Was it his voice calling her name among the clamour and noise when she tried to contact Dan? Could she speak to her father from beyond the grave? Mary felt light-headed; her chest constricted. On the edge of tears, she inhaled a long breath, stilling her emotions.

"Can I get you something to drink, madam? Tea, perhaps, or something stronger?" Harvey stood up, collecting the iPad from its precarious position and setting it down in a charging dock.

"I would get roaring drunk if I thought it would help. As it is, I have to attend that charity function with Shrimant Shinde tonight." She tucked her legs up on the settee and hugged a chintz cushion.

"Would you like me to call his assistant and cancel?"

"In truth, Harvey, I need to see him. I asked him for a favour about something important. I want to know what he has discovered. I won't be able to rest until I know that everything is resolved."

"Wouldn't a telephone call fulfil that objective, madam?"

"It would, but then I'd feel guilty about using his resources and then leaving him in the lurch for his function. No, I will have to attend. I just hope that I am not recognised by any paparazzi." A cup of steaming hot tea arrived on the coffee table, along with a full pot and milk jug on a silver tray. "Harvey, you are an angel."

Harvey tittered awkwardly. "You never know, you might enjoy yourself. I'm sure that Shrimant Shinde's assistant has prepared for every eventuality, including the management of the press."

There was a short period of silence, while Harvey busied himself replacing the towels in the bathroom and removing the midnight blue silk evening gown from the wardrobe. He placed a pair of navy suede stilettos and a small matching clutch bag next to the vanity unit and frowned. Returning to the sitting room he said, "madam, would you like me to enquire about a loan of some jewellery for this evening? I believe the whole ensemble would look a little plain without any at all."

"I have spent the last few weeks borrowing everything from everyone. People must be sick and tired of me. No, thank you, but it is kind of you to think of it." She scrambled up from the sofa and reached for her satchel. "I almost forgot. I have a brooch that I inherited." Mary pulled Grandma Phebe's jewel from her bag and held it up against the hanging dress. "What do you think?"

"A match made in heaven, madam." They both gave a titter.

"There you go then. I'm all set."

"There is the matter of your salon appointment downstairs, madam."

"Another one? I guess there are downsides to living like a duchess after all."

***

A gentle tap on the door signalled Karan's arrival. Harvey opened the door to the regal Indian gentleman; whose chin fell the moment he spied Mary in the silk gown. A single diagonal strap secured her modesty and negated the need for a necklace. The curls of her hair were piled high at the front and sides, but left to spill down between her exposed shoulder blades at the back. The overall effect rendered Karan mute. He handed a small, hand tied posy of violets to Harvey as he walked into the sitting room.

After a protracted silence, in which Karan just stood admiring her, she said, "thank you for the flowers," and blushing, she turned to Harvey, "Please could you put them in water?"

"Of course, madam. Have a wonderful time."

Still Karan said nothing. Bereft of speech, he offered his arm to her instead. With careful steps, Mary teetered on the heels and slid her hand under his forearm. The sensation was electric, even through the close woven cloth of his dinner jacket. Did he feel the spark of frisson too? Mary could not be sure. They strolled to the waiting elevator and absorbed the admiring stares of the operator.

Mary adjusted the neck strap several times before Karan found his voice. "Do not be uncomfortable, Mary. You are without fault."

She tried to assimilate his statement. Was that a compliment? Was he attempting to say that she looked nice? "Thank you, I think." The silk edged up her leg as she walked across the marble foyer. The cool night air stung her ankles, prompting her to flick the hemline back down her leg. *God, how do women deal with dress creep? Yelena wears silk all the time. She never has to wriggle her clothes back in place.* An elegant descent into the limousine was much easier than she had feared. She sat on the edge of the back seat and swung both legs together into the foot well. *So far so good.* Karan walked to the far side of the vehicle and slipped in beside her. Their thighs grazed whenever they rounded a corner. Mary found herself shallow breathing.

"Karan, do you think it would be better to drop me off at a service entrance to the venue?"

"Why would we do that?"

"What if I am recognised by the press? I wouldn't want to embarrass you."

"I doubt anyone would recognise you in that gown, Mary, but even if they did, you could never embarrass me. Just relax and enjoy yourself."

She couldn't relax. The side of his leg was firmly pressed against hers. It had been a long time since she had danced the tango of courtship. *This is flirting, isn't it? He doesn't normally like physical contact, so I guess this is particularly unusual behaviour for him. What am I supposed to do now? If I raise the subject of Alexi and the nuclear material, he might go all cold and formal on me. Better leave it until later to ask.*

They sat in silence, immersed in the warmth of attraction. The limousine cruised downtown, towards the financial district. Mary marvelled at the compact use of space; of how the old traditional churches rubbed shoulders with the concrete and steel of modern architecture. How the avenues would terminate with an impressive landmark building, reminding visitors and residents of its colonial history.

The tyres rumbled over the tight-packed cobbles, where once a canal ran. The Broad Street Ballroom lay just ahead. A queue of several stretched limousines inched forwards, delivering their passengers into the hands of an illuminated media circus. Mary shuffled forwards on the seat. She could see a flock of cameramen, presenters and sound engineers, each with their respected equipment thrust into the attendees faces. Mary panicked. "Can we get out here, and just sort of, well, hide from them?"

"You'll be fine. No one would expect to find you here." Karan tried to affect a calm air, but failed. He seemed equally perturbed by the spectacle.

"Please?"

They alighted from the car on the side furthest from the pavement. Karan swooped down and grasped her hand. Together, they rounded the back of the limousine queue, and strode confidently along the sidewalk towards the entrance. A red carpeted area, surrounded by roped cordons created a funnel shape for the arriving dignitaries. As they approached, a tall man with cropped silver hair and smiling blue eyes was seized by the crowds. Just above the neck of his dress shirt, Mary spotted a thin cotton dressing, attached to his skin with surgical tape. The paparazzi went wild. In a feeding frenzy of reporting, stark lights, woolly microphones and hooded video cameras jostled for prime position.

"Senator! Over here! How are you feeling, senator?"

"Luca, did your life flash before your eyes?"

"Did it hurt much, senator?"

"It did smart a bit, yes, but you know what they say; you can't keep an old dog down." He gave them the entire upper register of his perfect orthodontics, canines and all.

"What did it feel like, senator?" This, from a female reporter in a low-cut dress and a thick layer of cosmetics.

Luca held out his arm and stripped off the white cotton glove covering his left hand. The reporters gasped. A delicate branching pattern of scarring traced down his wrist to the end of his index finger. "They call it Lichtenberg Flowers. I'm told they will fade as they heal. It could have been worse. At least it flashed over my skin and not through my organs. Ruined my favourite suit though." The female reporter reached out to touch him, but he snatched his hand away.

"Is that all over your body, Luca?" The female reporter arched her back in towards him so that her chest was almost in his face.

"Just from my neck to this hand."

A larger man pushed his microphone between them. "Do you think your bill will pass through the second house?"

Another shouted, "What's next for you, Senator?"

Luca took a huge step backwards, disregarding the political enquiry. "Next, is attending this function for a very worthy cause… If you'll excuse me…" A man in a black suit and a curled cable stretching from his ear bud to the back of his collar, held out his arms and herded the press back to their cordoned area. Mary and Karan slipped in through the entrance immediately behind the senator. Luca did a double take at Mary, and then proceeded to fend off a variety of well-wishers. Karan and Mary glided right through to the ballroom without fanfare or issue.

A waiter presented a platter with champagne and fruit juices to Mary. She took the alcohol.

Karan gave her an awkward smile. "Will I need to carry you home later tonight, Mary?" The inference was clear. He did not think she could hold her drink and did not want a repeat of their encounter in London.

Mary chose to ignore it. He was beginning to remind her of Parth, and that would scupper more than one pleasant evening together. "So, is there something specific you have chosen to bid upon tonight or are you just here to be seen?"

"You make me sound so mercenary. It is a part of the job, you know." He checked himself, smoothing the ill-tempered frown into a forced smile. "Mary. Let us not quarrel tonight. Come, let's examine the lots."

She took his arm once more, allowing him to sweep her through the colonnade of pillars to the fake plaster plinths supporting photos and explanations of the items for auction. Between them, a fabric vertical banner advertised the charitable cause. The eight-foot image showed a turtle swimming through a soup of sun-bleached plastic, the nylon rings of a multi-pack binder cutting into the flesh of its limbs. Purposefully graphic, the picture silenced them.

Mary nodded. "A very worthy cause."

"You should see the massive build up off the shores of some of the Indonesian islands. This is a global issue, and it will require a global solution." Karan moved towards a photograph of a Yacht, picking up the booklet to read the terms of sale.

"Someone donated a yacht?" Mary peered around Karan's shoulder.

"No, just the use of it for a season."

"I was going to say... these people have more money than sense." The moment she said it, she wished she could take it back.

"You don't fancy a trip on my yacht then?" He grinned.

"I am sorry. This is a whole other world. I don't think I could ever understand it."

They both shuffled towards the next item; a Kandinsky original, resting on a display easel. As they drew nearer, a photographer ushered Senator Luca Bonovich to the canvas. Shouting directions for him to pose, the senator stood to one side of the easel, ill at ease, and sported his genial grin.

Karan steered Mary away. "Probably a good idea to avoid media attention." He winked at her and took a large gulp of champagne.

Maybe now is a good time to ask him about Alexi, he seems relaxed enough. In her peripheral vision, Mary spied an older woman bearing down on them. She could feel her upper lip curling the closer she drew. Her one and only meeting with this prominent CEO, left Mary in no doubt about her ethics and moral standing.

"Hey, Mary. Good to see ya again." Bernice Feinstein launched herself at Mary, her hand extended and rigid.

Mary edged backwards and filled her free hand with her clutch bag. "Hello."

"Got your eye on something in particular?" Bernice lowered her arm and then flicked her head towards the exhibited lots.

"No."

"I gotta say, that Kandinsky looks damn fine. Too rich for my blood though. How about you, Shrimant Shinde? You could get it for your bathroom wall." Her attempt at humour fell flat. Karan would not bite. "I made the Giving Pledge, this year, that's in addition to the charitable donations I make on Phlaxo's behalf. That reminds me, I meant to ask you about the permits for our India campaign…"

Before she could finish her request, Karan grabbed the sleeve of her couture dinner suit and dragged her into a corner. Mary watched Karan's features transform from displeasure, to anger and then full on fury. Their discussion intense, and conducted between set jaws and gritted teeth. Bernie appeared less flustered by their conference, although even at a distance, Mary could see Bernie's pulse throbbing in her neck. Glancing around her, Mary felt exposed. The guests seemed to be clustered in cosy groups at the far end of the room. The cavernous ceilings and opulent table decorations dwarfed her tiny form. Leaving her date to his business dealings, Mary made for the relative security of the buffet table. A lavish spread which spanned the width of the hall. She picked at an avocado hors d'oeuvre, trying to appear confident among the VIP guests.

As she leaned in for a second offering, she heard a high-pitched giggle. Mary glanced around her for the source and was blinded by a pulsing red beam. The giggles grew louder. Again, she scanned the room only to be blinded a second time. Mary averted her gaze and blinked until her vision was fully restored. Turning once more, she found Senator Luca Bonovich by her side.

He pointed to a low dome shape, sticking up above the buffet table, topped with sandy hair. Mary watched as the little boy bobbed up and aimed a laser pointer at Luca's face, before dipping low to hide.

Mary nodded. "There's always one, isn't there?"

"I'm afraid so." He looked at her as though he was making an analysis. Not in admiration or disdain, but an all-encompassing sweep of her presence. "Hi, Luca Bonovich." He shook her hand, holding on for a little longer than necessary.

"Hello, I'm Mary A… just Mary."

"Good to meet you, Just Mary." His eyes roved everywhere, without shame. She turned back to the table and collected her glass. He seemed keen to prolong their discourse. "It's ah… a real nice brooch."

"Thank you. It belonged to my grandfather's grandmother, so, you know, it's pretty old."

"It's unusual. Never seen anything like it before." He swiped a full glass from a passing waiter, and then tucked his gloved hand into his trouser pocket.

Mary saw him wince with pain. "Was it wise to discharge yourself from hospital so soon?" Mary surprised herself with her own candour. It was none of her business what he chose to do.

"Maybe not. But I got a lot of irons in the fire, so to speak. I cannot afford to leave things unattended." He sank the remainder of his champagne and gestured for another.

"You must be in a lot of pain." She squinted and tilted her head away from another laser foray. "You are lucky to be alive."

Luca shrugged.

The red beam wandered down Mary's cleavage and encircled the rushed silk covering her breasts. It wavered, jogging up and down in synchrony with the little boy's laughter. Straying to her left side, the beam hit the black jewel of the brooch at an oblique angle. At first, the gemstone glowed brightly with a golden hue. As Mary twisted her torso, a massive streak of light shot from the brooch and through the air, burning a gaping hole in the canvas turtle. The flames caught quickly, filling the sultry atmosphere with blackened smoke.

Luca grabbed a jug of water from the buffet table and dowsed the flames licking up the eight-foot sign. Nothing could be done for the scorch marks on the stucco pillar behind.

Empty jug in hand, the Senator stood slack jawed at Mary. Every CEO, celebrity and politician in the building, gaped in stupefaction.

Chapter Thirteen

Five hundred or more eyes settled first on the charred remains of the charity signage, and then on Mary. For a full ten seconds, everyone was still, perplexed by the origins of the fire. Mary shifted her weight from one stiletto to the other, glowing as hot as the embers. Luca plonked down the empty jug and lunged at the little urchin with the wicked red beam.

"It's okay, everyone. A bizarre mishap with a laser pointer and the lead crystal table vases. Who would have thought it possible, eh?" Luca dragged the boy from beneath the buffet and swung him from the scruff of his jacket. The laser pointer dropped with a clatter to the floor. Guests applauded Luca's quick thinking and rapid action. The boy squirmed and writhed, kicking out and complaining, until his parents came to claim him.

"Thank you." Mary was humbled and equally confused. "But it wasn't refraction from the vases." Her utterance barely audible.

"I know. I would keep that little gem under lock and key if I were you. My gut tells me that brooch was not meant for public display." Luca tapped a waiter's shoulder. "Can you bring me some ice? Good man." He took out a cotton handkerchief from his pocket. His complexion greyed.

"Are you alright?"

Luca nodded, grabbing at the ice bucket and making his way towards the vestibule, while unbuttoning his jacket.

Mary trailed after him. He stopped outside the gents; leaning heavily on the wall, his eyes closed, his mouth pinched.

"Let me help you." Mary took the pail of ice and opened the door to the men's room. Luca rushed in and staggered to the wash basins. The two men standing at the urinals stood closer to the porcelain to shield their attributes from Mary's view.

Luca shucked off his dinner jacket. The cotton glove hampered his dexterity. He could not unbutton his dress shirt. His eyes squeezed, his brow furrowed; every attempt brought a fresh wave of agony. Mary threw down her clutch bag, and carefully unwound his bow tie, loosening the pressure on his neck. The burns wept through the lint of the bandage. Every time he swallowed the surgical tape on his neck pulled at his skin. The wound had begun healing within the cotton weave. Each movement Luca made, tore the wound open further. One gentle gesture at a time, Mary undressed the senator until he stood bronzed and naked to the waist. With a handful of ice chips bundled into his handkerchief, she cooled his fractal scars with light dabs, from his index finger, along his forearm and finally his shoulder. The neck wound required the lightest of touches. Mary peeled the tape from the bandage and inspected the inside edges of the cotton wadding, its yellowed patches evidence of further oozing.

"It needs to come off, but it will really hurt when it does. And it could do with a thorough cleaning. You really ought to go back to the emergency room for sterile treatment." Mary replaced the surgical tape and tamped it down against his skin.

"Can't, there's too much at stake right now. Just rip it off for me."

"No, it will get infected. You need proper medical care."

"Come on, Mary. I did you a solid, payback time."

"That is crazy. You'll end up with septicaemia… blood poisoning, on top of everything else."

"I have to keep going, I have a schedule; really important events. There's a green sticker with a white cross on it behind you. That has to be first aid supplies. Patch me up, and I'll be forever in your debt." Her stubbornness faded when he produced the most alarming smile and took her soft hand in his. "Please, Just Mary?"

How could she resist those mischievous blue eyes? She could swear they were faceted, glinting as brightly as Grandma Phebe's brooch. "Fine. But don't go suing me if you drop dead from some nasty secondary infection. Not that I have any money for you to take."

"How could I sue my very own Florence Nightingale?" His comedic tone dissolved in a spasm of pain. "Don't suppose you could get me a nip of Brandy while you're at it, could you?"

Mary grabbed the first man to enter the rest room since the two others had departed and commanded him to go and fetch strong alcohol, preferably brandy. The man, at first bewildered, thought it a charming eccentricity of the little British woman in the men's room issuing directives. He disappeared for no more than a couple minutes, returning with two tumblers of the establishment's finest. By the time the man handed her the alcohol, she had unpacked the first aid box and donned latex gloves over her glamorous nails. Well-wishers and noisy onlookers gathered at the door. Mary shooed them away. Among them was Karan. He stood on tip toe, shouting her name above the chatter. Tasked with the job of keeping everyone at bay, her new errand boy closed the door and stood guard.

"I really don't understand why you couldn't get a professional to do this. You could at least have a local anaesthetic." Nervous rambling. She knew it, but couldn't stop herself. Stalling, she lined up the sterile bandages and fresh tape along the vanity unit.

"What's the time?"

"Oh, I shouldn't worry about that. Sounds like they have delayed the auction until you are fit to attend - you being a senator and all." The jibe felt small, spiteful. Why was she behaving in this petulant way?

"They can't do that, it'll ruin everything. Tell them to go ahead."

"What's the hurry? Besides, after I have plucked up the courage to rip this off, it should be a quick turnaround. Remember, it's okay if you want to cry..."

Luca began to laugh. Loud, self-assured guffaws. When he threw his head back, Mary leaned forwards, grabbed the cotton wadding and yanked. Luca's laughter transmuted into a howl, an intake of rapid breath and a series of expletives that made Mary cringe.

"Sorry." She looked at the remnants of his blistered flesh, still attached to the wadding. His neck was a mess. The impact of the lightning strike missed his jugular by a mere fraction. Medics had clearly debrided the blackened, necrotic skin, leaving raw, unprotected tissue. The fine tracery of scarring radiated from this wound in delicate tendrils of red welts. It could almost be mistaken for an elaborate tattoo. "It really needs a saline flush. The best I can offer is some of this antiseptic spray." She waved the aerosol from the kit. "Any chance of an allergic reaction?" Luca shook his head. Sweat shone on his temples, dampening his hair. She grasped his hand with her left and let him squeeze it tight, as she sprayed the stinging powder coating on his skin.

"Nearly done." She said, tearing open the sterile strips and laying the gauze and wadding across his neck. "Hold this here." He did as she commanded, while she attached fresh tape to secure the bandage. "I think we can dispense with the tie, don't you?" Luca smiled, and raised her hand to his lips, never taking his eyes from hers.

A splash of cold water, a quick tidy up and they were good to go. Mary held on to the cotton glove while he buttoned his shirt over his toned stomach muscles and pectorals. Mary could feel the heat rising from inside.

"Come on, Just Mary. We need to get a move on." He took the glove from her. Restored to his former ebullience, Luca charged through the rest room door to the waiting crowd.

"Why do we need to get a move on?"

He didn't answer her. She slipped out of the men's room behind Luca and tried to mingle with his entourage. The questions began immediately.

"Do you need us to call an emergency team? Are you fit for service, senator? Will this prevent you from presenting your bill to the house next week? Have you got the votes, Luca?" and so on, in a barrage of interrogating questions mixed with sycophantic platitudes. He slipped the cotton glove back onto his left hand and held both aloft. The group quietened down.

"I am fine, thanks to my new friend, Just Mary…" He looked around at the faces before him. "Oh, where did she go? Anyway, a little medical pit stop, and I am ready to bid on something expensive and unnecessary. Can we get back to the auction, ladies and gentlemen? It is, after all, why we are all here tonight. I will answer your questions regarding my proposals tomorrow."

Karan pushed through the spectators and approached Mary. "I looked everywhere for you, until someone said that you were in the men's room with the senator for California."

"Yes, what of it?"

"What was I to think? UN Ambassador and Indian royalty not enough for you? You go chasing after the Chief of the Environmental Protection Agency."

"I didn't chase after him. He was suffering, I helped. He was struck by lightning you know. Besides, you went off with your buddy from the Extermination Squad… oops, sorry, I mean the CEO of pharmaceutical giant, Phlaxo. What was it this time? The cost of sterilising little girls was too much so she agreed to drowning puppies instead?"

"Don't be like this, Mary. Yes, we argued, but it's not what you think."

A gong resonated throughout the ballroom, indicating a start to the auction. Luca's crowd dissipated, wandering through to their allotted tables. More glasses of champagne were delivered as the compere took centre stage and adjusted the microphone. The first of the lots sold quickly. A warm up, staged to whip the crowds into a fever. It was a luxury safari holiday to Kenya, capturing the wildlife through a digital lens with an expert photographer. A woman in green taffeta and hair like spun sugar outbid a gnarly business executive by ten thousand dollars.

The second, third and fourth lots followed in much the same way. Mary yawned. Karan's diplomatic flag was at full mast again. He smiled, replied in curt sentences and nodded at the appropriate moments, but the Karan she had met beneath the arches of The Grand Temple in the estate grounds at Ditchley in Oxford, had gone. There seemed little point in explaining her actions. She doubted he would have listened anyway. *No matter how hard we try we seem to always end in a fight. I owe him so much. He has been nothing but kind and generous towards me and I repay him with snippy retorts.* Mary twisted in her seat to face Karan. Her movements caught his attention. She lay her hand over his and leaned into his ear. "I'm sorry. I don't want to quarrel either."

He smiled his reply and patted her hand with metered affection.

The next lot was a diamond encrusted tiara, bequeathed to the charity along with a substantial number of necklaces and bracelets. The recently deceased patron had written her wishes for the auction into her will. The garish pieces sat on cushioned pillows, encased in glass boxes and wired with trip alarms for protection. From a side door, a young lady in a red gown, sashayed to the tiara stand, waited for the guard to unlock the alarm mechanism and lifted the headpiece high above the front row of tables. The crowd murmured their praise for the obscene item, and the bids commenced.

The compere slowed the bidding to enunciate clearly how many hundreds of thousands of dollars the guests were pledging. With each rising bid, the crowd cooed their approval, egging the buyers on in their gambits.

That was when the first masked man entered the hall. Jack boots, camouflage fatigues and a full cover latex hood, fashioned to resemble the president of the United States of America. The host stammered, his chin wobbled and he stepped back from the podium.

"What is happening?" Karan said, rising from his chair to achieve a better view. The masked man fired a volley of shots from his semi-automatic weapon at the ceiling. Karan sat down, ducking his head behind the woman to his right. Plaster fell in ugly lumps onto the tables, sending crockery and silverware crashing. Guests coughed through the dust clouds, and moved away from the broken glass and debris.

Three more masked men, and one woman, entered through the waiters' entrance, each of them carrying similar firearms and shoving numerous staff into the hall. They marched themselves around the edges of the ballroom and aimed at random people seated before them. The leader strode to the podium, flicking the barrel of his gun at the compere. "Move!"

The host scampered down the podium steps. A dark stain of liquid seeped down the leg of his suit.

The gunman took hold of the microphone from its stand. "Do exactly as you are told and no one will get hurt." The murmurs grew in volume. These people were not used to taking orders. This was not Mary's first encounter with malicious gunmen. Her heart raced, but she kept her wits about her. There was little she could do to help matters, but stay cool-headed and comply with demands. Karan trembled at her side. She stole a glance over to Luca. Unlike those on his table, there was no outward appearance of hysteria. *Perhaps he has a military background. So many of those political types seem to over here. Why is he looking at his watch?* Before Mary could fathom an answer to her own musings, the leader of the group stepped up.

"First and foremost, shut the fuck up. All of you." The gunman yelled. It had the desired effect. Old wealth and newly powerful, all did as they were instructed. "Leave your purses, phones and shit on the tables and line up along that wall." He turned to the guard on stage. "Don't be a hero. Hand over the firearm and keys." The guard unclipped the gun holster and retractable key chain from his belt, and passed them over. "Now go stand over there."

Karan, Mary and all the other dignitaries jostled and shambled in a disorderly mass to the farthest wall. The single armed woman made a point of cracking the butt of her semi-automatic into Luca's shoulder blade. He fell forwards onto Karan, who braced himself to steady the senator's gait.

"Are you alright, Senator Bonovich?" Karan enquired. His innate manners manifesting even in times of peril.

"Shut it! Speak again and I will fire." She waved the end of the weapon beneath Karan's nose. Chastised, he stared at the floor. The trembling multiplied into violent shakes. Mary grasped his hand tight.

The gunmen had assigned duties, and got to work fast. The woman patrolled the line of elite guests. Mary watched one man take a plastic sack and scoop up all the mobile phones, purses, wallets and bags from the tables. Another systematically emptied each of the display plinths of valuables, while another zipped the Kandinsky into a portfolio. Waiting until the woman with the gun reached the end of the line, Mary unhooked Grandma Phebe's brooch from her dress, and dropped it down her cleavage into her underwear. *Knives, brooches, spilt food and drink. Let's just hope they don't make us strip. They can have everything else, but not Phebe's brooch.* Still Mary held onto Karan's hand. He gave her a brief look of incredulity, at the risk she had taken to conceal her inheritance.

The gun woman returned to the centre of the line. She took immense pleasure in goading the senator. Shoving him backwards with her gun until his head connected with the wall behind, before continuing her patrol. The man with the portfolio, leaned the Kandinsky against the door frame of the exit and returned with a small fabric bag. Starting at one end of the line, he gestured towards the woman's ruby necklace and matching earrings. "Off" was all he needed to say. The woman immediately, removed the items, dropping them into the bag.

"You want my rings too?" She said. The man tutted and sighed. She peeled each ring from her fingers, trying to force the tightest band over her wrinkled knuckle. Stripped of all her baubles, he moved on to the next in line. As the gun man walked along the row, guests made ready with their treasured belongings. The woman with the semi-automatic shadowed her colleague, aiming at each of the attendee as they disgorged their Cartier, Tiffany's and Patek Philippe watches and jewels into the bag.

The pair were closing in on Mary's right-hand side. Karan let go of her hand and crossed his wrists together in front of him. Mary peeked down. He was trying to flick the clasp of his watch open with the nail of his thumb. It made a metallic clink, the strap sagged and the watch slid down his hand. For all his charm, Karan was not subtle. His attempts to pocket his watch was noticed.

"Hey, hey! What's this one up to? Show me your hands." The woman said, aiming her firearm at Karan's chest. "Come on, show me your hands."

"It's nothing…" Karan let go of the watch, it made another loud chinking noise as it hit the bottom of his jacket pocket. Karan displayed his empty hands. "See, I have nothing."

Mary knew what was coming, she could sense the antagonism building within the sadistic woman.

"Didn't I tell you to shut the fuck up? Get whatever is in your pocket and show me." She pointed the end of the semi-automatic from his jacket side to his chest.

"It's nothing…"

The woman took a pace forwards, raising the weapon to shoulder height. At a distance of no more than six feet, there was no chance of her missing. Karan closed his mouth. His eyes widened and fixed. The fear paralysed him. Mary touched Karan's sleeve, turning to face him. Luca edged closer to Karan from the opposite side, delivering an imploring look to Mary. A look which said, *don't interfere; don't involve yourself.* Still Karan blanched on the spot.

"Last chance. Give me what you got." She meant business, Mary could see that. The woman's fingers twitched against the trigger.

Karan was rooted, unable to move.

"You asked for it." The woman fired.

"No!" Luca lunged, holding his hands up to push Mary away. A single shot rang out. The bullet's path veered away from Karan in a wide sweeping arc, and bored a clean hole in the side of her silk gown, until it embedded deep in her abdomen with a squelching thud.

Chapter Fourteen

Mary swayed and fell backwards against the wall. The initial pressure in her gut now burned in a narrow channel right through to her spine. A warm wet trickle flowed down her right hip and leg. Blood pooled at her feet. Within moments, the numbness in her abdomen receded, and an aching pain took hold. As she slumped to the floor, Karan rushed to cushion her fall.

"Fuck. Grab what you can... get going." The leader fired another volley at the ceiling, picked up the Kandinsky, and ran. The other gun toting criminals followed suit, each swiping their spoils and leaving via the servant's entrance. Luca took his cell phone from his jacket and dialled the emergency services. He sat on the cool floor alongside Karan, who cradled Mary across his lap. Mary hyperventilated with shock. The hypoxia was dizzying. Guests yelled, screamed and cried, some crowded around Mary, others ran for the cloakroom facilities.

"I think you should lay her flat." Luca announced.

"Don't tell me what to do. This is your fault." Karan snarled.

"How is it my fault? What did I do?"

"If you hadn't donated that painting, they would not have thought to have raided the place." Karan's teeth gritted, his voice reduced to a hiss.

"Really? And the millions of dollars' worth of jewellery didn't attract them at all? Anyway, this is your fault. If you hadn't tried to stash your watch from that manic bitch, she wouldn't have fired on you."

"If you hadn't interfered, the bullet would have missed Mary."

"I didn't do anything."

"How did it miss me then? She aimed the gun right at me?"

Mary tried to move. She grunted and moaned, and then inhaled. "Um, guys. I can't feel my right leg."

"Oh, this is bad, really bad. Should I lie you down or keep you still like this?" Karan asked, but Mary did not answer. She was retreating into her thoughts, battling against the worst case scenarios playing out inside her mind. Karan held on, trying to keep as still as possible.

"We need to stop the blood flow or she'll bleed out before we can get her to hospital." Luca grabbed a couple of table napkins, scrunched them up into a ball and pressed them against Mary's side. She cried out in agony. "I'm so sorry, Mary. This was never meant to happen."

The police arrived before the ambulance crews. Filing in through the main entrance, they were afforded the VIP treatment. Cameras clicked and whirred, reporters clamoured for attention, shooting questions to the plain clothes detectives lingering on the red carpet. Medics arrived shortly after, pulling the gurney stacked high with medical equipment in green bags.

The ballroom was a scene of total mayhem. Scene of Crime Officers issued orders to hysterical women and quarrelsome men. Local Enforcement Officers swept through the entire building, directing the guests back to the ballroom. One uniformed man approached a plain clothes officer, who appeared to be in charge. “Sir, we have a body in the kitchen.” His tone grave and quiet.

“Show me.” The man in the long coat, left the medics to work on Mary and headed for the waiters’ exit.

Mary drifted in and out of comprehension. One moment she was lucid, the next, unaware of her surroundings bearing the pain. Karan held on so tightly, that paramedics had to force open his arms to release her. In the jerked movements, Mary slipped further down his knees, landing with a stomach clenching grunt on the hard floor.

Luca shoved Karan aside. “You are not fit to take care of her.” And to the medics, he said, “Mary complained of loss of feeling in her right leg earlier.”

With their swift and experienced care, the medics braced her neck with a plastic collar, and tipped her onto a rigid backboard. They hoisted her onto the gurney as though she was made of feathers. Karan dashed after them, wiping the moisture from his face with a swipe of his hand.

Luca’s long legs outpaced him. “I’ll go with her. You stay and give details to the police.”

“You will not. She is my responsibility. I will go.” Karan scurried faster, grabbing onto the framework of the gurney. As they all reached the doorway, the detective called after them.

“Senator Bonovich, sir. I need you to come with me. We believe that the fatality is one of your security team.”

Luca huffed, but stopped walking, watching Karan fly from the building with a sideways glance of triumph thrown in his direction. “Tell Mary that I will get there as soon as I can.”

The bump down the kerbside onto the cobbles, jarred Mary alert. Shallow breaths rattled her abdomen further.

The blood congealed, sticking the silk to her skin. Loaded in the back of the ambulance, Karan stepped in and sat on a folding seat attached to the cabin wall. The sirens were activated immediately, forging a path through the steady traffic of downtown Manhattan.

With thick cotton wadding plugging the gaping hole in her abdomen, Mary lay as still as her heaving and shuddering body would allow. All she could discern was Karan's presence, clearing his throat with a nervous cough and the medic jabbing her arm with a cannula needle. In her woozy state, she was aware of her brother establishing a telepathic link into her mind. From over three thousand miles away, she heard him enthuse with the latest piece of their family puzzle. His excited message, allowed her to deduce that Dan had persuaded Yelena to give up their grandfather's personal effects, and that one of those items was another journal. The passage Dan read to her was troubling in the extreme. Among the phrases of chaos, Mary picked out the fated word, *premonition*. It stung her almost as much as the bullet had. She tried to listen to the warnings and the concerned tone of her brother, but she could not will her mind to concentrate on anything except that one excerpt: *"I cannot recall a moment within the premonition which could indicate a potential date for this catastrophic event, but from the technology I saw, it will be soon. More importantly, we must be prepared..."*

Reeling from the pain and the disconnected memories of her grandfather, Mary momentarily lost Dan's transmission. *How could this be? Why would Grampy keep this enormous secret from me? Did he really have the ability to see into future events?* Tears prickled the inside of her sinus cavity. She tried to hold them back, but they escaped the confines of her eyelids and streaked across her temples to the backboard.

Dan reconnected the neural link. "*Mary, what's happening? Tell me what is going on...*"

More than anything, she wanted to tell him. Have her brother come and protect her like he had in the London hospital. To reassure her and hold her hand, make her feel that she would never be alone again. But what could he do to help from England but worry? She had to tell him, it might be her last chance to convey how much he had meant to her since they found one another. But how could she inform him without inducing alarm, and a headlong rush to the airport? *"Now is not really a good time, Dan. I've been shot."*

"What? You're having a laugh. Don't tease me, Mary. This is serious."

"So am I. Look, I am okay. I'm on the way to the emergency room now. I will get in touch again when things calm down a bit."

"No way, I am booking a flight right now..."

"Dan, really. It'll be okay. You stay there and take care of your mum. She needs you."

"Well, yes, she does, but I am sure we can make some sort of arrangement..."

"Dan..."

"Mmm?"

"Stay there. I will keep you informed."

"Right, well if you are sure?"

"I am. And... you know I love you right?"

"Me too, little sister."

Mary severed the connection, and sobbed great, fitful tears. They hadn't had enough time. One summer to form the unique bonds of siblings had made her happy beyond reckoning. He had pulled her from the depths following Pip's murder, the result of another stray bullet. He had saved her from the clutches of MI6 agents, twice. He was her anchor. The thought of never seeing him again was more than she could take. The seven-block journey to the Presbyterian hospital on Gold Street, culminated in a jolting motion as the vehicle reversed onto a ramp. The medic at her side, stood up, open the back doors and gestured for Karan to disembark. He directed him towards the check in desk, just as a team of surgeons and nurses scrambled to unload Mary from the waggon.

Mary drifted in and out of consciousness, the blood loss manifesting as severe weakness. Her lips tinged blue with oxygen depletion. Keeping track of reality, of time passing, was an effort and inaccurate. She was aware of feeling constricted on the backboard, of her head and neck completely immobile, of being carried and passed from place to place in jerky motions, like a theme park ride. In one of her more lucid moments, she heard; "Need to get onto the mid-town hospitals, see if they've got any AB neg in stock." Machines came and went around her. Some buzzed, others beeped, another cleared the room of all personnel. There were now two intravenous lines into her body, each pumping fluids of different viscosities and colour.

The pain was replaced by a sensation of lightness; a peculiar drug induced euphoria. A face loomed over her. *Was that Parth?* She squinted, blinking to clear the fog. *No, not Parth. He's like him, but better.* A second face appeared. *Ooh, he's nice too. Lovely teeth, dashing. I wish I could scratch my nose.* As her body adjusted to the increased level of opiates in her system, she grew more aware of the men at her bedside. Their bickering had not abated.

"What are you suggesting? There is nothing improper going on. She needed help, I provided it, and continue to do so. I should take it." It was Karan's voice, loud with a clear and confident intonation.

"What are you saying, you met her once before and now you are her benefactor? Oh, come on… could it be any fishier?" Luca scoffed.

"You think because you donated your blood to her, that it gives you some rights? You only met her a few hours ago."

"And because you've known her longer you're to be trusted? I am a United States Senator, my friend. I will keep the brooch safe, you can be assured of that."

Mary opened her eyes wide. Her lips were gluey and her mouth parched. Luca noticed her immediately.

"Hi there. Remember me?"

She attempted a nod, but the head strap prevented all movement. Swallowing was difficult. She croaked a weak "yes." Clearing her throat, she tried again. "Yes." A nurse leaned across her chest, pushed down on her chin and swabbed her tongue with a tiny sponge stick. "Thank you."

"I can't get you a drink, Mary," the nurse replied. "You're gonna need surgery. I'll be back to prep you in a minute." Her face disappeared from view, replaced by Luca's.

"How bad is it?" She asked.

Luca looked towards Karan. The nurse was asking him about insurance. Mary could hear their voices growing quieter and their steps clicking against the solid flooring. Karan had gone with the nurse to deal with the paperwork. Only Luca remained in view.

"Tell me straight. No sugar coating it, Luca."

"The x-ray shows that the bullet is lodged against your spine. They're not sure that it can be removed without causing further damage." He inhaled, opening his mouth to say more, but checked himself.

"Go on…"

His brows pinched together. "They got to repair a tear in your uterus. You're bleeding internally so they got to go in anyway, but if they can't remove the bullet, there is a chance that you'll never walk again." His face disappeared from her view. He coughed and sniffed, and then leaned over her once again.

"I see." Mary exhaled, a long slow thoughtful breath. "I am guessing from the discomfort in my lower regions, that there would also be issues with incontinence."

Luca gave her a piteous look. "I'm so sorry. This should never have happened to you." He touched her. The spark was immediate. An electric shock spread across her forearm.

"Sorry." He attempted a grin. "Static."

The nurse returned with a syringe, filled with a brown liquid. She removed the safety cap, inserted the end into the valve of the intravenous tube and squeezed. "This will make you sleepy and relaxed, before we take you down to theatre."

"I'll stay with her until you're ready to take her, nurse." Luca pulled the visitor chair across the floor and sat closer.

"Just don't go upsetting her, you hear me?" Her footsteps faded upon her retreat. "And get that dressing changed on your neck, while you're here."

The drugs seeped into her veins, slowing the world down into a dull illusion. She could almost pretend it was all a bad dream, that she would wake any moment to discover her grandfather plonking a hot cuppa down on her nightstand. This was not a dream. This was her life now. Assassins and agents, heists and deadly hospital trips. This could very well be her last hospital visit.

"Mary…" the voice dissipated into silence.

"Mmm?" She struggled to open her eyes.

Luca stood up and angled his face to match hers. "What is it?"

Her mouth wouldn't work, the drowsiness eroding her senses. *I thought he called my name. Dan, perhaps.* She listened again, keen to discover the owner of the voice with the strange cadence. Her eyelids drooped. Luca still loomed over her. He did have the most beguiling eyes, dark blue with a violet band around his irises. Salt and pepper hair framing his distinguished forehead. *I do like those little canine teeth. I hope I get to see them again.*

The surgical tape holding the protective wadding tugged at her skin. *What is he doing?* She could feel his hot palm laid against the wound site. The pressure barely registering, the pain suppressed by the analgesic drugs. There was a mild tingling which grew in intensity, and then warmth. Deep within her belly, she sensed movement. Her tissues pulled taught against a solid lump. By slow and gradual increments, the hard object burrowed through her clipped organs and stopped close to the surface of her shredded skin. She tensed her abdomen, the hard surface knocked against the nerve endings. Pain coursed through her entire torso, the drugs unable to dampen the synaptic transmissions.

Her skin was clammy, her pallor grey. Luca replaced the bandage. "I am, so sorry. See you when you get back, Just Mary." His face disappeared from her view. She could hear his footsteps moving away.

No wait...don't go. What did you do? I have questions, I can't... For a single moment, before the sedatives took away her awareness, she mustered a tiny vestige of strength. Straining against the tight straps of the backboard, both of her legs moved.

Chapter Fifteen

The post-op waiting area was stifling. Mary gagged on the tube obstructing her trachea, her arms flailing and thrashing in agitation. A male nurse with a narrow face and a sweet smile, grabbed at her hands. "It's okay, sugar. I'm gonna take it out…don't fight me." He pulled the tube in one swift movement, the rigid end rattled against her teeth. Mary gasped, coughed and flaked out unconscious once more.

When she came to, she found herself in a single room, wearing a neat patterned gown and surrounded by orchids and daisies. She lifted her head from the pillow and immediately wished she hadn't. Her entire abdomen ached as though she had been kicked by a street thug. In her hand, she found a plastic casing surrounding a large red button. She traced the attached cable back up the fluid stand to the morphine pump and gave it a press. The sensation was frightening. As the drug entered her arm, she could feel the burn coursing through her veins and across her chest. It took her breath away.

Despite the bright airy windows and the transparent door section through to the nurse desk, she had an uneasy feeling. One which took her back to a disused cottage hospital in Britain, with large bolts to keep her securely inside. A nurse made eye contact with her through the panel. She immediately picked up the telephone and made a call. Mary wished she could lip read. The woman did not take her eyes off her for the entire duration of the conversation. The nurse replaced the receiver and entered Mary's room.

"Hello, my name is Chantelle. Can you tell me your name and where you are?" The nurse adjusted the flow rate on her IV and made a note on Mary's chart.

"I'm Mary. I have no idea where I am. It's somewhere in Manhattan. That's all I can tell you."

The nurse chuckled. "You got everyone talking round here. There's a bunch of 'em waiting for you by my desk. Are you feeling up to seeing them? One of them is Senator Bonovich. Girl, I would hock my granny for a date with him."

"Why are they all talking about me?"

"That's what the Surgical Chief wants to discuss with you. Got him all in a sweat too. Shall I let them in?"

"You haven't told me how the surgery went?"

"That's just it, some of it never went. Didn't need to." The nurse flicked the bedsheets over and tucked them into the frame.

Mary could guess as to what she was referring and chose not to press the matter. "What about my uterus?"

"Oh, they stitched that back up. Only a nick in the wall as it turned out. Ain't you surprised about the bullet?"

"What about it?"

"Prep team went to swab you down with antiseptic and the bullet fell out of your side! Never seen anything like it before." She waved through the glass panel at Karan and Luca loitering outside. They bundled in and each took a side of the bed. The nurse hovered, arranging the flower pots and gaping at the senator.

Mary peered up at Luca, waiting for an explanation for his actions. He beamed back at her, content to remain silent.

Karan broke the deadlock. “It’s wonderful news, is it not?”

“The walking again and not being incontinent, yes, fantastic. How do you suppose that happened, Luca?” She maintained eye contact. He did not flinch. Not a hint of duplicity lurked in his features. He just went on smiling at her.

Karan moved closer and lowered his voice. “You mean the bullet working its way out of your wound?”

Mary nodded.

“You used your electromagnetic abilities, didn’t you?” Karan frowned. “You did, didn’t you?”

“No, I didn’t. Luca? Are you going to tell him, or shall I?”

“Tell him what?” Luca looked puzzled.

“That you removed the bullet.”

“I did what now? That’s hilarious.” His snort turned into an infectious laugh. He leaned on the bed frame, as if this humour made him too weak to support his own weight. Even Karan managed a titter. “Aww.” Luca drooped his bottom lip. “We shouldn’t make fun of her. They are some mighty powerful drugs served up here. I could do with a dose or two myself.” Karan summoned his personal secretary into the room. “Ah, Gupta. I want you to arrange for a permanent medical presence for Mary’s suite at The Plaza, from the moment she is discharged from here.”

“Certainly, Shrimant Shinde.” Gupta dipped his head to his employer, and then turned to Mary. “I am very glad that you are through the worst, madam.” Again, he bowed his head in respect.

“Thank you. You are very kind.” She said.

Gupta swung his tablet PC up onto his forearm and immediately began one finger typing at speed as he left the room.

Despite her desire to steer the conversation back around to Luca's involvement in her recovery, a more pressing matter came to the fore. Behind her visitors, Mary could see one uniformed and two plain clothes officers talking to the nurse at her desk.

The men noticed Mary's dismay. A quick peek through the window and they each comprehended her fear.

Karan turned to the senator. "A chance for you to make a name for yourself." His raised brow and hint of smugness was a challenge.

"I already have a name, Shrimant Shinde, and one which packs a punch in this great country. Leave this to me." Luca straightened up, slipped the cotton glove from his scarred hand and held it to his chest in full view, as he strolled through the door.

Karan skipped around the bedside to the visitors chair and sat close to Mary. "Mary, you should not trust Senator Bonovich. He is not what he says he is. I have Intel on him and his dealings which is highly suspicious."

"Intel from corporate pirate, Bernie Feinstein? I can't imagine what damning information she would concoct about an environmentally conscious politician who strives for an increase in alternative energies. He has got to be rarer than hens' teeth. What, did his true philanthropy disrupt her bogus one?"

"Hens' teeth? No, none of that. The intelligence came from a contact of mine at the UN."

"I'm more interested in what your contacts found out about The Summerfield Retreat in New Jersey. Did you alert the authorities about the nuclear material?"

"Mary, I am serious. Bonovich may seem all sweetness, but I assure you that it is only skin deep."

"And you don't think that your assertions could be biased at all?"

Karan's features flashed with a pained contortion, before settling back into his diplomatic veneer. A forced smile flourished. "Who am I to judge. You must do as you see fit, Mary, but know this, I warned you." He stood up and walked around the foot of her bed. "If you'll excuse me, I have an important call to make."

As he reached the door, Mary called to him. "I am grateful, Karan, truly. You have been so kind to me, I don't know how I will ever repay you."

"I do not expect repayment. Please remember that."

He left. Mary could just make out the back of his dinner jacket through the glass as he exited the department. Gupta followed on behind, engrossed in his tablet computer. A little part of her weakened. How could she have treated him with such disdain? *I am a horrible person. Just because he reminds me of Parth, it does not give me licence to abuse his kindness. What if I never see him again? I will never be able to apologise.* Acid rose and burned her oesophagus. *Must tell Dan that I'm okay, he'll be out of his wits with worry, bless him.* In a rapid linkage with her brother, Mary conveyed the news of her survival, and promised to fully update him of events as soon as she knew more. She felt his relief wash over her as though it was her own, such was the closeness of their bond. As she allowed the telepathic transmission to decouple, she felt his absence acutely. She was an injured fledgling in a wide and uncompromising world. He was all the family she had left, and he was too far away to provide her with a sense of security.

Mary looked about the hospital room. The orchids were everywhere; large pots of mosses and bark, balanced on every surface in her room. The waxy fronds were multicoloured and gaudy. It was as though they were trying too hard to be beautiful. For all their exotic charm, it cheapened them. A single vase of daisies stood on the nightstand. There was a handwritten card leaning against the base. It said: *Like the meadows at Ditchley. K.* Mary rubbed her forehead, inwardly chastising herself.

Luca returned, pushing a wheelchair which supported a large paper carrier bag. He beamed his empty smile. "Well, I managed to delay the cops, but not for long. They will want to speak with you about the shooting, and then there will be awkward questions regarding your identity. That is supposing that they are not already aware of your infamy."

Mary took a sharp breath. "You know about me?"

"This is the United States of America, Mary. Land of opportunity and saturated surveillance. LEO's might not know you yet, but you can guarantee that you are on the FEDs radar." He pulled out a fluffy cotton robe from the bag and held it up by the lapels.

Mary was dumbfounded. Why would a lauded senator assist a felon? Had he known who she was right from the beginning? Had he engineered their meeting? She couldn't see how, unless Karan only pretended to dislike Luca, which she doubted. How could Luca have known that she would attend the charity auction? Unless Gupta had registered her name when the invitation was extended, but that would have been as Sedgewell, not Arora. She inched closer to the edge of the bed, cradling her lower abdomen against the impact of movement. He disconnected the bag of fluids from the morphine pump, and then from the stand. Raising a metal armature from the rear of the wheelchair, he slid the bag through one side of the robe and hooked it to the bracket.

Groggy, she threaded one arm at a time through the sleeves. “Where are we going?”

“Home to California. You’ll love it.”

“But what about Karan, and my things at The Plaza?” His voice was a delayed echo inside her head, the anaesthetic lingering and clouding her reason.

He gently urged her to sit in the wheelchair with his hands pressing down on her shoulders. “I’ll getcha new stuff.” He spun the chair around, pushed her out of the room and down the corridor to the elevators.

She tried to stand up, balking from the pain. “I have to get my satchel, and the brooch…oh god, where’s my brooch? I had it on me last night…”

“Stop worrying, it’s safe and sound. I have it.” The elevator pinged its arrival and opened the doors. “And I’ll buy you a new satchel.”

“Not like that one. My grandfather bought it for me.”

A car waited for them at the kerbside to the main entrance. Another large man in a black suit, with the curly wire of an ear piece trailing to his collar, opened the passenger door for her. She turned to Luca. “I am sorry about your security man. I heard the detectives saying that he was killed last night.”

“Thanks. He was a good man. I will pay my respects to his family as soon as we get back.”

Mary slowly climbed into the spacious town car, and shuffled over to allow Luca in beside her. The bodyguard slammed the door, which wobbled the vehicle on its shock absorbers, and then made his way to the front passenger seat.

“Please can I have my brooch?” She hung the fluid bag on the suit hook above the door post.

“Yeah, sure, when we get there. It’s packed in my luggage.”

Mary was not sure why this response irked her so. He knew of the jewel's peculiar properties. If he had wanted to steal it, he need only leave her at the mercy of Law Enforcement Officers at the hospital and make off with her inheritance. Why was he being so squirrelly?

As they pulled away down the street, Mary felt a pang of sadness. A sorrow borne of unfinished business and trampled feelings. What would Karan think of her now? She tried to convince herself that there were no other options open to her, but it wouldn't stick. Why did she go with Luca so easily, without a murmur of protest? It boiled down to instinct. He was like her. He knew it, she knew it. Only time spent together would uncover the extent of his abilities. And, if Karan was reluctant to help her to discover what was happening at The Summerfield Retreat, perhaps the Senator of California would instead.

Mary turned to look at him. His features were so symmetrical, his countenance calm and self-assured. He removed the cotton glove and flexed his hand. The tracery of scars was still angry. "Are you in much pain?" She asked.

He held up his strong, masculine hand and examined the welts. "A bit. Less than before. Aren't we a couple of old invalids?" He laughed. The wrinkles bunched up around those impish eyes, drawing her gaze into his soul. The temptation was too great. She had to know what he was thinking. Did his future plans include her? Within that protracted glance, Mary tried to lock on to his consciousness. To forge a tether into his stream of thoughts and extract all she could. Projecting her will towards him, she concentrated hard. Her thoughts attempted to synchronise to his fluctuating wavelength, but it slipped by her like a swarm of eels, slithering around her connection. Perplexed, Mary halted her foray into his mind. She frowned. Luca's grin widened.

Was that just a coincidence? Did she fail because she was weakened by the post-operative stress on her body, or was he fully aware of her abilities and knew how to block them? One side of his mouth turned up in a cavalier curl. He had her measure. Her secrets were laid bare. The internet had taken care of her more visible assets, now he knew her strength with mind reading. She was no match for his blockade. The realisation unsettled her.

Over the last few horrifying weeks, her abilities had given her a confidence unlike ever before. An odd comfort in knowing that she would be able to blast her way out of most unpleasant situations. She had finally learnt how to protect herself. This new development silenced her on the journey back to the airport. Luca seemed to bask in his triumph, allowing her an undisturbed hour or so of contemplation. He made telephone calls to assistants, tracked data on his laptop and wrote notes for an upcoming speech to the senate. Mary wrapped her robe around her bare legs and tucked them up along the back seat, watching him. He did not seem to mind the audience. He gazed at her every now and again, accompanying it with a dazzling smile; the one he reserved for publicity photos and reporters.

The town car by-passed the airport terminal and drove along a slip road, turning directly towards the hangars for privately owned jets. Luca packed away his gadgets and helped Mary out of the car onto the asphalt. The wind stung her legs and tousled her hair. He led her to the small metal treads at the jet entrance, and steadied her ascent.

"As soon as we take off, I'll wrap you in a warm blanket. There's a tonne of clothes at the house. They'll keep you going for now."

The swanky jet taxied, took off at an alarming incline and eventually levelled off in the clouds. The seat-belt light extinguished and Luca called the flight attendant and asked for a blanket. Cocooned in wool, Mary lay back in the reclining leather seat, and watched Luca conduct his business affairs, thirty-six thousand feet above the ground. Scattered papers rested in little stacks on the folding table, on seats and on the side of his leather briefcase. Tiny fluorescent labels directed his attention to sections requiring his signature, others pointed out potential conflicts in his various campaigns, and some were attached to glossy brochures of luxury items for sale.

One prominent lever arch folder, stood tall with around four inches of A4 paper, enclosed within its bindings. Colour coded tabs poked out at the edges, delineating raw data from summaries. Luca flicked through its contents. His concentration manifested in squinted looks into the distance, followed by a habitual rubbing of his chin. Mary studied his features, from her half-closed eyes, for more than an hour. The volume of paperwork he could consume was impressive to say the least. He was no slouch in the due diligence department. Mary ached to broach the topic of his latent gifts, but she surmised that interrupting his work flow would not yield the information she desired. What was it about his features that so appealed to her? Was it his perpetual bad boy persona? His passion for his environmental crusades? The desire to replicate the Californian successes in alternative energy supplies to the rest of the country? Or was it simply animal attraction? Her gaze drew him from his reading. He peered up at her and smiled.

"Here." He grabbed one of the colour brochures, and chucked it over onto her lap. "Make yourself useful. Pick out a menu for a soiree I'm having next week at the vineyard."

"Why, because that's all women do; arrange parties and make dinner?" She caught the caterers file and chuckled.

He gave her a pronounced eye roll.

Half indignant, she whined. "I know nothing about posh food." She peered at the lavish pictures and gasped at the prices.

"Sure you do. Pick anything. I don't care."

"For how many guests?"

"Not many, two-hundred or so."

Her mouth gaped open. He flicked a pen in her direction and returned his focus to the hefty folder. As he read the concluding summary to the vast report, his expression darkened. Mary was just circling a variety of canapes and finger food choices, when he drew a sharp breath across his teeth, pounded his fist into the table and stood up. Reaching for the massive folder, he slammed shut the cover, lifted it high and hurled with some force onto the chair opposite his. Its sheer weight and momentum embedded the corner in the soft leather folds, tearing a hole in the calfskin. He turned on her, his stance threatening, his eyes crazed. Mary froze.

Chapter Sixteen

Her shocked reaction immediately reined in his temper. He took a cathartic breath and apologised.

"It's something I've been working on for a really long time. I had hoped that the conclusions in the report would support my campaign. They don't." Luca analysed her features. Mary remained tense and guarded. Her jaw was rigid, her hands poised in defence. "It's no excuse for my outburst. Can I get you anything to drink? That fluid bag ran dry an hour ago. We ought to see if we can disconnect it somehow." He took a step forward and leaned in towards the cannula.

Mary pushed back on her reclining seat, moving her arm further away. "I can manage. Thank you." She gave the plastic valve a jerked tug, freeing the delivery tube from her vein. It had adhered to her skin. The ripped tissue was reddened, sore and leaking. She licked her thumb and pressed it against the puncture site.

"I'm sorry. This must all be really confusing for you. You hardly know me, and yet here we are, high in the sky together having met only yesterday."

Still, she said nothing.

His desire to get back in her good books, seemed to be loosening his tongue and mellowing his temper. "It's just, this report was going to be my lynch pin. The evidence to sway the other senators to back my bill. It allows residents the right to veto the proliferation of new cell phone Wi-Fi systems which use untested ranges of high frequencies from the electromagnetic spectrum." He paused, looking for signs of forgiveness. Mary remained resolutely still, and silent.

As she predicted, he filled the uncomfortable void. "I wanted to take it further, follow the good examples set in Hawaii. They have threatened to hold anyone who installs smart meters or 5G personally liable for any health issues suffered as a result. It's a brilliant plan for Hawaii, wouldn't work in other states though. My goal was to make telecom companies accountable. Their response was to commission this study into the effects of 5G bandwidth. And as is usual for these types of situations, those who fund the research are able to skew the results in favour of their proposals. I don't got a leg to stand on."

Mary listened to his articulate outpouring. Even if his temper had flared, his motives were sound. After such a long campaign, anyone would be frustrated with this result. He sat heavily in his chair, raking his close cropped hair with both sets of digits. She slid the catering pamphlet on the table and rested a hand on his arm. He looked up at her, those roguish eyes searched hers for clues to her emotional state.

"Are there any other studies from which you could draw? Isn't fifth generation cellular technology on the cards in European countries too? They will have independent sources of research."

Luca rubbed his chin absently, staring at her and nodding his head. "Yes, I looked into that. They were what alerted me to the issues in the first place. Jeez, The World Health Organisation lists radio frequency radiation as a class Two-B carcinogen. It is not rocket science. Using frequencies that are borderline microwaves will cause untold damage. DNA strand degradation, unchecked levels of stress proteins and cell metabolism destabilisation…the list goes on and on." Luca jumped back up and paced along the narrow walkway within the confines of the jet. Mary empathised. Supersaturation of the airwaves was a global issue. Anything the United States could sanction, would soon propagate elsewhere, regardless of the hazards. She let him bluster.

"They are blurring the lines between ionising and non-ionising radiation. Opening up this bandwidth is just one step closer to irradiating everything and everyone of us, twenty-four-seven." He huffed a sigh and scooped up the cognac decanter from a hospitality tray. Holding it up towards Mary, he invited her to join him.

She shook her head and murmured, "no thanks."

Luca sloshed two fingers of the syrupy Baron De Sigognac into a tumbler and sipped it neat. Mary had no words of wisdom to sooth his anguish. There was nothing she could offer other than to listen. Something told her that this was a personal quest. There was an element of desperation driving his fervour. Someone close to him had or perhaps will suffer from this decision, but who?

"Ah… I shouldn't bore you with my work issues. You have enough to deal with right now." He held a mouthful of Cognac over his tongue, savouring the flavour and watching her responses. Swallowing, he returned to his seat, maintaining his intense eye contact. Mary's cheeks coloured. His attention was unabashed and obvious, nothing like the gentle overtures from Karan. She tucked the blanket around her naked legs. It unnerved her that she was without undergarments, a fact of which he seemed all too aware.

"Do I make you uncomfortable?" There it was again; direct, open, brazen.

"I… um… no. It's um…"

"That's a yes. I'm used to it. Women tell me that I am too forward. I can't change the way I am, and I make no apology for it." The rest of his brandy disappeared down his gullet. He clonked the glass down with a determined thud.

"Neither should you. I doubt you would have reached your position if you had been a timid wallflower."

"Why do I get the feeling that your wallflower days are behind you too?" He sat back, folded his arms and took a long look at the entire length of her. "How did it feel to be on that stage in Parliament Square, with fifty-thousand Christian worshippers hanging on your every word? Must have given you a buzz?"

"You've seen the videos?" She acknowledged his nods. "Poor choice of words then, surely. The equipment received more than a buzz, I can tell you." She allowed herself a brief giggle in recollection.

"Can you really do all those things? The turning water into wine, the healing of the sick…"

"Oh, no. I can't heal the sick. I assisted in a medical procedure, and it was completely misreported."

"Okay, but you can do the wine trick though, right?" He flicked his brows towards the lead crystal tumbler.

"I am not performing for you. I'm not a circus act."

He batted his eyelashes in a ridiculous display, flashing his cute canine teeth.

"And that won't work either."

He tittered, pouring himself another drink.

Mary gauged his temper, and took the plunge. "When are we going to talk about what you did at the hospital?"

The topic unnerved him. His reluctance was evidenced by him picking at the bandage on his neck. A diversionary tactic to pull her attention to his vulnerable side. It didn't work. She pressed him. "You are like me, aren't you? When did you discover your abilities?"

He tipped a double shot into his glass and cleared his throat. "To a lesser degree, all my life. Even from a kid, I felt weird. I could blow light bulbs, fuse electronics, you know... minor stuff, but er..." he looked at the scarring on his left hand.

"The lightning strike? It boosted your abilities?"

"Seems so, yeah. I don't know how, maybe a DNA expression shift or something unlocking in my brain? You'd probably know the biology of it all better than me, but now I feel really empowered. Bit like those kids who can suddenly play the piano to concert level after waking from a coma."

"You tried to deflect the bullet from Karan."

Luca nodded. "Yeah, well, tried to. Didn't mean for it to hit you instead."

The events from the auction tumbled into place. Everything made sense now; the guilt, the claiming responsibility, the undue attention he paid towards Mary's injury, the insistence on moving her away from the clutches of the law. One interview with the cops and she would be extradited on the first plane back to Britain, with a cautionary order to assess her mental welfare.

"And since it was your fault, you used your electromagnetic gift to remove the bullet from my spine."

"I practised in the men's room first. Make sure I could pull steel objects towards me. Didn't want to do more damage."

"Well, thank you. I am grateful for what you did. I would appreciate a little help with clothing, but as soon as I am respectable again, I will get out of your hair.

Having a religious pariah hanging around will harm your political career."

"Don't you worry about that. I have a top-notch spin doctor on my team. He could make Himmler sound like a nice guy."

The jet's intercom crackled into life and sounded a ping. "We are moving into our final descent in just a moment. Please return to your seats and fasten your safety belts. It is one-thirty, Pacific Standard Time and the sun is shining." Another crackle and the intercom switched off. Luca handed his glass to the stewardess, who stowed the hospitality tray in a secure locker before strapping herself into a seat at the rear of the plane.

Mary pushed open the window visor and marvelled at the parched brown peaks of Death Valley. The fractured barren landscape marking the shifting tectonic plates in the earth's crust. It was a humbling experience. The Gulf stream G280 cruised across the Nevada border into greener territory, the great bank of national parks, drawing a line across the landmass. Another five minutes saw them traversing the skies above the alluvial farmland and mosaic urban sprawl surrounding Sacramento.

They were flying low enough to make out the massive salt flats, brackish plains and deltas of the Californian coast. Each length of artificial causeway straddling the bays, made Mary sit up and gape at their ability to defy gravity. The stilted roads appeared to hover above the water unaided. A sharp bank in their flightpath, had her leaning on the window ledge and bracing her side against tearing her stitches. The pilot lined the aircraft up parallel to the headland suburbs of Mountain View and Palo Alto, and angled the wing flaps to land at San Francisco International Airport.

They taxied to the private jet enclosure, some distance from the main terminal. A car awaited their arrival, with a team of his aides in a second vehicle alongside.

"What about my documents. How will I get through border control?" Mary unhooked the seatbelt and folded the blanket neatly.

"Officials don't tend to bother me, especially at busy times like this. They know it's my jet by the tail number. It won't be a problem."

The aircraft came to a full stop and the stewardess unlocked the exit, lowering the steps to the concrete below. Mary disembarked first. Luca's staff exchanged glances upon seeing her peculiar attire. Despite the lateness of summer, the breeze was warm on her skin. She stood among the lean, tanned and suited figures and felt very pale and small. Luca was fast to her side, opening the car door for Mary and fending off the multitude of questions from his entourage. "Not now. Let's all get back to the ranch and we'll deal with everything there. Can someone grab my luggage, and there is a large folder in the jet." He left Mary to the backseat, and sat up front with his driver. On the dashboard were three mobile phones, all chiming and singing their various tunes. He had been out of contact with his public for too long. He picked up the first, unlocked it with his thumb print and listened to the caller. The scratchy, barely audible sounds leaked into his ear and then stopped. Without a word, he switched the phone off and picked up the second. This he repeated, uttering monosyllabic words on occasion, for the hour-long drive from San Francisco to the foot of the Napa Valley.

Here, at the southern foothills of the Sonoma, they turned off the main roads and began the climb up the mountainside. Row upon row of neatly spaced wire work, supported the finest Chardonnay, Pinot Noir and Merlot grapes for miles around. The yellowing leaves clipped back to reveal vines laden with swollen fruit, and workers toiling with care to harvest the precious load into plastic crates.

They sped through the ornate ranch gates, along the dust encrusted drive up to a long terracotta building. It would not have looked out of place in Andalusia or Tuscany; uneven pan tiles, covered terraces, potted plants and raised herb beds. It had its own stately charm, clinging to the mountainside in defiance of the arid conditions all around. Every square inch of southern facing roofs supported solar cells, with evidence of more modern additions lower down the valley. A cluster of circular metal dishes were embedded into the ground. In the centre, one dish was hinged open to allow a telescopic trunk to emerge. From this stem, a fanned array of solar fronds tracked the movements of the sun across the sky.

Mary stepped out from the car onto the courtyard, and surveyed her surroundings. It was inspiring. She shielded her eyes from the sun's glare and breathed in the dry heat and musky earthen scents. A little oasis of order, among a vast expanse of natural chaos had Mary captivated.

"This place is enchanting."

"It's my sanctuary. I come here when my Washington DC life gets too much." He directed his driver to collect the luggage from the second car and take it into the building. Returning to Mary's side, he pointed to the crest of the mountain behind her. "From the very top, you can see right along to San Pablo Bay on a good day. It's a bit hazy right now. You need bed rest young lady." He grappled her shoulders playfully, marching her towards the entrance. "I'll call a top class MD from Napa. He does house calls to a few select clients."

Mary resisted. "If I could just borrow some clothes and get my brooch back, then I can..." She stopped mid thought. Her money, passport and satchel were all back in Manhattan at The Plaza. How could she make a fresh start wearing a hospital gown and slippers? The morphine and anaesthesia had left her system and fresh waves of cramping stabbed her abdomen. *This is what happens when you let other people make decisions for you. Okay, think. I need Grandma Phebe's brooch back, I need clothes, I need painkillers. Stay one night, two tops.* She allowed him to steer her through a terraced patio, and into the cool of the entrance hall.

Double thickness walls insulated them from the blazing heat outside, and a refreshing breeze funnelled along the length of the building from French windows opening out onto the mountain view. His interior styling was an odd mixture of minimalist modern artwork and old world comfort. A lesser Picasso hung above a stone fireplace. A slouchy fabric wing chair, sat in a reading nook next to an impressive selection of hardbacks on a redwood bookcase. She longed for her own home; her own knick-knacks, a home cooked meal and a long soak in a familiar tub. The home she had built with Parth, with her grandfather's help, with the money from her parents' life insurance. A wisp of sadness funnelled up from her gut. She pushed the melancholy back down, and walked to the patio windows. The searing heat made her squint, but the need to find her bearings drove her out onto the terrace. Luca followed her outside and watched her take in the scenery.

Below her, further down the mountainside, a man aimed a handheld device at the retractable solar array. It immediately began folding itself up and inching back into the ground. Something about witnessing his action awoke a memory. It was as if she was standing on her luxury cabin balcony looking out across the Summerfield Retreat. She turned to Luca. He sensed her agitation. He locked onto her neural pathways the moment they made eye contact. Mary blinked rapidly. His incursion began at her optic nerve, tracing the neural links to the limbic region, right in the centre of her brain. Mary gasped, the intrusion was instantaneous and activated a sensory overload of emotions. All at once she wanted to cry, scream, fight and flee. The indecision rooted her to the spot.

Luca gave her a serene smile, content to dredge her thoughts and extract whatever notion took his fancy. She felt his raw power surging into the hippocampus of her brain, trawling her subconscious for recollections. He saw the curve of her mother's neck, felt the touch of her father's kiss upon her forehead, tasted the salty bacon from childhood breakfasts at her grandfather's house. He nudged further into her mind, sifting through the memories entombed in a desolate pall. The terror of airbags deploying, of rolling at speed down a motorway embankment, the stench of diesel and blood seeping from mangled bodies trapped inside the wreckage of their family car. Locked inside her bleak and pitiful despair, he shed a single tear.

There was nothing she could do to deflect him. His hold over her was absolute. The pity he felt for her derailed him, redirecting the intrusion towards her recent memories. A scene replayed in her mind's eye. It showed an ill-lit stairwell, coiling down flight after flight into the dankest recess, like a pit. He heard breathless wheezing and experienced pained shin muscles. A door opened to reveal vaulted ceilings in an underground cavern, filled to capacity with machinery, vehicles, food banks and clothing. His sight merged with the replay of her memory. It glided between the tractors and trucks towards a side room adjacent to a computer suite. Luca felt the cold sensation of frozen air blasting his skin from the open chest freezer, saw the contorted hand set in a rigid claw and the cataract of dead eyes staring back at him.

Chapter Seventeen

Luca jumped backwards, breaking his connection into Mary's stream of consciousness. She knew what had brought him hurtling back into his senses. The chilled corpse of MI6 agent, Jasper Flynn.

The force with which Luca abandoned her mind, left him panting. "Was that for real? You really saw that?" His breathing calmed, transmuting into concern.

"I did. And we have a lot to talk about, but next time you want to know something about me, just ask. Don't go rummaging through my brain for answers." Freed from his neural grip, she whapped him on his right arm.

"Ow! You can throw a good punch for someone so little."

"Yeah, and don't you forget it. Now make me a cup of tea and start taking notes. We haven't even got to the nuclear bit yet." The invasion into her mind, shook her confidence, but she was determined not to let it show. He was more like her than she cared to admit. Had he acquired every one of her gifts?

Should she mention the strange excerpt that Dan read from her Grandfather's journal, describing a catastrophe of epic proportions; a vision documenting the future of civilisation reduced to one of riots, looting, blackouts and the western world set ablaze? Would he believe her if she did relay the premonition? At the back of her mind, she knew that her grandfather was alluding to a global threat requiring the senior politicians of all western countries to solve. What impact could she possibly have on such a complex and international plot? The most she could do was to raise the alarm. Pinpoint the perpetrator and let the national security experts do their jobs. She assessed Luca's emotions. He was buoyed and compliant. Hardly conducive to discussing such serious matters.

Partly amused by her demands, partly concerned, Luca order his house staff to make up a guest room and bring them a tray of refreshments. Mary chose the warmth of the patio to divulge her story. She reclined on a sun lounger and refilled her vitamin D requirement, before settling under the shade of an awning. Luca handed his cellular phones to a man with a permanent scowl, instructing him to hold all calls. He then sat beside Mary and listened to her descriptions of the Summerfield Retreat site, of the team of new recruits with untapped potential, of seeing Jasper Flynn at the airport and of finding his body in the storage bunker. She left the most crucial fact until last.

"One of the lads with abilities helped me to find a bicycle. I rode up this enormous ramp, which circled around like in a multi-storey car park, until I reached the top most level. There were military personnel everywhere. I hid, and watched them loading up large crates onto a convoy of army trucks. Each crate was marked with the hazard warning for nuclear material."

"And then what?" Luca sat forward, sipping from a long glass of iced lemonade.

"Then I got out of there, pretty damn smartish, I can tell you." She poured the dregs from the teapot into her cup and grimaced at the stale film it formed on its surface. "I did tell Karan about what I saw. I asked him to investigate through his contacts at the UN, but nothing ever came of it. Only, I promised Lachie and Oona that I would find a way to get them out. They're good kids really. It's not their fault that they have become ensnared in Alexi's criminal activities." She watched Luca rubbing at his chin and wondered if it was an action derived through necessity more than unconsciously applied. Did it provide him with an air of gravitas and time to think of his next move? She was impatient to hear his thoughts. "Well? Can you help? Are there departments of people you can contact to chivvy the little weasel out of his lair? Nuclear material, Luca…this is serious."

"Yeah, I realise that. I'm thinking."

A glinting light in her peripheral vision made Mary snap her head towards the valley. Shielding her eyes, she peered across the acres of vines and saw the flash a second time but could not make out the source.

Luca put his glass down and straightened his spine. "As EPA Chief, I have oversight of the removal and processing of nuclear waste, but authorising specific companies to deal with materials is tightly regulated, and delegated to someone beneath me. I would have to put together a team to look into this allegation more thoroughly."

"EPA?"

"Environmental Protection Agency. It's quite a prestigious title to hold, Mary."

"Well, what can I say. I'm British. Prestige is in the eye of the beholder. Does that mean you will send your team in to arrest Alexi, and stop whatever he is up to? What is that bloody annoying flashing light?" Again, she was attracted by its dazzling brightness.

"Probably one of the solar arrays realigning, or a local media hack with a long lens camera. They're always lurking about these parts."

Mary moved seats, taking her further away from the edge of the patio and out of view. "So, you will have him arrested?"

"I'm not making promises, Mary, but yes. I will look into your story."

"Good. Any chance of a shower and a change of clothes?"

"Yeah, sure. You must be exhausted. I'll get Viktor to set you up."

Mary thanked Luca and followed him back inside the house. She waited for polite introductions to Luca's personal assistant and all round go-to person. Expecting to be directed up the main staircase, Mary was surprised to be taken to a ground floor guest apartment instead. Luca's tastes were evident here too, but with the odd addition of a central fish tank, supporting a variety of exotic species. Viktor said barely a word as he guided her through the sitting room, past a small kitchen area to the bedroom and en suite at the farthest end. It was practically an entire wing of the ranch. He backed away from Mary and headed towards the door.

"If there is anything you require, please dial zero on the land line and it will divert to me."

"Thank you. Luca had an item of jewellery that belongs to me in his luggage. Please could you bring it here the moment it is unpacked?"

"Certainly. I will direct the doctor through to you when he arrives." He closed the door, and as Mary listened for his footsteps on the corridor tiles, she wondered where Viktor was born. His accent was faint, but distinct. She just couldn't place its origins.

The cool shower was perfect. A ceiling rose sprayed rain-like drops down over her head and face, soothing the pent-up anguish she had held in for days. Alexi was Luca's problem now, that's if Karan had not already acted. *I just need to catch up with Dan and the news. What time would it be in England? It's plus eight hours from Pacific Standard Time to Greenwich Mean Time, plus another hour for British Summer Time, that makes it, oh, the middle of the night. Dan will be asleep. I could ask Viktor if I could borrow a laptop to search for news on the Prime Minister. If she has recovered, my arrest warrant may have been dropped. She might have even kept her word over repealing the Mental Health bill proposals.* Mary yawned. *Maybe I should have a bit of a nap first. Getting shot is tiring.* She dried off with the most enormous bath sheet and wrapped it around her torso while she cleaned her teeth. One eye lid fell as she brushed. *Just forty winks, as Grampy would say, and then I will get dressed for dinner.*

Mary lowered herself onto the bed, still shrouded in the towel, and sighed. *Just forty-winks…*

***

The doctor jogged Mary's shoulder until she was fully awake. He wore an open necked, short sleeve, lilac shirt and chinos. It did not inspire confidence. "Hi. Senator Bonovich has requested an examination. Can you show me the wound site?"

"Are you a proper doctor?" Mary struggled to sit upright, clutching the towel tight to her chest. "Where is your stethoscope and white coat? You don't look very professional."

"Apologies, Ms Arora. I can assure you that I am fully qualified, with a great many years of experience. Are you in any pain?"

The use of her marital name, threw her. Why on earth had Luca given him her real details? It provoked her more belligerent side. "Some. I've had worse. Where did you train… what's your specialism?"

"Cardio-thoracic. UCSF." He put his bag down on the nightstand, opened it and took out a pair of latex gloves the colour of his shirt.

"I don't know what that stands for, but it had better be good. Hang on." She wriggled and re-positioned the towel until she could reveal the bullet wound without exposing the rest of her private areas. The doctor nodded and murmured at the stitch work securing the edges of the small hole together, and then applied a fresh dressing.

"That is some fancy work there. I have seen some pretty messy lesions in my time. Bullets tend to rip the flesh up bad, especially if the surgeon has trouble removing it. Yours is one of the neatest I've ever seen. You'll hardly have a scar when it's healed." He taped the gauze and cotton pad against her skin, and whipped off his gloves. Mary did not comment. The less he knew about Luca's magic bullet trick, the better. He took out a small pad and Biro from his top pocket and scribbled at speed. "Get this filled as soon as you can. Take two, every four hours for the tenderness. I'll leave you some spare dressings. Change it once a day, and if you can, bathe it with a saline solution to keep it from infection."

Mary took the prescription slip from him. "Thanks. And sorry about earlier. I'm not the trusting soul I once was."

"Perfectly understandable, given your malady, Ms Arora. Take good care of yourself, try to move about as much as you can; it helps to break up potential blood clots. I'll come and remove those stitches in a week or two, if you are still here. I'm surprised that they didn't use soluble ones." He picked up his bag and walked out of the open French doors in the sitting room onto the paved area beyond. It was clearly not his first visit to the ranch.

Mary tried to read his scrawled moniker from the slip but it was unintelligible, as was the name of the drug he had prescribed.

A light-weight cotton dress with a small floral design, hung from the wardrobe door, and a pair of single post sandals sat beneath. Mary surmised that Viktor must have left them for her while she slept. The thought of him wandering in while she was so vulnerable gave her the creeps, but as far as she could tell, there were no locks with which to keep him out. There was a pair of folded cotton knickers on the dressing table. The labels were still attached. She chewed through the plastic tags with her incisors and put them on. They were a little on the tight side, but better than nothing. The dress swamped her. What would have been knee length on the average Californian beauty, now skimmed the base of her calves.

For once, her air-dried curls had tamed themselves during her nap, falling to her shoulders without frizz. Feeling a little self-conscious, she ventured from the apartment and into the main part of the house. From the setting sun she estimated the time to be around eight o'clock. Where was everyone? Had they eaten without her? The thought of food made her stomach growl. She wandered through the main living area towards the terrace and found Luca, leaning on the guard rail overlooking the valley. Behind him a table was set for two; crisp white linens, wine flutes and a flickering lantern at its centre.

Luca heard her movements and turned to greet her. "Sleeping beauty awakes. Would you like a drink… it's our best vintage?"

Mary thought for a moment. Artificial pain killing drugs, or a natural anaesthetic? "Yes please. That would be lovely."

He poured her a glass and topped up his own. They leaned against the iron railings and stood in silence, listening to the rustling leaves and the insects waking for the night shift. The burnt umber glow of the sky threw regimented shadows across the landscape. They reminded Mary of barbed wire fencing on old war films.

"Did you send the troops to New Jersey?" Her stare insistent, unyielding.

"Give me a chance, Mary. I have..." He took a sip of wine to consider his answer. "Made a couple of calls." His response did not seem to appease her. She continued to stare in silence, goading him into further action. He broke the stalemate by inviting her to sit at the laid table. "I didn't know what to ask cook to make for you. And since you may have slept until quite late, we decided a variety of salads might best suit." Luca gestured towards a loitering Viktor, who wheeled a steel trolley out onto the terrace. It supported a range of dishes, all covered with silver or glass domes to deter insect invasion.

Mary sat at one end of the table and watched as Viktor set about delivering each of the platters in turn. Her gaze fell back on the trolley. It reminded her, all too painfully, of the hospital gurney which carried her into surgery. With stoic aplomb, Viktor served filo parcels of goat's cheese and spinach, two kinds of rice salad, a tasty Waldorf and slices of marinated tomatoes the size of cricket balls. There were other untouched dishes, yet to be unveiled, but Mary's plate already overflowed.

Luca poured more wine as Mary sated her grumbling tummy. He nibbled on a few chunks of celery, as though he had already eaten and was forcing more down through polite manners. She looked out across the darkening vista.

"Where is the wine made? I can't see any other buildings." She took a sip of the rich Burgundy and then continued to shovel more of the food down.

"The winery itself is just over that peak over there." Luca pointed to a crest in the hillside, its top-most ridge still bathed in the last rays of the sun. "The grapes are all picked by hand to preserve the quality and reduce damage. Then they are dropped into a layered hopper, that reaches deep underground into the natural cave system, where the ageing process is more easily controlled."

"Caves? There are caves here?"

"Sure. These mountains are riddled with them. It's one of the reasons why the vintage is such a success. I'll show you around when you feel well enough."

Mary gave him a polite smile and a forced nod. The thought of an underground cavern system chilled her spine. She imagined the low ceilings and dripping stalactites of fantasy fiction, and shivered. "How long have you been making wine? Is it just a side line to your politics?"

"No, it has been in the family for some time. We have a few other sites as well as this one. I say we, but I mean other relatives. I like to think of this one as mine, although I have a general manager to keep everything ticking over."

"It is a beautiful part of the world, Luca, and this wine is quite moreish." She gulped at another mouthful. Her cheeks glowed.

"Is that Brit-speak for tasty?"

Mary giggled and snorted, spluttering on the tangy liquid as it trickled down her throat. He was amused by her childlike approach to intoxication, resting his tongue against expensive dental work in a genuine grin. The lingering stare was different this time. Not invasive or strained, but mellow and thoughtful. He had such impish eyes. They could literally penetrate her soul. How different he was to Karan. The pale locks and salt and pepper stubble glinting in the candlelight from his angular jaw. There was a maturity and presence that was both comforting and exhilarating. He had an air of danger about him that Mary could not place. He was far from the privilege that Karan's regal background afforded him, yet he had a similar degree of self-possession. It was a heady mix.

Two powerful men from the east and the west. What could they possibly want with me? I can almost understand Karan's interest, since he has no other access to people with electromagnetic sensitivity, but Luca has gifts of his own. Why on earth would he take all this trouble over me? Her internal musings allowed for a noticeable hiatus in their conversation. She stared for a moment too long, and blushed.

Luca's smile widened. "Dessert? Cook makes an incredible Death by Chocolate?"

"I shouldn't really, but it has been a long time since I had a treat." She nodded at Viktor, who stood with a cake knife poised in his grasp. "Thank you."

Viktor delivered the sweet, rested a small fork against her plate, and re-covered the cake platter.

"Are you not having pudding?" She said, suddenly self-conscious.

"No, I don't tend to do sweets." He noted her disappointment, and added. "Really, it's fine. You go ahead."

"Well if you are sure." Mary did not wait for further entreaties. She plunged the side of the fork into the soft ganache and savoured its smooth sweetness. When her mouth was clear of sticky chocolate she remarked, "wow… you were not kidding. This is divine." Another forkful disappeared as quickly as the first. Mary scooped up another portion and paused to waft it near to her host. "Are you sure I cannot tempt you?"

There was that beatific smile once again. The hazy eyed look of desire. "Yes, Mary. I think you can tempt me." He leaned forwards and gently held her wrist, guiding her utensil into his mouth. He wrapped his lips about the morsel and slid the fork slowly out. Mary was transfixed.

Chapter Eighteen

Luca did not let go of her wrist. He chewed the chocolate torte, swallowed, and then pulled her arm close until her face was inches from his. All she could focus on was a tiny fleck of escaped pudding on his top lip. With her free hand, she reached around and wiped her thumb across his mouth. Before she could transfer it elsewhere, he leaned in and kissed her. At first, it was a delicate brush of the lips, eliciting a tingling sensation that made her draw breath. He slid his hand along her shoulder and up her neck, cradling the back of her head. He kissed her again. This time, the sensory rush awoke every erogenous zone in her body. Eyes closed, she waited for more, expecting the firm pressure of his face against hers, but he had pulled away. Perturbed, her eyes flickered open. He was reaching for his glass. *Is that it? He sets me on fire and then stops? What kind of monster is he? Am I that awful to kiss or does he prefer the chase to the capture?*

Luca cocked his head and looked at her. "I'm not going to seduce you, Mary, as much as I would love to. You're fresh out of surgery. I'm not a monster."

Had he read her mind without her knowing? An embarrassed flush heated her skin. It bloomed from her forehead, right down to her cleavage. She folded her arms across her chest and sat back in her chair. That was when she noticed the flash of light, reflected from an angled lens.

Luca spotted it too. “This late in the day, that couldn’t possibly be the solar arrays. Gotta be a tenacious reporter.”

“We should go indoors then.” Mary ventured with reluctance. “If they recognise me, your career will be over.”

He shrugged.

“Seriously, Luca. Why are you helping me?” They stood up from the table and wandered through the French doors into the spacious lounge. “If the authorities discover that you are harbouring a fugitive and illegal immigrant, they would throw the book at you.” She sat on the edge of a leather settee and rearranged the excess fabric of the dress around her legs. Luca launched himself down next to her, stretching out an arm across the back of the sofa.

“As far as I can tell, the only thing you are guilty of is trying to assist a stubborn parliamentarian in the UK. As for the authorities, Mary Sedgewell is my house guest. She is lawfully permitted to visit the United States under the visa completed at the airport.”

“You didn’t answer my question. Why help me? You could have left me with Karan at the hospital.”

Another shrug. “I like you.”

Mary shook her head, exasperated. “That reminds me. I need to call him and explain where I went. That’s if he is still speaking to me after ditching him like that. He has shown me nothing but kindness.” She waited for a moment, hoping that Luca would offer to let her use his mobile phone. He didn’t. She frowned. “His telephone number is printed on a card in my satchel, which of course, is back in Manhattan.” She released a big sigh and buckled in the middle, blanching at the renewed discomfort in her abdomen. "What must he think of me?" She murmured it to herself, ashamed.

"I wouldn't worry about Shrimant Shinde, Mary. I dare say he has a fair few Indian princesses at his beck and call to entertain him."

Before Mary could leap to Karan's defence, Viktor arrived through the doorway and whispered something inaudible to his boss. Luca dipped his head in response and then jumped up from his seat.

"Excuse me, Mary, I have to take an important call." He hurried from the room without a backward glance.

I guess that means dinner is well and truly over. And yet again, I have managed to make a total fool of myself with a gorgeous and eligible man. Well done, Mary. I thought things were supposed to get easier when you got older. I don't remember being this inept dating Parth, but then he was probably instructed to entice me. The reminder of her marital turmoil hit her hard. Had she ever had a genuine relationship? To what extent had the British Secret Services monitored her, and for how long? A sudden urge to speak to her brother came over her. *I'll just borrow one of Luca's books to read and then go back to my rooms and see if Dan is available.*

Wandering over to Luca's reading nook, she traced a finger across the spines of the hardbacks, making a note of the titles. There were almost two shelves full of biographies. Mary recognised a few of the subject's names, the rest she supposed were political figures and rivals of Lucas. A couple of travel journals propped up a stack of glossy photographic books and a few chunky reference tomes. *Hmm, Luca does not appear to be into fiction. I don't really want to read about politicians.* She chose a photographic book. It had a dramatic image of an icy lake printed on the cover sleeve. Where the ambient temperature had plummeted, streams of rising bubbles had frozen into chains of glassy air pockets. The effect was striking. *Wow, where was this taken?* She opened the fly leaf and read the description. *Lake Baikal, Siberia.* She flipped it over and read the blurb on the back cover. *Oh, all the images are from Russia. It is stunning.*

Mary glanced through the remaining photographic books. Four more focused on images from Russian and Baltic states, one showed scenes of the mountains in Colorado and another on the Scottish Highlands. *Nothing eclectic about his tastes then.* She was just contemplating returning to her room with the book, when Viktor rushed through the room and along the passageway leading to where she assumed Luca had an office. He looked distressed. There were no utterances or pleasantries. He dashed through as though she were a minor inconvenience. He wore a gun holster clipped to his waistband. Mary sat up and assumed a defensive posture. A few weeks ago, timid Mary would have minded her own business and made herself scarce. Those days were gone, and with them, her manners.

"Hey, Viktor…What is going on?" She called after him.

He halted his speed walk and shot her a glacial stare. "It's confidential, miss. Nothing to concern yourself with." He did not wait for any further discourse, but instead resumed his trajectory, bashing open a heavy door at the end of the passageway with his fist.

Mary wrinkled her nose up. *Miserable git. Luca should employ a lovely personal assistant, like Gupta or Harvey. Poor Harvey. I never did get to say cheerio to him. Everyone seems to have some kind of man servant these days. Why people can't do their own packing and answer their own phones, I'll never know.* She took the book and sat down on the reading chair, determined to keep a watchful eye on proceedings. Folding her legs up on the seat, she settled down with the publication open across her lap and thumbed through the pages; The Kremlin at sunset, Mongolian Monasteries, open cast diamond mines, remote island labyrinths, geyser fields, Siberian craters, the Russian president shaking hands with two westerners and spectacular photographs of the Lena Limestone Pillars. Each glossy picture slipped beneath her fingers, as she idly glanced at them while straining to hear the raised voices at the rear of the ranch house.

Another door slam and Viktor reappeared, glistening with sweat. His look warned Mary off further discussion. He was a man on a mission. Viktor darted through the French windows and padded down the steps at the side of the terrace. *What was that boxy thing he was carrying?* Mary placed the book to one side and hurried after him, peering into the darkness of the courtyard beyond. As she reached the edge of the terrace and shielded her eyes from the patio lamps, all she could make out was his silhouette watching the tail lights of two large trucks heading for the gates at the property boundary.

"There you are. I wondered where you had got to." Luca stood so close to her, she could feel his breath on her neck. She twisted her head over her shoulder. There was that false grin again; the toothy one he gave to voters and reporters.

"What's all the commotion?"

"Ah, just a little mix up - the um…wrong tables and chairs delivered for the party. Viktor has it under control."

"At this time of night? Seems a little late for deliveries?"

They could hear his footsteps crunching on the gravel as he made his way back to the terrace. Luca grabbed Mary by the shoulders and spun her around. "Now, where were we?" He lowered his face to hers and kissed her; a fervent, all-consuming embrace of some duration. From the second he touched her, a tiny electrical buzz tingled her lips and travelled in one long, erotic surge through her torso. By the time he released her, Viktor had re-entered the house, still carrying the device Mary had spotted earlier. She tried to identify the object, without appearing impolite to Luca's advances, but Viktor was gone.

"Now, do you wanna fool around some more or are you gonna leave a guy hanging?" He led her gently by the hand back into the lounge.

"I thought you said I was too fragile to seduce?"

"I can work around fragile."

Mary gave it a moment's thought and allowed him to lead her through the guest apartment and into her bedroom. *Something about this situation feels all too familiar... Do all men use sex to distract women? Another tactic to shut us up? I should say no, but he is adorable, and wow, what a buzz.*

***

Mary lay awake in the dark, listening to the rhythmic wheeze of Luca's sleep. Moonlight poured in through the open windows, illuminating the fractal scars on his body. Rather than spoil an otherwise perfect physique, it was enhanced by their existence. He was beautiful. An ethical Adonis to rival the Gods. She reflected on their compatibility. Nothing in her past experience had prepared her for such definitive pleasure. It was as though he could pre-empt her movements, exploiting territories of her body to their fullest potential while avoiding those areas that might cause discomfort or pain. Either he had mastered the craft of love making with a great many partners, or more likely, was reading her mind throughout the entire encounter. Endorphins coursed through her body, giving her a sense of tranquillity like no other. How could she sleep after such exhilaration?

Gliding out from under his arm, she groped around the room for the bathrobe from the hospital and slipped it over her naked form. Pulling the bedroom door to a close, she walked to the kitchen area and collected a bottle of water from the fridge, before leaving the guest wing. The lounge lights were still on, and she could hear Viktor barking out orders in the office at the end of the building. She presumed that he was making international telephone calls on Luca's behalf.

The book from earlier was back on the shelf. She tried to find it again, among the thick spines of reference books. Something about the images she saw, gnawed at her subconscious. She needed to see them again, but could not explain why. Her first pass across the titles failed to find the book's location. A second glance found it behind a series of photo frames that she had not noticed before. They depicted a little blond girl in various pursuits; bouncing tennis balls on a massive lawn, playing with a golden retriever in a Wendy house, performing on stage in a pink tutu with her classmates, and finally, in the arms of her father, Luca. Mary scooped up the frame and peered closely at the image. His look of contentment was supreme. She was his world. As she replaced the frame back on the shelves, Mary could feel a presence looming behind her.

"Ava." Luca said, his features set like stone.

Mary evaluated his character. Sadness and fury lurked in abundance. She chose to stay silent, employing her previous successful gambit of waiting for him to elucidate. The pause went on too long. It was clearly a sore topic for him. She softened her gaze, exuding as much sympathy as she could. He stepped forwards and took the photo from her hands, his intense stare trained on his daughter's angelic face.

"Leukaemia."

"I am sorry."

Luca placed the frame back on the bookshelf with careful reverence. "It's a while ago now, but I still find it difficult to talk about."

"That's understandable. I cannot imagine what you must have been through." She touched his arm, felt his muscles contract beneath her hand and quickly removed it again.

Luca turned away, folding his limbs over his bare chest. Mary thought that he was signalling an end to the conversation. That she had reached a boundary over which she should not cross. This was his grief, and his alone. To her surprise, he took a moment, swallowed and turned back towards her.

"Her mother and I broke up. The divorce was… well, it was exactly how most divorces go, I guess. Messy, protracted, not nice. She refused to move into any of the buildings which belonged to me or my family… wanted complete independence, so I agreed to buy her a place as part of the settlement. She chose a penthouse apartment, mid-town NYC. She got full custody of Ava, since I was on the campaign trail, and judges thought it was best for a little girl to be with her stay at home mom. At first, we couldn't figure out why Ava was sick. Took her to all the top-class doctors and specialists, but she just got worse. When they diagnosed her, we were devastated."

Luca's voice broke. He coughed, and cleared his throat, cuffing his knuckle to his nose. Mary stood still and ashen. She could feel the remorse, his anguish and suffering as though it had happened only yesterday.

"I paid for tutors to come and home school her. Her mom let me stay over during the really bad times. How were we to know that the roof of her apartment block was stacked sky high with cell phone masts." His knees wobbled, and he sat heavily on the reading chair.

"I am so sorry." Mary repeated, at a loss as to how to comfort him.

"Afterwards, after she had... I campaigned, but got nowhere fast. Investigators claimed that the frequencies were within acceptable parameters for human health. No matter what independent analysts reported, State departments refused to accept any responsibility. The phone companies set their own safety limits." He tipped forwards, resting his head in his hands. "Ava just slipped away from us. How could we have known?"

She laid her hand against his shoulder. This time, she detected no impulse to push her away. Mary sensed that it was a breakthrough moment for him, for them both. Opening his inner sanctum of dark emotions was a bonding experience she had never felt with Parth. This was a completely new level of understanding. It was like they were in tune; his innate presence harmonised with hers. She stroked the hair on the back of his head.

His weakness was endearing. He looked up at her and saw the pity painted across her face. A millisecond of understanding passed between them, before his alpha male carapace concealed his vulnerability once more. The moment had passed, and with it, all her chances to read his thoughts. He smoothed his hair, brushing her hand from his head, and stood up. "Are you coming back to bed? I have a busy start in the morning." All evidence of his former state of upset vanished. He was composed and confident in an instant. How could he switch emotions so swiftly?

"I'll join you in a bit. I'm having trouble adjusting to all these time jumps."

He started walking towards the guest wing, and then stopped. "Hey, I don't suppose you want to come with me to DC in a few days, do you? You'll need to shop for some warmer clothes... I can give you my credit card and a set of car keys..." He waited for her answer, and when there was no response, he continued; "Decide in the morning. No pressure. What were you looking for when I came in?"

"Oh, there is a photography book about Russia..."

"You'd rather look at pictures than come to bed with me? You wound me, Mary." He held out his hand to her and smirked. She couldn't help herself. It provoked a giggle. He knew just how to play her. But then, why resist such an offer? She could always have a proper snoop in the morning. Why waste the chance to relive those exquisite sensations? Another round of endorphin release would dampen the residual soreness of the bullet site. Mary approached Luca and glanced down at his jockey shorts. His intentions were more than obvious.

"Come on then, old man. Try and keep up this time..." She slipped a finger beneath the elastic of his waistband and tugged it towards her, leading him back to her guest apartment and the king-sized bed.

"Less of the old. Are all you British women so domineering?"

"Shut up and kiss me."

"Yes ma'am."

Chapter Nineteen

Mary awoke to an empty bed. Luca had risen early. Donning her bathrobe, she went in search of him. The table on the terrace was laid once more, but this time for breakfast. There were American-style pancakes, jugs of maple syrup, burned streaky bacon, cereals, steaming hot pots of coffee and a large pot of tea. She sat down opposite him and watched the muscles in his jaw undulate as he chewed his muesli.

"Morning." She made a grab for the teapot, drawing it close like a long-lost friend, before searching out the milk jug.

He looked up from a tablet PC balancing on the edge of the table. "Did you sleep okay?" He shovelled another spoonful into his mouth, chomping down on the seeds and dried fruits with vigour.

"Not too badly, thanks. What's so engrossing?" The amber brew gushed out into her teacup, leaving bubbles at the surface. Without waiting for it to cool, Mary drank several gulps down.

"We are." He said, pausing to deliver that playful grin.

"What?"

"Well, I am at any rate. You are the blurry date of the most eligible divorcee in California, apparently." He put his spoon down and lifted the tablet up to show her. The headline for the tabloid article read; Is Senator Bonovich

Officially Off The Market? He plonked it down and thumbed through the commentary beneath the images.

"It doesn't bother you?"

"Why would it? Publicity is good. Great in fact. The lightning strike followed by the charity heist has me hitting international headlines. I can't put a foot wrong."

"I wouldn't count your chickens just yet, senator. What if they work out it is me? British heretic and general hater of all things Christian…"

"Then I would probably get an invitation to appear on Jerry Springer. It's all good."

"Not if I get arrested it's not. Speaking of arrests, is there any news from your contacts about the Summerfield Retreat? Has Alexi been detained yet? Have they recovered the nuclear materials?"

"Whoa! Hold your horses. One step at a time. They have to collect the intelligence first. You can't just go barging in on private property without the warrants, and warrants require proof."

"Sorry, but you did stress to them how dangerous Alexi can be, didn't you? He must surely be on some kind of CIA watch list."

One of his eyebrows kinked. He stopped chewing and swallowed. "Mary, let me do my job. You need to get some clothes if you are going to come with me to DC. You'll need a dress for the party too."

Mary knew she had pushed him too far. Ordinarily, she would have argued the point about attending a party in which she could easily be recognised, but she chose to let the matter drop. Leaning across the white linen clad table, she took two slices of toast from a rack and covered them with butter and marmalade. They ate in silence until Luca took his napkin from his lap and laid it across his plate. Standing up, he slid a set of car keys from his trouser pocket and handed them to Mary.

"I take it you can drive?"

She nodded. From his back pocket, he produced a credit card and a business card with his own and Viktor's contact details listed.

"If you have any troubles with the retailers, get them to call Viktor." Luca held out the cards.

"What if they ask for ID? I'd be screwed. If only you had let me go back to The Plaza in New York, I had plenty of cash I could have used." She did not take the card from him.

They stared each other down, until Luca heaved an exasperated sigh. "Fine. You want cash, I'll get you cash." He stomped off inside the house, and disappeared into his study. Mary trotted after him, but the stiff door hinges slammed it shut as she approached. She had just enough time to see Luca crouching at a safe beneath a side cabinet, before the keypad lock activated, locking him inside. Mary stood in the corridor, awaiting his return and another chance to catch a glimpse inside his mysterious room.

"Here." Luca thrust of roll of notes into her hand.

"That's far too much."

"You need clothes. Clothes cost money. There is about ten K there." He dangled the car keys in front of her.

She didn't want to make him angry. Mary took the keys from him and turned around, ready to go.

"It's the blue car in the courtyard, you should be able to find it. And get a nice cocktail dress while you're there."

Mary wandered through the lounge room holding the bank notes in one hand and car keys in the other. She heard the door of his study slam shut as he returned inside. *What's got to him all of a sudden? I don't know why people think that women are temperamental. They should try State Senators.* She paused on the terrace, contemplating her next move. Ten thousand dollars would be more than enough to start somewhere new. She could drive off to a train terminal and phone Viktor to collect the car. With cash to tide her over, she could slip into one of the central American countries and lay low until her name was cleared. The more she thought about it, the more she hated herself. *I am quite possibly the most selfish person that ever lived. My friends and complete strangers have bailed me out again and again. They have given me money, paid for surgeries, put me up in luxury, and what have I done in return? Run away from them. I don't want to be like this. I promised Lachie and Oona that I would find a way to help them. Luca is my best chance of achieving that. I need to stay.*

At the top of the terrace steps, she spotted the blue vehicle, and laughed. She had convinced herself that all Americans were addicted to their gas guzzling, muscle machines. Instead, she found a hybrid electric Smart Car, its leather seats warming in the morning sun. *How on earth am I going to fit any shopping in that?* She scurried to the open topped car and got in. The driver's seat was a perfect fit for her small form. A quick adjustment of the mirrors and she was away.

As she passed the ranch gates, at the entrance to the drive, she was aware of a glinting light in her peripheral vision. *Shit! That bloody reporter is still lurking.* Putting her foot to the floor, she caned the tiny engine down the street to the junction with Napa Road. A quick glance in her rear-view mirror confirmed her suspicions; the reporter was following her in a dark coloured jeep.

Mary tapped the destination into the touchscreen navigation system and floored the accelerator. *It may be small, but it's nippy. I'll lose him when I get to the town.* The jeep stayed at a respectable distance from her along

Highway Twelve, as she cruised past vineyards, wineries, ranches and smokehouses. The first cluster of large buildings she came to was signposted as an exclusive spa resort. It was rapidly followed by a similar advertisement for luxury kennels. *This really is a celebrity haven. There are more places to pamper yourself than to buy food.* The Highway rounded a curve at the base of the valley, running parallel with the Napa River. Following the signposts, Mary took the exit ramp and overpass taking a convoluted route through a maze of streets to lose the jeep behind her.

In the retail parking lot, Mary found a tiny space flanked by huge cars all around and squeezed the Smart Car into position within the white lines. With a quick look in all directions, she felt content to leave the safety of the car and hurry into the shopping precinct.

What is he expecting me to buy with ten thousand dollars, diamond encrusted knickers? Mary by-passed the elite shops which carried all the most expensive labels and cut a diagonal path to the high street stores. A pair of standard trainers, or sneakers as the assistant called them, in the sports shop and she was kitted out for a whirlwind shopping spree before lunch.

She began with the casual wear. Three pairs of jeans, a selection of plain t-shirts and a half dozen pairs of socks. Next, was a small boutique for the obligatory little black dress. Mary winced at the cost. She caught one of the assistants sniggering behind her back as Mary tried on the gown. She looked down at her feet. Her bare feet in black trainers did look comical, but Mary sensed that she was laughing at her frizzy halo of unkempt hair. It seems that dashing about a retail park in the heat of a late Californian summer, induced a kind of mania with her locks. She looked at herself in the full-length mirror. *Dear God, I am a mess.*

Leaving the change booth, Mary paid for the dress and asked the girl on the tills where the nearest salon was located. She made a detour back to the car to deposit the shopping and returned as a walk-in customer, waving crisp dollar bills at the receptionist. That seemed to get their immediate attention. Roughly ninety minutes later, Mary emerged with sleek clipped hair, painted nails and the lingering after burn of a full wax. She was just on her way to purchase lingerie and a decent trouser suit, when she heard an echoing voice inside her head. Stopping outside a diner, she tucked herself close to the shop windows and plugged her ears with her fingers against the traffic noise.

"Hello?" The greeting was projecting from within her mind, extending the frequency out into the ether. *"Is that you Dan?"* Another wait. She concentrated hard on amplifying any feedback or sensations that she could pick up on. *"Hello... Lachie?"*

"Mary...help us." It was faint, but definitely someone trying to make contact. *It can't be Dan,* Mary reasoned. *He has a strong ability to connect with me.*

"Am I speaking to Lachie and Oona at the Summerfield Retreat?"

There was that echo again. It was infused with unrestrained emotion. Mary could feel the terror and sadness welling up through the transmission.

"Who is Lachie and Oona?" The voice came back, clearer this time, and with a notable Russian inflection. Mary gasped.

"Captain? Is that you?"

"Mary...at last we have found you."

"Captain Thirty-Four?" Mary steadied herself against the wall of the diner. It could not be. Was this really the captain of Alexi's Hive Mind? The leader of a team of conscripted personnel who were kept in a constant state

of coma, with the sole purpose of exploiting their mind control capabilities? The very same unit that the British Secretary of State for Defence had blown to smithereens in a diverted US Airforce drone strike? Mary stayed quiet, hoping that whoever was pranking her would make a tell-tale error.

"Mary...Can you hear us? We have been without direction or orders for such a long time. What is happening?"

There was no mistaking his accent. The rush of military presence was exhilarating. Her head filled with excited chatter and noise. It made her giddy. She pushed through the door of the diner and slumped onto a bench seat.

"What can I getcha?" The waitress said, flicking her lank hair out of her eyes.

"Oh, um...tea please, and a cheese sandwich, if you have it?"

"Grilled cheese for table six, Arnold." She shouted, scribbling in her notepad.

Mary was too bewildered to correct her. She held her head in her hands and listened to the building clamour of voices crowding her senses. How could she still hear their thoughts? Their physical bodies perished in the inferno at Fairfax Airport in Alaska. How could she possibly explain to the unit that they were not able to return to their families and loved ones, that they were cast adrift in the upper atmosphere, to end their days, slowly dissipating into space? *Oh God. That means that Parth's theory about consciousness and the Ionosphere could be true. He will be unbearable, and the fall out for all the religions across the world could lead to decades of conflict.*

Her warm milk and teabag arrived. She thanked the waitress and hid her face with her hands. *I can't put it off. These poor soldiers need to know. "Captain, are all your troops with you?" "No, Mary. A while ago we lost over half our unit at once. We assumed that since they were recruited together, they completed their service at the same time and went home to their families."*

Mary decoupled from the neural link. She did not want the Hive minds detecting the sadness welling up inside her and she needed a moment to think. A large fraction of those who died, also lost the retention of their consciousness within the ionosphere, but some did not. A small number remained accessible. What if she were still able to connect with her grandfather, or her long deceased parents? The thought buoyed her spirits a little. *First things first. I have to tell these men the truth.*

"Mary, where is the Colonel? We have not been given orders for a considerable time."

This could not be put off any longer. *"Captain, Colonel Visser is dead. There was a drone strike which blasted him, and all the shipping containers that you and your unit were stacked in. I am sorry to tell you this, but all of your bodies perished in the flames."*

All at once, the mutterings transmuted into loud howls, concurrent strings of angry Russian rants and sobbing. These men knew that something had gone dreadfully wrong, but the glimmer of hope that they might see their families once more, was extinguished. Anger, frustration and pent up seething, boiled into Mary's neural circuitry. She felt their pain as acutely as if she had suffered the same fate. She was their only link to the living world. *"I am so sorry."* She repeated over and over, but she knew the weight of her words was nothing. The grilled cheese order arrived, slammed down onto the table without fanfare or cutlery. Mary was not sure she could eat. With the roiling mess of emotions filling her entire being, refuelling her flesh seemed insensitive.

Sipping her tea, she allowed the dead to express their grief. The energies surged and bubbled inside her head, overloading her frontal lobes. What use was she to them now? After a few minutes, Mary felt as though her presence within their frequency was an intrusion. What if they stumbled upon a stray thought that gave away her part in their demise. That would add further insult to an already impossible situation.

"Captain, I feel your grief, and that of your comrades, but you all need time to come to terms with this awful state of affairs. If there is anything I can do to ease the suffering, contact me again. In the meantime, I can only convey my deepest sympathies."

"We understand, Mary. At least now we have our answers. Thank you."

The disconnection was not as abrupt as she expected. Instead, they seemed reluctant to cut her psyche loose. Again, Mary waited patiently, until she could feel the last consciousness drift from hers. She ate her cooling lunch, while the waitress slopped more hot water into the dregs of her tea, expecting her to re-use the same teabag.

Was it too soon to try? Mary couldn't wait any longer. She took a slow breath and cleared her mind of trivia. With renewed hope she sent her message out into the airwaves. *"Grampy, can you hear me? Hello...Grampy?"* The acid burn of her sinuses stimulated her tear ducts, until they erupted into a stream of saline down her cheeks. *"Grampy...please, I need you." He has to be one of the few to survive physical death. He is too precious to lose forever. "Please."*

“Are you alright, Hun?” It was the hair flicking waitress. She rested her hand upon Mary’s shoulder and squeezed.

Mary used the napkin to dry her face and sniffed. “Fine. Thank you. I say, please may I have a clean cup and a new teabag?”

“You’re English, right?” The waitress smirked.

“How could you tell?” Mary found the energy to smile. Maybe it was just too soon for her grandfather to find his way back to her. Maybe.

The remainder of her expedition was completed in a pall of grief, but the distraction of shopping was welcome. With the Smart car boot and the passenger seat jam packed with bags, Mary set the navigation system to take her back to the ranch, and depressed the accelerator. The sun disappeared behind the clouds, casting the Napa Valley into a dejected bleakness. Even the vines lining the hillsides looked weary. Turning off Highway Twelve, she slowed for the junction that would take her up to Luca’s home. A wide old school bus, painted a garish turquoise, chugged and strained with the incline, it’s exhaust belching out plumes of black smoke.

The bus wound around the roads, at a pace that would frustrate a sloth. Mary shifted into second gear and crawled behind, keeping a sharp eye out for an opportunity to overtake. *Where could they be headed? There are only two ranches along this road, and one of those is Luca’s.* Eventually, the coach slowed, and pulled onto a dusty lay by at the roadside. Mary passed them slowly, taking in the collection of people disembarking the vehicle. Such a broad cross section of the population was represented by the passengers, Mary could not neatly pigeon hole them at all.

It was only when she peeked in her rear-view mirror and spotted the daubed placards leaning against the front of the bus, did comprehension dawn. The word had spread. Christians across the globe had united in their hatred of Mary. The faithful were raising an army.

Chapter Twenty

The moment Luca's automatic gates closed behind her, Mary knew she was trapped. The reporter must have posted her image online the second he snapped her leaving the ranch. How quickly the troops rallied. *This is a massive country. One coach load of locals is just the start. The longer I leave it, the more they will come. I need to get my brooch back and get out of here.*

With a determined plan fermenting in her mind, she carried her shopping up the terrace steps and into the lounge room.

"Luca? Viktor? I'm back...Hello there." Mary wandered down the corridor to the study and tried the door. As usual it was locked. She pushed her ear to the wood and listened for voices, but only heard the dull roar of her own auditory chamber. "Where is everyone?" A quick circuit of the kitchen and utility rooms yielded nothing more than empty spaces. She returned to the terrace and looked over the valley towards the ranch gates. Christian protesters were positioning themselves across the entrance. The dark jeep was parked at the boundary; the reporter's vehicle.

Mary skipped back down the terrace steps to the courtyard. This was an area she had yet to explore. The first of the buildings housed plastic crates for the fruit collection. Workers were visible through the windows, stacking them into high leaning towers. She rapped on the glass.

"Have any of you seen Senator Bonovich?"

They all shook their heads and returned to their task. *Weird. He must be around here somewhere or the ranch would be locked up.* She looked in each of the out buildings, but found more store rooms and equipment. It was when she reached the end of the courtyard that she sighted a gate and a pathway leading around the rear of the ranch house. Quickening her pace, she unlatched the gate and left it to swing open behind her. At the end of a long narrow walkway, sloping down into the hillside, were two large steel doors. "Holy shit. Luca has his own bunker."

A thousand connections whirred in her brain. A flood of unfounded suspicions and worries, fixing her to the pathway. Why would he have a bunker? Was this the start of the wine caves, or something more sinister? The similarities with the underground storage bunker at The Summerfield Retreat rang alarm bells in her prefrontal cortex. "But he's a Senator…"

"Yes I am. You're back sooner than I expected." Luca loomed up behind her, his soft shoes muffling his footsteps.

"Jeez…you scared the…" Mary didn't know what to say. She couldn't take her eyes from the steel doors ahead.

Luca took in her defensive posture and lack of speech. "It's my sanctuary. Part of the cave system around here. Would you like to see?"

Mary was not sure that she did. Could Luca be trusted? Her judgement of character had been way off the mark for years. Was Karan right to warn her off him? A hasty risk assessment persuaded her that she still retained the upper hand. After all, she could always give him a jolt of electricity to match his lightning strike. "Okay." She tried to sound nonchalant but it came off as haughty.He beamed, stepping ahead to wrench open the heavy doors. She dipped under his outstretched arms and entered the cavern inside. Disorientated, she blinked until her eyes adjusted to the ambient glow from the walls. "I'd turn on the lights for you, but it's best to view the tanks in the dark like this." He touched her shoulders and gently pushed her forwards. At first, she thought the walls were moving, but closer inspection revealed an underwater world of elegant species, each with their own magical powers. Electric eels, medusae jelly fish, cuttlefish, catfish, stingrays, different sub-species of sharks; the aquarium virtually surrounded them with bio-luminescence in one form or another. The effect was hypnotic. Mary lost herself in their depths. So many creatures existing in harmony together.

"How is it that they aren't eating one another?" All thoughts of distrust dissolved into the waters.

"I feed them well. There have been a few mishaps, but on the whole, it works…somehow." He watched Mary. Her fascination with his pride and joy made him smile. "I come here when I need to block everyone else out. The rocks here are rich in iron minerals, dozens of feet thick. It acts like a Faraday cage. Blocks out all other frequencies. It's very peaceful."

"And yet you let me in." She turned to him, honoured by his invitation into his personal space.

He nodded, slipping his fingers into the belt loops of her jeans and pulling her towards him. "Uhuh. You had your hair cut. It's nice."

Mary stood on tip toes and reached up to kiss him. He obliged, bending low to meet her. She wondered if he was digging around inside her mind as they smooched. It broke her concentration.

"So how far back do these caverns go?" She needed to distract him. It was hypocritical of her to worry about him trawling through her thoughts, but she couldn't help herself. It unnerved her. Now she knew how Shrimant Karan Shinde felt when he thought she was reading him.

"Oh, miles. There are a series of larger and smaller caves, right across the mountains. Most contain wine casks. We had to blast some with explosives to open them out, make them more useful, others only needed passageways dug between them."

"Don't you ever feel claustrophobic?" She turned back to the aquarium glass as a reef shark drew close.

"Can't say that I do, really. It's the only place where no one bothers me."

"What's through there?" Mary pointed to a bolted door on the far side of the space.

"Just access to the tanks." He moved towards the exit, grabbing her wrist and tugging at her arm. "Come on, I'll ask Viktor to make us afternoon tea."

"Can we go and feed the fish?" Mary resisted his pull, leaning back towards the locked door.

"Another day. It's a mess back there. Come on."

Mary grumbled, but complied. She didn't want to push her luck. He had shared his grief over losing his daughter and now allowed her into his private sanctum. The least she could do was to respect his boundaries.

They returned to the ranch house. Mary stowed her shopping away in the guest quarters, Luca answered a call on his mobile phone and Viktor arranged their refreshments. Mary was first to arrive back at the terrace. The Christians at the gates were growing in number, their placards hoisted high for the news crew setting up just beyond. *Oh hell. Not again. CNN must have news crews in every bloody state.* She turned back and walked inside the lounge. Luca's muffled voice bled through the study door. What was it about those books that drew her attention? It was like someone was tugging at her neurons, urging her to confirm a nebulous fact. Grabbing the photographic book from the shelves, Mary settled cross-legged on the reading chair and flicked through each of the pages. It was an excellent vantage point. Kitchen staff, winery managers and Viktor bustled through to the study door, and not one noticed her quiet presence.

Monasteries, volcanic craters, The Kremlin… She turned each page with an urgency that she could not explain. Viktor reappeared with a tray of muffins and coffee, slamming it down on the coffee table with a grunt which said; *I am not their fucking slave.* He left the room muttering sour and guttural noises which made no sense to Mary whatsoever. The next page in the book made Mary gasp. It depicted a snowy day in Moscow, The Royal Citadel clearly visible behind the Russian President. The two western figures clad in thick ski wear, were indisputable. Those mischievous blue eyes twinkling beneath the beanie hat as he shook the president's hand. The same blue eyes that had lulled her into submission in his sanctuary only minutes before. The second man was Viktor.

Mary couldn't move. Her arms rigid and trembling, her breath quickened by the adrenal spike in her central nervous system. A few weeks ago, her immediate response would be to run. Experience had taught her to learn more first. With Luca's image burned into her memory, she took a few calming breaths and returned the book to the shelves. Moving to the settee, she poured two cups of coffee from the cafetière, and added a splash of cream to one. With her arms crossed, she leaned back and waited, framing her interrogation questions in her mind. She was just considering whether to simply present the photograph to Luca and demand an explanation, when he walked into the room.

"Sorry about that. So much for a few days of downtime, eh?"

She flashed him a lack lustre smile. He paused, and frowned. "What's wrong now?"

"Nothing it's fine. Have you any more news about Alexi and the Summerfield Retreat? Did agents track down the nuclear materials?" She could not prevent her eyes from narrowing as she spoke.

It made him more guarded in his response. "As it happens, yes. It is all dealt with. Big raid, materials recovered, everything sown up. You were right, he is a dangerous little crook." He reclined on the settee and balanced his left ankle on his right knee. "So, you can relax now. Everything is under control."

"And there were no fatalities, no opposition to the raid?"

"Casualties, I believe. No one died, I don't think. I haven't seen the report yet." He gazed at her dark irises and frowned again. "What's eating you? I thought you'd be glad."

"Oh, I am, it's just hard to believe that it's all over with, so easily." It took the wind out of her sails. She had geared herself up for a confrontation, but now saw no need to question him. He wouldn't stop staring. A pincer grip took hold of her thoughts. She felt him lock onto her consciousness with such brute force, it made her woozy. Sifting through her worries, he alighted on the image of him and Viktor with the Russian President. Laughing, he released her at once.

"Is that it? My you are a suspicious one. I don't suppose you read the dedication in that book, did you?"

Mary shook her head.

"My cousin was the photographer. It's his book. He came with Viktor and me on a diplomatic trip to visit the Kremlin. My one and only chance to meet the president was captured in a book, which he dedicated to me." He unfolded his legs and sat forwards to reach his coffee. "Anything else you want to grill me on, Ms Arora, or do I get a pat on the back for my efforts?"

"What about Lachie and Oona? Have they been arrested? Can you do anything to help them?"

"Who is Lachie and Oona?"

"Alexi is blackmailing them. They didn't want to be involved in his plot, he forced them." Her plea was urgent and desperate.

Luca cocked his head to one side, evaluating her earnestness. "I'll see what I can do."

"Oh, thank you." Mary leaned forwards and pecked him on the lips. "Thanks. They are such innocents. All of them really. They are not in Alexi's league, by any stretch of the imagination."

"I have said I will do what I can, Mary. That is the end of it. Okay?" He thumped his coffee mug down on the table, stood up and walked out onto the terrace. Mary was dumbfounded. What had provoked his temper? For a few seconds, she debated whether or not to follow. His moods were so difficult to predict. By the time she had made up her mind to join him on the patio, she found him descending the steps, out onto the courtyard.

Mary watched Luca meet up with a black Lexus as it slowed down and drew level with him. Luca bent down to the tinted driver's window as it lowered. He greeted the man in the grey pinstripe suit, who then handed him a small plastic box and a documents folder. The window rose and the car drove in a circle, before leaving the property entirely. *Another party delivery? Too small.*

Now where's he going. Mary sneaked down the edge of the terrace steps. Luca clutched the folder and parcel tight to his chest, opened the gate to the narrow pathway, and headed for his sanctuary. *Whatever that is, it is not meant for public viewing.* She waited for him in the lounge, but Luca did not return from his sanctuary until later in the evening, after Viktor had fetched her from the guest apartment to dine.

The gathering of Christian protesters and reporters had doubled in size, in just a few hours. Mary shied away from the terrace and their intrusive long lenses. Viktor called to some of the vineyard staff to assist with a large delivery of hired furniture and crockery for the party. With everyone busy at their labours, Mary was free to explore. Her nosiness took her up the main staircase and into the master suite. She tapped gingerly on the door and entered. The room was immaculate. Minimalist furnishings, a bathroom the size of a municipal pool and a large area devoted to his clothes and possessions. She wandered past the modern artwork, taking note of the collection of expensive watches suspended on individual stands on a tallboy dressing unit. Here, she found more photographs of his daughter. Ava was cradled in the arms of a slender blond woman, who looked to be in her early thirties. Mary supposed that she was Luca's ex-wife. It seemed odd that he should display pictures of a woman to which he was no longer married. Another frame showed the three of them together, all wearing fur lined Cossack hats, and playing in the snow. Luca beamed with happiness. *Must have been take during that trip to Moscow.*

It stirred something inside Mary. Men who adore little children have a strange appeal. It heightens their attractiveness exponentially, even if there is no intention to have children with them. Mary always thought that the allure must be written into the biological blueprint on the X chromosome. Shaking off her suspicions, Mary glared at the rows of business suits and formal shoes, the back lit wall of sneakers perched on shelves and the array of shaving equipment. *He is certainly very neat and tidy. A place for everything and everything in its place. A bit of a control freak, like Parth.* Thinking of her own ex-husband brought its own level of sadness. One that laments the past as a failing, her failure to see through his charade. Parth was unfinished business. One day, she would have to confront him and lay the matter to rest.

"Hey little sister, can you talk? I have good news." Dan's ebullient tone inside her head was unmistakable. His warmth and affection bathed her brain in happy dopamine.

"Dan, it's lovely to hear from you. We seem to be prisoners of international time zones. *How's your mum?"*

"Good thanks. Tonnes better, and so is the PM. Yelena called me today to say that the warrant for your arrest has been dropped. She wants you to come back home."

"I bet she does."

"Isn't that great news? Your name will be dropped from international ports warnings."

"Yeah, I guess. Did she say anything about the Mental Health Bill being scratched?"

"Nope, I suppose that will take longer to sort out. The Secretary of State for the Environment has been shuffled to the Defence Department. She is now in charge of Yelena and her team at GCHQ Buckinghamshire."

"Oh great. She's almost as bad as the last Defence Minister. Almost."

"At least you can come home if you want to. Yelena has asked for our help. She said that Alexi was back on the radar. There has been chatter via Stoneghost metadata and the dark net; something to do with the transportation of radioactive materials?"

"Oh no that's all sorted now apparently. I told Senator Luca Bonovich about my findings in New Jersey, and he alerted the Feds. He told me earlier today that they raided the retreat and detained everyone."

"Not according to Yelena. She said satellite imagery show the retreat is very much still a going concern."

Mary was taken aback. She halted her rummaging in Luca's dressing room and stood fully upright. *"Why would he lie to me?"*

"What does your gut tell you? Can you trust this man?"

"He's a politician, of course he can't be trusted. I just don't know why he would lie about something so serious as this." Before she closed the cupboard, door something caught her eye. A large flat item, wrapped in folded fabric, leaned against the back wall of the cupboard.

"Perhaps you should get out of there. Has he threatened you in any way?"

"No, he hasn't. In fact, he saved my life. He is like us, Dan. He used his abilities to remove the bullet from near my spine. It's thanks to him that I can walk at all after the heist. And besides, he has Grandma Phebe's brooch in his safe. I couldn't leave until I get that back."

"The second you feel under threat, get out of there, do you hear me?"

"I hear you, Dan."

"Promise?"

"Uh uh. I promise."

"Catch you later little sister." The connection broke between the siblings, leaving Mary feeling as though she had let Dan down. He wanted her to run back to England and settle down with her PhD studies. She wanted that too, but not if it meant being under the MoD yolk.

The flat object was heavy. She knelt down on the polish oak floor boards and reached in with both hands. Tipping it towards her, she unwound the fabric from the corner. A steel frame surrounded a canvas. She peeled the covering back a little further to reveal the multicoloured overlapping circles of a familiar work of Kandinsky. The very same artwork stolen during the heist.

Chapter Twenty-One

Mary could not believe what she was seeing. There was only one possible explanation for the Kandinsky being in his closet. Luca arranged the heist. He was responsible for the death of his own security guard. It was his fault that Karan nearly got killed. Luca was to blame for the bullet lodged next to her spine.

Why would Luca do such a thing? What could he possibly gain from such actions? He'd garnered enough publicity through the lightning strike. Was he trying to play the hero? Mary wrapped the Kandinsky in its fabric covering and slid it back in the cupboard. She had to keep her cool. Was Luca involved in the Summerfield retreat? She knew it was risky, but she had to play along with him to get Phebe's brooch back. More importantly, she had to find out what else he had planned. Perhaps Yelena could be of help after all. If she knew about Alexis plans, then surely MI6 were aware. No longer being a fugitive was an immense relief. She was free to do as she pleased. At least, she would be, if her sense of duty was not so pronounced. It was hard to believe that Alexi's activities had flown under the radar for so long. Luca had to be helping him. Was she really the last line of defence from the general's latest plot?

There was one thing about Mary's decision that bothered her. What if, in her quest to find answers, Luca reads her mind? If he found out that she suspected him of collaborating with a known terrorist, she would be placing herself at his mercy. What if he too could discharge electromagnetic pulses too? She had to take that chance. Mary closed the cupboard, left the room and ran downstairs. Victor gave her a scowl as she walked into the lounge. *Just act normal, Mary. Don't give Luca an excuse to read me.*

They dined on the terrace as the sun sank beneath the horizon, painting the sky in tones of pink and orange. The food was delicious. Wild mushrooms and pine nuts in a parcel with fresh salads, and new potatoes in a lemon and dill sauce. It gave Mary the opportunity to focus on her plate. She did all she could to avoid looking into Luca's eyes.

"Have you seen the protesters at the gate." Mary looked up briefly and then straight back down to her meal.

"Yeah, but what can we do about it? If I get Viktor to drive them away, reporters will tell the world that I'm a tyrannical hater of religion. I'm dammed if I do and I'm dammed if I don't."

"You know they're here for me, don't you? If you ask Victor to take me to the nearest station, they'll leave you alone. I just need my brooch back. I mean, I'm very grateful to you, but I really think it's best that I leave."

"What and miss the party? Victor tells me that you're no longer a wanted woman. You have every right to be here." There was that charming smile again, the one she had trouble resisting.

How did Viktor find out before me, I wonder? Mary kept her musings to herself. This was not the time to rile him. "How on earth are you going to explain my presence at your party to all of your visiting dignitaries? What if they have seen the footage on You Tube and have heard of Miracle Mary?"

"I don't care if they have. It's all good publicity for my campaign."

"You'll drive away all the religious votes if they think we are together." She risked looking up into those expressive eyes. He was gazing into the distance. He swallowed his food and washed it down with vintage wine of his own label.

"Doesn't matter anymore. Looks like I have lost most of the house anyway. My proposed 5G bill will get heard as a matter of procedure. It hasn't a hope in hell of being passed." Still he looked towards the gates and the silhouetted placards waving in the twilight.

"I am sorry, Luca. I know how much it meant to you. Are there any other avenues you could pursue? Could you, perhaps, fund more research into the dangers it poses?"

"I could fund a hundred studies into the dangers of fifth generation cellular technology, it won't make a shred of difference." He analysed her perplexed air, and offered an explanation. "This president is a low bureaucracy capitalist. He has already scrapped all legislation and proposals that benefit public health and the environment, all to favour commerce. I have had to fight tooth and nail to get this far, and he'll use my failure to boot me out of the EPA Chief position. He has one of his pets lined up for my job already."

Mary didn't know how to console him. She could understand his frustration, almost sympathise with his plight, but anyone assisting in Alexi's plots had to be stopped, whatever part he had to play. After an almost silent, barely eaten dessert, it was obvious that Luca was not in a talkative mood. The noise from the floodlit chanters at the front gate, soured their meal. They rose from their seats and walked into the lounge. Luca offered Mary a cognac as he poured one for himself. She declined.

"Luca, please could you fetch my brooch? I'd like to wear it tomorrow."

"Yeah, sure. In the morning. It's in the sanctuary."

"I thought you said it was in your safe?"

"It is. There is a safe in the cave too." He swilled the rich liquid around the glass and sipped. "It's late. Let's go to bed."

Mary opened her mouth to protest, but he was already walking towards her guest rooms. She huffed a sigh. "Why don't we sleep in your bed for a change?" She wanted to see his reaction to her suggestion, but he had anticipated her question.

"You get more of a breeze through the ground floor rooms. Are you coming, Lady Sedgewell? Come and ravage me."

She froze. *Lady* Sedgewell? What did he know that she did not? *Can't let him know that I am rattled. Keep it together, Mary. I can do this.* She trotted along after him and kicked the door shut behind her.

***

Luca already seemed settled into a routine. Again, he rose before Mary and sat searching through news reports online, while he ate his muesli on the terrace. She slouched in the chair next to him, pulling her robe around her against the intrusion of long lens cameras.

"Do you have time to show me around the winery today?" She felt sure that he would jump at the chance to show off his accomplishments, but he did not even look up from his tablet PC.

"I'll ask Viktor to take you on a tour."

"Oh. Don't bother."

That made him look up at her. “You don’t like him?”

“He doesn’t like me. Always snarling and grimacing. He’s like a bad-tempered goat.”

“A goat?”

“It’s that nasty little straggly beard thing on his chin.”

Luca erupted in laughter. He put the tablet down and focused on her. It made her feel uncomfortable. Was he trying to read her again, or was this more of a lover’s analysis? She couldn’t tell.

“How about this...? I have the State Governor coming over for a meeting. He’ll stay for the party later this afternoon. I’d appreciate your help entertaining his wife while we talk. We can meet up at lunchtime and I’ll take you all around the winery then. What do you say?” He grabbed hold of her hand across the table. Mary envisioned the headlines in the evening news; *Senator bewitched by Miracle Mary*. She shuddered at the thought.

“You want me to play hostess? That’s a bit dangerous isn’t it?”

“Why? You aren’t planning on electrocuting them, are you?” His humour bubbled over into an irritating smirk. Was she just a source of amusement to him?

“Fine.” She grabbed a pancake from the stack on the table and stood up. “What about my brooch?”

“I’ll get it, don’t nag me. It’s not going anywhere is it? Besides, from what I have seen, it’s safer locked away.”

Mary wandered off, muttering under her breath. *Hmm, and while you have that jewel captive, I can’t go anywhere. May as well put me in shackles.*

After her shower, Mary stood in front of her new clothes hanging in the guest wardrobe, and sighed. *I’m pretty sure that nothing I bought will be suitable for what’s in store today. I am not cut out for entertaining*

Californian politicians and local celebrities. Ah well, who cares what they think. Jeans it is. No matter how she blow-dried and combed her hair, she could not make it behave in the same way as the hairdresser had at the salon. An awkward section stood up in a cow's lick on the left side of her forehead. Defeated, she made her way out to the courtyard, to meet the Governor and his wife with Luca.

They arrived in a black limousine with two large bulletproof security cars either side. The team of agents spread out along the perimeter of the courtyard, and dispatched others to patrol the grounds and ranch gates. It was beginning to resemble Fort Knox.

"Welcome to my humble grove, Millicent, Zak. Good of you to join us." Luca offered his hand to the tall woman in the linen suit as she spilled out of the rear of the limousine. Her husband rolled out from the opposite side.

"Say, what's all the rumpus down at your gates? We barely made it through." The governor levelled his waistband over his paunch with a tug, and buttoned up his light cotton jacket.

"Ah, it's not so bad. They have a right to voice their opinions, providing they do not trespass or cause damage." Luca waited until the fat man had rounded the back of the limousine before making the introductions. "Mary, this is Governor Zak Cooper and his long-suffering wife, Millicent."

Mary stepped forwards at shook their hands in turn. "Hello there, I'm Mary, Luca's…um…guest."

The governor grabbed her with both hands, jogging her entire body with his exaggerated greeting. His wife's hand was limp and clammy. Neither she nor Mary relished the physical contact, retreating at the earliest opportunity. As one decisive group, they mounted the steps and hovered next to the freshly cleared breakfast table.

"May I get either of you some refreshments? Tea, coffee, a soft drink perhaps?" Mary clasped her hands together and searched their faces for any clues as to their intentions.

The governor looked at Luca and then at his wife. "Soft drinks? Do you mean soda? Hell, if I wanted to raid the kids stash, I'd have stayed at home."

Millicent peered down at Mary. "He'll take a bourbon on the rocks."

Mary's eyes reduced to slits. "I'm sorry, I just thought that Luca and Zak would need to keep a clear head for their meeting."

"Zak?" Millicent boomed, from a husky, smoke damaged larynx. "You are addressing the governor of the great state of California in the greatest country in the world. Show a little respect and use his title."

"Greatest…? I meant no disrespect, but on what evidence are you basing this assumption? If we are talking about the sheer volume of gun and drug related crime as a parameter, then yes, the US wins hands down."

The governor bit down on his bottom lip, sucking in enough breath for his retort. "Now look here, young lady…"

"Why is it that men immediately resort to condescension whenever their arguments can't be justified?" Mary feigned bewilderment, and wandered off into the lounge room to pour his midmorning bourbon. She returned to the terrace with the tumbler, half-full and without the ice. "There you go, Gov. Bottoms up."

Luca curled up from laughter, holding his sides and wiping tears from the pronounced wrinkles at his temples.

Mary was on a roll. What did she care if this power hungry and pretentious couple hated her. That she could live with. Now that the warrant for her arrest was nullified, she was free to do exactly as she liked. "I'm going to make myself a pot of tea. Millicent, would you care for a cup?" Mary didn't wait for an answer, but turned on her heels and sauntered towards the kitchen. As she did so, she heard the governor bluster;

"Who does she think she is?"

And Luca responding with, "Believe me, she has no idea who she truly is."

The caterers arrived early, and took over most of the ground floor in their preparations. Mary worked around them, searching in cupboards for a tea service, and accompanying items. Eventually, she found a bone china set in the mahogany unit of the formal dining area. She gave it a good rinse, warmed the pot with hot water and added four teaspoons of leaf tea while the kettle boiled. Stacking the rest of the set onto a carved wooden tray, she carried her elevenses out into the sunshine.

Millicent sat, with a thunderous scowl scoring through her Gucci sunglasses. "I'd prefer coffee." The men had disappeared into Luca's study, leaving Millicent to commandeer the seat at the head of the table.

Mary laid the tray down with care, and sat opposite the governor's wife. "I'm sure you would." She said, lifting the lid of the pot and creating a mini typhoon inside with a whirling spoon. "Milk?" She splashed a little into her own cup, and suspended the jug over her guest's.

Millicent shook her head. Mary shrugged, balanced the strainer over her cup and poured. Unpacking the items from the tray, she placed a small china plate and napkin in front of Millicent, along with tiny pots of jam, cream and the butter dish. "Would you care for a scone?"

"No, I would not. Don't you Brits know what carbs do to your body?"

"Indeed, we do. They provide us with starch based energy. An essential food group, in moderation. Although moderation appears to be something you Yanks struggle with." Mary looked up at the skeletal woman with fresh insight. "Aren't you just a teensy bit hungry?"

Millicent glared her response, but the loud rumble from her intestines betrayed her. Mary smiled, piling the clotted cream onto the scone and slowly lifting the cake to her mouth. "Mmm. You are missing a treat."

"So, how did you bag the most eligible man west of the Rockies?"

"Oh, I didn't 'bag' him. He got me shot and felt guilty. I suppose he could have left me to die, but he didn't. I still haven't worked out why."

"You were shot?" Millicent sat fully upright in her seat. "When, how?"

"Surely you heard about the heist at the charity auction at the Broad Street Ballroom?"

"That was you? The reports said that someone was shot and killed." Millicent reached for her teacup, through habit more than necessity.

"One of Luca's security team was killed. I survived."

The governor's wife opened her mouth to deliver platitudes, but decided against such an action. They sat in silence for an interminable time, each supping from their teacup and listening to the incessant chants from the valley floor. Mary could see that Millicent was itching to ask about the Christians at the gate, and that her abstention was to avoid acknowledging her fame.

Mary did not want to fuel hostilities. She was supposed to be hosting these people, however odious they were. Her grandfather would have berated Mary for her rudeness. She offered Millicent an armistice. “Were you born in California?”

“Can’t you tell from my accent? I’m Texan, through and through. Met Zak at college.”

“Goodness. And how do you feel about the shunning of oil based energy supplies in favour of alternatives?”

Millicent balked. Mary had stumbled over grazed nerves. She watched her compose herself and formulate a guarded response.

“It’s wonderful. If only other states would take the bull by the horns and diversify.” The collar of her blouse stuck to the damp skin on her neck. She pulled at the fabric, grimacing at the indiscretion. “Of course, it has been a terrible blow to old families who built their fortunes around oil, but progress is progress.” A nervous giggle erupted subconsciously and deflated.

Mary wondered just how old she classed, ‘old families’ to be, but kept it to herself. “I guess they can still move their wealth into new technology, avoiding complete disaster?”

“Sure, but which technology do you invest in that will provide the same security as oil?”

“I see the dilemma. If only we had a crystal ball…”

Millicent snorted. It was an involuntary display of mirth. Despite herself, she was warming to Mary.

Steering the conversation down less contentious pathways, the women waited for their partners to return. When they did, Zak had a fresh tumbler of alcohol balancing on his outstretched palm.

Millicent noticed immediately. "Oh Coop, you said you'd go easy."

"This is easy, darlin'. I promise I'll make this one last." Zak stood at the edge of the terrace, shielding his eyes from the glare of the sun. "You should chase those noisy bastards off your land, or your guests will never get through to your party later. What's their beef? You bin shooting your mouth off, baiting good Christian folk, Bonovich?"

"Not me, Zak. They're here for Mary."

"Then for God's sake, give her to them. This could ruin your career." The fat man tipped the bourbon down his throat as though it was a lifeline.

Luca grinned his famous laminated, plastic smile. "They are not on my land. They are exerting their First Amendment rights."

"I'll get it under control. I can have the National Guard here within a couple of hours tops. I got them stationed at Travis Air force Base, testing something out for me. I'll get the way clear." The governor fished in a trouser pocket for his mobile phone, wandering out of earshot as the connection was made. "Cell reception around here is shit." Zak raised the phone high until he spied additional service bars on the device, and then hit a re-dial number.

Luca called after him. "Just leave it, Zak. They are not doing any harm." But it was too late. The order had been made.

Chapter Twenty-Two

Luncheon was awkward to say the least. Luca had his staff set up a table at the winery so that the ranch could be laid out and decorated ready for the guests. Mary detected a new friction developing between the two alpha males; their body language defensive and gruff. It seems as though their meeting was cut short, and did not end with the resolution for which Luca was hoping. The governor insisted that they travelled the short distance over the mountainside in his limousine, flanked by his security detail. The pretension was sickening. Mary covered her face with her hair as they nudged through the crowds of protesters, but it did not stop them from rushing at the stretched car and hurling abuse at the windows. Zak's stoic guards, jogged alongside the vehicle, growling at each Christian to back off. A flash of their holstered weapons was enough to clear a pathway large enough to drive through.

The menace of the religious zealots rendered the passengers silent. The men seemed buoyed by the experience, adrenalin fuelling their vibrant discourse.

At lunch, Millicent nibbled on a single oat cracker with a tapenade spread just thin enough to discolour the surface, while the men tucked into cold cuts of honied ham, cheeses and relishes of all distinctions. Mary ate a little of the French bread and tuned out the small talk. They were feet away from a sign which indicated a stairwell. Was this another entrance to the cave system? Memories of the Summerfield Retreat returned to give her indigestion. How did Luca fit into Alexi's scheme? What was he going to use the nuclear material for? Surely, he wasn't planning to detonate it as part of a nuclear attack, that would be suicide?

If she could just hang in long enough for Luca to slip up. Then she could get a message through to… to whom? Who could help her against such powerful men? The governor would have been a safe bet, if he hadn't spent the last hour hidden away with Luca in his private office. She popped a few grapes into her mouth, and grabbed the rest of the bunch before they could be cleared away. Luca announced the tour idea to Zak and Millicent, who seemed grateful for the distraction.

Taking control, Luca paraded them through the production lines, from the giant hoppers where the grapes are washed to the lower levels where the first presses still oozed from a recent batch. From there, the shiny stainless steel vats and chutes gave way to more traditional wood and glass as they descended into the cave system below. The temperature dropped by at least ten degrees with each level they traversed. It stabilised at precisely fifty-eight degrees Fahrenheit. Millicent shivered, pulling her jacket together at the front. Luca led them into a bank of shelving which supported the oldest of vintages, and invited them to sample three of his best wines.

The governor was most eager, swilling the first of the ruby liquids around its glass and neglecting to spit out the tasted mouthful. By his third glass of the prime vintage, his judgement failed him. Clanking the glass down heavily onto a wine cask, he fractured the stem, spilling the remainder of the liquid across the barrel and down the leg of his wife's trousers.

"Oh Coop. You clumsy oaf." She jumped backwards, brushing the wine further into the fibres with a swipe of her hand.

"Mary, there's a sluice sink the other side of that door, just behind you. You should find a clean cloth too." Luca gestured for Mary to take the governor's wife into the preparation room and assist her in the clean-up. Mary obliged, nodding and guiding Millicent through the swing door.

The sink was mounted to their left, and, as promised, clean cloths were stacked neatly in the cupboard beneath. Mary doused the cloth in cold water, wrung out the excess and handed it over. While the governor's wife rubbed ineffectually at the stain, Mary wandered the length of the preparation area and peered through a second set of doors. *So many gas cylinders.* She mused to herself. I know they use *Nitrogen to push the oxygen from the wine bottles, but who knew they needed this much? Must have a gas generator somewhere... oh, just there, in fact.* Mary closed in on the large metal cased machine, delivering freshly pumped gases into massive cannisters at its end.

Heavy booted footsteps came from a room beyond, along with a repetitive squeaking noise of trundling wheels. Someone was headed towards them. Mary did not move. Her heart rate quickened, and the desire to slip away grew ever more urgent. Taking a few paces closer to the gas machine set a cascade of neurotransmitters into her brain. The cylinders were each marked with a large H2. Luca was generating the explosive gas Hydrogen. For one terrified moment, Mary allowed the data to percolate through her senses. *What does he need that for? They need inert gases to stop the oxidation of wine, not something as volatile as Hydrogen.*

"Hey, what are you doing back here. This is for staff only." The man in the boiler suit, pushing a sack barrow bellowed at them.

Mary snapped back to her senses. "We're with Senator Bonovich. Just clearing up a minor accident, won't be a minute." Mary stepped aside, allowing the worker to see Millicent making a hash of cleaning away the wine stains.

"Well, it ain't safe back here, lady. Better go and clean up elsewhere."

"Right, yes. Of course. My apologies." Mary grabbed Millicent's sleeve and dragged her through the door, still clutching the wet cloth.

"These are ruined. Coop, I could strangle you."

"I'm sorry, honey. Maybe we can getcha something else to wear for the party?" The governor looked pointedly at Mary. She, in turn, looked at Luca.

"Perhaps Luca could ask his friend, Viktor, to pick something up for her from Napa?" Mary offered.

"He's got a rather important errand to run this afternoon, but I'm sure I can find someone else. Leave it with me." And with that, Luca cut short the tour, guiding them back to the main stairs, out of the winery and back to the limousine. The governor and Millicent barely noticed the abrupt alteration in the cordial atmosphere, but Mary saw the mercurial change in Luca. There was tension in the muscles surrounding his eyes and mouth. The easy smile plasticised into his media ready one, and the churning thoughts weighed down his brows. Had he read the Governors thoughts while Mary was in the sluice room with Millicent? What information had he gleaned that so altered his temper?

Their return to the ranch was stressful. Two further coach loads of militant faithful blocked the gate entrance, jostling and barging the limo from every angle, making it rock on its shock absorbers. Mary braced herself for a stream of rude language from the Governor, bemoaning the right to protest and the shoddy way in which Luca was handling the invasion, but it failed to manifest. Instead, he looked smug and calm, as if he knew something that they did not. The security team battled through the crowds and held them back with outstretched arms, allowing the limo to cruise through onto the property.

The courtyard was decked with festoons of twisted hops, interwoven with meadow flowers. Large patio flares stabbed the gravel at intervals, awaiting darkness to be lit. Small lanterns picked out the steps up to a canopied terrace. The buffet table spanned the length of the patio, laid with crisp linen and floral and fruit displays.

Luca directed his guests towards his own suite upstairs, allowing them time to freshen up and rest prior to the party.

"You don't mind me sharing your bathroom, do you?" This he uttered into her hair, heaving her close to his body. He smelled of faded cologne and the salt residue from a day in the heat.

"Please can you get my brooch first?"

"Yeah, sure." He kissed her fully on the mouth, and squeezed her tight, his arms enveloping her entire torso. It was as if he needed her to bolster his courage. A moment of vulnerability rising to the surface, quelled by her intimacy. She patted his back and then let her arms relax to her sides. He did not take the hint, but held onto her for a few seconds more. When he did release her, she wandered towards the guest apartment, stopping near to the bend in the corridor to look back at him. He had not moved. There he stood, watching her walk away from him, a contented expression smoothing out his frown lines.

Slightly perturbed, Mary entered the guest quarters and closed the door behind her. Why was he so difficult to fathom? How could someone be so duplicitous and so sweet at the same time? How could he campaign so diligently for environmental considerations and yet be tied somehow to Alexi and the Summerfield Retreat? Why had he gone to such lengths to keep her with him, even while ravening Christians were practically beating down his door?

Mary stripped off her dusty clothes and stepped into the shower. She washed quickly aware that Luca would return, and seeing her naked and wet, would initiate another round of carnal gymnastics. As much as she enjoyed him, she did not want to flood her brain with endorphins. She needed a clear head, and her wits about her. Clad in a layer of expensive lingerie and protected from advances with her towelling robe, Mary grappled her unruly hair as Luca entered the room carrying a garment bag, his formal dress shoes and a grey plastic box.

He took one look at her advanced state of dress and remarked, “Jeez, that was quick. I was hoping for a …”

“Have you got my brooch?”

Luca held out the grey container. It was the same box she had seen Luca take delivery of in the courtyard. Mary drew breath, and then checked herself, reining in her reaction. She took it from him and opened the case. It looked the same. The black jewel appeared unmolested, but she had to be sure. She ran her index finger over its surface, giving the setting a little wriggle to test its strength. The gem did not budge. Mary closed her eyes and offered up a prayer into the ether that it was the original jewel and not some fake knock off that Luca's colleague had swapped out.

"Where did the box come from?"

"Just one I had lying about in the sanctuary. Thought it might save it from any damage." The lie slipped from his tongue as easily as butter. "Is it really a good idea to wear it tonight, considering what happened last time?"

"It'll be fine as long as no one shines a laser pen in my direction."

"If you're sure…"

"I am." As she pinned the last slide into her curls, they were deafened by a droning roar changing pitch overhead. Mary rushed to the windows, leaning out over the sill. "Holy shit! It's one of those massive Chinook thing helicopters."

"That fucking bastard. I didn't think he'd have the balls. Serves me right for lowering his inhibitions with my finest vintage." They dashed from the apartment to the terrace as the Chinook hovered above the massing group of protesters carrying a large military vehicle from steel cables beneath. The pilot lowered the aircraft in an expert manoeuvre until the wheels of the truck made contact with the ground, before detaching the coupling device. While the helicopter found a landing site further down the road, the personnel inside the vehicle raised a motor driven array of equipment from its roof. They were approximately one hundred metres from the ranch gates.

Mary and Luca watched helplessly from the terrace. They were soon joined by the governor and his wife.

"See Bonovich, told you I would get it squared away for you." Zak's face shone from the effects of high blood pressure and alcoholism. Luca seethed, but there was little he could do.

Mary watched the flat square of metal reposition, controlled remotely by the passenger inside. “What is it?” She said it out loud, without thinking.

“They call them Active Denial Systems.” Luca growled, shooting the governor a lethal glare.

“Best invention since the internal combustion engine.” The governor grinned, teetering back on his heels.

“What does it do?” As Mary said it, the crowds of worshippers and faithful screamed in terror, protecting their faces with their arms and scattering in all directions. One tiny cluster remained, howling in pain while they pushed wheelchairs over uneven and tufted ground. “I don’t understand, what happened to them?”

“It fried their skin. It’s little more than a giant microwave, blasting one hundred kilowatts of energy in concentrated bursts. No sound, no sight, no warning. Just a rush of volcanic heat penetrating and cooking your skin through your clothes.” Luca turned to the governor. “Call them off, Zak. It’s inhuman.”

“Nonsense. They’ll be fine if they get out of the way. It’s perfectly safe.” He was posturing, exhibiting his importance and perceived superiority.

“And the infirm and elderly protesters who cannot move as quickly as the more able?” Mary reared up at the politician, spitting her question through clenched teeth.

The governor did not answer.

“I mean it, Zak, call them off. It’s barbaric and completely unnecessary.”

The flat antennae repositioned again, ready to fire more bursts into the fleeing crowds. An older woman tripped and fell, knocking her head on a rock during the landing. Within her unconscious state, the invisible beam continued to cook her from a distance of two hundred yards. Blisters the size of golf balls bubbled and popped with the prolonged exposure.

"Stop them, now!" Luca bellowed. He turned to Mary. "Call emergency services. I'll go down and see what I can do to help them." He rounded on the governor again. "For god sake, call off the guards."

Governor Zak Cooper waved his cell phone above his head, straining to see the absence of bars on the screen indicating signal strength. Luca ran towards the terrace steps but Mary called after him, halting him in his tracks.

"I don't have access to a land line phone."

"Use the one in the study. Door code is nine, five, one, nine, eight, one. Do it straight away." He ran down the steps two at a time, and disappeared from view. Mary skirted the lounge furniture and hurried through to the secure door key pad, barring access to Luca's private study. Sympathy for the injured and her thirst for knowledge spurred her on. As she punched in the numbers he had shouted. *Nine, five, one, nine, eight, one... No way.* She released what it meant. *The ninth day of the fifth month, nineteen eighty-one...the day I was born.* Mary shuddered. How much did he know of her background, and for how long? Her heart thumped in her chest as she stepped closer to his desk. *First things first. That poor woman needs an ambulance.* Dialling the emergency services, Mary told the operator as much as she knew, and asked if there was any possibility of sending an air ambulance, or the coast guard helicopter. The operator listened to the story and suggested that the Home Guard re-direct the Chinook to deliver the woman to the nearest Emergency Room. Mary did not think that a likely course of action, since they were the cause of the severe burns, and would claim no responsibility for their actions. She was out of options and of plausible reasons to offer up in explanation. The fate of the burned Christian was in the lap of her God.

With Luca busy at the gates and his guests looking on from the terrace, Mary risked a quick scan of his study. She guessed that anything too divisive would be under lock and key, long before the governor was permitted entry, but she could not miss the chance to snoop. The in-trays of brushed steel were laden with paperwork. A quick flick through them informed her that it was a stack of orders and subsequent shipments of wines, cleaning fluids and raw ingredients. Other files showed the enormous costs of transporting the cases of Luca's finest across the world. Everything appeared to be perfectly fitting for the manager of a family vineyard. *It's obvious he would not have told me the door code if there was anything incriminating for me to see. Luca is much too careful for that.* A quick examination of the room showed that he was as neat and tidy in his work dealings as with his wardrobe. Even the framed diplomas and winery awards were mounted to fit a precise rectangle on the far wall.

With a disappointed sigh, she moved towards the door. As she ambled, a logo for a meteorological supplies company caught her attention. It showed a cumulus cloud, bisected with a wind vane. Half of the A4 sheet was masked with papers, piled on the opposite side of Luca's desk. Mary tugged the paper clear of the rest of the letters. She read through the top section at speed, and then went through it a second time, looking for the company or people responsible for the order. None were present. All that she could discern, was that it was an invoice for five hundred high altitude weather balloons, to be delivered to the tiny town of Summerfield, New Jersey.

Chapter Twenty-Three

The implications of this information took a few moments to slot into place. The hydrogen gas generation, shielded alternative technologies, the high-altitude weather balloons and Alexi's test flights at the retreat, the transportation of nuclear material all pointed towards one conclusion. They were planning a global attack on electrical equipment emitting harmful frequencies. A choreographed series of electromagnetic pulses to fry all circuitry, barring those protected underground. The Summerfield Retreat was no military training ground, it was an end of days compound, and Luca was funding them.

Mary's mind ran through the multitude of systems and life-preserving services which would be wiped out during the attacks; hospitals, emergency services, public transportation… the list was endless. Inside her head, she recalled her brother's voice as he read out a passage from her grandfather's journal. The same passage that predicted disaster on a cataclysmic scale, but when and where would it take place? If she had any chance of stopping them, she needed the details. Returning to her senses, she found herself hyperventilating. *Grampy's premonition was right. These lunatics are going to plunge the western world back into the dark ages. I wish that wise old bird was with me now. He would know what to do. Okay, think, Mary. What would Grampy do?*

She sat heavily in Luca's office chair, glancing periodically over her shoulder at the corridor beyond the open door. *He would keep calm, and search for dates, times, places, potential targets.*

With something concrete to focus on, Mary opened each of the drawers in the single filing cabinet and those in the desk, but found nothing but stationary. She found his appointment diary in a zipped leather portfolio on the shelves behind her. A quick flick through its contents revealed a packed itinerary of meetings, committees and appointments. None shed any light on Luca's side line of terrorism. She levered the laptop lid open, and watched the software cycle through its greetings. A finger tap on the track pad brought a log on screen to the fore. There was no time to figure out password combinations. She hammered in her birthday digits in a futile bid to unlock the contents. It warned her of the consequences of repeated password failures. She was about to try Luca's daughter's name, when she heard loud footsteps approaching. Slamming shut the computer, Mary tucked the chair beneath the desk just as Viktor reached the doorway.

"How did you get in here? This is out of bounds." His growl was particularly vehement.

"Luca gave me the code. An ambulance is on its way for that injured woman by the gates." Mary stepped around Viktor, who scanned the room for any evidence of tampering. She could feel his scowl boring a hole in the back of her head like the microwave emitter of the National Guard. Hurrying back through the lounge, she found the governor helping himself to more bourbon on the terrace. They stood together for a moment, Zak watching the commotion at the gates with an obscene amount of pride, and Mary clinging to her bathrobe looking on in horror. The Chinook was silhouetted against the coral skies of the setting sun, its roar reverberated in her chest as it took off, hovered momentarily, and finally lifted the truck clear of the ground. Leaves, powdered dirt and twigs all swirled in a funnelled-up draft, coating everything in debris. All that remained, were the injured and a TV crew, delighted to have captured the entire scene, plus the added bonus of the Californian Senator attempting to administer first aid to the afflicted.

"Where did all the Christians go?" Mary ventured. The governor shrugged his response, grabbing a handful of the freshly delivered buffet morsels, and cramming them into his dribbling mouth.

Mary wandered back to the guest apartment and sat on the bed. She considered her jeans, laying over the back of an occasional chair, her trainers on the floor beneath. *If I run now, I may never find out when and where they will strike. If I stay, I am in danger of Luca reading my thoughts. How can I behave as though I am unaware of their plans? I am worse than useless at acting as if everything is fine.* The memory of her grandfather's vision flitted through her mind. He saw iconic buildings and structures from cities across Europe and America fall. This attack was meant for the entire western hemisphere, perhaps even more. He recounted the sight of impaled children, explosive fires at electrical sub-stations, colossal crashes on highways and roads.

She knew what a large EMP could achieve. Aircraft would fall from the sky, train signals would fail, life support as we know it, would cease to be - permanently. No economies, no banks, no food distribution, nor water, nor sewage treatment. It would take mere hours, rather than days, for civilised behaviour to disintegrate into the chaos of every man for himself.

Mary shook herself alert. She shed the bathrobe and slipped into her black evening dress, pinning Phebe's brooch to the neckline.

"There but for the grace of God, go I." A favourite quote of her father's, whenever he was battling with her mother. She inhaled a long, slow breath and released it through pursed lips. "I can do this." She stepped into her new sling backs and marched from the room.

Mary re-joined the governor, helping herself to a stiff drink from the hospitality tray. Together, they watched Luca shake hands with the paramedics arriving first at the scene. Floodlit and holding a fluffy microphone in his scarred hand, Luca talked his way through an impromptu interview with the reporter at the scene, his brow furrowed in mock concern. Mary could imagine what propaganda spilled from his fake smiles, in an attempt to bolster his popularity further still. He would gush with messages of support for those injured and point the finger of blame squarely at the Home Guard. After he had extracted every ounce of media coverage possible, he took a direct route up the hillside, through vines and rough ground, climbing the last few feet like a mountain goat, up to the patio.

Luca held Mary loosely around the waist, dipping low to speak quietly into her ear. "I have to shower and change. Can you welcome the guests as they arrive? I saw a couple of limos heading this way a minute ago." He didn't wait for her to respond. He bounded down the corridor to the guest apartment and slammed the door behind him.

Mary stood at the top of the terrace steps, shaking hands and directing guests towards the catering staff for drinks. The first few visitors made mention of the emergency services crew bundling victims into several ambulances. Their inquisition provided an excellent means of deflection, should any of the visitors recognise her as Miracle Mary. Her nerves began to dissolve the moment she realised that most of the guests already knew one another. It was a tight circle of friends, acquaintances and political adversaries, each attending the same gatherings month in month out. Mary was the outsider, and that was her preferred status.

The only guest that Mary actively avoided was CEO of global pharmaceutical giant, Bernice Feinstein. Bernice, however, had other ideas.

"Hey, Mary. I wondered whether I would catch you here..." She broadcast her greeting across the crowds milling about in the lounge. Mary looked for an escape route, but she was fleet of foot. With her arm held out towards Mary's chest, she could not feasibly rebuff her with so many onlookers. Mary took her hand and gave it a perfunctory shake, and then dropped it as though it scalded her skin.

"Bernie. Fancy seeing you here." It was as toneless and sarcastic as she could manage. Mary stopped just short of an eye-roll. "You certainly get about the place, don't you?"

"As do you. Guest of the most eligible Indian nobleman one minute, then of the most eligible and gorgeous man on the west coast the next. You sure set your sights high. Kudos." Bernie stood towering over Mary, in spiked heels that gave her an extra four inches above her naturally tall frame.

"What do you want, Bernie? Why are you here?"

"Me? I came to enjoy myself. Luca's parties are legendary, and this one seems to have started before his guests arrived." She tucked her tongue into her cheek and winked. "Come on... dish the gossip. What's all this I hear about Chinooks and the army and some sort of ray gun?"

"I'm sure you will be able to see it all in glorious Technicolour later. There was a camera crew at the scene." As much as she loathed the woman, Bernie did seem to have all the insider knowledge. It grieved her to ask, but Mary just had to know. "How is Karan? Have you seen him?"

"My dear girl… Shrimant Shinde has scurried back to India with his tail between his legs. What did you do to the poor boy? Crushed his heart, after he was courageous enough to offer it to you…?" She dragged a cerise acrylic nail across her forehead, inching the lacquered blond fringe away from her eyes.

Mary thought about her response. She wanted to say that it was not her fault, that events had overtaken them before she had the chance to explain or to make amends, but the truth caught in her throat. Karan reminded her too much of her ex-husband. She was just starting to feel the liberation of making her own choices and decisions, after her split with Parth. She could not let Karan wrap her up in cotton wool and neuter her hard won freedom. In retrospect, she realised that she should have discussed her concerns, instead of railing against him like a petulant teen. Bernice Feinstein was waiting for her answer, sipping a cocktail that was little more than coloured vodka.

"If you do see him, please tell him that I am sorry… for everything." Mary hung her head in shame. There was nothing she could do to make things right, and no way of contacting him.

Bernice raised a single brow, narrowing her eyes in analysis. She must have concluded that Mary was genuinely contrite, since she lowered her voice and said, "my offer still stands. Your own department, pick your own team of researchers and name your salary. I like a woman who'll stand up to the establishment. Mary, you got balls." She downed another inch of vodka, slapped her hand on Mary's back and pushed her towards a group of people on the patio. "Come on, I'll introduce you."

One of the women in the gathering was familiar. Was it the head flick to accentuate her thick and shiny copper locks, or the tiny freckles decorating the bridge of her nose?

"Hey everyone, this little stick of dynamite is Mary. She's staying here with Luca. She's a Brit." Bernice aimed a paw at each the people in the circle, listing their names and occupations in turn. Mary heard only one. The name of Philippa Chambers, heiress to the Chamber's fortune and US media chain. *Where have I seen her before? Think, Mary.*

"Hi there. Good to meet you."

"And you, Phillipa. Do you know, I have the oddest feeling that we've met before." Mary confessed.

"Really? Can't think when. And hey, call me Pip. Everyone does."

As Mary extended her hand towards Philippa, a chill ran down the length of her spine. *She is the one who took the memory stick from Flynn at JFK; the now dead and frozen Intelligence Agent Flynn. Did Alexi also witness the exchange? Did Philippa get him killed? So, she has ties with MI6. I wonder if Yelena knows her? Maybe she is also an agent, but undercover. I simply cannot call her Pip. That is Grampy's name.*

A similar looking older woman called to Philippa from across the room. They shared the same bone structure and texture of their hair, even if the older woman required chemical enhancements to support the flaming red colour. Philippa looked heavenward at the summons, and then addressed Mary and Bernice.

"Would you excuse me, ladies?" She twisted her mouth in an approximated smile. "Yes, mother. What is it now?"

Her mother, of course. That makes sense.

Luca skipped into the room, straightening his collar. He tucked his hand into the impression above Mary's hip and kissed her cheek. "Thanks for that."

Mary couldn't help but beam. For all his devious and underhanded dealings, he still trusted her capabilities more than any other man in her life. He glared at the mother-daughter duo and leaned into Mary's ear. "Be careful what you say to those two."

"How so?" She whispered back.

"They who control the media, control the hopes and fears of the nation."

"Mmm, quite. I've had enough of hack reporters to last me a lifetime."

Luca propelled himself away from Mary, into a natural clearing among the guests and grabbed a glass of fizz from the tray of a waiter. "Ladies and gentlemen, you have my sincere apologies for my tardiness. Thank you all for coming. I hope that you have availed yourself of my best wines and spirits. There's more where that came from so don't be shy, fill up. Let us toast to success in the upcoming mid-terms - cheers!" Luca guzzled half the contents of his glass down and watched the crowd. They mirrored him, with a rousing 'cheers' in response. "Please, everyone, the buffet is open so dig in and let's make this a night to remember."

The older red head stepped forward. "From what we hear, senator. You have already made this a night that no God-fearing Christian will ever forget. You and the governor's little stunt earlier, will make our viewing figures rocket, so cheers for that. Advertising revenue alone will be enough for another condo in Malibu."

"You're all heart, Tawnie, you know that? It was not my idea. Zak made the decision alone."

"So, the team at the scene tell me. Makes for a hot story whichever way you look at it. I should thank you for keeping all my publications and broadcasting houses so busy of late. Are you auditioning for the role of Superman, by any chance?" Those guests surrounding the media boss edged further from her side and sucked in air.

"You're the only woman I know who can make a compliment sound like an insult."

"It's a talent I have." Her stance was wide and confident, her hand perched on her jutted hip. She knew how to work a room for all its worth. Every visitor and staff member focused on her jibes. Mary looked first at Luca and then at Tawnie, sizing up the depth of their dislike for one another. Was it a superficial hatred, borne from the role each of them played in the deviating political landscape, or a more personalised malice? Surely the aim of a senator would be to keep the controllers of news outlets placated, or bribed, whichever action could bring about the desired outcome? As she was assessing this peculiar relationship, Mary failed to notice Tawnie's shift of focus. Her gaze now fell directly on Mary. There was a moment of puzzlement, then of appraisal, and finally of recognition. "When were you going to tell us all that you have been harbouring Miracle Mary?"

Mary almost choked. The urge to flee gained momentum in her legs, but her muscles failed to respond to her will.

Tawnie pressed home her advantage. "She's the reason all those Christians were at your gate, isn't she?"

The swift change in direction left Luca unready for the fight. Any preparatory explanations he had worked out to explain her presence evaporated from his mind. He stood, mouth agape, hoping a common sense approach would rescue the moment.

"I didn't think it warranted a mention. Mary is my guest. How Christians perceive her is their problem, not mine."

"Really," Tawnie emphasised her mastery over the situation, moving her weight from one hip to the other and throwing out a slender ankle to her side. "So, you have *that* many supporters that you can ignore the Christian voters entirely, or did you think that a few drinks and a couple of blinis would sway our opinions of your new 5G proposals?"

He was backed into a corner. Revealing his imminent defeat in the House of Representatives was tantamount to signing his resignation. Mary shuffled backwards out of the firing line. Luca was stalling for time. He only needed to appease them for so long. If the Summerfield plan came to fruition, the entire government would topple overnight. The debate was no more than a moot point.

Ducking under and around the elbows of Luca's guests, Mary crept towards the study. There had to be something that she had missed. If she could just spend more time digging around in there, while Luca was occupied, she might uncover dates, times and locations for the attacks. Keeping her eye on the verbal combatants, Mary stepped back another pace until her spine connected with something immovable. A quick peek over her shoulder triggered more shivers throughout her core. Viktor impeded her progress.

"Out. Of. Bounds." He enunciated each word so close to her face that she could smell the remains of salty fish on his breath.

Luca's wits returned. "Tell me this then. If I intended to antagonise all my Christian voters, why did I rush to their aid the moment they were under attack, eh?"

A single ping sounded on the terrace. A text message arriving via the temperamental network coverage. Tawnie opened her mouth to answer Luca. Her own mobile phone whooshed with an email notification. She closed her mouth, and squinted at her screen. As she did, it rang. More text alerts, beeped, pinged and buzzed, until the airwaves were saturated with alarmed warnings. Others on lesser networks waved their devices in the air, attempting to catch a signal. Luca took out his phone from a pocket in his trousers. The message, displayed in block capitals, said it all:

MASS TERROR AS LAS VEGAS SUFFERS TOTAL BLACKOUT

Chapter Twenty-Four

The party guests all began speaking at once. Murmurs of tempered panic underpinned a louder request from several people for Luca to switch on a giant flat screen television. Mary observed Viktor and Luca engaging in a silent, gesticulated argument. They knew what had happened. Their reaction was as anxious as the visitors. This event was not part of the plan.

Viktor aimed a remote control at the wall units and pressed a button. From a hidden compartment, a large screen descended and flickered into life. The dark pixels warmed and radiated until the primary colours coordinated, showing a news team high in the night sky above the Nevada plains. A female reporter shouted out her story above the rhythmic drone of the rotor blades, her cheeks were blotchy, her eyelids swollen and red.

"We were filming a world record tight-rope walk attempt at the Grand Canyon when the call came through. We scrambled into the air as soon as we could, and were utterly floored by what we saw. This footage was taken just forty-five minutes ago, from the camera units mounted beneath our aircraft." The programme cut to recorded footage. It was shaky, and at times disorientating, with a perpetual muted engine whine, in the background. Punctuated with a running commentary from the cockpit, the video feed panned across the Colorado River, the valley floor flooded and funnelled towards the Hoover Dam. The smooth concrete arc, once a halo of blue, sometimes amber flood lights, was dark as pitch. Its eerie rush of white waters rumbled below, without a single lamp to indicate the hydroelectric facility was operational. The helicopter flew on, rising above the peaks of the gorge walls and towards Boulder City. Here the last of the ambient glow from the setting sun, showed the extent of the blackout. Every light source was extinguished for miles. Cars sat steaming in junction collisions in the heart of town, the traffic signals failing as the evening traffic was at its height.

There was one notable source of light just south of the city. You could hear the reporter directing the pilot towards the blaze that was visible for tens of miles. "Just below us, you can see the Mead sub-station burning out with the most ferocious heat. Our pilot won't fly any closer for fear of erratic columns of smoke and secondary explosions throwing debris into our path, but if we switch over to the heat sensing cameras for a moment, you'll get an idea of how hot this is burning." She waited while her crew flicked a switch. The video altered to night vision. Dazzling white flames licked the copper coils at the centre of the fire.

Lucas guests were mesmerised. Some held their hands over their mouths, others made ineffectual comments, suggesting potential reasons for the blackouts, from solar storms to alien invasions. The governor harrumphed, and began punching out telephone numbers on his mobile as he wandered out to the terrace. Mary kept her eyes trained on Luca. His surprise was genuine, his annoyance growing, evidenced by an involuntary scratching at the scars on his neck as he viewed the scenes.

The Crew of the helicopter began choking from the soot laden clouds of smoke rising into the cabin, forcing them high into the sky in avoidance. An amateurish cut in the video tape, took away the flight time between catastrophes. They were now cruising in a north westerly direction over the suburbs of Paradise on the outskirts of Las Vegas. Swooping low between the lifeless streets and over Sunset park, the reporter stopped speaking. Her commentary drying up with scenes unfolding before them.

The enormous tracts of asphalt at the McCarran International Airport, was lit up with several large fires, each of them emanating from a plane wreckage. One had ploughed through the back of a Walmart situated at the end of a runway. As the helicopter drew nearer, the video picked up survivors rolling on the ground trying to dampen the flames from their burning bodies. Charred and blackened victims could be seen through the ripped metal of the fuselage, still strapped into their seats. Burning embers floated on the air currents, igniting the ruptured fuel tanks, lessening any chance of further survivors making it clear of the wreckage. The recording picked up the low sounds of sobbing, and an end to the reporter's commentary.

Mary's mind flitted between the images on the screen and the memories of the devastation witnessed on another giant screen at GCHQ Buckinghamshire, with similar results at Fairbanks Airport in Alaska. *Alexi…how can he sleep at night? This is all his doing… again. He has no regard for life at all.*

Moving to the main terminals, hordes of people could be seen fleeing the building, most were dragging cases and bags out to the taxi ranks. Some even joined the queues before realising that all transportation systems had failed along with the electricity supplies. The pilot turned the aircraft north, skirting the last of the airport buildings and following the route for the Las Vegas Boulevard. As they passed the famous unlit 'Welcome to Las Vegas' sign, the pilot flicked on the helicopter spotlight and trained it on the thousands of people, haemorrhaging from cars, coaches and buildings, out onto the streets. Harley Davidson showrooms, the Las Vegas Fire and Police Departments, the convention centre and aquarium attractions, all spilled confused occupants out into their parking lots.

Fights broke out in the forecourts of the casinos and hotels, looting shortly after, as residents and visitors all concluded the same thing. The emergency services, police and national guard were all stricken by the same electrical disaster.

The reporter sniffed and wiped away the saline build up at her tear ducts, and resumed her duties to the live television feed. "Ladies and gentlemen, with such extensive electrical failure to services, to supply networks and autonomous vehicles, it can mean only one thing. This is the result of a heinous act of terrorism. A premeditated Electro-Magnetic Pulse attack, and I urge the President, if you are watching this, to declare a state of emergency and send help immediately."

The governor returned to the lounge and called to his wife. "Get your things together, we are leaving now. Luca, action stations."

People scattered, grabbing partners, belongings and taking last gulps of fortifying drink. Most made a run for their cars and limousines. Luca hooked an arm over Viktor's shoulder and walked off into the study, leaving Mary to fend for herself. She stood in the deserted lounge for a moment, before deciding what to do next. The sensible course of action, would be to take this opportunity and run. Grab the keys to one of Luca's cars and get as far away from the entire rats' nest of liars and deviants as possible, but she did not. The most critical information was to be had right there, in the study, at this moment in time.

Plucking the brooch from her neckline, Mary ran to the guest apartment and wriggled out of her dress and into her jeans, T-shirt and trainers. She knew that any physical attempt to enter the study, would be met with Viktor's disapproving pout and a bad-tempered instruction to go away. With the brooch tucked into her pocket, she lay down on the guest bed, closed her eyes and tried to relax her muscles. Humming the Beatles tune, which had proven so successful in the past, Mary slowed her brain waves to fluctuate between seven and eight Hertz, harmonising with the Earth's natural frequencies. Within moments, she detached her psyche from her body and flew.

Mary's nebulous form passed the lounge and headed to the study at the rear of the ranch. Viktor was shouting at Luca. She pushed through the solid door, and hovered close above them.

"I swear I had no idea that he would do this. The plan was laid out in clear, time reactive steps."

"Then he has gone rogue. He's trying to isolate us from the end game. First, he targets the Hoover Dam, then he will go for something more central, perhaps Cisco itself. Get Judith online." Luca paced, and fumed. His nose whistled from the pressure of his shortened breath.

Judith? She is working with Luca? I knew that there was something off about that girl.

Viktor sat at the desk, clicking the application buttons for encryption software to protect the video link. A pop jingle sounded, along with a few unrelated electronic noises and Judith appeared on the laptop at an oblique angle. Her breasts and nasal passages looked unnaturally large. She must have spotted her image on the feedback window, since she adjusted the lid to a more favourable angle.

"What the fuck, Judith? You were supposed to keep an eye on him." Viktor's more argumentative side spilled out before pleasantries could be observed.

"I tried! He must have mobilised during night hours. Don't you think I would have told you if I had known?"

"Where is he now?"

"I have no idea. Honestly, he has not said one word to me in weeks."

"Then what use are you, eh?"

Luca pushed Viktor's shoulder, encouraging him to move out of the chair. Sitting down in front of the laptop, Luca employed his more disarming smile. "Hey you…"

"Looking good, senator." Judith fingered the golden cross suspended on a chain around her neck. "When am I gonna see you again?"

"You're seeing me now."

"You know what I mean." She attempted a coy demeanour, twisting her shoulders and rocking to accentuate her bust line for the web cam.

Luca said nothing, choosing to wait for her to volunteer useful information, but her objective did not match his. "You aren't fucking that stuck up British skank, are you? Tell me you ain't."

"No…of course not."

"You'd better not be. When can I fly out to the ranch? This place is boring as hell."

"Soon, my love. Hang tight. Right now though, I need you to get Alexi online…can you do that for me?"

"But then he'll know that I've been working for you all this time." She moved backwards, suddenly vulnerable.

"I'm guessing he already knows. Go fetch him, Jude, there's a good girl."

Her face dropped from adoration to irritation, her pinched face receding from view as she left the laptop running and walked to the door of her bedroom.

"Oh, and Judith?"

The girl turned back and faced the camera.

"You didn't divulge Mary's presence here to anyone did you?"

There was that sliver of spite that Mary had detected the first time they met. A self-righteous sneer spread across her face. "I might have mentioned it on one or two forums and a couple of Christian Facebook groups." And with that she flounced from the room. Mary listened to their discourse and seethed. *She deserves thirty pieces of silver, bitch.*

Her door slammed shut behind her. Viktor raised his hands to his head, squeezing his skull and massaging his fingertips into his scalp. "I told you we couldn't trust her."

Luca sighed. He had bigger problems to deal with. "Don't start."

Alexi blustered into Judith's bedroom and sat down at her desk. Thin branches from a windblown tree screeched against the window pane behind him, yet still he wore his baseball cap and sunglasses. "Yes? I very busy."

"Explain yourself." Luca folded his arms across his chest and scowled.

"Ah, Las Vegas? Yes, little test, that is all. Height of detonation now more…um… accurate. Yes."

"That was not authorised and for good reason. The entire plan is now in jeopardy thanks to your little *test*."

"Not problem. Equipment and people almost in place already. Nothing for jeopardy for to stop. They wait now for final orders."

Luca absorbed the former Soviet general's muddled sentences and deconstructed their meaning. "You don't understand. The moment this news goes global, every intelligence agency and military unit will be put on notice." Luca paused and looked at Alexi's expression. His slack mouth and wrinkled nose conveyed his confusion. "We have to move the schedule forward."

"Da…I understand. Peoples look for us." Alexi gave an exaggerated nod.

That's weird. Alexi's English is better than this. Why would he deliberately appear dumb to Luca? Unless he is planning to double-cross him…

Luca shook his head. "Just get the last of the electronics shielded or packed away. Use the land line until the final Go order, got it?"

"I got it."

Mary had heard enough. She had to get her body out of there before Luca noticed her missing. Just as she was commanding her mass of consciousness back to the guest apartment, Viktor walked right into her frequency cluster. It was a frightening experience, and one which delayed her return. Viktor was charging down the corridor, closely followed by the senator.

Luca paused in the lounge, taking out his mobile phone from a pocket. "We need to deal with the governor. Can't have him interfering again, especially now he has access to all those new military toys."

"It's already in hand. Cousin Gregori leads his security team. He won't make it home in one piece tonight."

"Providing he follows orders and doesn't screw things up, like he did the heist."

"Hey, he dealt with your head of security, didn't he? Would you rather have a CIA agent still on the team?"

If there was any vestige of affection Mary had left for Luca, it now dissolved into hatred. *Their complete contempt for human life is staggering. I have to get help, but who can I tell?* She concentrated hard, pulling the discordant and scattered frequencies of her psyche back into one coordinated mass, and launching herself through to the apartment and into her physical form. With anxiety building in her gut, Mary took the remainder of Luca's shopping money and slid it into her back pocket. She grabbed a light jacket and opened the door a fraction to check her path of escape. Viktor stood at the entrance to the lounge room. She was cut off.

Shit. That bloody man. Treading on the occasional chair in the bedroom, Mary threaded her leg through the open window and knelt on the sill. With great care, her other leg followed, until she could lower herself down the outside wall of the apartment to the steep hillside beyond. The ground was rough, and hard to traverse. Her trainers slid in the sandy soils, making tiny but noisy landslides as she skittered across the exterior of the ranch house towards the garages near the courtyard.

Keeping her head down, Mary scrambled around the edges of the terrace steps. She could hear Viktor shouting from the guest apartments.

"Mary has gone."

"What? She has to be around here somewhere." The volume of Luca's voice lessened as he ran to the guest bedroom, and increased as he turned back towards the lounge. "She can't have gotten far. She doesn't have access to the garage codes. Search the grounds… bring her back."

"You said that we don't need her abilities anymore, now that the lightning strike boosted yours." There was a loud ratcheting noise, as Viktor chambered a bullet in his handgun. "I'll track her down alright, but I don't plan on bringing her back."

"Do as I ask, Viktor. Her bloodline is a critical bargaining chip."

My bloodline? What was his plan, to keep me like a brood mare? At the base of the steps, her footsteps crunched on the gravel courtyard. She tried to tread lightly, but her slow pace put her at risk of Viktor catching up with her.

Taking the chance, she dashed across the expanse, weaving between the party lanterns and tall flares, until she reached the end of the stores. Pulling the handle of the back entrance to the garage, she found it locked. A quick assessment of the door furniture told her that breaking a window would not help; it was secured with an internal Yale lock.

Her heart pounding with fear, she bolted around the corner of the buildings to the drive side. Another handle rattle of the locked car entrance, left Mary with no other option but to run. The loose chippings in the courtyard ground against Viktor's rapid steps. He was already on her tail. Mary took a sharp left off the drive and between the equidistant rows of grapevines as they stabbed the undulations in the hillside. Within a hundred feet of her escape, she realised that she was trapped. The supporting cables and old wizened growth fenced her into the narrow lane. All Viktor had to do, was aim and fire. There was no way of dodging the bullets, nowhere to hide. Her only hope was to outrun him, and pray that he would stay faithful to Luca's wishes to keep her alive.

The descent gave her a strange momentum, almost as though she was flying. She knew that if her legs did not keep pace with the forward thrust, she would topple down the remainder of the track, with two potential results; capture or serious harm. Adrenalin surged through her muscles, her heart metabolising glucose fast enough to make her nauseous, but still she ran on. Through the aching cramp of lactic acid building in her calf muscles, through the oxygen depletion strain in her chest, past the dry mouthed gasping; she neared the floor of the valley. *This never seems to get any easier.*

A dark mass of vegetation lay ahead, marking the end of the vines and the property boundary. A thicket of trees coated the parched dust like an ominous blanket. *Finally, some cover. I can lose Viktor in there.* Scrambling over the wire fencing, Mary crawled across a small ditch and into the woodland. It took a moment for her sight to adjust to the darkness, but at least the sandy soils limited the low-level shrubs. Zig zagging between the rough trunks, she could hear the sound of snapping branches, behind her, and also ahead. Confused, she stood still, looking back to gauge Viktor's position. He was at least fifty yards away. If only she could get to a road, perhaps flag down a car. She turned to resume her running and…thud - A rifle butt smashed her in the face.

Chapter Twenty-Five

Mary's head throbbed. Blunt force trauma ripped open the thin flesh of her forehead. Blood trickled, dripping from her hairline as her upper body swung against the back of her assailant. His shoulder dug into her abdomen, tearing open the stitched wound from the bullet. A muscular arm clamped her legs together against his chest. Every step he took jarred, adding to the distress. *How did Viktor...?* A woozy fever flooded her logic from the pressure building in her inverted skull. *I don't understand? I was almost away...* She passed out of consciousness briefly, until the man dropped her into the boot of an old car. She could feel the spare wheel digging into her ribs. Mary forced open her eyes just before the lid slammed shut. In the orange glow of street lights, she saw his face. He was young and lean with long hair pulled back into a ponytail. Mary detected not a hint of malice from his features, just a self-satisfied smile of success. He had captured his quarry.

The heady mixture of stress hormones, kept her in a state of high anxiety as she bumped along the cramped space. The stink of spilled petrol made her gag, and contracted the membranes in her sinuses. Exhaust fumes seeped in while they idled at a junction, before the roar of speeding tarmac sucked away all noxious gases, leaving her gasping and cold. With a judicious wriggle,

Mary pulled a tissue from her jacket pocket and applied increasing pressure to her head. The gash still exuded enough blood to leave her faint, but she needed her wits about her. With every fibre of strength, Mary fought to stay awake and aware of their journey.

I am okay. As confined as it is, I can still move. There are some advantages to being a pip-squeak after all. Swallowing back her claustrophobia, Mary ripped at the plastic casing holding the tail lights in the rear body panel. She got a shock from the exposed wires delivering electricity to the indicators. Riled, she summoned an electromagnetic surge and blew out the remaining lights. Scraping and pushing at the charred plastic, Mary managed to dislodge the entire fitment, and push it out onto the roadside. Lying on her side, she looked out at the freeway, hoping to signal a driver or passenger for help. The road was clear; the nearest vehicle was miles behind them, their headlights mere sparks in the distance.

Road signs were dimly lit, facing the wrong way to be useful or unintelligible. The only thing she was sure about was the direction they were headed. West for approximately fifteen minutes and then due south. Not that this information helped her any. Calming her nerves, she had one final chance to secure help. With a few clean gulps of air from the narrow aperture in the rear panel, she laid flat and centred her mind.

"Dan! I am in terrible trouble. Can you hear me?" She wasn't sure what assistance her brother could supply, being over five thousand miles away, but he was her last hope. *"Dan...please don't be asleep."*

"Not asleep. I'm here. What's happened?"

Mary could not contain her relief. *"Thank God. I need you to call Yelena and see if she can pull some strings with her US contacts."*

Tears erupted from her ducts and spilled down her temples, but she maintained the connection with the one person she could always rely on. Over the course of her journey, Mary relayed as many details as she could, emphasising the urgency with which Yelena needed to infiltrate the Summerfield Retreat.

"How can I convince her that this is a genuine threat? What evidence can I give?" His anxiety for his sister's welfare transmitted down the connection to Mary. She felt it as keenly as her own.

"Tell her that Senator Bonovich has put a hit out on the Californian governor. He'll be dead within hours, that should be enough to convince her that I am telling the truth."

"Jesus, Mary. What have you got yourself tangled up in?"

"Please don't. I can hardly believe it myself. So much for lying low, eh?"

"Have you any way of us tracking your whereabouts? Road signs, highway numbers...anything?"

"Not really, we headed South from Napa."

"South? Do you know how big the state of California is? There's a whole lot of land south of Napa." His frustration manifested in hurried transmissions. He was trying his best not to sound alarmed, but their neural networks were inextricably linked; whatever filtered through his mind, passed directly into hers.

"Wait... the car is slowing down. The tyres are rumbling over rough ground. I think this is it."

"How long have you been travelling?"

"No more than an hour. Got to go, we've stopped moving."

"For God's sake, Mary, do whatever needs to be done to protect yourself. Do you understand? Forget morals and ethics, get the bastards before they get you."

"Love you, Dan." Cuffing the tears from her eyes, Mary severed the connection. She couldn't let Dan feel her terror.

The car shook as the man left the driver's side and slammed the car door. Mary held her breath, holding up her hands and tensing her stomach muscles against attack. No sounds of footsteps, no voices, coughs or snuffles, no way to ascertain his location. Her own breathing laboured in anticipation. Was he going to leave her in the back of his car? What was the delay? Was he preparing a kill room with plastic sheeting to foil forensics? Either way, Mary psyched herself up to deliver a jolt of energy powerful enough to make him piss himself, or worse. If he lived, he would regret having ever heard of Miracle Mary.

She cocked her head closer to the gap in the panel, sure that she could hear distant mumbling. As it grew louder, she knew that her assailant had alerted another person to her arrival. Could she feasibly fend off two attackers at the same time? Kneading her hands into tight fists, she readied herself for the onslaught.

The boot lid hinged open, revealing two male silhouettes, against a stark porch lamp. Squinting, Mary bolted upright.

"I'm warning you now, let me go or you may not live to regret it. I will hurt you." She reared up at them, bearing her palms and panting with indignation. The younger of the two men moved away from her threats. The older man, blinked slowly and acknowledged her fear.

"We welcome you into our lives and our home. Be at peace, Mary. I am Abraham, this is Isaac." They stepped aside to allow her to scramble from the car boot and adjust her clothing. "I apologise for the methods employed to bring you here. Let us break bread together and talk." He signalled for Mary to enter the large wooden structure behind them. Mary looked Abraham up and down. The long grey hair and beard, the cotton robes and sandals, all a perfect cliché for a religious commune leader.

"Why would I trust you? You bashed me over the head with a big gun and kidnapped me." She started walking along the service road, oblivious as to the direction she was heading. "If you don't follow me, I may not report you."

Isaac's boots scuffled along the tarmac drive. He raced ahead of her and lifted the hem of his polo shirt, allowing her sight of a hand gun tucked into the waistband of his jeans.

Abraham called after her. "Of course, we would rather this was all done without any violence or bloodshed, but if we must resort to extreme measures, we will." He gave her time to consider his statement, before repeating his offer of hospitality. "Would you like some tea?"

Isaac was huge against her tiny frame. The thought of enduring another bullet, with the potential for a more final outcome, did not appeal. She turned to face her new captors. "Just tell me what you want from me. If I can be of service, I will consider it. Otherwise, I really don't have time for all this. I am sorry if I insulted your religious sensibilities, really I am, but I never intended offence to anyone."

The older man smiled, tucking his hands into the sleeves of his robe. "Please, it is late, and you must be tired. Let us take tea together."

Mary gazed all around for signs of life in other buildings. There were no other lights, or properties unconnected to Abraham's for miles. He seemed to comprehend her impulse to flee.

"Five miles." He said.

"What is?" She looked back at his smug face.

"Five miles to the nearest neighbour, in any direction." Again, he gestured towards the entrance. Five miles was too far to run with a younger, fitter Isaac on her tail. Without a mobile phone or access to a vehicle, Mary had few options open to her. Isaac grew impatient with her indecision and took the gun from his waistband. He flicked his wrist, waving the pistol towards the door. Flattening her palms in readiness, she took a breath and charged through the entrance, arms raised in defence. Three young women stood before her, each supporting a look of shock for a moment, before approaching her in greeting.

Mary surveyed her surroundings. The foyer in which the ladies fussed about, opened onto a massive communal room, packed with people of all ages. A staging area was just visible at one end of the hall, as was the high-level stained glass, which looked modern and dulled by the darkness outside. This was clearly their room for collective worship. The young women peeled her jacket from her arms, and ushered her towards a smaller anteroom at the end of the foyer.

"Ladies, please don't rail road me. I really need the use of a telephone, if you would be so kind?"

They ignored her request, shuffling and jostling until Mary was sitting on a pile of cushions next to a square coffee table with a tea tray set down at its centre. Abraham sat opposite Mary, the ladies sat either side of her, while Isaac blocked her escape in the doorway. A loaf of homemade bread nestled in a napkin lined basket in front of the old man. He picked it up and ripped it in two, passing one half directly to Mary. She leaned forwards and took it from him, suspicious of its ingredients. Peering up through her brows, she frowned at Abraham and slowly laid the bread down on the table.

Abraham laughed. "You think we would poison you?" He split his half again, passing chunks around the room. Each woman tore a piece and ate the offering, muttering their thanks to the lord. Abraham chewed on a large mouthful himself before lifting the tea pot and offering it to his guest. "We thought you might like Earl Grey, being from England and all." He poured the pale liquid into her teacup, pushing quarters of lemon on a saucer towards Mary. "There is milk if you prefer…?" It was all so civilised after such a rude delivery and introduction. In truth, Mary hated Earl Grey; the Oil of Bergamot was too scented for her tastes, but an hour or so of travelling in a car boot had given her a thirst. She took a few sips, trying to keep her look of revulsion at bay.

"We have watched your story unfold online for a number of weeks now, Mary. You cannot imagine how excited we were when we discovered that you were staying nearby. We gave thanks to God for bringing you to our humble dwelling."

The women genuflected and muttered, "hail Mary, full of grace."

Mary finished the tea and rose from her uncomfortable, cross-legged position. "Well, it's been a blast. Thanks for having me. Now if you could direct me to the nearest town…" She held her head. *That bash must have given me a slight concussion*. "Whoa…" The room spun in one of her eyes, the other remained closed tight. Balancing with outstretched arms, Mary staggered, clutching onto the obliging women at her side, and finally, lost consciousness as she slipped from their grasp and slumped to the floor.

***

It was hard to choose between the throbbing of her head wound or the pulsing in her temples from the drugged Earl Grey, both seemed to accentuate every movement and sound and translate it to her brain as pain. *This cannot be happening again.* She tried to forge a connection to her brother's mind, but the drug appeared to be hampering her attempts. *How is it that people think it's okay to make me bend to their whims? I doubt they would do the same to Dan or Lachie.* She tried to touch her forehead but found her wrists tied together. Focusing her efforts on sitting up, she spied her jeans and t-shirt folded neatly on a chair, her trainers sitting on the floor beneath. A cold damp sensation jolted her awake. One of the women from the foyer was applying a wet sponge to her feet. She moved it in long strokes from her ankles to her toes, each time muttering an incantation which included her name. 'Our new messiah, the prophesy is made whole. Mary, daughter of David, second king of the Holy Land, is with us. God sent us his son to show us our folly, forgive our sins and pay for our weaknesses. Now he sends us his daughter."

The other two women were on bended knee at their side. Each intoned their agreement of the prayer with a collective, "Mary, full of grace."

As the swirling inside her head lessened, it dawned on Mary that these women had stripped off her clothes and dressed her in a thin cotton gown, similar to a nightdress favoured by grandmothers. Her underwear had been replaced with fabric bindings, wound around her bust and a second woven between her legs and around her pelvis. *This is too weird. If I can just get out of these bonds, I could give them a small shock, not enough to kill them, just enough to make them run away.* She chewed at the nylon rope, tugging the knots with her incisors. That was when she noticed Isaac standing in the darkest corner of the room, his arms folded across his chest, the barrel of his handgun resting on his left elbow. He gently shook his head in warning. *Plan B. Wait for an opportunity to take out Isaac first.*

The more dominant woman, laid the sponge down and picked up a small wooden bowl which glistened with aromatic oil. Dipping her thumb into the viscous liquid, she reached up to Mary's forehead and made the sign of the cross on her skin. Next, she dabbed perfume on her neck and wrists. It was sweeter and spicier than the bow resin Mary once used, prior to her violin lessons at school. The other woman rose from their kneeling position and combed her hair, braiding two plaits either side of her face and joining them together at the back of her head like a crown.

"There…" The foot washer said. "You are ready."

"Ready for what?" Mary batted the women away with her bound hands when they tried to help her to her feet.

"Now, we eat."

Isaac opened the door and lead the ladies and Mary from the anteroom, back through the foyer and main hall, and finally out via a fire escape into the cool night air. Braziers and flaming torches lit a pathway down the neat lawn to a circle away from the main building. Surrounded by her hand maidens, Mary walked down the dewy track, bare foot and shivering, partly from the frigid temperatures, partly through anxiety. Within the wide expanse of the circle, a long table was laid with simple bowls of fruits, nuts, bread and oils. The closer they got to the table, the more she could smell the caramelising of rendered fat. A whole pig turned on a roasting spit, the logs in a pit beneath covered in ash and glowing embers.

A procession of Abraham's flock followed them from the main hall. Some of the men took their seats at the table, the remainder plus women and children sat on blankets on the ground. Standing central to them all, was Abraham. *Is this for real? Am I hallucinating from that bloody tea, or am I still unconscious and this is some Alice in Wonderland type of dream? Look for a bong smoking caterpillar called Absalom, with the voice of Alan Rickman.*

Abraham beckoned Mary and untied her hands. "Sit here, if you will. We have much to discuss."

Mary complied, rubbing at the welts on her wrists and watching the women flitting around the table in a delayed blur. Wine goblets were filled and passed around the men, bread broken, meat carved from the turning pig.

"The day of reckoning is at hand. The city of Las Vegas is vanquished, and with it, the sinful will turn against one another and implode. If ever there was a sign from God to mend their wicked ways it was thus. We must celebrate." Abraham raised a goblet to the stars and those about him followed suit, and then drank heartily.

Mary slowed her breathing and tried to concentrate. Her mind still swam in a fog of conflicting chemicals. "What did you put in that tea?"

"Just a mild herbal sedative. Something my wife, Sarah, concocted from her garden. It's harmless."

"I find that hard to believe." She leaned on the table edge, supporting the weight of her head in her hands. A girl placed a wooden bowl before her. It contained steaming slices of pork with a dollop of apple sauce and a chunk of rustic bread.

"Oh, thanks, but I don't eat meat." She said, pushing the bowl away.

"You must, it was sacrificed in your honour. The Messiah's got to transubstantiate the body of Christ at her Last Supper."

Chapter Twenty-Six

"What did she say? Her Last Supper? You freaking wackos think I am the next Jesus Christ? Hell no. I am out of here." Mary stood up to leave, her legs failing to coordinate with her wishes.

Abraham caught her mid topple and forced her back into her seat. "There is nowhere for you to run, Mary. This is your destiny. Embrace it."

The foot washing woman returned with a cup in her hand. She grabbed hold of Mary's lower jaw, pushing her chin to her neck and pouring more of the Earl Grey liquor down her throat. Mary thrashed her arms about, clawing and flailing, until Isaac stepped in and held her down. *Definitely not a dream,* she concluded, when at last they released her to examine the bruises blooming on her upper arms.

Abraham drew close to her and looked into her eyes. "The New Covenant came with a promise of internal power; 'I will put my laws into their minds, and write them on their hearts.' Hebrews, eight, ten, B. What does God require of us in terms of obedience for The Next Covenant? What powers will he bestow upon the faithful, Mary?" Mary could not stay still. The spinning inside her head wreaked havoc on her spatial awareness, making her over compensate to remain upright. Her upper body resembled a sleepy toddler fighting to stay awake.

Abraham was determined. "What are the tenets of The Next Covenant? Will this be the final forgiveness of all sins, such as that mentioned in Hebrews eight to twelve? 'For I will be merciful towards their iniquities, and I will remember their sins no more.' Mary?" Again, he attempted to rouse her into debate, shaking her shoulder with vigour. "Sarah, you fool. You gave her too much. Now I cannot get any sense from her."

Sarah returned to Abraham's side, and made a quick evaluation of Mary's state. "The daughter of God will deliver the terms of the New Relationship, so that Abraham, Father of Many Nations, can claim great riches and unlimited abundance - There will be a promise of intimate knowledge through the body of Christ." Sarah announced her statement in a loud and confident manner, asserting her authority as the first wife of Abraham. She reached down and grabbed a handful of Mary's hair. Snapping her head back, Sarah swiped the back of her hand hard across Mary's, cheek. Mary's eyes almost popped from the sockets. Every sense receptor in her face stung, sending a fresh wave of cortisol and adrenalin into her bloodstream.

"Start talking, Messiah, or I'll do it again."

"I don't know what you want me to say. I am not who you think I am." Mary cradled her face, and in the moments of lucidity, vowed that she would make Sarah scream before the night was out.

Abraham looked around at the table of elders, and then at the groups of followers on their blankets within the circle, and frowned. Leaning into Mary's hair, he said; "I can hear her words. She speaks… wait…she says that many more will come and be welcomed into this, our house of God. More cities of sin will perish in fire and torment. With her coming, our sins are forgiven, our faith strong…" He looked around at the angelic faces of his congregation and smiled. Fully in his stride now, he relaxed into the fabrication of The Next Covenant with God.

"Prepare yourselves for a modern day version of the Great Flood. An end to days of profligacy, greed, self-absorption and malice. An end to social media groupies and televisual manipulation. An end to lies and corporate greed. This new epoch will mark the age of temperance and fortitude, of sharing our harvest, our wisdom, ourselves with only the worthy within our flock." He blanked. He had exhausted the list of imagined promises. Throwing his arms in the air, he shouted, "Let us rejoice!"

The elders, their women and children all rose to their feet, and replied as one voice. "Hail Mary, full of grace."

Mary's lolling head twisted enough to spy the crowd. With a few exaggerated blinks and a scowl, she announced. "I didn't say any of that." Before she could protest further, Sarah drew closer, appearing to lend assistance to Mary's drooping body. With her back to the crowd, Sarah swung her elbow, catching Mary with such a clout to the head, she rendered the Daughter of God, unconscious.

***

"Mary...wake up." The voice was distant, and inside her head. She heard it a second time. *"You have to stay awake, protect yourself."*

"Captain? Is that you?" The confusion was justified. Concussion, drugged tea and the remnants of a Russian hive mind tethered to your brain, was enough to send the most stoic crazy. Mary opened her eyes. Flaming torches surrounded the blanket on which she was laid.

Her head rested on a pillow that smelled strongly of sage. As she regained her awareness and mental faculties, Mary realised that her situation had not improved. For one, her wrists were bound again. She scrambled to her knees and looked towards the feasting table. Abraham held them in awe with another of his lectures reaffirming his lordly position over them, as the Father of Many Nations.

Where is Isaac? If I can immobilise him, I can get away. An ominous presence loomed behind her. Isaac stood guard over her, his left hand gripping his right wrist, supporting the weight of the gun as it rested against his thigh. *Jeez, doesn't he ever sit down and rest?*

A quick survey of the high sallow moon, the exposed ribs of the roasted pig and the spilled wine on the feasting table, told her that she had lain unconscious for some time. All were in a frenzied state of religious fervour. Every platitude and falsehood that spilled from their leader's mouth, was met with cheers of Amen, or the laying of hands on his smock. He was worshipped and adored as the claimed descendant of the original Abraham; an unbroken line stretching centuries. She tuned into his sermon just long enough to hear a tirade regarding children.

"If it were God's message to procreate with his daughter, his word alone would be my bond. For ever is my faith in his wisdom, and our duty to bring forth many sons and followers of his will. Were it not for the love of my wives Sarah, Hagar and Keturah, I might break with tradition and take Mary as my fourth. No, we will not mix blood with the line of David. Mary will absolve us of all our sins this night." Abraham called to Isaac. "Bring her to us, my child, that she might bless us with the body of Christ."

Isaac dragged Mary up from the blanket by her arm, and propelled her towards Abraham. Sarah cleared the head of the table, brushing away crumbs and removing empty vessels. From an enamelled container, she took a chalice and some flat breads, laying them down on a cotton teacloth. A fresh bottle of red wine arrived via Hagar. She poured from the bottle into the chalice and handed it to Abraham.

Abraham whispered to Mary. "Do as you are told, and I will spare you Isaacs more lustful advances. He has yet to name a wife."

"I've killed bigger men than he, old man. Do your worst."

Abraham chortled. "You are spirited, I like that. You will make a fine sacrifice." He grabbed her bound wrists and touched the chalice to her hands. "This chalice of benediction we offer up to thee our Lord, that it be made into the blood of Christ..."

Mary made a swipe at the goblet, but Abraham was too quick. Only a small fraction of the wine was spilled. "Blood of our blood, in remembrance." Abraham took a sip.

Sarah made a show of dabbing the lip of the goblet with a cream linen cloth, before taking a sip herself. "I receive the Eucharist." She wiped it again, and passed it to Hagar.

Next was the bread, which Abraham touched to Mary's screwed up fists. He chanted, "This bread is his body. As we take the bread into our mouths, we take in the body of Christ, so that we may remember him first and always." He tore a small piece and ate it, passing the loaf to his wives. "We celebrate the Eucharist." The offerings went around the table first, and then to the blankets around the circle, each person consuming a tiny portion and muttering the incantation.

Abraham signalled to the elders sitting around the feasting table with a nod. They rose from the benching and walked beyond the fire pit with the sizzling pork. Mary struggled against Isaac, who clamped his meaty paws around her body and held her firm. Abraham signalled for Isaac to take Mary towards the men. This he did with an air of pure elation. The short walk around the fire pit, gave Mary an opportunity to run, but Isaac caught hold of her robe and yanked her back under his control, ripping the fabric across her back.

The wives took an easterly approach, the remaining men walked a westerly route, until all but the children were gathered around a huge wooden crucifix, laid in the damp grass. *Shit, these people are not messing about. They really mean to sacrifice me. "Dan! Dan, help me. I am in serious trouble."*

Sarah, and the other wives, removed what was left of her robe, leaving her with just the bindings to cover her modesty.

"See how her wounds mirror that which was suffered by our lord Jesus Christ, son of God." Abraham pointed to the weeping gash in her side where Isaacs rough handling had ripped her stitches. "See the lacerations in her scalp, just as Jesus endured with the crown of thorns."

The wives each took up their positions either side and behind Mary, forcing her down onto the cross, and pushing her limbs in place to allow the elders to strap her at the elbows and knees to the wooden shaft.

Panicked, Mary tried to channel her thoughts into a direct message to her brother, but her situation grew all the more serious as they produced a series of masonry nails and two hammers. "No…I am not the daughter of God, you have to let me go. Please don't do this, you are making a terrible mistake." Her wriggling and protestations, delayed the ritualistic nailing, while they added more straps to hold her still.

Mary closed her eyes. *"Dan. You have to hear me...please."*

"Hey, sis. What's happening, are you alright?"

"No, things have taken a really shitty turn for the worse. I thought I could handle things, but it has gone beyond blasting a few people. Did you get through to Yelena?"

"I did. She says the American Security Services are being awkward. Something about one British holiday maker is not their concern, when they have a state of emergency declared in Las Vegas. She is also trying to get verifiable facts about your Summerfield Retreat report."

"Dan, they are quite literally going to crucify me. Alert the media, get the British Embassy on board, whatever it takes, please. There is a massive fire and a whole bunch of flaming torches in a circle. It should be seen for miles from above."

"Hang in, Mary. I'll get Connie to help me. Delay them as long as you can." The connection severed, she was alone with her thoughts once more.

Delay them...Okay, I'm ready to audition for my Oscar. Mary ceased to struggle, the elder men let go their grip. Her body limp, her manner calm and compliant, she opened her eyes and searched out Abraham. "I am ready to disclose God's wisdom and give you all my blessings."

Wives, elders and children clapped their hands together in praise. Discordant choruses of "Hail Mary, full of grace," rang out.

Sarah scowled. "Go on then, Daughter of God. What do you got to say for yourself?"

"Untie me and let me up and I will tell you everything that God would wish you to know."

"No, tell us from there. We can all hear you."

As you wish, wife of Abraham, mother of Isaac. You must have been exceedingly young when you gave birth?" Mary watched Sarah's lips purse and her eyes narrow in contempt. "Never mind. It is the past. God wants you to know that you are forever in his thoughts, and that he loves each and every one of you. He would like to amend the teachings that dear Abraham has laid down, to include an abstinence of the consumption of animal flesh." She paused to think of her next amendment, allowing Sarah to interrupt.

"On which day of the week?"

"On all days. Does not the bible give the commandment of 'Thou shalt not kill'? It does not specify man or beast, but all of God's creatures. The spilling of blood saddens the Lord. A sacrifice is only worthy if it is of great value to those making the offering, something which would be of enormous cost and inconvenience. In biblical times, sheep and cows were all the material wealth a tribe had to offer. In today's communities, greater value is placed on technology. You should offer up your mobile phones and computers for sacrifice, to show that you love your God."

"She makes a fair point." Abraham said, stroking his beard.

"She is lying to save her skin. Only a life for a life can be offered. Her death will be our salvation." There was a spite to her intonation which bypassed Abraham's senses entirely.

"Can you take that risk, Abraham. Will you take the word of your first wife over that of the Daughter of Christ, descendant of King David, who slay Goliath with a simple sling shot? Would you rather incur God's wrath, than offend one of your women?"

Abraham contemplated her words, glancing from Mary, to his flock and then finally to a seething Sarah. A lengthy unspoken conversation took place between the couple, one played out in looks and non-verbal warnings. She had a power over him that was reinforced by Hagar and third wife, Keturah, as they moved to stand behind Sarah. Their folded arms and ill-disposed pouts, lent support to Sarah's plight. Mary was outnumbered. They could give him a life of undiminished pleasure, or round the clock aggravation.

"I think we have heard enough of your blessings, Mary." Abraham nodded again to the elders. The straps were tightened. There was absolutely no wriggle room.

"No, wait. I have more…um…Kill me and the western world will burn. Lightning strikes and mayhem in every major city will render this great country and others powerless. Hospitals will crumble, children will die, looters will take your home and your wives, Abraham… Abraham, this is a big mistake." Her last words were shrieked as the final bindings were made fast.

One of the elders forced open her left hand and pinned her fingers down against the wood. Another man took up a hammer and long nail.

"Don't do it…I'm warning you." Mary growled.

The man hesitated, looking to Abraham for approval. Another nod egged him on. The hammer high above the man's head, Mary could hear him whispering a prayer of forgiveness.

In a quieter, more conspiratorial tone, Mary said. "You don't have to do this. You know that it is wrong. You have free will to choose for yourself. If you truly believe that I am the Daughter of God, I will bless and forgive you, but you must do no harm and leave this place."

The elder looked across to her bloodied and bruised face. His eyes glistened with pity.

"Please, I beg of you." Mary implored, watching the elder crumple into tears and dropping the hammer.

Sarah rushed forwards. "Oh, for Christ's sake, I'll do it." She knelt in the damp grass and took up the nail, adjusting its position in Mary's palm.

"You shouldn't have done that, Sarah." Mary said, with calm assurance.

"Really? Enlighten me."

The moment the nail connected with Mary's skin, she sent a pulse of voltage through her palm, along the nail and into Sarah's body. The charge was sufficient to have her yelping and screaming, her hand charred and blistered. She smelled as delicious as the pig. Her screaming transformed into enraged shouting, for someone to get the cordless nail gun.

"You'll pay for that." Sarah spat. "Just you see."

Men scurried at her command to the tool sheds, others poured water from a table jug into a bowl and soothed her burns. Abraham stood back, struck dumb with the display of strength.

He came to his senses as the men jogged the length of the lawns carrying the power tool. "Perhaps we are mistaken. Let us consider for one moment, whether what she says is the truth."

Sarah scoffed. "You never were able to finish what you start, old fool. Give me the nail gun." Sarah grit her teeth against the agony, and held the gun with both hands until the nail at the terminal end was close but not touching Mary's skin. She fired.

Two nails shot into the soft tissue at the centre of Mary's palm, tearing through flesh and sinew, each of them grinding the small bones in her hand. Mary squealed. The initial shock of the steel driving through her dulled the lacerating pain, but as the weight of her hand pulled against the fixing, a fresh wave of agony jangled her nervous system.

Sarah smirked, and then stepped over Mary's body to her right hand and repeated the double tap procedure, basking in screams and wails from the Daughter of God. Blood oozed from her hands, between her fingers and painted the crucifix claret. The elders bent down to grapple the top of the cross, ready to hoist it into a prepared hole in the ground.

"Wait…" Sarah commanded of them. "She will take forever to die with such small wounds. Ideally, we need to hit a gusher." Standing one leg either side of Mary's arm, Sarah aimed the nail gun at the vessel rich wrists and fired another shot.

Chapter Twenty-Seven

Mary's nervous system had already reached the apex of pain reception. Sarah's additional malice was met with groans and pleas and a great deal more blood. There was an excited buoyancy in Sarah's keenness to exact revenge. A couple of additional nails embedded in Marys arms, and Sarah ordered that the men hoist her aloft.

The agony renewed in intensity with every movement, every twitch of her body. *If I can just survive until they find me. Dan won't leave me to die. He will summon help. I can do this. Bodies heal, I just need to slow my heart rate so that I don't bleed out.* Mary tried everything to calm her muscles and reduce the pounding in her chest to control the blood loss, but it was not working. It was impossible to tell herself not to feel the nauseating throb of ripped flesh and scuffed bone. It seemed hopeless.

"Mary..."

Even her breathing caused her muscles to jolt against the hard steel of the nails, preventing any potential clotting to stem the blood flow.

"Mary... leave your body. Come with us and you will no longer feel anything." The Russian inflection was distinctive. Captain Thirty-Four, former leader of the Russian Hive mind, urged her to disassociate her psyche from her physical form.

"Oh Captain, it hurts so much, but if I leave now, I may never be able to return to my body. What if... forgive me... like you and your comrades, my flesh and blood dies and I have nowhere to return to?"

"Then we welcome you into our unit permanently, Mary."

"But didn't you say that not all members of your unit survived the drone strike, that some also perished on a psychological level too?"

The captain's silence was answer enough. These were her options. To suffer a slow and agonising death, with a lingering hope of rescue, or to leave her body to endure the torture, risking mental extermination on the ethereal plane.

"I could really use Grampy's advice right about now. Why has he not come back to me, as you have done?" There was a moment or two of sympathetic murmurings from the captain's team. They felt her torment and knew its strength. The loss of their bodies denied them access to their living kin too.

"We cannot answer that question, Mary. All we know is that many of us remain. Perhaps your grandfather has simply lost his way. One thing is for sure, your body will not take much more of this punishment before you blackout, and then it will be too late to join us here."

Battling through the misery, Mary listened to the logic of the former military man. It made sense. There was only so much a body could endure before its systems failed irrevocably. Chances were high that her personality and energy would persist after physical death. The captain and her men could guide her and keep her safe, even if there was only a slim possibility of ever seeing her parents and grandfather in the afterlife. Would Dan understand her choices? The brother that had been lost to her for so long. Who had given her more support in the short time she had known him, than a husband of nine years.

"Hail Mary, daughter of Christ, descendant of Solomon and David..." Abraham raised his palms heaven wards and closed his eyes.

His followers chanted. "Hail Mary, full of grace."

"We recognise you as the final fulfilment, our obedience and faith are rewarded." Abraham continued in his prayer.

"Hail Mary, full of grace."

"With your coming, we are blessed, sanctified and forgiven..."

"Hail Mary, full of grace."

"We give thanks for every miracle, every soul saved, every sinner redeemed."

"Hail Mary, full of grace."

Blood dribbled from the punctured vessels in her wrists and streamed down her arms to her torso. She felt dizzy and weak, her resolve fading with each minute. Beneath her the chosen faithful knelt, heads bowed in contemplation. Only Abraham kept his sight trained on Mary.

"You are right, Captain. I have little choice but to leave my body."

Abraham drew closer, curious as to why Mary's lips were moving. "Wait, what is she saying?"

"Who cares. She will be dead soon and The Next Covenant is yours for the taking. Unlimited prosperity and abundance are ours."

"She is singing, heaven be praised, she is singing."

Sarah rose to her feet, cushioning her charred right hand with her left. "Singing what? A hymn to our lord?"

They leaned in and concentrated on her lips. "I think...I think it's a Beatles number." Abraham and Sarah looked at each other, frowning.

Mary equilibrated her brain waves to the Schumann frequencies of the earth, and extracted her mind from the suffering of her physical form. The moment she felt herself blend with the Captain and his squad, she felt immense relief. Relief from torture, from solitude, obligation and from responsibility. The fate of the western world was no longer her problem. She had only Dan to worry about, now that she was freed from the restraints of a messy body. Dan and Connie, his girlfriend, and possibly her only friend, other than Yelena. She too had supported Mary in times of crisis, despite their estrangement. And of course, the old Walrus himself, Professor Haas, who had helped her to secure the PhD study and funding. Not forgetting Karan, and his endless kindness and chivalry, and Harvey at The Plaza. There was more to lose than she originally thought. These people had provided more than material assistance. They were her friends. The people who deserved the same care and loyalty in return. How could she leave them now, when Alexi and Luca were days, perhaps hours away from destroying civilisation in the western hemisphere?

Abraham and Sarah observed her battered body, limp and serene, suspended high above the crowd. With her heart at rest, the blood flow slowed to an occasional drip, allowing the platelets to cluster in the embryonic phase of clots. Sarah collected a chair from the feasting table and set it down near Mary's feet. Climbing up to gain a closer view, she prodded a blood stained leg, and waited for a response.

"Is she dead?" Abraham asked. His tone one of disappointment.

Sarah cautiously applied her index and middle finger tips to Mary's ankle. "No, I can feel a strong pulse."

"Has she passed out?"

"Her face would droop if she had. This has to be some kind of trick. No one could withstand pain like that and have a smile on their face." She tugged at a leg, jogging Mary's body against the nails. Blood flowed in fresh spurts. Sarah sighed, her hands on her hips. She shuffled around on her chair until she stood facing the kneeling followers. "WE ARE DECEIVED!" The crowd looked up at Sarah, baffled. She had their attention, their adoration, and she had the determination to exploit their weakness. "She is NOT the daughter of God. Like the good doctor, Hugo Blom said. She is a pretender. No one could withstand the crucifixion without suffering. She is the Daughter of Satan… a witch, sent to test us."

Someone at the back of the crowd shouted, "BURN HER!" It gave them a new purpose.

"Yes, my dear ones. We must be sure that Satan is not given the opportunity to make any of us his servants. Go now, collect brushwood and oil. We will watch her die in a blaze of glory."

The Captain voiced what all his unit members were feeling. *"It is good to have you back with us, Mary. Everyone is thrilled to have you directing us again."*

Mary looked down, watching the life ebb away from her body. *"Truth is, Captain. I don't want to die. There is still so much I want to achieve. I have people that I care deeply about."*

There was a moment of thought and another of murmuring within the ranks. *"Then we must hurry."*

"How so?"

"We must increase the chance of rescue before they light the fires of your doom." In a collective ball of energy, the Hive operatives carried Mary's mind with them, high into the night sky. For once, not a single entity made a noise, their military training kicking in to

stealth mode. *"What are we doing?"* She enquired of them.

Before the Captain could answer her, a string of unintelligible Russian came from one of the crew. The captain translated. *"There is a CNN helicopter in a north easterly direction, Mary. We must divert its course."*

Their plan came to Mary in a seamless stream. Her thoughts and theirs were one. As Abraham's followers prepared the fuel for her burning, her hive mind rushed her several miles through the cloudless sky and into the cockpit of the news helicopter.

"Can you get inside the pilot's head, Mary?" The Captain instructed, as Mary caught up with the unfolding events. Hovering level with his face, Mary concentrated on the man's eyes until she could sense the stirring frequencies in his mind. Latching onto transmissions in his optic nerve, she harmonised with his thoughts until she could dominate his entire nervous system. His strong character was tough to combat, more so than the old woman at the guest house, but within seconds, Mary was in charge.

"I've never flown a helicopter before. What do I do?"

"Just relax. We have several former pilots here to guide you." The Captain almost laughed at her anguish. With their combined energies, Mary moved the cyclic stick instinctively, aiming the aircraft towards the orange glow of torches in the distance. At first, the reporter and crew wondered why they had altered their path, until Abraham's circle of flames came into view. With the camera mounted on the underside activated, and the reporter spurred into action, their live feed broadcast via satellite link to CNN studios.

"You can let go now, Mary. That will give friends at MI6 way to find you."

As she unhitched her mind from the pilot, Mary replied, *"That is assuming Yelena can convince the US forces to help me."*

"A British woman being burned on big cross? Mary, there would be international outrage if they do not."

The helicopter swooped lower, fanning the ashes from the fire pit and blasting the followers with embers from the down draught. Many of the faithful scattered. Abraham and Sarah stood firm. Isaac drew out his weapon and fired on the aircraft, prompting a retreat to a safer distance. Sarah was riled. With only a small clump of brushwood and sticks at Mary's feet, she yanked a torch from the circle and threw it into the kindling. Its weight crushed the layer of thin branches, dousing the flame in the damp grass. Fuming, Sarah kicked the firewood from the back side of the crucifix, stacking it up in one pile beneath Mary. The throbbing from her scorched hand prevented her from fulfilling her goal. She turned to look for Hagar and Keturah, but they had vanished along with the elders, women and children. Only Abraham remained.

She picked up the extinguished torch and thrust it at her husband. "Here. Take the lid off and pour the paraffin over the sticks."

Abraham took the item from her. "Sarah, it's over. The authorities will be here any minute."

"Do it!"

He took his time, unscrewing the hot mechanism with his cuff protecting his hand, and sloshing the fuel over the wood. Sarah collected a second torch, throwing it against the base of the cross. A third torch followed suit, and a fourth, until a small blaze flickered into life. She looked up at Mary's body, waiting for her expression to alter from serene to hysteria.

"Burn, damn you!" Sarah squealed, collecting chairs from the feast table to add to the pyre.

Abraham placed his hand on her shoulder. "It's over." The rhythmic clatter of double rotor blades joined that of the CNN aircraft. Within a few minutes, the re-directed Californian National Guard were on the scene detaining Abraham and restraining Sarah, as she kicked out with flailing limbs against them.

Mary watched the guards clearing away the burning brushwood from the bottom of the cross.

"You should go back to your body now, Mary." The Captain said. She felt their combined remorse mingled with a little fear.

"You're right, I should, but this is not the last you will hear from me. When all this is over, I promise I will contact your families. Perhaps I can find a way to help them, as you have helped me. I am so grateful to you all." The hive let her consciousness drift back to her pitiful body. Pain coursed through every nerve ending, her thought processes weakened by blood loss. Three burly guards supported her weight as another climbed up and carefully removed each nail and binding. With surprising gentleness, they laid her on a stretcher and carried her to the Chinook. Every moment of her rescue, broadcast via CNN to every channel.

Before they could take off, Mary shouted at a medic. "Wait…you have to get my clothes from the building. They are in a little room just off the main corridor."

"Don't worry about those now. Let's concentrate on your injuries."

"You don't understand. I have something very valuable in my pocket…please?"

The man looked at her pitiful state. She tried to sit up, raising her knee in a weak attempt to leave the aircraft. He relented. "Fine, I'll go."

The medical team waited for him to return, administering nitrous oxide to Mary while they bandaged her wounds and secured a line into her veins to replenish lost blood. Eventually, the man with her clothes returned, placing the folded stack on the floor next to her stretcher. They took off. The noise was immense.

With sound cancelling headphones protecting her ears, she heard none of the guard's orders. Mary batted the mask delivering the laughing gas to her lungs, from her face. "Where are you taking me?" She shouted at the medic taping cotton wadding to her hands and arms.

Her headphones clicked and a tinny voice echoed in her ear. "Orders are to take you to Travis Air Force Base so that you can be Medevacked back to the UK." The medic slipped the microphone stem closer to Mary's mouth.

"I'm going home?" Her elation was magnified by the effects of the gas, a massive beaming smile spread across her face.

"That's all I can tell you, ma'am."

"And Sarah and Abraham? Those people who tried to kill me?"

"The authorities will deal with them. They will pay for what they put you through." He reached across and replaced her mask over her face. It left Mary to contemplate her homecoming, safe in the knowledge that the military would arrange everything.

The short trip in the Chinook culminated in a brief landing at Travis where her stretcher was lifted onto a second military aircraft bound for the east coast of America. This transporter plane, was met by a small medical team and their portable equipment. During the four-and-a-half-hour flight, Mary's injuries were flushed with saline, stitched and re-bandaged by expert hands.

She even found time to exploit the analgesics and sleep for a while. When she awoke, it was to remove the intravenous connection from her veins and transfer her into a standard upright seat.

"We are coming into land now, ma'am." The military nurse accompanying the flight remarked. "I'll just attach your seat belt for you." The kind woman buckled Mary into the chair and sat beside her. There was an awkwardness about the nurse which made her uneasy. She avoided eye contact and fussed with the tape securing Mary's dressings.

Mary felt obliged to make small talk. "I'm so looking forward to seeing my brother, and sleeping in my own bed. What a luxury that will be." She looked directly at the nurse, whose puckered frown and pitiful look betrayed her. "I am going home, aren't I?"

"You must be a very important person, Mary. We are to transfer at McGuire in New Jersey and I am to accompany you to London. Special arrangements have been made for a landing at Heathrow Airport." She automatically patted Mary's shoulder, a comforting gesture.

"Heathrow? That's fine, I can catch the tube from there; maybe stay at my friend Connie's until I am feeling stronger." Mary scrutinised the nurse's features. She was still pensive, as though there was more to reveal. "What aren't you telling me?"

The nurse shrugged. "Do you need more pain relief? I am permitted to use my judgement over your requirements." Her evasiveness did not go amiss. Their small talk petered out as the aircraft landed, and then taxied to a siding. The nurse unbuckled Mary's seat belt and helped her to the exit. From the top of the steps, Mary could see that more military personnel waited next to a floodlit hangar with a wheel chair to ferry her, and her neat pile of clothes, to the next aircraft and more banal chatter.

The prospect of a further eight hours listening to her nurse evading more pertinent questions, tired Mary. She ate the rations of disgusting flight food and then settled down to sleep across three empty seats of the aeroplane. The nurse laid a blanket over Mary's shoulders and retreated within sight of her patient.

Mary did manage to snooze for some of the journey, but the soreness of her injuries awoke her with every bump of turbulence and movement she made. In addition to the sharp stabbing sensation, Mary could not stop the jumble of anguish building inside her head. Flashbacks of her ordeals mixed with anxiety over Luca and Alexi's plans. One city in turmoil was just the start of their attacks. If other targets were to be ambushed at the same time, emergency services would be completely overwhelmed and unable to coordinate their efforts. With communications destroyed and electronic circuitry fried in every vehicle and all medical equipment, very little could be deployed to help anyone. Her hope remained with Yelena, and that Dan had managed to persuade her and the rest of MI6 to act.

Mary did not have to wonder for long. They landed and taxied to no fanfare or press; the military aircraft camouflaged by the night. The nurse wheeled Mary across the tarmac towards a stout man in a black coat standing next to a grey car. Mary thanked the medics and bid them farewell, just as another man spilled out from the vehicle. He held up a smart phone to Mary's face.

Yelena Plender, MI6 agent and friend, effused from the screen with relief. "We are thankful that you are back in one piece. We have been concerned." She twisted the phone's camera to show her brother Dan at her side. “These men will bring you to us as quickly as possible.”

“Yelena, there was no need to drag Dan into this. Can’t you handle things without us?”

“You did the dragging, and as well you did. Without Dan you would be dead. We have a problem with proof. There is no evidence to corroborate your claims. I’ll explain when you get here. And Mary… hurry.”

Chapter Twenty-Eight

Yelena's agents drove the grey car into and across London via a police escort, with Mary hiding on the back seat. She checked and re-checked that Phebe's brooch was still tucked into the pocket of her folded jeans. The green smock provided by the US medical team did little to hide her battered body or keep her warm in the early autumnal breeze. One of the less crotchety agents, took off his great coat and helped Mary to thread her bandaged arms through the sleeves. At Euston Station, female agent met them, carrying a pair of trainers. She offered to help Mary get changed in the public toilets.

When she was fully clothed, they boarded a solitary train with only one carriage. It stood on an empty platform, quite separate from all others. Mary expected the station to be sparsely populated, it being well past midnight, but it was as though the place had been cleared just for her. The train carriage was old, but in pristine condition, with a crimson lacquered coating. It had no other markings on the outside, except for a tiny golden logo; a crowned circle surrounding crossed swords, an eagle and an anchor. The agents corralled her towards the footplate, and encouraged her to board.

The inside was like no other train she had ever experienced; a plush modern interior with comfortable armchairs, each swivelled to the direction of travel or to face the fixed table between them. Wall sockets, laptops and printers, lined one end of the carriage, while the other looked more like a dining car from the Orient Express. As Mary boarded, a man in matching livery greeted her.

"Would you care for some tea?" He said, all teeth and hair gel.

"Absolutely. And keep it coming. Thanks." She was directed to one of the armchairs where a laptop connection to Yelena was already established. Mary spied her red headed friend on the monitor. "Where am I going? Can't be the Ministry of Defence building, we could have driven there."

"Back to your favourite place, GCHQ Buckinghamshire."

Mary's heart solidified. The one place she had fought tooth and nail to avoid, and she was hurtling there at a colossal speed. There was no way out. They had Dan secreted in their Tactical Room, surrounded by armed guards and barbed wire. That, Mary could see from the video link. MI6 were similar to the Canadian Mounties; they always get their man, or woman in this case. She inhaled profoundly. *One problem at a time.*

"What's the latest news on Las Vegas?"

Yelena signalled to someone off-screen and then returned her attention to Mary. "We are not yet sure. We are a bit short staffed since Flynn's disappearance. I have had to draft in a new techie onto my team."

"Hmm, I think I can help you with that issue, although you should be sitting down to hear what I have to say." Mary drank the rest of her tea, using the time to frame her explanation regarding Flynn's death and subsequent burial in Alexi's freezer. However, the information was phrased, it pointed to the same conclusion. Flynn was selling information to any group prepared to pay, most likely data regarding Parth's discovery of people with similar abilities to Mary, and for that Alexi took his life. It may not have been his hand on the trigger, but it was on his orders that Flynn was silenced.

"I am sorry for your loss, Yelena. I know that he was a part of your team for a long time." Mary watched her friend for a reaction. There were no tears, no noticeable signs of upset. Whether or not Yelena had mastery over herself or thought less of Flynn than she anticipated, Mary could not tell.

Her entire response amounted to two words; "I see."

The carriage steward deposited a tray with more tea, and breakfast pastries far exceeding the standard of the average British Rail fare. Mary thanked him, and balanced a croissant between her bandaged hands, taking large bites to satisfy her hunger. "I'm sorry," she tried not to speak with her mouth full, "But I am starving. I'm still on Californian time."

"We will make sure that there is more waiting for you when you get here."

"Hmm. Great. What's happening with the cabinet re-shuffle? Have they put that Defence Minister bastard behind bars yet?"

The former minister for the Environment and Rural Affairs bobbed into view. Mary almost choked.

"If you are referring to my former colleague, then he has been suspended pending investigation. I have the helm now. You will be a valuable addition to this little team, Mary. Glad to have you on board."

Mary glowered. "I have not agreed to anything, madam secretary, and you cannot force me to assist."

"We shall discuss your involvement after this current threat is neutralised." The new Secretary of State for Defence peered down her nose at Mary on the screen.

Mary slammed the lid of the laptop shut, cutting her off. "She can sod off, for a start." Her escorting agents struggled to keep their faces straight. The steward made no attempt to hide his amusement, snickering as he retreated from the carriage into a small preparation area at the rear of the train. Eating the rest of her breakfast, Mary contemplated her fate.

By her fourth cup of tea, an idea coalesced in her pre-frontal cortex. One that could potentially deliver both her and her brother from an isolated life of service, trapped in a secure government base in the heart of the British countryside.

Their exclusive train slowed but did not stop at Milton Keynes, trundling through the industrial and warehouse districts and out into the Buckinghamshire fields north of the town. Within a few minutes, they slowed once again, allowing a speedier train to hurtle past, rocking them all in a unified sway. Mary heard a clinking noise, as the track linkages altered and the diesel engines strained and lurched in a forward motion once more. Veering away from the main line, their locomotive pulled them around a steep bend bordered either side by a thicket of trees. Leaning to squint out of the windows, Mary jumped backwards as the carriage entered a close walled tunnel. Her ears popped and buzzed with the pressure changes. One of the accompanying agents spoke quietly to Mary.

"I must remind you that you are bound by the terms of the Official Secrets Act, which prohibits you from exposing anything you may see, hear or surmise while you are at GCHQ Bucks, and..."

"And you can sod off too. I am fully aware that I have signed my soul to the devil. This is not the first tunnel entrance I have been through at this place, although in retrospect, I should have known that there would be an underground railway connection directly from London. Are all the government bases linked to the rail network?" The agent took another breath and paused with his mouth agape. Mary rolled her eyes. "Never mind. I don't care."

The engine trudged along and drew to a full stop at an underground platform. Mary swiped the last of the pastries from a platter and thanked the attendant as she disembarked. Two uniformed officers awaited them, one a woman, brandishing a handheld metal detector. She brushed it against Mary's body, front and back and declared her clear for entry.

Following the other agents, Mary ascended via the elevator to the surface and walked into the floodlit grounds, less than a hundred metres from the pyramidal building, where tactical command waged war. An agent waved her towards the concrete ramp, past the drainage pond to the reception area.

"I know where I am going, thanks all the same."

Dan waited in the lobby, pacing his giant strides across the polished flooring to gather her up in his arms. "I am so happy to see you." He lifted her from her feet, burying his face in her hair. "I've been out of my mind with worry." Mary grunted from his constricting hug, enduring the painful constriction of her injuries. Dan let her go, stepping back to examine her face. "What did they do to you?" His countenance morphed from elation to pity and then to anger. He touched her forehead and her cheek with such tenderness, Mary could feel the corners of her eyes burning.

"Don't be nice to me. I can't lose it now, we have a terrorist to stop."

Dan slipped his arm over her shoulder. He lowered his voice, bending closer to her ear. "The new Defence

Secretary wants to see you immediately. Are you up to it?"

"Take me to her, Dan. I'm warning you, this could be a blood bath."

They walked in silence, along a corridor of locked doors and shuttered internal windows. Every office was empty. All agents had scrambled to assist in foiling the terror plot. The Tactical Room was just as oppressive as she remembered. The giant screen of electronic snow gave the darkened room enough illumination to highlight the computer terminals lined up in serried ranks facing the back wall. Yelena rushed with outstretched arms, until Mary pushed her back with her bandaged hands. Their friendship and Mary's trust had eroded beyond hugs and platitudes. There were too many unanswered questions; a suspicion which festered in the pit of her stomach. Mary was still not convinced about the Russian born MI6 agent's loyalties.

The older woman in the blue suit beside her, dispensed with pleasantries and took control. "Yes, good to have you back, blah, blah, now can we get down to business?" The new Defence Minister, strutted over to Mary and pushed the spectacles up the bridge of her nose. "We have Dr Arora's old lab back in commission for you to use and…"

"He's not here, is he? Yelena, tell me you did not bring Parth into this?" Mary held her palm up to the politician, and over talked her. She snapped her attention to the red head with the St. Petersburg accent.

"No, rest assured, he is not here, but we do need your help. I have called in every favour I can to get US cooperation but without evidence they will not act against a senator who has considerable clout at the White House. We sent a team of our own into the New Jersey compound, but it was locked down. They couldn't get eyes on the underground bunker that you mentioned. None of our checks have managed to link Bonovich to Alexi at all. How did you make the connection?"

Mary folded her arms and exhaled slowly. This could be her only chance to secure her freedom. She looked at Dan, then Yelena and finally raised an eyebrow at the minister. "I have a few conditions that I want agreed and put in writing, before I can assist your efforts."

The minister laughed, turning on her block heels towards the main screen.

"I am perfectly serious. I know precisely what you expect me to do, and what you plan to do with me afterwards. I will not be your puppet, madam secretary. Think carefully about what you are asking."

"Oh really, Ms Arora. And what would that be?"

"You cannot get the support of the US military or even their intelligence agencies. They are too busy treating the Las Vegas blackout as an isolated incident. You know how dangerous Alexi can be, and you would rather he was neutralised to save further high altitude EMP attacks. You cannot kill a civilian on US soil without massive diplomatic fallout. Therefore, you expect me to enter his mind, stand down those teams poised at his command, and then force him to kill himself."

The minister paled. Her dry mouth made a smacking sound when at last she did speak. "You may have anticipated our mission, but we cannot have you doing just as you please…"

"Madam secretary, if I can control a terrorist three thousand miles away, imagine what I can do to you." Mary watched the woman judging her tone and stance. Every muscle in her body conveyed her conviction. As if she needed more, Mary added, "you could drop me in the deepest darkest dungeon, and I could still infiltrate your mind… make you swallow rat poison or walk in front of a bus. I won't, but I could." She indulged in a moment of victory. Her power over them absolute. "Now then, call your legal team in here. We don't have a great deal of time before Alexi strikes again."

Despite some initial posturing, the Defence Secretary crumpled in submission. Having Mary on side would allow her career to soar. She too knew when to strike, and when to lay down arms and wait patiently for better opportunities. Within fifteen minutes, Mary had dictated her terms of service. They included extraction and a full pardon for Lachie, Oona and the rest of the team barring Judith. In Mary's words, "That skinny bitch can rot for all I care." The minister had one or two concessions of her own, but Mary agreed to a compromise. The printed agreement was signed and notarised, and then taken away for duplication and filing.

"Right then." Mary said, taking centre stage in front of the viewing area. "Luca had an invoice for five hundred weather balloons. That shouldn't be hard to track down, get your techies onto that. He was also generating huge quantities of hydrogen at his winery. Follow the shipments of gas cylinders and you should track down the launch sites for the nuclear materials. At least in the US anyway."

"What do you mean? You think he will target other countries too? How do you know this?" Yelena glared at Mary, urging a response.

Mary looked at Dan. The siblings continued the discussion privately, via a telepathic link. *"Should we tell them about Grampy's journal, and his premonition about the Eiffel Tower, the London Eye and other targets?"*

Dan's breathing quickened. He recalled the threats their grandfather had issued to Yelena before his death. *"No, if we can stop Luca and Alexi, other nations will no longer be at risk. Pip did not trust Yelena. We shouldn't either."*

Mary nodded. "I could be mistaken of course. It was just a feeling I got while I was rifling through Luca's study. Wouldn't it be wise to get your Five Eyes surveillance systems, Echelon and Tempora searching for communications about balloons, altitude and detonations in the ionosphere, as a precaution? If Alexi has teams stationed across the western hemisphere ready to plunge us all back into the dark ages, I guess your home nation would be in a particularly strong position to take over, wouldn't they Yelena?"

"Now look here, Mary. You cannot go throwing unfounded accusations at our top people. Save your vitriol for your lover." The minister's retort stung. It crystallised her inadequacies. Her judgement of character had failed her on every level for years. Marrying the terminally deceitful Parth, her vacillating trust of Alexi and her complete fascination of Luca and his environmentally conscious crusades. He had enveloped her into his private life so fully, it was inconceivable that someone so righteous, with gifts so similar to hers, could orchestrate such a heinous plot. Mary felt suitably chastised. She took a seat in the viewing area and allowed Yelena to lead once more.

"Mary is correct." Yelena said, offering an olive branch. "We should send out the alert." She nodded to an Asian lad with a teal blue streak dyed into the front of his jet black hair. Mary surmised from Yelena's treatment of him that he must be Flynn's replacement. His fingers danced across the keyboard and the main screen refreshed until it showed horrifying images.

"Ma'am." Tech boy said, tapping Yelena on the arm. "Satellite's within range now. This is live."

A few more taps and the images magnified. The minister walked closer to the monitor. "What am I looking at Quan?"

"I believe the large fire in the centre is The Bellagio, ma'am."

"Pan across towards the east please, Quan."

The famous 'Welcome to Las Vegas' sign hung askew from its pedestal, every lamp and bulb blown. Several buildings and a few cars were ablaze, dotted across the outskirts of the city. Long lines of stationary or crashed vehicles blocked their highways. There was no access for emergency services to get to those hurt when their electrical circuits fused, causing engines to fail. Some bodies were thrown clear at the time of impact. Others had dragged themselves to the roadside, and there lay dying slow and agonising deaths from their injuries. Others used the chaos to loot the casinos and shops. Glass shards and broken electrical equipment littered the streets. Trains of shopping carts piled high with groceries and bottled water snaked through the abandoned cars. Gangs formed protection details for the spoils, their sub-machine guns cocked and held at shoulder height. Security teams were overpowered. Many lay dead at their posts, their mangled bodies drenched in spattered blood and tissue.

Everyone watched in silence from the Tactical Room. This was but a taste of what was to come. The minister held her hand up to the back of her head. "Now I see why they call it the wild west. How long has it been now… twenty-four hours… less perhaps? Where are their military units? Who have they drafted in to keep order?"

"It will get worse when the sun sets." Mary muttered, articulating what they were all thinking. "I hope you have plans in place for when it happens here."

"Rest assured," the minister gloated, "our vulnerabilities have been assessed and our main assets protected. Nevertheless, we must stop these attacks at their source. Show other would-be terrorists that we are on top of this threat."

Mary listened to her claims and decrypted their meaning; the royal family, the House of Lords and those in parliament would be protected first, military installations second, and the rest of the population could fend for themselves. It was not a surprise.

"Let us take this one step at a time. You say that their base of operations is that compound in New Jersey, yes?" The minister's and all other eyes focused on Mary.

"Well, yes, but by now, Alexi would have teams of his personnel stationed near cities all over the place, waiting for the go order… that is unless the charges attached to the balloons have timer switches to coordinate detonation."

"Let's hope that is not the case. Can we have the air force seek and destroy the balloons mid-air?"

Yelena piled into the conversation. "Not unless you want nuclear fallout raining down on civilian populations."

"Mary, we have no other option, you must neutralise him now."

Chapter Twenty-Nine

Dan followed Mary out from the Tactical Room and into the side room that was once her husband's makeshift laboratory. The reclining dentist chairs gleamed under the strip lighting.

"Are you sure you can do this?" He closed the door behind them and sat in the chair at the side of the room.

Mary clambered up on to the central seat. "What choice do I have?" She knew what he meant. Her lifetime of pacifistic beliefs and vegetarianism would be blown to kingdom come. She had killed people before in self-defence or through Alexi's trickery, but this was premeditated murder. Would she have nightmares over his death in the same way as the others? Had her innate faith in human kindness degraded so completely that killing no longer gave her pause for thought.

Dan sensed her conflict. "He is not an innocent victim. He has killed hundreds, harmed thousands and is set on a course for total destruction of western civilisation."

"I know. And we don't have time for debate. Are you coming with me?"

"Yeah, I promised Yelena that I would update her on your progress, or if you get into trouble."

Lying back in the seat, Mary closed her eyes and hummed her tune. It took only one verse of *Let it Be*, to wrench her consciousness from her weary body. She hesitated for a moment to shelve her emotions, and then she flew high into the atmosphere, beyond the clouds to where she could see the curvature of the Earth. It was a magnificent sight. The blinding glow of sunlight as it fell beyond the horizon, picked out the swirls of cloud covering mountain ranges in the distance. Mary took a direct route straight to New Jersey, across the wide expanse of the Atlantic Ocean.

Descending to a lower altitude, she zoomed over Liberty offering her a subconscious salute. *Us women need to stick together. We will lead men into a better and equal future. Keep the faith.* She half expected her brother to laugh at her proclamation, but he remained a quiet passenger of her thoughts. In essence, he agreed with her.

The urban scars of the east coast zipped beneath her as she aimed for the wooded stretch of New Jersey. Here, she passed low over conifer plantations and homesteads until she spotted the retreat, with its inactive wind turbines and rows of polytunnels. The service roads criss-crossing the compound were deserted. There were a few lights visible from the windows of the communal centre, but everywhere else appeared to be in darkness. Had the attacks already begun? Were the inhabitants all hunkered down in the underground storage caverns, awaiting a signal akin to an air-raid all clear?

A quick sweep of the centre seemed to corroborate Mary's suspicions. One or two staff members loitered in the medical wing, plus a few guards in military uniform carrying automatic weapons were dotted around the place. It was as though they expected imminent trouble. Mary turned away from the centre and floated to the building from which she and Lachie accessed the staircase into the bunker. Squeezing her presence through the gap between the steel door and its frame,

Mary entered the dark corridor, passed through the entrance at the furthest end, and began her descent.

It was much easier going as a ball of energy. Mary bypassed the steps and hurtled through the central space between the banisters. In less than three seconds, she was at the base of the stairwell, and entering the main cavern. The same farm vehicles and military trucks filled the middle of the cavity, the storage units flanking either side. Without fear of detection, Mary drove her presence above the equipment, passed the freezers containing Flynn's body and the computer suite where Lachie and Oona had their first kiss. *Where is everyone? The place is empty.*

As soon as her thoughts assembled as coherent sentences in her mind, Dan heard them and responded. *"Didn't you say that there was a second level, after you stole the bicycle and rode up a ramp?"*

"I did, good thinking." Retracing her escape route, Mary wound her way around the helical ramp to the cavern leading directly to the surface. This area was buzzing with activity. Military personnel packed and stowed electrical equipment, from solar arrays to battery units, cables and fuse boxes. Others manned a camp kitchen area, slopping out chilli and rice, potatoes and veg into trays with irregularly shaped indentations. *There must be some sort of operations headquarters down here, but where?*

She was right. At the far end of the cavern was a large room, set back into the right-hand wall of the bunker. It was sectioned off with stud walls and high Perspex windows, but from her vantage point, she could see Alexi in his hat and sunglasses, standing next to a large oval table. Behind him, a screen similar to that of the Tactical Room at GCHQ Bucks. He was addressing those sitting at the table. She needed to hear what he was saying.

Pushing her nebulous form through the stud partition, Mary positioned herself above Lachie's head. She spotted Ronica and Raeni, for once silent and attentive. The two quiet lads, who had never given Mary their names, sat opposite them. Oona and Judith were both missing. *That can't be a good sign. I wonder where Alexi has them stashed?*

Tuning into Alexi's lecture, Mary tried to ascertain how close he was to implementing the next wave of attacks. In his broken English, he warned the twins and young men about their contracts and penalties should they fail to follow orders. Each of the crew looked more than chastened, they looked terrified. What had Alexi done to reduce these confident youngsters to nervous wrecks? The screen behind Alexi showed a map of the US states. At regular intervals it updated the positions of red dots overlaying the satellite image.

"They must be the teams transporting the balloons and devices." Dan muttered. *"How is Alexi communicating with them?"*

"I don't know, but if I am to get each unit to stand down, then I have to find out."

Alexi's shirt pocket pinged. He took out his mobile phone and swiped at the screen. Mary rushed in closer as he touched his thumb to a green icon, opening a dialogue box.

"They're using WhatsApp!" Mary couldn't believe the simplicity of it all. *"But his unit won't be able to communicate with him after the attacks... ah."* The remainder of his plan fell into place in Mary's mind. *"That's why he has been training Lachie and the others. Their telepathy will instruct Alexi's personnel."*

"So, all you need to do, is to take Alexi over and message his men to stand down and return to the compound." Dan said. *"You could Even make him turn himself in, instead of killing him."*

"Let's hope so. Here goes."

Mary lowered until she was level with Alexi's face. Those weaselly eyes looked grey through the tint of his glasses. Concentrating hard, Mary tried to detect his brain waves to initiate a merging of her frequencies with his. After a few moments, Mary moved higher and tried again. Nothing, not a wisp of his energy anywhere. She moved to another spot and tried again. No luck. *"His glasses must have some kind of polarisation in the tint. I cannot get through."*

"Can you detect anything from his brain at all? Perhaps you could find a channel via his auditory nerves?" Dan suggested.

Mary moved to the side of Alexi's head. Again, no brain waves could be traced. In a ditch attempt, Mary tried to push her way through the fibres in his hat; a brute force attack on his brain. Once again, she was repelled.

"He has some sort of metallic shielding surrounding his head. I cannot get to him."

Alexi turned and watched the screen refresh. The red dots were now pulsating in stationary positions. "All US teams in position. There is only unit in Rome to hear from, then we are go."

Mary could feel the anxiety building in her brother's neural pathways. *"Stay cool, Dan, I have an idea."* Abandoning the plan to infiltrate Alexi's mind, she moved rapidly across the table to Lachie. His brain waves surged and ebbed with contradictory emotions; a veritable open book of frequencies. Mary blended with him in an instant, shocking the young Scottish lad into an audible snort, followed by a jerked movement of his upper body.

"Is something wrong?" Alexi asked of him.

Mary isolated his mind from the others in the group, taking over the nervous control of his auditory channels. *"Lachie, it's me, Mary. Don't let on that you can hear me, okay?"*

"Okay." He replied, confusing Alexi.

"Okay, something is wrong, or okay, you are okay?" Alexi enquired, his suspicions fully aroused.

"Everything is fine general. Apologies for the interruption." Lachie tried to keep his face neutral, and in doing so, made himself appear unnaturally focused. The twins glared at him, as though they had tried and failed to communicate with Lachie telepathically, blocked by Mary's control.

"Listen. I have secured a deal for you, Oona and the others with MI6. You will be fully pardoned and can go home, just as soon as we stop this despot. All you have to do is overpower Alexi." Mary said, in slow, well enunciated words, allowing the information to percolate through his mind.

"I cannae do that, Mary. He has Oona locked up somewhere. He said he'll kill her if I don't do as he says."

"I don't believe for one second that he would. He values people with abilities too much."

"No? Tell that to Judith. She's in the freezer next to your pal Flynn."

This revelation sent Mary's brain waves into a frenetic beta rhythm, temporarily detaching her from Lachie's consciousness. Dan helped her to regain her composure, soothing her frequencies with his own calm presence.

"You are going to have to kill him, Lachie. It's the only way. Then I'll help you to find Oona and we can release her from wherever she is being held."

"That's cold-blooded murder. I cannae do that."

"What do you think will happen when multiple EMP devices wipe out all electronics in the west? How many people will die from lack of emergency services, no medicine, water or food, no police to maintain order, no functioning hospitals...how is that different from murder? Kill this one man, and we can stop it all." Mary knew it was a lie. Alexi was not the only threat. They still had Luca to deal with, but she kept that to herself.

Every person in the room, faced the giant monitor opposite the one showing the United States of America. This screen glowed with little red dots over every major city in Europe. Mary persisted. *"Look at that map, Lachie. Do you think your family in Scotland will survive with no medicines, or sanitation or fresh water? What if they are driving when the blast hits, and their cars go careening off the road into a ditch?"*

"Am sorry, Mary. I cannae." A single tear spilled down his cheek. Alexi had his back turned to Lachie. He need only face him to know that something was afoot, putting Lachie's life in danger.

"Then I am sorry too." Mary said, taking control of Lachie's entire body and forcing his consciousness into sleep mode. Before Alexi could turn around, Mary stood Lachie up, and walked him around the table. With both strong hands raised to Alexi's head, she grabbed hold and twisted with such force, she heard the vertebrae in his neck dislocate. Every muscle in his body sagged, his eyes glazed, the mobile phone skittered across the floor. Mary released Lachie's grip, allowing Alexi to crumple in a heap.

For a moment, the team of telepaths just stared at the body on the floor. Mary directed Lachie to pick up the phone and use the dead man's thumb to open the screen lock.

"That's cold, man." Ronica said, shaking her head. Her sister, Raeni, hugged herself, petrified that Lachie would come for her next.

Mary bellowed from Lachie's voice box. "Don't just sit there. Go and find Oona, and then collect your things together. The British are coming. And hurry, before Alexi's men realise what has happened." Mary agreed with Ronica. It was cold. Killing people could not be anything else. Thumbing through Alexi's WhatsApp files, she could not make sense of any of his messages. The Cyrillic letters were beyond her abilities. She tucked the mobile phone into Lachie's jeans pocket and then concentrated on the screens. Every single red dot pulsed from its city location. The last unit was in place. All Senator Luca Bonovich had to do, was say the word to end all of western civilisation.

"Dan, can you tell Yelena to get her team here asap. They must get the phone from Lachie and find someone who can message in Russian."

"Way ahead of you, sis. Come on home now."

Mary released her control over Lachie and allowed him a moment to assimilate all that had occurred. He glanced down at the body. Alexi's legs were tangled around the table struts and urine seeped into his army fatigues. His eyes were still wide open and glassy.

"You made me into a murderer without my consent." His anger boiled, his brain waves fluctuated from beta into gamma, making her linkage hard to maintain.

"I'm sorry, Lachie. MI6 know that you are not responsible. You were merely my weapon. You know it

had to be done. At least you and Oona are now safe, and can come home."

"I'll ne'er forgive yea for this."

Mary left Lachie's mind, quite sure that he would not forgive her. She had used him in much the same way that Alexi had used her when first they met. On her journey back to her physical body, she felt most wretched. Despite the justifications, she had taken another life. A life of someone, who had put her in harm's way and manipulated her into committing terrible crimes, but had ultimately been kind to her. Alexi was full of unfathomable dichotomies. Why had he rescued her from imprisonment following the poisoning incident at The Houses of Parliament? He could have implemented the EMP plan without her aid. Why did he go to such lengths to keep her close? It was clear that his connection to Luca was one of convenience and not loyalty. Both men wanted leadership of the attacks. Luca would hardly lose sleep over Alexi's demise. And what of Yelena's connection? She had uttered his name during her sleep that afternoon at the Ditchley Estate in Oxford. Did she retain her Russian connections even after she joined MI6?

The clamour of questions distracted her from her mission. There was still much to achieve in order to safeguard the west. She reconnected with her body and roused herself awake. Dan was waiting by her side when she opened her eyes.

"How are you doing? That could not have been easy for you." He said, resting his hand on her shoulder.

Mary peered up at her sweet brother. "You know what is most frightening? That it didn't bother me at all. What have I become?" There was a moment where she detected his pity infused with pride, but he could not articulate his emotions.

Rushing from the lab, they bounded into the Tactical Room and instructed Yelena and the minister to look for the evidence they required in Alexi's control room.

"With the WhatsApp messages and the digital trail from the bunker, you shouldn't have too much trouble co-opting the CIA to lend support, but first and foremost, you need to decipher the messages from Alexi's phone."

Yelena smiled. "I have just the man for the job. An old colleague of mine is nearby. I will appoint him to lead the team."

Dan and Mary exchanged glances. The minister saw the tension building between them.

"No, by all means have your man there to assist with language issues, but I want someone senior at the scene." The minister tapped a few shortcuts on her phone and walked from the room to make her private call.

Yelena looked beaten. Her former youthful complexion looked desiccated and lined. The hollows beneath her eyes grey and lacklustre.

Mary pressed her. "One down eh? Alexi can never again cause mayhem." She watched her friend closely. Was that a tear rising to the surface of her lower lids? The implacable Yelena, close to crying? The old Mary would have offered comfort, a shoulder on which to cry. The new Mary did not have time for such niceties. There was a hanging thread to Alexi's tale, and she was determined to see it unravelled. "How did you know him?"

Yelena picked at fluff on her jacket, dipping her gaze from Mary's inquisition. She swallowed, looked up and then cleared her throat. "We, um… he was, er…fostered by my family. We grew up together."

"Jesus, Yelena. Don't you think we should have known this? What the hell were you thinking?" Dan fumed.

"Six know about it. It was registered as a conflict of interest in my files. It is all as you say, *above the boards*."

"But you have known all along what he is capable of?" Mary tried to keep the note of contempt from her tone, but failed.

"He was an intelligent child. His inquisitive nature made him genius at science and mathematics. Papa thought he might one day make great breakthrough, change the world." Her eyes glowed for a few moments in recollection, until reality dulled them once more.

Dan rounded on her. "What happened?"

"National Service. Met some very bad people, and now this…" She gestured to the screen showing the live feed of street riots Las Vegas.

Chapter Thirty

Everything fell into place. Yelena's reactions during previous dealings with Alexi, the cryptic message Mary saw on a mobile phone thanking the sender for the warnings about the drone strike in Alaska; she was behind his escape. She was treading a thin line of treason. Mary fumed, but kept control of her facial muscles. Yelena had been her biggest champion throughout every ordeal at the hands of the government and of terrorists. She had campaigned tirelessly to bring Mary onto her team full time.

And now, Mary had agreed to their terms. She was an active MI6 operative, with a duty to uphold. If she reported all that she knew about Yelena, her friend would end her days in a prison cell, or worse still, would meet with a timely accident to silence her once and for all.The minister returned from the corridor, tucking her phone into her handbag. Yelena stared at Mary. There was a pensive look of fatalism etched in her eyes. She fully expected Mary to betray her. In the split second before the minister could relate her update, Mary made a momentous decision; better the devil you know. She chose to keep the information regarding Yelena's treachery to herself. There was nothing to be gained from outing her at this juncture, but it could prove useful much later. Her cold calculations stunned Dan, but he maintained his composure.

"I have an extraction team going in now. The CIA are on standby with a join task force to clear up this mess." The minister retrieved a handkerchief from her bag and swiped it beneath her nose. "Bloody grandchildren and their germs."

"Madam secretary, this is not over, don't you see?" Mary loomed closer to the Defence Minister, puzzled as to her relaxed attitude. "Senator Bonovich could initiate the attacks right now, as we speak."

"Ah yes, well we discussed that, and there is absolutely no evidence linking the senator to any wrong doing at all. Now that Russian general is out of the way, we can stand down the terror alert."

"I don't know how you can say that after all I have told you."

"Mary, I have said it before, you cannot go around accusing old lovers of crimes, particularly one as powerful as him." She blew her nose and rummaged in her bag for more tissues.

Mary, Dan and Yelena shared incredulous looks. Even Quan appeared to be perturbed by her stance. Yelena tipped her head towards the door. Mary did not need further permission to leave the room. She and Dan hurried back to the lab and sat in their respective chairs.

"You know what has to be done?" Dan said, with a mixture of apprehension and admiration plastered across his face.

"I do. Let's get on with it."

Her trip across the Atlantic was speedy, as was the journey across land; ethereal journeys annihilating distance and time zones. She reached Luca's ranch a little after sunset. Centring herself and calming her nerves, she entered his lounge via the terrace and followed the raised voices back to his study.

Luca was yelling at Viktor. "Well something's got to have happened, neither Judith or that two faced little Trotskyite are answering messages. Can't get them on Skype either. This is your fault."

"I am not to blame. You wanted her here. I said she would be a liability. You should have let me kill her when I had the chance."

"You let her run. Out foxed by a little woman. For shame." Luca sat at his desk, opened his laptop and typed in a password. "We will need to coordinate things from here."

"If you hadn't got stupid idea in head about her giving you son with immense power, none of this would have happened." Viktor stepped forward, indicating to Luca that he should pass control to him. "Here, let me. I can do that if you give me the codes."

"You've done enough. Go and stow the last of the equipment down in the sanctuary. Did you arrange the flights from Moscow? I want our family around me when all this is over."

"Yes, yes… It is done." Viktor stormed off muttering, what Mary assumed from the vehemence of his snarling, a string of Russian invectives. Pushing her nebulous form through the open door, she hovered above Luca's head, trying to locate files containing go codes on his screen. She watched him click a few more icons until she saw a file which looked promising. He was going to initiate the attacks, now was the time to act.

Shifting herself to face him, Mary directed her energies towards his eyes, trying to detect his frequencies. A steady high alpha wave emanated from his brain. With no time to reflect on her actions, Mary surged forwards to forge a link into his mind.

"Mary." Luca smirked, "I can feel you trying to burrow your way into my head."

Shocked, she took a moment to equilibrate before trying again. A second approach was met with laughter.

"You are wasting your time. I am far stronger than you will ever be. You should have stayed here and together we could have started a new dynasty of telepathic people." He continued to type furiously on the keyboard, decrypting files and pasting codes ready to send to the teams scattered across the western world.

She had no other option but to try brute force. With every ounce of concentration, she forced her cluster of energy through the lens of his right eye, across the viscose liquid and into the centre point of his optic nerve. With this tenuous connection to his nervous system, he stopped typing.

"Get out of my head." He barked.

Now she could make herself heard, but he fought against her binding with every fibre of his being. *"Please don't do this, Luca. The destruction will kill hundreds of thousands of people."*

"That is true, but I will not be among them, and those who do survive will be the fittest and strongest society has to offer. Mother Earth has too many parasitic humans to support as it is. This solution is both elegant and environmentally sustainable." His little speech made him relax a fraction. Mary used the lull in activity to advance along his optic nerves towards the seat of his consciousness. "It's a shame that you had to run away like that. What tipped you off?"

"I saw the Kandinsky from the charity heist, and then an invoice for Alexi's weather balloons. Not to mention your staff at the winery churning out cylinders of Hydrogen as if their life depended upon it."

"Their lives do depend upon it. All must pull their weight in the new world."

"You need help, Luca. I know that you are still upset over losing Ava to Leukaemia, but you cannot seek revenge on every country in the west, just because politicians have sanctioned more powerful cell phone technology."

"I tried political methods and was outnumbered by capitalists. They will never stop developing their networks until our airwaves are completely saturated and cancer becomes a certainty. No, this is the only way." His hands moved over the keys again, sending Mary into a frenzy. It was clear that Luca could not be reasoned with. She had exhausted her options.

Inching ever closer, Mary could feel the full force of his resistance. His gift was incredibly strong. She could feel the pounding of his heart, the adrenalin coursing through his vessels, his extreme excitement of beating her back. Exuding waves of gamma frequencies, he radiated his energy in every direction from his head, cancelling out her own meagre bursts of power. At one point in the furious onslaught, Mary felt her consciousness disperse, and with it her mental agility. It took a few moments to coalesce her mind into one united entity.

"Mary, this is not working. You cannot withstand much more of this. Your body is starting to break down." She noted the anxiety in Dan's voice. His concern for her wellbeing was acute. *"I'm serious, can you hear me? It is damaging your body. You have already burst capillaries in your eyes. You cannot do battle with him and maintain sub-conscious control over your organs."*

"I don't have a choice. He has to be stopped." She collected her wits and forged ahead, clamping onto his brain stem and attempting to harmonise with his waveforms.

"Forget it, Mary. This is a done deal. You cannot stop me." Luca gloated.

He had a point. The more she strained, the greater damaged she incurred on her physical body. Dan screamed at her to stop trying. He ran into the Tactical Room and explained the situation to Yelena, but without the minister's support, she did not have the authority to sanction a hit.

Mary was all but spent. Her strength ebbed and waned.

"Captain…if you can hear me, I could really use your help right about now." She sent her distress signal out into the atmosphere, daring to hope for assistance. His response was almost instantaneous.

"We are at your command, Mary." Captain Thirty-Four and his Hive Operatives merged with her amorphous mass, quadrupling her amplitude and restoring her weakened faculties.

"Bless you, Captain. Bless all of you." Bolstered, determined, and with renewed vigour, Mary drove a pathway right through Luca's brain and took complete control of his entire body. *"You are not the only one with friends in high places."* She batted Luca's consciousness into the reptilian section of his brain stem, overpowering his ability to move or speak. With his computer screen already unlocked and the files open in front of her, she stared through Luca's eyes at the strange symbols on the screen. *"I have no idea what any of this says… what shall I do?"*The captain stifled a snort. *"It is written in Russian, Mary. It is not even in code. We can guide you."*

It took a few minutes for the Hive Mind to stand down Alexi's troops, and for Dan to relay a message to Yelena regarding the location of each team. Mary found a series of files denoting the exact coordinates for the strikes on

Luca's hard drive. She emailed directly from Luca's account to Yelena and carbon copied it to the minister as a backup. *"That should be enough proof for the CIA."* Mary exclaimed. One last thought passed through her mind as she was preparing to leave Luca's body. The captain heard her concerns the second they were formed.

What if Luca tries again? His mind is so powerful, he could easily manipulate key people in the senate. One failed attempt could spur him onto greater things.

"You know what we have to do, Mary, as gruesome as that may be." The captain did not want to spell it out for her, but she seemed reluctant to act. *"He has to die. It's the only way we can be sure of no further related attacks."*

Why was she so hesitant, when Alexi's death was achieved with barely a thought? Had he made such an emotional impact on her that she could not face his death? She searched his office. There were more photographs of his daughter, Ava, staring back at her. She let the muscles in his eyes relax, his focus shifted to a muted reflection. Luca was so handsome, so full of life. How could she simply snuff it out as though he never existed at all?

"Mary. It must be done now, before that other brute returns." The captains voice was insistent, the longer she pondered his demise, the harder it would be.

"That's a point. What shall we do with Viktor?"

"Leave him to the authorities. Log out of Luca's account, and he can do no more damage."

"I suppose so." Mary did as the captain suggested, shutting the lid of the computer to delay the inevitable. As she retreated from his motor functions back to the centre of his brain, Mary noticed a thinning of a blood vessel wall. She hovered stationary inside his mind, watching the vessel bulge, and finally tear in a

longitudinal rip. Blood gushed in spurts into the fragile tissues, his arm spasmed, one side of his face drooped until drool spilled out of the side of his mouth.

"Mary, you must leave now!"

This she did, and within a second, found herself witnessing his downfall. "Looks like the pressure was too great for even Luca to handle."

Mary could not stay to watch his final moments, for her the anguish was too near. She let the Hive transport her psyche back across the globe, to merge with her beaten body in the laboratory.

With Dan in tow, they wandered into the Tactical Room, and stared down the sniffing Defence Secretary.

"It's done. Luca is dead, or soon will be. He ruptured a vessel in his brain." Mary announced. She could not in all honesty explain what she was feeling. Her connection with Luca was too intense not to lament the loss, but she did not think anyone would understand. She would have to tame her emotions if this was to be her new path in life.

A role which would see her mould and shape the lives of other fresh-faced telepaths and sensitives. To lead and manipulate them into protecting the ignorant masses from groups and individuals who would see our countries burn.

How could she explain to Lachie and his friends, that sometimes you must become the villain, to ensure continued stability of a nation. There are no clear-cut boundaries between good and evil.

Luca was sure he was protecting the vulnerable from the barrage of harmful frequencies at the hands of greedy communications empires. Alexi remained wholly convinced that the destruction of bee colonies would lead to global crop failures and the downfall of mankind. Who could tell if they were ultimately right?

Mary had acted to protect the immediate future, even if that might lead to a more agonising and protracted end to civilisation. She had become judge and jury, her subjectivity ruling her heart and her actions. She was reminded of a school production, in which she watched from the wings in awe, as Shakespeare's Richard the Third played out;

"And thus I clothe my naked villainy
With odd old ends stol'n out of holy writ;
And seem a saint, when most I play the devil."

In which of those guises would Lachie now view her? How was she to win him over, having forced him to commit so grievous an act? When first she met the group, each of them had the innocent spirit of childhood about them. Their weeks at the Summerfield compound had rent that veil wide open. Would they consent to working with her and MI6 to secure a better future?

Mary looked at Yelena. Had she trodden the same tightrope of terror between the changing guard of the Defence Department and loyalty to her kin? Was losing your moral compass the cost of protecting those whom you love?

The Midlands, England.

Dan knocked on the windows of Mary's laboratory at the University's Genetics Department, and stood outside waiting for her to unlock the door. His teeth rattled together as he hopped on the spot, his hands in his coat pockets, his breath misting up the air about him. Chuckling to herself, Mary replaced the lid on the bottle of ether and removed her latex gloves.

Opening the door, she said; "What's up buttercup?" and moving back to her stool, let him shut the door after entering. Dan plucked a folded newspaper from his armpit and waved it at her.

"Have you read this?"

Mary nodded slowly, tidying the Perspex containers which had earlier housed her mating fruit flies. "Lots of congratulatory pats on the back for foiled terror plots, and isn't it a good job that their all-pervading surveillance network caught it in time."

"Hmm, indeed. Doesn't say anything about Luca's involvement I notice." He unfolded the sheets and poked his nose into the middle section of the story.

"Well that wouldn't look too good at the White House, would it? Besides, there is little honour in pointing the finger of blame at a rich philanthropist who lost his daughter, got struck by lightning and then suffered a major stroke forcing him to retire from political office. In some respects, I think he would have been better off dead." She gazed at her anaesthetised flies, lying on their backs with their tiny feet in the air. "Is that why you came to find me?"

"No, I wanted to speak with you in person." He put the paper down on the benching and looked at his sister. "I got a call from the solicitors dealing with Pip's legacy. They want us to go down to London and meet with them. Apparently, the old boy who looked after the estate on Pip's behalf is too infirm to travel, but didn't want to pass it off to some underling."

"Did he say why he was being so cloak and dagger about everything?"

"Kind of. When I joked about Pip's diary and the mention of the Eighth Earl of Sedgewell, he went silent for ages. You could have heard a pin drop. Then he said that there was an element of truth to it, and that we shouldn't discuss it over the phone." Dan raised a brow at Mary.

"You're suggesting that our family is titled? That's ridiculous."

"Is it? Think about it. Your passport, the agents who ransacked Pip's place in Brighton, all of it fits. Besides, we will find out soon enough." He shoved his nose back into the newspaper, leaning back to turn the large pages and whacking them into place with a swift back-hander. "Do you want to come over for dinner tonight? Connie is cooking, so you won't get poisoned."

"Thanks, but I can't."

"Oh?"

"I'm going down to Heathrow to meet Harvey from the plane. He had some holiday owed to him so I invited him to stay. He's bringing the satchel that Grampy bought for me."

"Aw, that's nice of him. Do you want to borrow my car?" He fished in his trouser pocket and prised out the keys, chucking them across the work surface.

"That's so nice of you, thanks. It'll save me having to catch the train and then battling across London again."

"You never know, Harvey might have Shrimant Shinde's contact details. Didn't you say that his secretary arranged a private annuity for Harvey to look after you while you stayed at The Plaza?" He beamed up at her, goading her in his usual cheeky way.

"I did, but I doubt Karan would want anything to do with me after the way I treated him." A cerise glow surged across her cheeks. She didn't mention the fact that she also had Karan's numbers printed on a business card tucked into her satchel. More than anything, she wanted a chance to put right the mistakes she had made. To explain why she had behaved so shamefully towards him and beg his forgiveness. But that was for another day. She stacked the boxes next to the sink in the sluice room and stretched fresh gloves over her hands.

"Hey, didn't you say that you had a jeweller friend from the North Laines in Brighton?"

"I did, I have…why?"

"It says here that police are investigating the suspicious death of a jeweller from Brighton, who had attended a precious gem symposium. He met with the guest speaker for a drink after the conference and was later found with his head smashed in, on the canal towpath in Camden Town."

"Holy shit. You don't think it has anything to do with me showing him Phebe's brooch, do you?"

Dan shrugged. "Somehow, I just knew that this would not be the end..."

***

If you have enjoyed The Aurora Manifesto, and can spare a moment of your time, **a review would be greatly appreciated**. Reviews play a crucial role in raising visibility of books on distribution websites, thus supporting sales.

www.samnash.org

The next book in The Aurora Conspiracies Series is entitled, The Aurora Prophecy

Also by this author:

The conspiracy thriller novella series,

The Aurora Journals

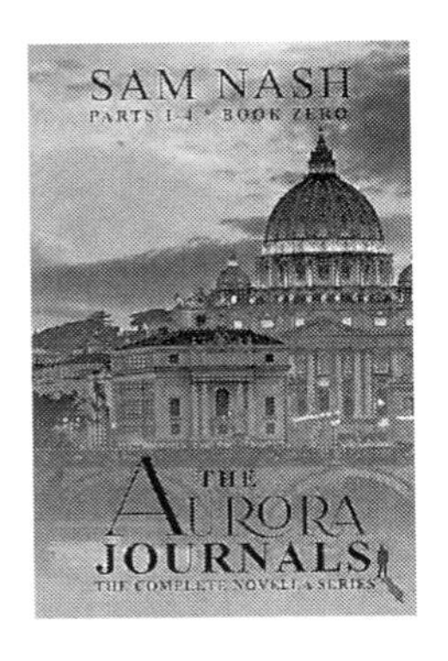

Doctor Pip Lawrence discovers the astounding truth behind his family's heritage, placing himself and those he loves in imminent danger. This four part novella prequel series, uncovers the secrets behind their lineage and how they became entangled in government controversy and intrigue.

Pip is forced to comply with the dubious commands of more than one ruthless international group, taking him on a journey through some of Europe's most beautiful cities. Can he devise a plan to circumvent their hold over him? This thrilling conspiracy, cuts at the roots of democracy, religion, wealth and power.

About the Author

Sam Nash taught science and technology for twenty years in British schools, before turning her hand to writing science fiction thrillers full time. She lives in a small market town in Leicestershire, in the U.K, and dreams of one day owning a woodland on the Cornish coast.

Acknowledgements

I cannot begin to express the love I have for my family. All I can do is to appreciate their continued support to the fullest, and thank them each and every day.

I would also like to thank Nick Phillips and Rae Else, for their unrelenting kindness, useful advice and constant friendship. I don't know what I would do without you.

Printed in Poland
by Amazon Fulfillment
Poland Sp. z o.o., Wrocław